POWERS

URSULA K. LE GUIN

POWERS

• • • • • • • • • • • •

HARCOURT, INC.

Orlando   Austin   New York
San Diego   Toronto   London

www.HarcourtBooks.com

Library of Congress Cataloging-in-Publication Data
Le Guin, Ursula K., 1929–
Powers/Ursula K. Le Guin.—1st ed.
p. cm.
Summary: When young Gavir's sister is brutally killed, he escapes from
slavery and sets out to explore the world and his own psychic abilities.
[1. Fantasy.] I. Title.
PZ7.L5215Pow 2007
[Fic]—dc22   2006013549
ISBN 978-0-15-205770-1

Maps created by Ursula K. Le Guin
Text set in Adobe Jenson
Designed by Cathy Riggs

First edition
A C E G H F D B

Printed in the United States of America

POWERS

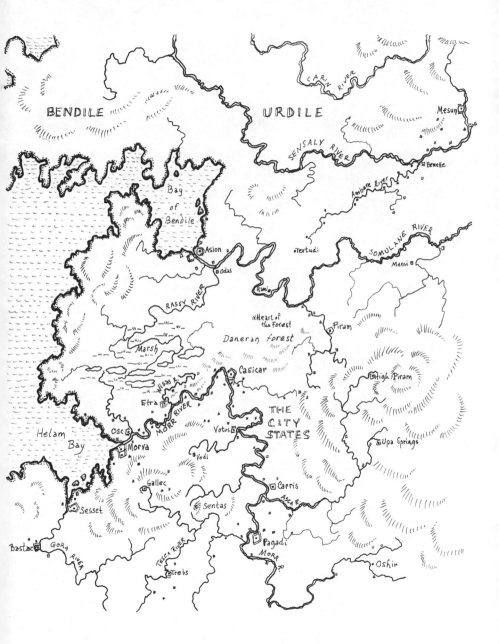

PART ONE

◆ 1 ◆

"Don't talk about it," Sallo tells me.

"But what if it's going to happen? Like when I saw the snow?"

"That's why not to talk about it."

My sister puts her arm around me and rocks us sideways, left and right, as we sit on the schoolroom bench. The warmth and the hug and the rocking ease my mind and I rock back against Sallo, bumping her a little. But I can't keep from remembering what I saw, the dreadful excitement of it, and pretty soon I burst out, "But I ought to tell them! It was an invasion! They could warn the soldiers to be ready!"

"And they'd say—when?"

That stumps me. "Well, just ready."

"But what if it doesn't happen for a long time? They'd be angry at you for giving a false alarm. And then if an army did invade the city, they'd want to know how you knew."

"I'd tell them I remembered it!"

"No," Sallo says. "Don't ever tell them about remembering the way you do. They'll say you have a power. And they don't like people to have powers."

"But I don't! Just sometimes I remember things that are going to happen!"

"I know. But Gavir, listen, truly, you mustn't talk about it to anybody. Not anybody but me."

When Sallo says my name in her soft voice, when she says, "Listen, truly," I do truly listen to her. Even though I argue.

"Not even Tib?"

"Not even Tib." Her round, brown face and dark eyes are quiet and serious.

"Why?"

"Because only you and I are Marsh people."

"So was Gammy!"

"It was Gammy that told me what I'm telling you.

That Marsh people have powers, and the city people are afraid of them. So we never talk about anything we can do that they can't. It would be dangerous. Really dangerous. Promise, Gav."

She puts up her hand, palm out. I fit my grubby paw against it to make the vow. "I promise," I say as she says, "I hear."

In her other hand she's holding the little Ennu-Mé she wears on a cord around her neck.

She kisses the top of my head and then bumps me so hard I nearly fall off the end of the bench. But I won't laugh; I'm so full of what I remembered, it was so awful and so frightening, I want to talk about it, to tell everybody, to say, "Look out, look out! Soldiers are coming, enemies, with a green flag, setting the city on fire!" I sit swinging my legs, sullen and mournful.

"Tell me about it again," Sallo says. "Tell all the bits you left out."

That's what I need. And I tell her again my memory of the soldiers coming up the street.

Sometimes what I remember has a secret feeling about it, as if it belongs to me, like a gift that I can keep and take out and look at when I'm by myself, like the eagle feather Yaven-dí gave me. The first thing I ever remembered, the place with the reeds and the water, is like that. I've never told anybody about it, not even Sallo. There's nothing to tell; just the silvery-blue water, and reeds in the wind, and sunlight, and a blue hill way off. Lately I have a new remembering: the man in the high room in shadows who turns around and says my name. I haven't told anybody that. I don't need to.

But there's the other kind of remembering, or see-ing, or whatever it is, like when I remembered seeing the Father come home from Pagadi, and his horse was lame; only he hadn't come home yet and didn't until next summer, and then he came just as I remembered, on the lame horse. And once I remembered all the streets of the city turning white, and the roofs turning white, and the air full of tiny white birds all whirling and flying downward. I wanted to tell everybody about that, it was so amazing, and I did. Most of them didn't listen. I was only four or five then. But it snowed, later that winter. Everybody ran outside to see the snowfall, a thing that happens in Etra maybe once in a hundred years, so that we children didn't even know what it was called. Gammy asked me, "Is this what you saw? Was it like this?" And I told her and all of them it was just what I'd seen, and she and Tib and Sallo believed me.

That must have been when Gammy told Sallo what Sallo had just told me, not to talk about things I remembered that way. Gammy was old and sick then, and she died in the spring after the snowfall.

Since then I'd only had the secret rememberings, until this morning.

I was by myself early in the morning, sweeping the hall outside the nursery rooms, when I began remembering. At first I just remembered looking down a city street and seeing fire leap up from a house roof and hearing shouts. The shouts got louder, and I recognised Long Street, running north from the square behind the Forefathers' Shrine. At the far end of the street smoke was billowing out in big greasy clouds with red flames inside them. People were running past me, all over the square, women and men, most of them running towards the Senate Square, shouting and calling out, but city guards ran by in the other direction with their swords drawn. Then I could see soldiers at the far end of Long Street under a green banner; they had long lances, and the ones on horseback had swords. The guards met with them, and there was deep shouting, and ringing and clashing like a smithy, and the whole crowd of men, a great writhing knot of armor and helmets and bare arms and swords, came closer and closer. A horse broke from it, galloping up the street straight at me, riderless, lathered with white sweat streaked red, blood running from where its eye should be. The horse was screaming. I dodged back from it. And then I was in the hall with a broom in my hand, remembering it. I was still terrified. It was so clear I couldn't forget it at all. I kept seeing it again, and seeing more. I had to tell somebody.

So when Sallo and I went to get the schoolroom ready and were there alone, I told her. And now I told her all over again, and telling it made me remember it again, and I could see and tell it better. Sallo listened intently and shivered when I described the horse.

"What kind of helmets did they have?"

I looked at the memory of the men fighting in the street.

"Black, mostly. One of them had a black crest, like a horse's tail."

"Do you think they were from Osc?"

"They didn't have those long wood shields like the Oscan captives in the parade. It was like all their armor was metal—bronze or iron—it made this huge clanging sound when they were fighting with the guards with swords. I think they came from Morva."

"Who came from Morva, Gav?" said a pleasant voice behind us, and we both jumped like puppets on strings. It was Yaven. Intent on my story, neither of us had heard him, and we had no idea how long he'd been listening. We reverenced him quickly and Sallo said, "Gav was telling me one of his stories, Yaven-dí."

"Sounds like a good one," Yaven said. "Troops from Morva would march with a black-and-white banner, though."

"Who has green?" I asked.

"Casicar." He sat down on the front bench, stretching out his long legs. Yaven Altanter Arca was seventeen, the eldest son of the Father of our House. He was an officer in training of the Etran army, and away on duty much of the time now, but when he was home he came to the schoolroom for lessons just as he used to. We loved having him there because, being grown up, he made us all feel grown up, and because he was always good-natured, and because he knew how to get Everra, our teacher, to let us read stories and poems instead of doing grammar and logic exercises.

The girls were coming in now, and Torm ran in with Tib and Hoby from the ball court, sweating, and finally Everra entered, tall and grave in his grey robe. We all reverenced the teacher and sat down on the benches. There were eleven of us, four children of the Family and seven children of the House.

Yaven and Torm were the sons of the Arca Family, Astano was the daughter, and Sotur was their cousin.

Among the house slaves, Tib and Hoby were boys of twelve and thirteen, I was eleven, and Ris and my sister Sallo were thirteen. Oco and her little brother Miv were much younger, just learning their letters.

All the girls would be educated till they were grown and given. Tib and Hoby, having learned to read and write and recite bits of the epics, would be let out of school for good, come spring. They couldn't wait to get out and learn to work. I was being educated to be a teacher, so my work would always be here, in the long schoolroom with its high windows. When Yaven and Torm had children, I would teach those children and the children of their slaves.

Yaven invoked the spirits of his Ancestors to bless our work today, and Everra reproved Sallo and me for not setting out the schoolbooks, and we got to work. Almost immediately Everra had to call up Tib and Hoby for scuffling. They stuck out their hands palm up and he whacked each one once with his yardstick.

There was little beating in Arcamand, and no tortures such as we heard of in other Houses. Sallo and I had never even been struck; the shame of being reproved was quite enough to make us behave. Hoby and Tib had no shame, and as far as I could see no fear of punishment either, and hands as hard as leather. They grimaced and grinned and all but sniggered when Everra struck them, and indeed his heart wasn't in it. Like them, he couldn't wait for them to be out of his schoolroom. He asked Astano to hear them recite their daily bit of history from the Acts of the City of Etra, while Oco helped her little brother write his alphabet, and the rest of us got on with reading the *Moralities* of Trudec.

Old-fashioned, the old ways—those were words we heard often in Arcamand, spoken with absolute approval. I don't think any of us had the faintest idea why we had to memorise tiresome old Trudec, or ever thought to ask. It was the tradition of the House of Arca to educate its people. Education meant learning to read the moralists and the epics and the poets Everra called the Classics, and studying the history of Etra and the City States, some geometry and principles of engineering, some mathematics, music, and drawing. That was the way it had always been. That was the way it was.

Hoby and Tib had never got beyond Nemec's *Fables*, and Torm and Ris depended a good deal on the rest of us to get them through Trudec; but Everra was an excellent teacher, and had swept Yaven and Sotur and Sallo and me right into the histories and the epics, which we all enjoyed, though none so keenly as Yaven and I. When we'd finally finished discussing the Importance of Self-Restraint as exemplified in the Forty-first Morality, I snapped Trudec shut and reached for the copy of the *Siege of Oshir* that I shared with Sallo. We had just started reading it last month. I knew every line I'd read by heart.

Our teacher saw me. His long, grey-black eyebrows went up. "Gavir," he said, "will you now please hear Tib and Hoby recite, so that Astano-ío can join us in reading."

I knew why Everra did it. It wasn't meanness; it was Morality. He was training me to do what I didn't want to do and not do what I did want to do, because that was a lesson I had to learn. The Forty-first.

I gave Sallo the book and went over to the side bench. Astano gave me the book of the Acts of the City and a sweet smile. She was fifteen, tall and thin, so light-skinned that her brothers called her the Ald, after the people in the eastern deserts who are said to have white skins and hair like sheep; but "ald" also means stupid. Astano wasn't stupid, but she was shy, and had perhaps learned the Forty-first Morality almost too well. Silent and proper and modest and self-contained, a perfect Senator's daughter: you had to know Astano very well to know how warm-hearted she was and what unexpected thoughts she could think.

It's hard for a boy of eleven to play the teacher to older boys who are used to bossing him around and roughing him up and who normally call him Shrimp, Swamp Rat, or Beaky. And Hoby hated taking orders from me. Hoby had been born on the same day as Torm, the son of the Family. Everybody knew but nobody said he was Torm and Yaven's half brother. His mother had been a slave, he was a slave; he received no special treatment. But he resented any slave who did. He'd always been jealous of my status in the classroom. He stared at me frowning as I stood before him and Tib, sitting side by side on the bench.

Astano had closed the book, so I asked, "Where were you?"

"Sitting here all along, Beaky," Hoby said, and Tib sniggered.

What was hard to take was that Tib was my friend, but whenever he was with Hoby he was Hoby's friend, not mine.

"Go on reciting from where you left off," I said, speaking to Hoby, trying to sound cool and stern.

"I don't remember where it was."

"Then start over from where you started today."

"I don't remember where it was."

I felt the blood rise in my face and sing in my ears. Unwisely, I asked, "What do you remember?"

"I don't remember what I remember."

"Then begin at the beginning of the book."

"I don't remember it," Hoby said, carried away with the success of his ploy. That gave me the advantage.

"You don't remember any of the book at all?" I said, raising my voice a little, and Everra immediately glanced our way. "All right," I said. "Tib, say the first page for Hoby."

Under our teacher's eye he didn't dare not to, and set off gabbling the Origin of the Acts, which they'd both known by heart for months. I stopped him at the end of the page and told Hoby to repeat it. That made

Hoby really angry. I'd won. I knew I'd pay for it later. But he muttered the sentences through. I said, "Now go on where you left off with Astano-ío," and he obeyed, droning out the Act of Conscription.

"Tib," I said, "paraphrase." That's what Everra always had us do, to show we understood what we'd memorised.

"Tib," Hoby said in a little squeaky murmur, "pawaphwase."

Tib broke into giggles.

"Go on," I ordered.

"Go on, pawaphwase," Hoby whisper-squeaked, and Tib giggled helplessly.

Everra was talking about a passage in the epic, lecturing away, his eyes shining, the others all listening intently; but Yaven, sitting on the second bench, glanced over at us. He gazed at Hoby with a sharp frown. Hoby shrank into himself and looked at the floor. He kicked Tib's ankle. Tib immediately stopped giggling. After some struggle and hesitation he said, "It uh, it uh says, it means that uh, if the City is threatened uh with uh an attack the uh the Senate will uh what is it?"

"Convene," I said.

"Convene and debilitate—"

"Deliberate."

"Deliberate the conscription of able-bodied free-men. Is deliberate like liberate, only the opposite?"

That was one reason I loved Tib: he heard words, he asked questions, he had a strange, quick mind; but nobody else valued it, so he didn't either.

"No, it means talk something over."

"If you pawaphwase it," Hoby muttered.

We mumbled and stumbled through the rest of their recitation. I was putting away the Acts with great relief when Hoby leaned forward from his bench, staring at me, and said between his teeth, "Master's pet."

I was used to being called teacher's pet. It was inevitable—it was true. But our teacher wasn't a master, he was a slave, like us. This was different. Master's pet meant toady, sneak, traitor. And Hoby said it with real hatred.

He was jealous of Yaven's intervention on my behalf, and shamed by it. We all admired Yaven and longed for his approval. Hoby seemed so rough and indifferent, it was hard for me to understand that he might love Yaven as much I did, with less ability to please him, and more reason to feel humiliated when Yaven sided with me against him. All I knew was that the name he'd called me was hateful and unfair, and I burst out aloud, "I'm not!"

"Not what, Gavir?" said Everra's cold voice.

"Not what Hoby said—it doesn't matter—I'm sorry, Teacher. I apologise for interrupting. I apologise to all."

A cold nod. "Sit down and be silent, then," Everra said. I went back to sit by my sister. For a while I couldn't read the lines of the book Sallo held in front of both of us. My ears kept ringing and my eyes were blurred. It was horrible, what Hoby had called me. I'd never be a master's pet. I wasn't a sneak. I'd never be like Rif—a housemaid who'd spied on the other maids and tattled, thinking to gain favor. But the Mother of Arca told her, "I don't like sneaks," and had her sold at the Market. Rif was the only adult slave who had been sold from our House in all my life. There was trust on both sides. There had to be.

When the morning lesson was over, Everra gave punishment for disturbing the class: Tib and Hoby were to learn an extra page of the Acts; all three of us were to write out the Forty-first Lesson of Trudec's *Moralities*; and I was to copy out thirty lines of Garro's epic poem *The Siege and Fall of Sentas* into the fair-copy book and have them memorised by tomorrow.

I don't know whether Everra realised that most of his punishments were rewards, to me. Probably he knew it. But at the time I saw our teacher as old and wise beyond mere human feeling; it didn't occur to me that he thought about me at all or could care what I felt. And because he called copying poetry punishment, I tried to believe that it was. In fact, I was clamping my tongue between my teeth most of the time I was writing out the lines. My writing was scrabbly and irregular. The fair-copy book would be used in future classes, just as we used the books that previous generations of students had copied out when they were children in this schoolroom. Astano had copied the last passage in this book. Under her small, elegant writing, almost as clear as the printed books from Mesun, my lines went scrawling and straggling pitifully along. Looking at how messy they were was my real punishment. As for memorising them, I'd already done that.

My memory is unusually exact and complete. When I was a child and adolescent, I could call up a page of a book, or a room I'd seen, or a face, if I'd looked at it with any attention at all, and look at it again as if it were in front of me. So it was, perhaps, that I confused my memories with what I called "remembering," which was not memory but something else.

Tib and Hoby ran outdoors, putting off their tasks till later; I stayed in the schoolroom and finished mine.

Then I went to help Sallo with sweeping the halls and courtyards, which was our perpetual task. After we'd swept the silk-room courts we went for a piece of bread and cheese at the pantry handout, and I would have gone back to sweeping, but Torm had sent Tib to tell me to come and be soldiers.

Sweeping the courts and corridors of that enormous house was no small job; it was expected that they be clean always, and it took Sallo and me a good part of the day to keep them that way. I didn't like to leave Sallo with all the rest of it, when she'd already done a lot while I did my punishment, but I couldn't disobey Torm. "Oh, you go on," she said, lazily pushing her broom along in the shade of the arches of the central atrium, "it's all done but this." So I ran out happily to the sycamore park under the city walls a few streets south of Arcamand, where Torm was already drilling Tib and Hoby. I loved being soldiers.

Yaven was tall and lithe like his sister Astano and the Mother, but Torm took after the Father, compact and muscular. There was something a little amiss with Torm, something askew. He didn't limp, but he walked with a kind of awkward plunge. The two sides of his face didn't quite seem to fit together, so he looked lopsided. And he had unpredictable rages, sometimes real fits, screaming, hitting out wildly or tearing at his own clothes and body. Coming into adolescence now, he seemed to be growing together. His furies had calmed down, and he was making an excellent athlete of himself. All his thoughts were about the army, being a soldier, going to fight with Etra's legions. The army wouldn't take him even as a cadet for two years yet, so he made Hoby and Tib and me into his army. He'd been drilling us for months.

We kept our wooden swords and shields in a secret cache under one of the big old sycamores in the park, along with the greaves and helmets of leather scraps Sallo and I had made under Torm's direction. His helmet had a plume of reddish horse-hairs which Sallo had picked up in the stables and sewn in, so it looked quite grand. We always drilled in a long grass-alley deep in the grove, right under the wall, a secluded place. I saw the three of them marching down the alley as I came running through the trees. I snatched up my cap and shield and sword and fell in with them, panting. We drilled for a while, practicing turning and halting at Torm's orders; then we had to stand at attention while our eagle-eyed commander strode up and down his regiment, berating a man here for having his helmet on crooked and a man there for not standing up straight, or changing his expression, or letting his eyes move. "A shoddy lot of troops," he growled. "Damned civilians. How can Etra ever defeat the Votusans with a rabble like this?" We stood expressionless staring straight ahead, resolving in our hearts to defeat the Votusans come what might.

"All right," Torm said at last. "Tib, you and Gav are the Votusans. Me and Hoby are Etra. You go man the earthworks, and we'll do a cavalry attack."

"They always get to be the Etrans," Tib said to me as we ran off to man the earthworks, an old, half-overgrown drainage ditch that led out from the wall nearby. "Why can't we be the Etrans sometimes?"

It was a ritual question; there was no answer. We scuttled into the ditch and prepared to meet the onslaught of the cavalry of Etra.

For some reason they took quite a while coming, and Tib and I had time to build up a good supply of missiles: small clods of hard dry dirt from the side of the ditch. When we finally heard the neighing and snorting of the horses, we stood up and hurled our missiles furiously. Most of them fell short or missed, but one clod happened to hit Hoby smack on the forehead.

I don't know whether Tib or I threw it. It stopped him short for a moment, stunned him; his head bobbed strangely back and forth and he stood staring. Torm was charging on, shouting, "At them, men! For the Ancestors! Etra! Etra!"—and came leaping down into the ditch. He remembered to whinny as he leaped. Tib and I fell back before the furious onslaught, naturally, which gave Torm time to look around for Hoby.

Hoby was coming at a dead run. His face was black with dirt and rage. He jumped into the ditch and ran straight at me with his wooden sword lifted up to slash down at me. Backed up against bushes in the ditch, I had nowhere to go; all I could do was raise my shield and strike out with my sword as best I could, parrying his blow.

The wooden blades slid against each other, and mine, turned aside by his much stronger blow, flicked up against his face. His came down hard on my hand and wrist. I dropped my sword and howled with pain. "Hey!" Torm shouted. "No hitting!" For he had given us very strict rules of how to use our weapons. We were to dance-fight with our swords: we could thrust and parry, but were never to strike home with them.

Torm came between us now, and I had his attention first because I was crying and holding out my hand,

which hurt fiercely—then he turned to Hoby. Hoby
stood holding his hands over his face, blood welling between his fingers.

"What's wrong, let me look," Torm said, and Hoby
said, "I can't see, I'm blind."

There wasn't any water nearer than the Arca Fountain. Our commander kept his head: he ordered Tib
and me to hide the weapons in the usual place and follow at once, while he led Hoby home. We caught up to
them at the fountain in the square in front of Arcamand. Torm was washing the dirt and blood off Hoby's
face. "It didn't hit your eye," he said, "I'm sure it didn't.
Not quite." It was not possible to be sure. The rough
point of my wooden sword, driven upward by Hoby's,
had made a ragged cut above or on the eye, and blood
was still pouring out of it. Torm wadded up a strip torn
from his tunic and had Hoby press it against the
wound. "It's all right," he said to Hoby. "It'll be all right.
An honorable wound, soldier!" And Hoby, discovering
that he could see from his left eye at least, now the
blood and dirt was no longer blinding him, stopped
crying.

I stood at attention nearby, frozen with dread.
When I saw that Hoby could see, it was a huge relief. I
said, "I'm sorry, Hoby."

He looked round at me, glaring with the eye that wasn't hidden by the wad of cloth. "You little sneak," he said. "You threw that rock, then you went for my face!"

"It wasn't a rock! It was just dirt! And I didn't try to hit you, with the sword I mean—it just flew up—when you hit—"

"Did you throw a rock?" Torm demanded of me, and both Tib and I were denying it, saying we had just thrown clods, when suddenly Torm's face changed, and he too stood at attention.

His father, our Father, the Father of Arcamand, Altan Serpesco Arca, walking home from the Senate, had seen us by the fountain. He now stood a yard or two away, looking at the four of us. His bodyguard Metter stood behind him.

The Father was a broad-shouldered man with strong arms and hands. His features—round forehead and cheeks, snub nose, narrow eyes—were full of energy and assertive power. We reverenced him and stood still.

"What is this?" he said. "Is the boy hurt?"

"We were playing, Father," Torm said. "He got a cut."

"Is the eye hurt?"

"No, sir. I don't think so, sir."

"Send him to Remen at once. What is that?"

Tib and I had tossed our headgear into the weapon cache, but Torm's crested helmet was still on his head, and so was Hoby's less ornate one.

"Cap, sir."

"It's a helmet. Have you been playing at soldiers? With these boys?"

He looked us three over once more, a flick of the eye.

Torm stood mute.

"You," the Father said, to me—no doubt assessing me as the youngest, feeblest, and most overawed— "were you playing at soldiers?"

I looked in terror to Torm for guidance, but he stood mute and stiff-faced.

"Drilling, Altan-dí," I whispered.

"Fighting, it looks like. Show me that hand." He did not speak threateningly or angrily, but with perfect, cold authority.

I held out my hand, puffed up red and purple around the base of the thumb and the wrist by now.

"What weapons?"

Again I looked to Torm in an agony of appeal. Should I lie to the Father?

Torm stared straight ahead. I had to answer.

"Wooden, Altan-dí."

"Wooden swords? What else?"

"Shields, Altan-dí."

"He's lying," Torm said suddenly, "he doesn't even drill with us, he's just a kid. We were trying to climb some trees in the sycamore grove and Hoby fell and a branch gashed him."

Altan Arca stood silent for a while, and I felt the strangest mixture of wild hope and utter dread thrill through me, running on the track of Torm's lie.

The Father spoke slowly. "But you were drilling?"

"Sometimes," Torm said and paused—"sometimes I drill them."

"With weapons?"

He stood mute again. The silence stretched on to the limit of endurance.

"You," the Father said to Tib and me. "Bring the weapons to the back courtyard. Torm, take this boy to Remen and get him looked after. Then come to the back courtyard."

We all ducked in reverence and got away as fast as we could. Tib was crying and chattering with fear, but I was in a queer, sick state, like a fever, and nothing seemed very real; I felt calm enough but could not speak. We went to the cache and hauled out the wooden swords and shields, the helmets and greaves, and carried them round the back way to the rear court-yard of Arcamand. We made a little pile of them there and stood by them waiting.

The Father came out, having changed into house clothes. He strode over to us and I could feel Tib shrinking into himself with terror. I reverenced and stood still. I was not afraid of the Father, not as I was afraid of Hoby. I was in awe of him. I trusted him. He was completely powerful, and he was just. He would do what was right, and if we had to suffer, we had to suffer.

Torm came out, striding along like a short edition of his father. He halted by the sad little heap of wooden weapons and saluted him. He kept his chin up.

"You know that to give a slave any weapon is a crime, Torm."

Torm mumbled, "Yes, sir."

"You know there are no slaves in the army of Etra. Soldiers are free men. To treat a slave as a soldier is an offense, a disrespect to the army, to the Ancestors. You know that."

"Yes, sir."

"You are guilty of that crime, that offense, that disrespect."

Torm stood still, though his face was quivering terribly.

"So. Shall the slaves be punished for it, or you?"

Torm's eyes opened wide at that—a possibility that clearly had not occurred to him. He still said nothing. There was a long pause.

"Who commanded?" the Father said at last.

"Me, sir."

"So?"

Another long pause.

"So I should be punished."

Altan Arca nodded very briefly.

"And they?" he asked.

Torm struggled, and finally muttered, "They were doing what I told them to, sir."

"Are they to be punished for following your orders?"

"No, sir."

The brief nod again. He looked at Tib and me as if from a great distance. "Burn that trash," he told us. "Consider this, you boys: obeying a criminal order is a crime. Only because your master takes the responsibility do you go free.— You're the Marsh boy— Gav, is it?— And you?"

"Tib, sir, kitchen, sir," Tib whispered.

"Burn that stuff and get back to work. Come," he said to Torm, and the two of them marched off side by side under the long arcade. They looked like soldiers on parade.

We went to the kitchen for fire, brought back a burning stick from the hearth there, and laboriously got the wooden swords and shields to burn, but then we put the leather caps and greaves on the fire and they smothered it. We scraped up the half-burnt pieces of wood and stinking leather, getting a lot of small burns on our hands, and buried the mess in the kitchen midden. By then we were both sniveling. Being soldiers had been hard, frightening, glorious, we had been proud to be soldiers. I had loved my wooden sword. I used to go out alone to the cache to take it out and sing to it, smooth its rough splintery blade with a stone, polish it with grease saved from my dinner. But it was all lies. We had never been soldiers, only slaves. Slaves and cowards. I had betrayed our commander. I was sick with defeat and shame.

We were late for afternoon lessons. We ran through the house to the schoolroom and rushed in panting. The teacher looked at us with disgust. "Go wash," was all he said. We hadn't looked at our filthy hands and clothes;

now I saw Tib's face all smeared with soot and snot and knew mine was like it. "Go with them and get them clean, Sallo," Everra added. I think he sent her with us out of kindness, seeing we were both badly upset.

I had seen Torm in his usual place on the school-room bench, but Hoby had not been there. "What happened?" Sallo asked us as we went to wash, and at the same time I asked, "What did Torm say?"

"He said the Father ordered you to burn some toys, so you might be late to class."

Torm had covered for us, made us an excuse. It was a great relief, and so undeserved, after my betrayal of him, that I could have cried in gratitude.

"But what toys? What were you doing?"

I shook my head.

Tib said, "Being soldiers for Torm-dí."

"Shut up, Tib!" I said too late.

"Why should I?"

"It makes trouble."

"It wasn't our fault. The Father said so. He said it was Torm-dí's fault."

"It wasn't. Just don't talk about it! You're betraying him!"

"Well, he lied," Tib said. "He said we were climbing trees."

"He was trying to keep us out of trouble!"

"Or himself," Tib said.

We had got to the courtyard fountain by now, and Sallo more or less pushed our heads underwater and rubbed and scrubbed us clean. It took a while. The water stung and then felt cool on my various burns and my puffy, aching hand. Between scrubs and rinses Sallo got the story out of us. She didn't say much, except, to Tib, "Gav is right. Don't talk about it."

Going back to the schoolroom, I asked, "Is Hoby going to be blind in that eye?"

"Torm-dí just said he was hurt," Sallo said.

"Hoby's really angry at me," I said.

"So?" Sallo said, fierce. "You didn't mean to hurt him, and he did mean to hurt you. If he tries it again he'll get into some real trouble." She spoke the truth. Gentle and easygoing as she was, she'd fire up and fight for me like a mother cat for her kittens—everybody knew that. And she'd never liked Hoby.

She put her arm around me for a moment before we got back to the schoolroom, leaning on me and bumping me, and I leaned on her and bumped her, and everything was all right again, almost.

❖ 2 ❖

Hoby's eye wasn't hurt. The ugly wound had cut his eyebrow in half, but as Torm put it, he didn't have much beauty to be spoiled. When he came back to the schoolroom the next day he was joking and stoical about his bandaged head, and cheerful with everyone—except me. Whatever the real source of his rivalry and humiliation, whether or not he really thought I'd thrown a rock at his face, he'd chosen to see me as an enemy, and was set against me from then on.

In a big household like Arcamand, a slave who wants to get another slave in trouble has plenty of opportunities. Luckily Hoby slept in the barrack while I was still in the house. —But as I write this story now, for you, my dear wife, and anybody else who may want to read it, I find myself thinking the way I thought back then, twenty years ago, as a boy, as a slave. My memory brings me the past as if it were present, here, now, and I forget that there are things to explain, not only to you but maybe also to myself. Writing about our life in the House of Arcamand in the City State of Etra, I fall back into it and see it as I saw it then, from inside and from below, with nothing to compare it to, and as if it were the only way things could possibly be. Children see the world that way. So do most slaves. Freedom is largely a matter of seeing that there are alternatives.

Etra was all I knew then, and this is how it was. The City States are almost constantly at war, so soldiers are important there. Soldiers are men of the two upper classes, the wellborn, from whom the governing Senate is elected, and the freemen—farmers, merchants, contractors, architects, and such. Male freemen have the right to vote on some laws, but not to hold office. Among the freemen is a small number of freedmen. Below them are the slaves.

Physical work is done by women of all classes in the house and by slaves in the house and outdoors. Slaves are captured in battle or raids, or bred at home, and are bought or given by families of the two upper classes. A slave has no legal rights, cannot marry, and can claim no parents and no children.

The people of the City States worship the ancestors of those now living. People without ancestors—freedmen and slaves—can only worship the forebears of the family that owns them or the Forefathers of the City, great spirits of the days long ago. And the slaves love some of the gods known elsewhere in the lands of the Western Shore: Ennu, and Raniu's Lord, and Luck.

It's plain that I was born a slave, because here I am talking mostly about them. If you read a history of Etra or any other of the City States, it'll be about kings, senators, generals, valiant soldiers, rich merchants—the acts of people of power, free to act—not about slaves. The quality and virtue of a slave is invisibility. The powerless need to be invisible even to themselves. That was something Sallo already knew, and I was learning it.

We slaves, we house people, ate at the pantry handout, where grain porridge or bread, cheese and olives, were always to be had, fruit fresh or dried, milk, and hot soup in the evening and on winter mornings. Our clothes and shoes were good, our bedding clean and

warm. Arcamand was a wealthy and generous house.
The Mother spoke with contempt of masters who sent
their slaves into the streets barefoot, hungry, or scarred
with beatings. In Arcamand, old slaves past useful work
were kept on, fed and clothed, till they died; Gammy,
whom Sallo and I loved, and who had been the Father's
nursemaid, was treated with special kindness in her old
age. We boasted to slaves from other houses that our
soup was made with meat and our blankets were
woollen. We looked down on the liveries some of them
had to wear—showy and shoddy, we thought them.
Not traditional, ancestral, solid, sound, like everything
at our house.

Adult male slaves slept in a big separate building
called the barrack off the back courtyard, women and
children in a great dormitory near the kitchens. Babies
both of the Family and of house people and their wetnurses had a nursery closer to the Family's rooms. The
gift-girls lived and entertained their visitors or lovers in
the silk rooms, pleasant apartments off the west inner
garden.

It was up to the women to decide when a boy ought
to move to the men's barrack. They had sent Hoby
across the court a few months ago to get rid of him, he

was such a bully with the younger children in the dormitory. The older boys in the barrack were hard on him at first, I think, but still he saw it as a promotion to manhood and sneered at us for sleeping "in the litter."

Tib longed to be sent across the court too, but I was perfectly happy in the dormitory, where Sallo and I had our own little nook with a lock-box and a mattress all to ourselves. Gammy had mothered us, and when she died they let us look after each other. Since slaves have no parents or children, in a dormitory a woman may take on a child or children to mother; no child is left to sleep alone, and some have several women looking after them. The children call all the women "aunty." Our aunties said I didn't need a motherer, since I had such a good sister, and I agreed.

My sister no longer had to protect me from Hoby's persecutions in the dormitory, but they grew worse elsewhere. My sweeping duties took me all over the great house, and Hoby kept an eye out for me in any court or corridor where nobody else was likely to be. When he found me alone, he'd grab me by the back of my neck, lift me up, and shake me the way a dog shakes a rat to break its neck, grinning all the time into my face; then he'd throw me down hard on the ground, kick me, and go off. It was horrible being held up like that, helpless. I kicked and struck at him wildly but my arms were so much shorter than his that I couldn't reach him, and if my kicks landed he never seemed to feel them. I dared not cry out for help, since a quarrel among slaves that disturbed members of the Family would be severely punished. I suppose my helplessness fed his cruelty, for it grew. He never shook and kicked me in front of other people, but he lay in wait for me more and more often, and he tripped me, knocked my plate of food out of my hands, and so on, and worst of all, lied about me to everyone, accusing me of stealing and sneaking.

The women in the dormitory paid little attention to Hoby's tales, but the older boys in the barrack listened to him and came to treat me as a worthless little spy, a master's pet. I didn't see much of those boys, whose work took them out of my way. But I saw Torm daily at lessons. Ever since the battle in the ditch, Torm had dropped Tib and me entirely and made Hoby his only companion. Hoby had taken to calling me "the dung," and Torm began to do so too.

Everra could not reprove Torm directly. Torm was the son of the Father. Our schoolmaster was a slave; it was his role, not himself, that was respected. He could correct Torm's mistakes in reading or measurements or music, but not his conduct; he could say, "You need to do that exercise over," but he couldn't say, "Stop doing that!" But Torm's fits of mindless rage when he was younger had given Everra an excuse and device which he still used to control him. When Torm began to shout and strike out, Everra used to lug him bodily out of the schoolroom and shut him up in a storage room down the hall, with the threat that if he came out, the Mother and Father would be told of his misbehavior. Torm would get over his fit there in solitude, and wait to be released. It may have been a relief to him, in fact, to be shut away; for even in the midst of a yelling, foaming rage, when he had grown too big and strong for Everra to manhandle, if the teacher said, "To the hall room, Torm-dí," he'd go running there and let the door be shut on him. He hadn't had a fit of that kind for nearly a year now. But once or twice, when he was unruly and restless, disturbing everybody else, Everra had said quietly to him, "To the hall room, please," and he had gone, obedient as ever.

One spring day in the classroom, Hoby was bent on persecuting me; he shook the bench when I was writing, he spilled the ink and accused me of trying to spoil his copybook, he pinched me savagely when I had to pass him. The teacher caught him doing that, and said, "Keep your hands off Gavir, Hoby. Hold them out!"

Hoby stood up and stuck out his hands palm up for the punishment, with his sheepish, stoical grin.

But Torm said, "He did nothing to be punished for."

Everra stood silent, taken aback. Finally he said, "He was tormenting Gavir, Torm-dí."

"That boy is dung. He should be punished, not Hoby. He spilled the ink."

"That was an accident, Torm-dí. I do not punish accidents."

"It was not. Hoby did nothing to be punished for. Punish the dung boy."

Though Torm was not going into the shaking frenzy of his old rages, he had the look of them in his face, a grimace, a blind stare. Our teacher stood silent. I saw him glance over at Yaven, who was on the other side of the room bent over the drawing table, absorbed in measuring an architectural plan. I too was hoping the older brother would notice what was going on; but he didn't, and Astano was not in class that day.

At last Everra said, "To the hall room, please, Torm-dí."

Torm took a step or two in automatic obedience. Then he stopped.

He turned to face the teacher. "I, I, I order you to punish the dung boy," he said, thickly, barely able to make the words, his face quivering and shaking as it had that day when his father reprimanded him.

Everra's face went grey. He stood still, looking thin and old. Again he looked over towards Yaven.

"This is my classroom, Torm-dí," he said at last, with dignity, but almost inaudibly.

"And you are a slave and I give you an order!" Torm cried, his voice, which had not broken, going up shrill.

Now Yaven heard and looked round, straightening up.

"Torm?" he said.

"I've had enough of this filth, this disobedience!" Torm cried in that thick, shrill voice. He sounded like a crazy old woman. Maybe that was what made four-year-old Miv laugh. His little giggle rang out. Torm turned on the child and struck him a smashing blow to the head that threw him right off the bench against the wall.

Then Yaven was there, and with a grave and hasty apology to the teacher, took his brother by the arm and led him out of the room. Torm did not resist and did not say anything. He still glared blindly, but his face had gone loose and confused.

Hoby stood staring after him with the same dull, stricken look. Never had I seen so clearly that it was almost the same face.

Sallo was cradling little Miv, who had not made a sound. He seemed dazed for a while, then he wriggled about and turned his face against Sallo's arm. If he cried it was in silence.

The teacher knelt by them and tried to make sure the child had suffered no injury except the bruise that would be swelling up soon across half his face. He told Sallo and Miv's sister Oco to take him out to the atrium fountain and bathe his face. Then he turned to Ris and Sotur, Tib and Hoby and me, the only pupils left. "We will read Trudec," he said, his voice still hoarse and faint. "The Sixtieth Morality. On Patience."

He had Sotur read first. She stumbled bravely through it.

Soturovaso was the Father's niece. Her father had been killed at the siege of Morva soon after her mother died giving birth to her, so she was an orphan within the Family, the last and least among them. She had much the same quiet modesty as her older cousin Astano, whom she trusted and imitated, but the temper underneath it was quite different. She was no rebel, but she was not resigned. She was a solitary soul.

She was extremely upset now by Torm's defiance and discourtesy towards our teacher, whom she loved. Because she was the only one of the Family in the room, she felt responsible for that injury and for the apologies that should follow. There was nothing she, a child of twelve, could do, except obey promptly and show the teacher the utmost politeness, which she did. But she read very badly. The book was shaking in her hands. Everra soon thanked her and told me to go on with the passage.

As I began to read, I heard Hoby, on the bench behind me, move restlessly and hiss something. The teacher glanced at him and he was silent, but not quite silent. I was aware of him there behind me all the time as I read.

We got through the rest of the morning lessons somehow. Just as we were finishing, Sallo came back. She reported that she had left little Miv and his sister with the healer Remen, because Miv was dizzy and kept falling asleep. The Mother had been told, and would come see to the child. That was reassuring. Old Remen was only a slave mender, whose cure for everything was comfrey ointment and catnip tea, but the Mother was a renowned and experienced healer. "Arca looks after her own, even the littlest," Everra said with grave gratitude. "As you leave today, go by the Ancestors and give them worship. Ask them to bless all the children of the House, all its children, and its kind Mother."

We all obeyed him. Only Sotur could go in among the Ancestors, whose names and carven images crowded the walls of the great, dim, domed room. We house people knelt in the anteroom. Sallo held her little Ennu-Mé in her closed hand and murmured, "Ennu bless us and be blessed, please make Miv all right. I follow you, Ennu-Mé, dear guide." I made the reverence and knelt to my chosen Ancestor, Altan Bodo Arca, Father of the House a hundred years ago, whose portrait, carved in relief on stone and painted, could be seen from where we knelt. He had a wonderful face, like a kindly hawk, and his eyes looked straight at me. I had decided as a very small child that he was my special protector, also that he knew what I was thinking. I didn't have to tell him that I was frightened of both

Torm and Hoby right now. He knew. "Great Shadow, Forefather, Grandfather Altan-dí, let me get away from them," I asked him silently, "or make them not so angry. Thank you." After a while I added, "And please make me braver."

That was a good thought. I would need courage that day.

Sallo and I did the sweeping together and kept together while she did her spinning and I wrote out our geometry lesson. We didn't see Hoby around at the pantry or in the house. Evening came, and I thought I'd escaped and was wondering if I should go thank the Ancestor, when as I came back from the privies to the women's court I heard Hoby's voice behind me, "There he is!" I ran, but he and the big fellows with him caught me at once. I kicked and yelled and fought, but I was a rabbit among the hounds.

They took me to the well behind the barrack, pulled out the bucket, and took turns stuffing me into the well head down, holding my legs and pushing my body down till my head was under water and I was choking and breathing water, then pulling me up just far enough to recover.

Whenever they brought me back up into the air, strangling and writhing and vomiting, Hoby would lean

over me and say in a queer flat voice, "That's for betraying your master, you little traitor. For sucking up to that
foul old teacher, you swamp rat. See how you like getting wet, swamp rat." And they would cram me down
into the well again, and no matter how I tried to brace
my arms against the stones and hold my head away from
the water they would push me down and down till the
water flooded into my nostrils and I gasped and choked,
drowning. I don't know how many times they did it till
I lost consciousness, but I must have gone limp at last,
and that scared them into thinking I was dead.

It's a capital offense for anyone but his master to kill
a slave. They ran off and left me lying there by the well-
head.

It was old Remen the slave mender who found me,
coming to the back well, which he always said had purer
water than the fountains. "Fell over him in the dark,"
he would say, telling the story afterwards. "Thought
he was a dead cat! No, too big for a cat. Who's been
drowning a dog in the well? No, it's not a drowned dog,
it's a drowned boy! By Luck! Who's been drowning
boys here?"

That was not a question I ever answered.

I suppose the boys thought their torture would not
leave visible injuries, so my claims against them could

be denied for lack of evidence; but in fact my arms and hands and head were lacerated and swollen with bruises I got in my struggles down in the narrow well, and even my ankles were black and blue from their merciless hands. Tough-bodied and hardy boys, they probably had no idea that they were doing me real harm, aside from terrifying me.

I came to in Remen's little infirmary sometime that night; my chest hurt and my head ached, but I lay peacefully floating in a shallow pool of dim, yellowish light, feeling the silence moving out from me like the rings on quiet water. Gradually I became aware that my sister Sallo was asleep beside me, and that made the wonderful peacefulness sweeter still. I lay that way a long time, sometimes seeing only dim gold and shadows, sometimes remembering things. I remembered the reeds and the still, silky, blue water, and the blue hill away off in the distance. Then it was just the pool of light and the shadows and Sallo's breathing again for a while. Then I remembered Hoby's voice, "There he is!"—but the terror was like the pain and the headache, remote, untroubling. I turned my head a little and saw the tiny oil lamp that poured out that endless pool of warm, golden light from its grain of fire. And I remembered the man in the high, dark room. He was standing at a big table covered with books and papers, with a lamp and a writing desk on it, under a tall, narrow window; he turned to look at me as I came into the room. I saw him very clearly this time. His hair was turning grey and his face was a little like the Ancestor's, both fierce and kind; but where the Ancestor was full of pride, he was full of sorrow. Yet seeing me he smiled, and spoke my name, Gavir.

"Gavir" again…and I was in the pool of dim light, looking up a long way, it seemed, at a woman's face. She wore a night wrapper of white wool drawn partly over her head. Her face was smooth and grave. She looked like Astano but was not Astano. I thought I was remembering her. Slowly I realised that she was the Mother, Falimer Galleco Arca, at whose face I had never in my life gazed openly. Now I lay staring at her as if she were a carven image, an Ancestor, dreamily, without fear.

Beside me Sallo, sound asleep, stirred a little.

The Mother laid the back of her hand a moment on my forehead, and nodded a little. "All right?" she murmured. I was too weary and dreamy to speak but I must have nodded or smiled, because she smiled a little, touched my cheek, and went on.

There was a crib bed near my bed; she paused there a while. That would be little Miv, I thought, drifting back into the silence of the pool of light. I remembered when we went to bury Miv, down by the river, how the willows were like green rain in the grey rain of spring. I remembered Miv's sister Oco standing by the small black grave with a flowering branch in her hand. I looked out across the river dappled with raindrops. I remembered when we all went down to the river to bury old Gammy; that was in winter, the willows were bare over the riverbanks, but I wasn't so sad then because it was like a holiday, a festival, so many people came to bury Gammy, and there was to be a wake-feast after. And I briefly remembered some other time there, in spring again, I did not know who was being buried. Maybe it was myself, I thought. I saw the sorrow in the eyes of the man standing by the lamp at the table in the high, dark room.

And it was morning. Soft daylight instead of the dim golden pool. Sallo had gone. Miv was a little lump in the crib bed nearby. At the end of the room an old man lay in bed: Loter, who had been a cook till he got old, and got sick, and now was here to die. Remen was helping him sit up against a pillow. Loter groaned and moaned. I felt all right, and got up; then my head hurt and went dizzy, and a lot of parts of me hurt, so I sat down on the bed for a while.

"Up, are you, marsh rat?" old Remen said, coming over to me. He felt some of the lumps on my head. He had splinted a dislocated finger on my right hand, and explained the splint to me while he checked it. "You'll do," he said. "Tough, you kids are. Who did that to you, anyhow?"

I shrugged.

He glanced at me, nodded shortly, and did not ask again. He and I were slaves, we lived in a complicity of silences.

Remen wouldn't let me leave the infirmary that morning, saying that the Mother was coming in to look at both me and Miv; so I sat on the bed and examined my lumps and cuts, which were extensive and interesting. When I got bored with them I recited from *The Siege and Fall of Sentas*, chanting the lines. Along near noon, Miv finally woke up, and I could go over and talk to him. He was very groggy and didn't make much sense. He looked at me and asked me why I was two. "Two what?" I said, and he said, "Two Gavs."

"Seeing double," said old Remen, coming over. "A

whack on the head'll do that. —Mistress!" and he went down in the reverence, and I did too, as the Mother came into the room.

She checked Miv very thoroughly. His head looked misshapen on the left from the swelling, and she looked into his ear and pressed his skull and cheekbones softly. Her face was concerned, but finally she said, "He is coming back," in her deep, soft voice, and smiled. She was holding him on her lap, and she spoke tenderly. "Aren't you, little Miv? You're coming back to us."

"It roars," he said plaintively, squinting and blinking. "Is Oco coming?"

Remen, shocked, tried to get him to address the Mother properly, but she waved him away. "He's only a baby," she said. "I'm glad you decided to come back, little one." She held him a while, her cheek against his hair; then she put him back in his crib and said, "Now go to sleep again, and when you wake up your sister will be here."

"All right," Miv said, and curled up and shut his eyes.

"What a lamb," the Mother said. She looked at me. "Ah, you're up, you're afoot, good for you," she said. She did look like her slender daughter Astano, but her face, like her body, was full and smooth and powerful. As-tano's glance was shy; the Mother's gaze was steady. I looked down at once, of course.

"Who hurt you, lad?" she asked.

Not to answer old Remen was one thing. Not to answer the Mother was quite another.

After an awful pause I said the only thing that came to me: "I fell into the well, Mistress."

"Oh, come," she said, chiding but amused.

I stood mute.

"You're a very clumsy boy, Gavir," said the musical voice. "But a courageous one." She examined my lumps and bruises. "He looks all right to me, Remen. How's the hand?" She took my hand and looked at the splinted finger. "That'll take some weeks," she said. "You're the scholar, eh? No writing for you for a while. But Everra will know how to keep you busy. Run along, then."

I bobbed the reverence to her and said, "Thank you," to old Remen, and got out. I ran to the pantry, and found Sallo there, and even while we were hugging and she was asking if I was really all right, I was telling her that the Mother knew my name, and knew who I was, and called me the scholar!

I didn't say that she had called me courageous. That was too immense a thing to talk about.

When I tried to eat, it didn't go down very well, and my head began thumping, so Sallo went with me to the dormitory and left me on our bed there. I spent that afternoon and most of the next day there, doing a lot of sleeping. Then I woke up starving hungry and was all right, except that I looked, as Sotur said, as if I'd been left out on a battlefield for the crows.

It was only two days since I'd been in the schoolroom, but they welcomed me back as if I'd been gone for months, and it felt that way to me too. The teacher took my injured hand in his long, strong-fingered hands and stroked it once. "When it heals, Gavir, I am going to teach you to write well and clearly," he said. "No more scrawling in the copybook. Right?" He was smiling, and for some reason what he said made me extremely happy. There was a care for me in it, a concern as gentle as his touch.

Hoby was watching. Torm was watching. I turned around and faced them. I reverenced Torm briefly; he turned away. I said, "Hello, Hoby." He had a sick look. I think seeing all my swellings and bruises in their green and purple glory scared him. But he knew I had not told on him. Everybody knew it. Just as everybody knew who had attacked me. There might be silence, but there were no secrets in our life.

But if I accused nobody, it was nobody's business, not even the masters'.

Torm had turned from me with a glowering look, but Yaven and Astano were kind and friendly. As for Sotur, she evidently felt she'd been thoughtless or heartless saying that I looked like I'd been left for the crows, for when she could speak to me without anybody else hearing she said, "Gavir, you are a hero." She spoke solemnly, and looked near tears.

I didn't understand yet that the whole matter was more serious than my small part of it.

Sallo had said little Miv was to be kept in the infirmary till he was quite well, and knowing he was in the Mother's care I thought no more about him or my fever dreams of the burial ground.

But in the dormitory that night, Ennumer, who mothered Miv and Oco, was in tears. All the women and girls gathered about her, Sallo with them. Tib came over to me and whispered what he'd heard: that Miv was bleeding from his ear, and they thought his head had been broken by Torm's blow. Then I remembered the green willows by the river, and my heart went cold.

The next day Miv went into convulsions several

times. We heard that the Mother came to the infirmary and stayed with him all that evening and night. I thought of how she had stood by my bed in the golden light. When we were sitting on our mattress in the evening, I said to Tib and Sallo, "The Mother is as kind as Ennu."

Sallo nodded, hugging me, but Tib said, "She knows who hit him."

"What difference does that make?"

Tib made a face.

I was angry at him. "She *is* our Mother," I said. "She cares for us all. She's kind. You don't know anything about her."

I felt I knew her, knew her as the heart knows what it loves. She had touched me with her gentle hand. She had said I was courageous.

Tib hunched up and shrugged and said nothing. He had been moody and gloomy since Hoby turned away from him. I was still his friend, but he'd always wanted Hoby's friendship more than mine. He saw my cuts and bruises now with shame and discomfort, and was shy with me. It was Sallo who got him to come over to our nook and sit and talk with us before the women put the lights out.

"I'm glad she lets Oco stay with Miv," Sallo said now. "Poor Oco, she's so scared for him."

"Ennumer would like to stay with him too," Tib said.

"The Mother is a healer!" I said. "She'll look after him. Ennumer couldn't do anything. She'd just howl. Like now."

Ennumer was in fact a foolish, noisy young woman, without half as much good sense as six-year-old Oco; but though her mothering had been random, she was truly fond of Oco and Miv, her doll-baby as she called him. Her grief now was real, and loud. "Oh my poor little doll-baby!" she cried out. "I want to see him! I want to hold him!"

The headwoman came over to her and put her hands on Ennumer's shoulders.

"Hush," she said. "He is in the Mother's arms."

And tear-smeared, scared Ennumer hushed.

Iemmer had been headwoman of Arcamand for many years, and had great personal authority. She reported to the Mother and the Family, of course, but she never gained advantage for herself by making trouble for other house people, as she might have done. The Mother had proved that she didn't like tattlers and toadies, by selling a tattler, and by choosing Iemmer as headwoman. Iemmer played fair. She had favorites—among us all, Sallo was her darling—but she didn't favor anyone, or pick on anyone either.

To Ennumer, she was an awesome figure, far more immediately powerful than the Mother. Ennumer blubbered a little more, quietly, and let the women around her comfort her.

Ennumer had been sent to us from Herramand five years ago as a birthday gift to Sotur's older brother Soter. She was then a pretty girl of fifteen, untrained and illiterate, for the Herra Family, like many others, thought it an unnecessary ostentation or even a risk to educate slaves, particularly girl slaves.

I knew Ennumer had had babies, two or three of them. Both Sotur's older brothers often sent for her; she got pregnant; the baby was given to one of the wetnurses, and presently traded to another House. Miv and Oco had been part of one of those bargains. Babies were almost always sold off or traded. Gammy used to tell us, "I bore six and mothered none. Didn't look for any baby to mother, after I nursed Altan-dí. And then you two come along to plague me in my old age!"

Very rarely the mother, not the child, was sold off.

That was Hoby's case. He had been born on the same day as Torm, the son of the Family, and alleging this as a sign or omen, the Father had ordered that he be kept. His mother, a gift-girl, had been sold promptly to prevent the complications of kinship. A mother may believe the child she bore is hers, but property can't own property; we belong to the Family, the Mother is our mother and the Father is our father. I understood all that.

I understood why Ennumer was crying, too. But to a boy my age women's griefs were too troubling to endure. I warded them off, walled them out. "Play Ambush?" I challenged Tib, and we got out the slates and chalk and marked the squares and played Ambush till lights-out.

Miv died as the sun rose that morning.

◆　◆　◆

THE DEATH OF a slave child would not ordinarily cause any disturbance to a great House such as Arcamand. The slave women would weep, and the women of the Family would come with kind words and gifts of burial wrappings or money to buy them. Very early in the morning a little troop of slaves in funeral white would carry the litter down to the riverside graveyard, and pray at the grave to Ennu to lead the small soul home, and come back weeping, and get to work.

But this death was not quite ordinary. Everyone in Arcamand knew why Miv had died, and it was a troubling knowledge. This time, it was the slaves who spoke and the masters who kept silence.

Of course the slaves spoke only to other slaves.

But there was talk such as I had never heard: bitter anger, indignation, not from the women only but from men. Metter, the Father's bodyguard, respected by all for his strength and dignity, said in the barrack that the child's death was a shame to the Family, for which the Ancestors would demand atonement. The chief hostler, Sem, a clever, vigorous, fearless man, said out loud that Torm was a mad dog. Such sayings were whispered around the courts and corridors and the dormitory. And Remen's story, too: he told us that the Mother was holding Miv on her lap when he died, and she held him close for a long time and whispered to him, "Forgive me, little one, forgive."

He told this in the hope it might console Ennumer, for she was wild with grief, and it did comfort her to know the child had been in tender arms when he died, and that the Mother grieved that she hadn't been able to save him. But others heard it differently. "She might well ask forgiveness!" Iemmer said, and others agreed. The story of how Miv had innocently laughed at Torm and how Torm had turned on the child and knocked him across the room—Oco had sobbed it out the day it happened, and Tib and Sallo had confirmed it, and as it was retold in the barrack and stables it lost nothing in the telling.

Hoby defended Torm, saying he'd only meant to slap the child for impertinence and didn't know his own strength. But Hoby was in ill favor. Nobody openly blamed him for my adventure at the well, since I hadn't accused him, but nobody admired him for it. And now his loyalty to Torm was held against him; it looked too much like siding with the masters against the slaves. I heard the stableboys call him "Twinny" behind his back. And Metter said to him, "A man who doesn't know his own strength ought to learn it fighting with men, not beating up babies."

This talk of blame and forgiveness was very distressing to me. It seemed to open cracks and faults in the world, to shake things loose. I went to the anteroom of the Ancestors and tried to pray to my guardian there, but his painted eyes looked through me, haughty and uninterested. Sotur was in the room, bowed down in silent worship; she had lighted incense at the altar of the Mothers, and the smoke drifted up into the high, shadowy dome.

That night after Miv died, I dreamed that I was sweeping one of the inner courts of the House and found leading from it a corridor I had never seen before, which led to rooms I did not know, where strangers turned to greet me as if they knew me. I was frightened of transgressing, but they smiled, and one of them held out a beautiful ripe peach to me. "Take it," she said, and called me by some name I could not remember when I woke. There was a shining like the trembling of sunlight all round her head. I slept and dreamed again, exploring the new rooms; I met no people now, but heard their voices in other rooms as I followed the high stone corridors. I came to a bright interior courtyard where a small fountain ran and a golden animal came to me trustingly and let me stroke its fur. When I woke I went on thinking about those rooms, that house. It was Arcamand and not Arcamand. "My house," I called it in my mind, because I had the freedom of it. The sunlight there was brighter.

Whether it was a memory or a dream, I longed to dream it again.

But the green willows by the river, that had been a memory of what was to be.

We went down to the river that morning to bury Miv. Light was just coming into the world, a long time yet till sunrise. Sparse grey rain fell among the willows and drifted over the river. I remembered it and saw it at the same time.

A great crowd of people followed the mourners in white and the white-draped litter, as great a crowd as had come to Gammy's burial, almost all the slaves of Arcamand. Only those were missing whose absence from their duties, even so early in the morning, even for a burial, was not permitted. It was unusual to see so many men at a child's funeral. Ennumer wept and wailed aloud, and so did some of the other women, but the men were silent, and we children were silent.

They covered the little white bundle in the shallow grave with black earth. Miv's sister Oco came forward, tremulous and bewildered by grief, and laid on it a long spray of willow with delicate yellow catkin flowers. Iemmer took her hand and standing by the grave said the prayer to Ennu, the guide of the soul into death. To keep from crying I watched the river and the speckle of raindrops on its surface. We stood quite near it. Not far from us, where the bank was lower, I could see where old graves were being washed away by the current as it worked against the curve of the land. The whole outer edge of the great slave cemetery was flooded by the river running high in spring. Willows stood far out in the water, trailing their new green leaves. I thought of the water coming up here to the new grave, oozing into the dirt around Miv wrapped up in white cloth, rising and filling the grave, washing him away with the dirt and the leaves, the white cloth trailing in the current like smoke. Sallo took my hand and I pressed close to her side. Everything was washing and drifting and trailing away with the water, except my sister Sallo, except her. She was here. With me.

◆ 3 ◆

We went back to the House and to work. Everra did not hold class that day. Sallo and I did our sweeping. When we were sweeping the silk-room court she came and took hold of my hand suddenly. She was in tears. She said, "Oh, Gav, I keep thinking about Oco— If I lost my little brother I would die!" She hugged me fiercely, and then seeing I was crying too, she hugged me again, whispering, "You won't ever go away, will you, Gav?"

I said, "Never. I promise."

"I hear," she said, trying to smile.

We both knew well enough what a slave's promise is worth, but still it comforted us both.

When we finished sweeping, she went with Ris to the spinning room. I went to the pantry and found Tib, and we loitered out to the back court. Some of the big boys were there. I held back—I had never been sure which ones had helped Hoby dunk me—but they spoke to us mildly. They were playing toss, and one of them lobbed the ball to me. I only had one hand to catch with, but caught and passed it creditably, and then stood back and watched them throw and catch. One of them asked, "Where's Hoby?" and another, Tan, said, "In trouble."

"What for?"

"Sucking up," Tan said, with a high loft of the ball to Tib. Tib fumbled it, another boy retrieved it and lobbed it back to Tan. He caught it, tossed it high and caught it, and turned to me. Tan was a stableboy, sixteen or seventeen years old, a short, thin fellow almost as dark-skinned as me. "You had the right idea, young Gav," he said. "Stick to your own. Don't go looking for gratitude up there." He glanced at the windowed wall of Arcamand towering over the courtyard and back at me, and winked. He had a keen, bright face. I'd always liked Tan, and was flattered by his notice. As the older boys left, another of them slapped me lightly on the shoulder, the kind of comradely notice that looks like nothing and means a lot. It brought a warmth to me I needed. I'd been down at the river in my head all morning, in the grey rain and the silence and the cold.

Tib ran off to the kitchen to his work. I had nothing to do. I went to the schoolroom because there was nowhere else to go. And because if any room in Arcamand was my room, it was that one. It was dear to me, with its four high north windows, its carved and grimy benches and desks and tables, the teacher's lectern, the bookshelves and stacked-up copybooks and slates, the big glass ink jug from which we filled our inkwells. Sallo and I were in charge of keeping it swept, dusted, and orderly, and though it looked quite neat and peaceful, I set to sorting and straightening out the books on the long shelves. All work was made awkward by the splint on my finger. Often I stopped and had a look into a book I hadn't read yet. Sitting on the floor by the shelves, I opened Saltoc Asper's *History of the City State of Trebs*, and got to reading about the long war between Hill Trebs and Carvol, which ended in the rebellion of the slaves in Hill Trebs and the utter destruction of the city. It was an exciting story, and troubling because it was about what I had glimpsed through those cracks in the walls. I was completely lost in it when Everra said, "Gavir?"

I leapt up and reverenced him and apologised. He smiled. "What's the book?"

I showed him.

"Read it if you like," he said, "though it might be better to read Asham first. Asper is political. Asham is above opinion." He went over to his lectern and looked through some papers, then sat on the long-legged stool and looked at me again. I was rearranging books.

"This is a heavy day," he said.

I nodded.

"I attended on Father Altan-dí this morning. I have some news that may lighten the day for you a little." He rubbed his hand over his mouth and jaw. "The Family will be going to the country early this year, at the beginning of May. I will go with them, and all my pupils, except for Hoby. He is henceforth excused from school and will serve under Haster. And Torm-dí has been granted leave to stay in the city and learn swordsmanship from a master teacher. He will join us in the country only at the end of summer."

This was a lot of news to absorb all at once, and at first I saw only the promise of a long country summer at the farm in the Ventine Hills. Then I saw the bonus—without Hoby! without Torm!— That was a moment of bliss. It was quite a while before I began to think about it in any other terms.

Tan and the other boys had already known it, this morning in the courtyard—news always got all over the House immediately: *Hoby's in trouble for sucking up...* Hoby hadn't been rewarded for his loyalty to Torm, but punished for it. "Serving under Haster" meant being sent to the civic workforce, to which every House contributed a quota of male slaves, to do the heaviest, hardest kind of labor and live in the city barrack, which was little better than a jail.

On the other hand, Torm hadn't been punished for killing little Miv, but rewarded for it. Studying the arts of war was the dream of his heart.

It burst out of me— "It's not fair!"

"Gavir," the teacher said.

"But it's not, Teacher-dí! Torm killed Miv!"

"He did not mean to, Gavir. Yet he is being made to do penance. He is not allowed to come with the Mother and the rest of us to Vente. He will live with his teacher and be subjected to a very severe discipline. Swordmaster Attec's pupils lead a hard, bare life of constant training, with no reward but their increase of skill. The Father spoke of it to Torm-dí while I was there. He said, 'You must learn self-restraint, my son, and with Attec you will learn it.' And Torm-dí bowed his head."

"But then Hoby—what did he do to be punished?"

The teacher was taken aback. "What did he do?" he repeated, looking at my scabs and swellings and splinted finger.

"But that—that didn't hurt the Family," I said, not knowing how to say what I felt. I meant that if Hoby was punished for what he'd done to me, it should be by his and my people, the slaves. That's why I hadn't said who hurt me. It was between us. It was beneath the Family's notice. But if Hoby was being punished for his attempt to defend Torm, clumsy as it had been, then it was so unfair that it must be a mistake—a misunderstanding.

"What happened to you was no accident," Everra said, "though in your loyalty to your schoolmate you say it was. But Hoby was insolent to me. And through me the authority of the Father acts in this classroom. That cannot be tolerated, Gavir. Listen now; come sit here."

He went to sit at the reading table, and I went to sit by him, as I would when reading with him. "Loyalty is a great thing, but loyalty misplaced is troublesome and dangerous. I know you're troubled. Everyone in the House is troubled. The death of a child is a pitiable thing. You're hearing wild, angry talk, maybe, in the barrack and the dormitory. When you hear such talk, you must think what this household is: Is it a wilderness? Is it a battlefield? Is it an endless, hidden war of sullen rage against implacable force? Is that the truth of your life here? Or have you lived here as a member of a family blessed by its ancestors, where each person has his part to play, always striving to act with justice?"

He let me think that over a minute, and went on, "When in doubt, Gavir, look up. Not down. Look up for guidance. Strength comes from above. Your part is with the highest in this House. Born wild as you were, a slave as you are, as I am, without family, yet you've been taken into the heart of a great household and given all you need—shelter and food, great Ancestors and a kindly Father to guide you. And as well as all that, nourishment for your spirit—the learning I was given and can pass on to you. You have been given trust. The sacred gift. Our Family trusts us, Gavir. They entrust their sons and daughters to me! How can I earn that honor? By my loyal effort to deserve it. I wish when I die it might be said of me, 'He never betrayed those who trusted him.'"

His dry voice had become gentle, and he looked at me a while before he went on. "You know, Gavir, behind you, in the wilderness you came from, there's nothing for you. In the shifting sands beneath you, there's nothing for you to build on. But look up! Above you, in the power that sustains you and the wisdom offered to you—there you can set your heart, there you can put your trust. There you will find treasure. And justice. And a mother's mercy, which you never knew."

It was as if he talked of the house I had dreamed of, that sunlit house where I was safe and welcome and free. He restored it to me in waking life.

I couldn't say anything, of course. He saw what comfort he had given me, though, and he reached out to pat my shoulder, as the boy in the courtyard had, a light, brotherly touch.

He stood up to break the mood. "What shall we take to read in the summer?" he asked, and I said without thinking, "Not Trudec!"

◆　◆　◆

THE FAMILY HAD STAYED in the city for the past two summers, since the farm had not been considered safe from roving bands of Votusan soldiers out for plunder in the Ventine Hills; but our army had a camp now near Vente and had driven the Votusans back to their city gates.

I remembered the farm as a marvelous place. It was as if I felt the warmth of summer whenever I thought about it. Even the preparations for going were exciting, and when we actually set off, a great straggling procession of horse-drawn chariots and wagons and donkey carts and outriders and people afoot going through the streets of Etra to the River Gate, it was as good as a heroes' parade, even if we didn't have drums and trumpets. The chariots in which the women and girls and old people of the Family rode were high and ungainly and seemed too wide for the bridge across the Nisas; but Sem and Tan and all the drivers and outriders were in their glory, guiding the teams across, hoofs clattering on the bridge, plumes on the harnesses nodding. Sotur's elder brothers rode ahead with Yaven on fine saddle horses. The wagons and carts came creaking behind, with a lot of shouting and whipcracking, and the inevitable donkey who did not want to cross the bridge. Some of the women and little children rode on the wagons, high on the piled-up goods and foodstuff, but most of us walked, and when people stopped to watch us go by, Tib and I waved at them with patronising pity, because we were going to the country and they, poor cockroaches, had to stay all summer in the city.

Tib and I were like dogs on an outing, traveling three times farther than anybody else because we kept running up the line of the procession and back to the back again. By noon we had become a bit less energetic and mostly stayed close to the women's wagon, where Sallo and Ris had to ride, because they were getting to the age where girls can't run loose; they had Oco with them, and several babies, and the kitchen women, who were always good for a handout of food when Tib and I came panting by.

The road was going up now, winding among small hillside fields and oak groves; ahead were the round green summits of the Ventine Hills. As we climbed we began to be able to look back over the countryside and see the silver curve of the Nisas where it ran down to the wider river Morr. Across the Nisas was Etra, our city, a hazy huddle of roofs of thatch and wood and red tile in the circle of its walls, with four towered gates of yellowish stone. There was the bulk of the Senate House, and the dome of the Forefathers' Shrine. We tried to make out the roofs of Arcamand, and were sure we saw the tops of the sycamore grove by the wall where we used to drill with Torm—miles away, years ago...

The wagons creaked slower and slower, the horses strained at the climb, the drivers flicked their whips, the gaudy tops of the chariots up ahead dipped and rocked as the high wheels lurched in the ruts of the dusty road. The sun was hot, the breeze in the shade of the road-side oaks cool. Cattle and goats in the wood-fenced pastures watched our procession solemnly; colts at a horse farm went bucking off stiff-legged at the sight of the chariots, and then came mincing back to have another look. Somebody came running down the line of carts and wagons, a girl—Sotur, who had escaped from the Family and now clambered up onto the wagon to sit with Ris and Sallo. She was flushed with the excitement of her escapade and much more talkative than usual—"I told Mother Falimer-ío I wanted to ride outside, so she said go ahead, so I came back here. It's all stuffy and jouncy in the chariots, and Redili's baby threw up. It's much better here!" Pretty soon she began to sing, raising her sweet, strong voice in one of the old rounds everybody knew. Sallo and Ris joined in, and the kitchen women, and then people walking or riding

in other wagons up the line sang too, so the music carried us up the road into the hills of Vente.

We came to the Arca farm after sunset, a long day's
journey of ten miles.

To look back on that summer and the summers
after it is like looking across the sea to an island, remote
and golden over the water, hardly believing that one
lived there once. Yet it's still here within me, sweet and
intense: the smell of dry hay, the endless shrill chant of
crickets on the hills, the taste of a ripe, sun-warmed,
stolen apricot, the weight of a rough stone in my hands,
the track of a falling star through the great summer
constellations.

All the young people slept outdoors, ate together,
played together—Yaven, Astano and Sotur and the
cousins from Herramand, and Sallo and I, Tib and Ris
and Oco. The cousins were a skinny boy and girl of
thirteen and ten, Uter and Umo; they had been unwell
and their mother, Sotur's elder sister, brought them to
the farm hoping the country air would be good for
them. There was a whole scrabble of little kids, too—
Family babies, Sotur's nieces and nephews, and slave
children being mothered—but the women looked after
them and we had little to do with them. We "big ones"

had lessons with Everra early in the morning and then were set free for the rest of the long, hot day. There was no work for us. The slave women from the city waited on the Family and looked after the huge old farmhouse along with its regular housekeepers, of whom there were plenty. Tib had been brought as a kitchen boy, but was so unneeded that he was released to study and play with us. Everything else on the farm was in the hands of its people. They lived in a fair-sized village, down the hill from the great house, in an oak grove by a stream, and did whatever it was farm people did. We city children knew nothing of them, and were ordered to keep out of their way.

That was easy. We were busy with our own doings from morning till night, exploring the hills and forests, wading and splashing in the shallow streams, building dams, raiding orchards, making willow whistles and daisy chains and tree houses, doing everything, doing nothing, whistling and singing and chattering like a flock of starlings. Yaven spent some time with the grown-ups but much more with us, leading us on expeditions up into the hills, or organising us to put on a play or dance to entertain the Family. Everra would write us out a little masque or drama; Astano, Ris, and

Sallo had been trained in dance, and with Sotur's pure, true voice to lead the singing, and Yaven playing the lyre, we put on some pretty shows, using the big threshing floor as our stage and the haybarn as our backstage. Tib and I were sometimes the comic relief and sometimes the army. I loved the rehearsals, and the costumes, and the tension and thrill of those evenings; all of us did, and as soon as we'd put on a show and been politely applauded by our noble audience, we started discussing the next one and begging Teacher-dí for a subject.

But the best times of all were the nights after the hot days of midsummer, when it finally began to cool off, and a little wind stirred from the west though heat lightning still played in the dark sky to the south, and we lay on our straw-stuffed mattresses out under the stars and talked, and talked, and talked…and one by one fell silent, fell asleep…

If eternity had a season, it would be midsummer. Autumn, winter, spring are all change and passage, but at the height of summer the year stands poised. It's only a passing moment, but even as it passes the heart knows it cannot change.

Good as my memory is, I'm not always sure what

happened in which summer of those three we spent at Vente, because they seem all one long golden day and starlit night.

I do remember from the first summer how pleasant it was not to have Torm and Hoby with us. Sallo and I spoke of it to each other with surprise, having scarcely known how Hoby's hostility oppressed us or how much we feared Torm's outbreaks. Miv's death, though we seldom spoke of it, had made our dread of Torm urgent and immediate. It was wonderful to be completely away from him.

Astano and Yaven seemed to be relieved and released by his absence as much as we were. They were older, they were Family, but here they played with us without observance of age or class. It was the last summer of Yaven's boyhood and he enjoyed it as a boy, active, high-spirited, careless of his dignity, joyful in his strength. With him and us and away from the restraint of the women of the Family, his sister Astano too became merry and bold. It was Astano who first led us on a fruit raid in our neighbor's orchards. "Oh, they'll never miss a few apricots," she said, and showed us the shortcut to the back of the orchard where the pickers hadn't come yet and wouldn't notice us...

Although they did, of course, and taking us for
common thieves, came shouting and hurling rocks and
clods at us with deadlier intent than ever Tib and I had
when we were being Votusans. We fled. When we got
onto our own land, Yaven, panting and laughing, recited
from *The Bridge on the Nisas*—

Then fled the Morvan soldiers,
The men of Morva ran,
Like sheep before the ravening wolf,
They fled the Etran van!

"Those men are horrible," Ris said. She'd barely got-
ten away from a big fellow who chased her to the bor-
derline and threw a rock after her, which luckily just
grazed her arm. "Brutes!"

Sallo was comforting little Oco, who had been following us into the orchard when we all came flying past
her in a shower of rocks and clods. Oco was scared, but
soon reassured by our laughter and Yaven's posturing.
Yaven was always aware of the younger children's fears
and feelings, and was particularly gentle with Oco. He
picked her up to ride on his shoulder while he declaimed,

Are we then men of Morva,
To flee before the foe,

Or shall we fight for Etra,
Like our fathers long ago?

"They're just mean," Astano declared. "The apricots are falling off the trees, they'll never get them all picked."

"We're actually helping them pick," said Sotur.

"Exactly. They're just mean and stupid."

"I suppose we could go ask Senator Obbe if we could pick some fruit in his orchard," said Uter, one of the skinny cousins from Herramand, a very law-abiding kind of boy.

"It tastes a lot better when you don't ask," Yaven said.

I was inspired by memories of our skirmishes and sieges in the sycamore grove, which I still missed despite their wretched outcome. I said, "They're Morvans. Cowardly, brutal, selfish Morvans. Are we of Etra to endure their insults?"

"Certainly not!" said Yaven. "We are to eat their apricots!"

"When do they stop picking?" Sotur asked.

"Evening," somebody said. Nobody really knew; we paid no attention to the activities of the farm workers, which went on around us like the doings of the bees and ants and birds and mice, the business of another species. Sotur was for coming back at night and helping ourselves freely to apricots. Tib thought they left dogs in the Obbe orchards to guard them at night. Yaven, taken by my warlike stance, suggested that we plan a raid on the orchards of Morva, but properly conducted this time, with reconnoitering beforehand, and lookouts posted, and perhaps some ammunition stockpiled with which to respond to enemy missiles and defend our retreat if necessary.

So began the great war between "Etran" Arca and "Morvan" Obbe, which went on in one orchard or another for a month. The farm workers on the Obbe estate soon were keenly aware of us and our depredations, and if we posted lookouts, so did they; but our time was free, we could choose when to strike, while they were bound to their work, to pick the fruit and sort and carry it away, all under the overseer's eye and his lash if they were slow or lazy. We were like birds, flitting in and stealing and flitting off again. We thought nothing of their anger, their hatred of us, and taunted them mercilessly when we'd made a particularly good haul. They'd learned that we weren't all slave children as they'd thought at first, and that tied their hands.

If a slave threw a rock and hit a young member of the Arca Family, the whole orchard crew might be in mortal trouble. So they had to hold their fire and try to intimidate us merely by numbers and by setting their cur-dogs on us.

To make up for their disadvantage we made a rule: if they saw us, we had to retreat. It wasn't fair, Astano said, to take fruit openly, under their noses, since they couldn't retaliate; we had to steal it while they were there in the orchard. This rule made it extremely dangerous and exciting, with only one or two tree-robbers per expedition, but any number of watchers and warners to hoot, tweet, chirp, and whistle when the enemy came close. Then, if we'd made off with some plums or early pears, we could pop up on the home side of the boundary, display our loot, and exult in our victory.

The great fruit wars came to an end when Mother Falimer told Yaven that a little group of our farm slave children had been savagely beaten by a group of orcharders at Obbe farm, who caught them stealing plums. One boy had had his eye gouged out. The Mother said nothing to Yaven beyond telling him what had happened, but when he brought the report to the rest of us, he told us that we'd have to stop our raids.

The farm children had probably hoped to be mistaken for us and so get away unhurt, but the trick hadn't worked, and the men from Obbe had taken their rage out against them.

Yaven apologised to us formally for his thoughtlessness in leading us into doing harm, and Astano, repressing tears, joined him. "It was my fault," she said. "Not yours, none of you." They took full responsibility, as they would do when they were grown, when Yaven was the Father of Arcamand and Astano perhaps Mother of another household, when every decision would be theirs and theirs alone.

"I hate those awful orchard slaves," Ris said.

"The farm people really are brutes," Umo said regretfully.

"Foul Morvans," Tib said.

We were all disconsolate. If we didn't have an enemy, we needed a cause.

"I tell you what," Yaven said. "We could do the *Fall of Sentas.*"

"Not with weapons," Astano said very softly and lightly.

"No, of course not. I mean, like a play."

"How?"

"Well, first we'd have to build Sentas. I was thinking the other day that the top of the hill behind the east vineyard, you know?—it's like a citadel. There are all those big rocks up there. It would be easy to fortify it, and make some trenches and earthworks. Teacher-dí has the book here—we could get the plans out of it. Then we could take different parts, you know—Oco could be General Thur, and Gav could say the Envoy's speeches, and Sotur could be the prophetess Yurno... We wouldn't have to do the fighting parts. Just the talking."

It didn't sound very exciting, but we all trooped up to the hilltop, and as Yaven paced around among the big tumbled rocks and described where we could build a wall or make an earthwork, the idea of building a city began to take hold. Later in the afternoon he got Everra to bring out the book and read us passages from the epic, and our imaginations caught fire from the grand words and tragic episodes. We all chose what characters we would be—and all of us were Sentans. Nobody wanted to be a besieging warrior from Pagadi, not even the great General Thur or the hero Rurec, not even though Pagadi had won the war and destroyed the city, so that now, after hundreds of years, Sentas was still a poor little town among great ruined walls. Usually we were on the side of the winners; but we were going to build doomed Sentas, and so her cause was ours, and we would fall with her.

We built Sentas and enacted her glory and her fall, all the rest of the summer. Building was hard work up there on the hilltop in the sparse dry grass with the sun beating down and no shade except under the rock walls and towers we piled up. The two little girls, Oco and Umo, toiled up and down the hill with water from the stream while the rest of us sweated and grunted. We swore with parched mouths when a stone refused to fit in its place or slipped and came down on a finger; we greeted the water carriers with praise and rejoicing. Astano's delicate hands were rough and bruised, as hard, the Mother said, as horse hoofs; but the Mother smiled and did not reprove. She even came out several times and walked up the Hill of Sentas to see how the work was going. Yaven and Astano showed her our triumphs of engineering, the Eastern Gate, the Tower of the Ancients, the defensive ramparts. Erect in her light summer robes, smooth-faced, smiling, she listened, nodded, approved. I saw her hand sometimes laid lightly, almost timidly, on her tall son's arm, and saw the yearning in the gesture though I didn't understand it. I think she was happy in our happiness and, like us, wanted it unshadowed by any thought of days past or days to come.

Everra also came up the hill frequently to oversee the plans and layout of the buildings and defenses according to the chart in his copy of the book; and we'd persuade him to stay and read to us from the epic while we took a break from rock laying and ditch digging. It was, he said, a most excellent educational opportunity, from which we would all profit. He was so enthusiastic about it that he might have been a real nuisance, demanding pedantic improvements and corrections to our architecture; but he'd begin to wilt in the heat by mid-morning and go back down, leaving us on the windy, white-hot hilltop, building up our stones and dreams.

◆ ◆ ◆

ALL THESE MONTHS, the great farmhouse had been a household of women and children. The Father stayed in Etra because the Senate was meeting almost daily. Sotur's older brother Soter rode out to Vente every now and then to spend a night or two with his wife and children, but the other brother, Sodera, a lawyer, was kept in town by what Sotur always called his "suitcases." Great-Uncle Yaven Herro Arca, in his nineties, had been brought along to sit out under the oak trees. Most of the time, our Yaven was the man of the house, though he chose not to play the role.

Among the farmhouse staff were a few old handy-men past much real work, but most of the house people were women. They were used to running things with no masters present and were more independent both in act and manner than the city house people. There was a lack of hierarchy and protocol. Everything seemed to go along quite well without the formalities and rigidities of life at Arcamand, the creaking and straining, the needless complications. When the Mother wanted to make plum jam the way it had been made at Galleca-mand when she was a girl, there wasn't the bowing and scraping there would have been in the great kitchens of Arcamand, nor the suppressed resentment at the inter-ruption; old Acco, the chief cook of the farm, stood over the Mother as she'd stand over a prentice, and was free with her criticisms. Babies were common property; slave women cared for Family babies, of course, but also the Mother and Soter's and Sodera's wives looked after slave children, and all the "tiny ones" crawled and staggered about together and fell asleep in promiscuous heaps, like kittens.

We ate outside at long tables under the oak trees near the kitchen, and though there was a Family table and a slave table, seating wasn't all by status; Everra usually sat at the Family table at the invitation of the Mother and Yaven, while Sotur and Astano, self-invited, sat with Ris and Sallo at ours. We sorted ourselves out less by rank than by age and preference. This ease, this commonalty, was a great part of the happiness of life at Vente. But it changed, it had to change, when the Father arrived for the last few weeks of the summer, bringing both his nephews with him, and Torm.

The first evening of their arrival seemed to bode ill. The Family table was full of men now. The Family women and girls all sat there, dressed up, looking far more ladylike than they had all summer, in modest silence, while the men talked. Metter and the valets, who had ridden out with the men, sat with us and talked with one another. Everra sat with us, silent. We children were frowned at if we spoke.

Dinner was served formally and went on a long time, and after it the children of the Family—Yaven and Astano, Sotur, Umo, and Uter—all went indoors with the adults of the Family.

We five slave children, left outside, loitered about, disconsolate. It was too late to go down to Sentas. Sallo suggested we walk down the road by the farm village to see if the blackberries in the hedges were ripening. Some of the children there saw us, and hiding behind the brambly hedges, they threw stones at us—not big stones, not to kill, only pebbles, but maybe they had slingshots, for a hit stung like fury and left a small black bruise. Poor little Oco, the first to be hit, shrieked out that there was a hornet, then we all began to get stung. We saw the missiles flying over the hedge, and got a glimpse of our assailants. One, a big boy, leapt up and jeered something in his uncouth dialect. We ran. Not laughing, as we had run from the orcharders, but in real fear. We saw the twilight darkening around us and felt hatred at our backs.

When we got back to the farm, Oco and Ris were both crying. Sallo quieted Oco down. We bathed our bruises, and sat on our hay-filled mattresses as the stars came out, and talked. Sallo said, "They saw there weren't any Family children with us."

"But what do they hate us for?" Oco mourned.

Nobody said anything.

"Maybe because we can do a lot of things they can't," I said.

"And their fathers hate us," said Sallo. "For the fruit wars."

"I hate them," Ris said.

"I do too," said Oco.

"Dirty peasants," Tib said, and I felt the same fierce contempt, and along with it the faint, sweet self-disgust of conscious prejudice, of despising what you're afraid of.

We were silent for a long time, watching the stars come out above the black crowns of the oaks and the roofs of the house.

"Sallo," Oco whispered. "Is he going to sleep with us?"

She meant Torm. Oco was utterly terrified of Torm. She had seen him kill her brother.

By "sleep with us" she meant would he come out, as the Family children had been doing all summer, to sleep as we did on hay mattresses under the stars.

"I don't think so, Oco-sweet," Sallo said in her soft voice. "I don't think any of them will, tonight. They have to stay in and be gentlefolk."

But waking before dawn, when the constellations of winter were fading in the brightening eastern sky, I saw Astano and Sotur get up from their mattress, wrapping their light blankets around them, and steal barefoot back to the house.

The Family children came out of the house much later than usual that morning. We hadn't decided whether we should go down to Sentas Hill without them, and were still discussing it when we saw them. Yaven called, "Come on! What are you all sitting around here for?"

Torm was not with him. The girls were in their country clothes, like us, tunics over trousers, ragged and dusty.

We joined the group. Yaven picked up Oco and put her on his shoulders. "Brave charioteer," he said, "drive your fiery steed to the high walls and gates of Sentas! Onward!" Oco gave a little squeak of a war cry, and Yaven galloped off down the path, neighing. We all galloped after him.

The phrase "a born leader" is a common one. I suppose many men are leaders by nature; there are a lot of ways to lead, and a lot of goals to lead to. The first true leader I knew was this boy of seventeen, Yaven

Altanter Arca, and I have judged others by him. By that standard, leadership means personal magnetism, active intelligence, unquestioning acceptance of responsibility, and something harder to define: a tension between justice and compassion, which is never satisfied by one without the other, and so can seldom be wholly satisfied.

At this moment, Yaven was divided between his allegiance to all of us "Sentans" and the protective loyalty he felt he owed to his younger brother. Along towards noon, when it was time to send a volunteer to fetch bread and cheese and whatever else the kitchen had for us for lunch, he said, "I'll go." He came back with the lunch sack, and with Torm.

As soon as she saw Torm climbing the hill, Oco shrank into the maze of rocks behind the Tower of the Ancients. Presently Sallo slipped away with her down to the stream that ran by the foot of our hill.

Yaven showed Torm all over our rock buildings and earthworks, explaining how they followed the historic plans, and telling him of the scenes that would be enacted when we'd finished building Sentas and were ready for the siege and fall. Torm followed him about, saying little, looking stiff and uncomfortable, but he did say some words of praise for the circumvallation—our masterpiece.

Our rock buildings were small and shaky and required the eye of love to see much resemblance to towers and gates in them, but our earthworks were, on their small scale, perfectly real. We had built a palisade right around the summit of the hill, with a steep-sided ditch, the circumvallation, outside it, piling up the earth against the inner side of the palisade to brace it and give foothold to the defenders. You really could not get into Sentas except by a long single-plank bridge across the ditch and through the single gate in the palisade. Torm still didn't say much but he was clearly impressed by the size and extent of our labors.

"Here," Yaven said, "I'll lead a surprise assault— Men of Sentas! to the walls! to the gate! The enemy comes! Defend our homes!" He went off down the hill a bit while we closed the gate and ran its big wooden bolt into the socket and swarmed up onto the slanting earth inside the palisade or atop the wobbly rock walls of the inner "citadel." Then Yaven came charging up the hill and across the plank, and we all yelled defiance and rained down invisible arrows and spears upon him. He rattled the gate mightily and then sank down and died in front of it while we cheered.

Torm watched it all, not part of our game but clearly drawn to it by its nature and by our excitement.

We opened the gate and welcomed Yaven in and sat down in whatever shade we could find to eat lunch. Sotur slipped off with some food for Sallo and Oco down at the creek.

"So what do you think of Sentas?" Yaven asked.

Torm said, "It's fine. Very good." His voice had deepened; he sounded like the Father. "Only…It's sort of foolish. People going *biwang*…" He imitated the way we pretended, with empty hands, to draw a bow and shoot.

"I suppose it does look silly. You've been using real weapons all summer," Yaven said with his easy, honest courtesy.

Torm nodded, condescending.

"This is just play. A play. It did get us out of lessons, though," said Yaven. And this was true. Everra had given up any pretense of holding class, once the building of Sentas had got under way. He assured the Mother and himself that it had actually been his idea, a means of teaching us the epic poem, the history of the war between Pagadi and Sentas, and the architecture of defense.

"If you didn't use the others, you could have swords and bows," Torm said. "There'd be six of us."

"They'd still be toy weapons," Yaven said, after the slightest pause. "Not like what you've been learning. Ho! I wouldn't give Sotur a sword with an edge, she'd have my liver out before I knew it!"

"But you couldn't give slaves weapons," Uter said, not having understood what Torm meant by "the others." Uter was always coming out with rules and prohibitions and moralisms; Sotur called him Trudec. "It's against the law."

Torm went black-browed. He said nothing. I glanced at Tib, who was cringing, like me, at the memory of our punishment for playing soldiers for Torm. And I saw Yaven glance over at his sister Astano. "Get us out of this!" his glance said, and she did, promptly, speaking fluently and almost at random, as women are trained to do.

"I'd hate to have even toy weapons," she said. "I like our air bows and arrows. I never miss with them! And they don't hurt anybody. Anyhow we're ages from any battles yet, aren't we? We'd have to do all the envoys' speeches first. The ditch took so long! We haven't got the Tower really steady yet. But the rocks are real enough, Torm. You'll see, when you've carried them around and piled them up all day. Even the little ones helped build, Umo and Oco. We're all Sentans."

So she fought, with what weapons she had been given, to defend the city we had built together all that summer, our city of sunlit air.

Torm shrugged. He finished chewing his bread and cheese in silence. He went down to the stream for a drink; we saw Sallo, Oco, and Sotur shrink back hiding from him among the tall grasses of the bank. He paid them no attention. He waved up at Yaven, shouted something, and set off alone back to the house on the white path by the vineyard, a sturdy, solitary figure, swinging his arms.

We went back to building for a while, but a shadow had fallen across our make-believe.

And though during what was left of the summer we all went down to work on Sentas almost daily, it was never quite the same. The Family children were called away often—Yaven and Torm and Uter to go on hunting parties with the Father and neighboring landowners, the girls to entertain the landowners' wives. Sotur and Umo, who passionately loved our dream-game, escaped these duties and joined us whenever they could, but Astano couldn't escape; and without her and Yaven we lacked direction, we lacked conviction.

But all the delights of Vente were still there, swimming and wading in the streams, figs coming ripe (which we didn't need to steal, because the fig trees were right behind the great house), talking together before we slept out under the stars. And we had one great final day of happiness. Astano proposed that we walk all the way up to the summit of the Ventine Hills. It was farther than we could go and return in a day, so we took food and water and blankets. One of the farm boys followed us with the baggage loaded on a jenny.

We set off very early; there was a chill in the air now before the sun rose, a foretaste of autumn. The dry grass on the hills was burnt pale gold, the shadows were longer than they had been. We climbed and climbed on an old track, a shepherds' path that wound among the great round hills. The scattered flocks of mountain sheep had no fear of us, but stared and challenged us with their harsh bleating, almost like roaring. There were no fences up here, since mountain sheep keep to their own pastures without fences or shepherds, but among the flocks were big grey dogs, wolf-guards. These dogs ignored us as we passed by. But if we stopped, a dog would begin to walk forward towards us, silent, very clearly saying, *Now you just move along and everything will be fine.* And we moved along.

Torm and Uter did not come with us. They had chosen to go wolf hunting down in the pine forests

with the uncles Soter and Sodera instead. Oco and
Umo, who though ten years old was not very much bigger than Oco at six, stumped along valiantly. Yaven gave
Oco a ride on his shoulders now and then, and during
the last, long, steep pull, in late afternoon, we took the
food and blankets off the jenny and put the two little
girls up on her pack saddle. She was a pretty creature,
grey as a mouse. I had no idea what a jenny was; she
looked like a small horse to me. Sotur explained that if
her father had been a donkey and her mother a horse
she would have been a mule, but since her mother had
been a donkey and her father a horse, she was a jenny.
The boy who had been leading her stood listening to
this explanation with the dull, glowering expression the
farm people seemed always to have.

"That's right, isn't it, Comy?" Sotur asked him. He
jerked his head and looked away, scowling. "It's all in
who your ancestors are," Sotur said to the jenny, "isn't it,
Mousie?"

The boy Comy tugged at the halter and Mousie
walked along peaceably, Oco and Umo clinging to the
saddle, scared and gleeful. We all trudged along with
our light burdens, which we certainly could have carried all day. But we were glad to come up at last onto
the very summit of the highest hill and stop climbing

and stand gazing at the great view that lay all around us, miles and miles of sunlit land, pale gold fading into blue, the long shadows of August falling in the folds of the hills. There was Etra, remote and tiny in the vast sweep of the plains; we could see farmhouses and villages all along the courses of the streams and the river Morr, and farsighted Yaven said he could make out the walls of Casicar and a tower above them, though I could see only a kind of smudge there on the deep bend of the Morr. East that way and southward the land was hilly and broken, but to the north and west it fell away and widened into immense, dim levels, green fading into the blue of distance.

"That's the Daneran Forest," Yaven said, looking northeast.

"That's the Marshes," Astano said, looking north, and Sotur said, "Where you and Gav came from, Sallo."

Sallo stood beside me and we looked that way for a long time. It gave me a strange, cold thrill to see that vastness, that unknown country where we had been born. All I knew of the people of the Marshes was that they weren't city people, they were uncivilised, barbarians, natives. We had ancestors there, as free people did. We had been born free. It troubled me to think about that. It was a useless thought. What did it have to do with my life in Etra, with my Family of Arcamand?

"Do you remember the Marshes at all?" Sotur asked us.

Sallo shook her head, but I said, to my own surprise, "Sometimes I think I do."

"What was it like?"

I felt foolish describing that simple memory or vision aloud to them. "Just water, and reeds growing in the water, and little islands…and there was a blue hill away far off…Maybe it was this hill."

"You were only a baby, Gav," Sallo said, with just a touch of cautioning in her voice. "I was two or three, and I can't remember anything."

"Not about being stolen?" Sotur asked, disappointed. "That would have been exciting."

"I don't remember anything but Arcamand, Sotur-ío," Sallo said in her soft voice, smiling.

We spread our feast out on the thin dry grass of the hilltop and ate it as the sun went down in glory, revealing the ocean to us by the gleam of the high horizon where it set. We sat and talked, in all the old ease and companionship of the long summer. The little ones fell asleep. Sallo fell asleep with her head on my lap. Ris brought me a blanket, and I tucked it round my sister as best I could. The stars were coming out. The boy Comy, who had sat all evening at a distance, between us and the picketed jenny, facing away from us, began to sing. At first I didn't know what I was hearing, it was such a thin, strange, sad sound, like the vibrations in the air after a bell has been struck. It rose and trembled and died away.

"Sing again, Comy," Sotur murmured. "Please."

He was silent for so long we thought he would not sing, but then the faint tremor of sound began again, the thinnest thread of music, the overtones of a tune. It was inexpressibly sad and yet serene, untroubled. Again it died away, and we listened for it, wanting it to return.

It was utterly silent now up on the wide hill, and the glimmer of starlight was stronger than the last blue-brown light far down in the west.

The jenny stamped and made a little huh-huh noise in her chest, and we laughed at that, and talked a little more, softly. Then we slept.

◆ 4 ◆

The next couple of years went along without excitement. Sallo and I swept the floors of the great house and went to our lessons daily. Nobody missed Hoby, not even Tib, I think. Torm, mentally practicing the discipline of the swordsman, was sullen, aloof, and obedient in the classroom. Once or twice when his impatience with the lessons or the teacher threatened to overcome him, he excused himself and left. Yaven was mostly away with the army. Etra had no ongoing war at that time, so young officers like Yaven were trained in exercises and drills or put on guard duty at the borders; now and then he was sent home on leave, looking very fit and cheerful. We went both of those summers to the Vente farm, and there too were no great doings, just the lazy, ordinary happiness of being there. Yaven didn't come with us; he spent the first summer in training, and during the second he accompanied the Father on a diplomatic mission to Gallec. Torm spent both summers at the school of swordsmanship. So Astano was our leader.

She led us to Sentas Hill the very first evening. That was a shock and a grief at first, for we found it almost in ruins. The moat had silted up with winter rains, the earthwork behind the palisade had slipped; the palisade itself had been torn down in several places and the rock piles that formed the Tower and the Gates had been knocked apart, not by weather, but by human malice.

"Those filthy peasants," Tib growled—he could growl now, his voice was changing. We all moped about the dilapidated place a while, feeling the same hateful, shameful contempt for the farm children we'd felt when they threw stones at us, and mourning the defilement of our city of dreams. But Astano and Sotur took heart, discussing how easily we could restore the palisade, and beginning even in the dusk to pile up rocks for the

Tower again. So we went back to the house, set out our pallets under the stars, and lay planning the rebuilding of Sentas.

Sotur said, "You know, if we could get some of them to help, to work on it, they might not hate it."

"Ugh! I don't want any of them around," said Ris. "They're foul."

"One couldn't trust them," said Uter, who was less skinny and bony this summer, but no less prim.

"The one with the jenny was all right," his sister Umo said.

"Comy," Astano said. "Yes, he was nice. Remember when he sang?"

We all lay remembering that golden, mysterious evening on the summit of the hills.

"We'd have to ask the foreman," Astano said to Sotur, and they briefly discussed the chances of getting any farm slave released to us. "Only if we said they were to work for us," Sotur said, and Astano replied, "Well, they would. We worked as hard as any of them do! Digging that moat was awful! And we never could have done it without Yaven."

"But it would be different," Sotur said. "Giving orders…"

Astano said, "Yes."

And there they left it. The idea was not mentioned again.

We rebuilt Sentas, even if not to Yaven's or Everra's standards. And when it was rebuilt, we held a ceremony of purification, circling the walls within, not in mockery, but as it was described in Garro's poem, with our teacher leading the procession as the high priest and lighting the sacred fire in the citadel. All summer we often went to that hilltop as a group or in pairs or singly, all of us feeling it to be, amid all the wealth of woods and hills and streamside that the farm offered, our dearest place, our fortress and retreat.

Aside from repairing Sentas, we had no great projects; we put on a few dance-plays, but mostly what I remember is swimming with Tib in pools under the willows and alders, and lazing about in the shade talking, and going on long, desultory explorations of the woods south of the house. We did lessons for a half-morning daily with our teacher, and Ris and Sallo were often kept on for music lessons with Sotur and Umo, for a singing teacher had come from Herramand. Sotur's little niece Utte had graduated from the "tiny ones" to run around with us, under Oco's particular care; and sometimes we took a whole batch of the older babies down to the stream and supervised the splashing and screaming and shrieking and sleeping, all through a long, hot afternoon.

Sotur's aunts and the Mother often joined us there, and sometimes Uter and Tib and I were sent away because the women and the older girls were going to bathe. Uter was convinced that the farm boys hid in the bushes to spy on them. He would patrol up and down officiously, ordering Tib and me to help him "keep the vile brutes away from the women." Knowing the terrible punishment for such a transgression against the sacredness of the Mother, I was sure the farm slaves would never come anywhere near our bathing pool; but Uter's mind ran on such things, fascinated by the idea of pollution.

I was slow in my adolescence. To me Uter's obsessions were as stupid as Tib's sniggering attempts at manly remarks about what you might see if you did hide in the bushes. I knew what women looked like. I'd lived in the women's quarters all my life. Just because Tib had been sent across to the men's barrack last winter, he acted as if there was something special about a woman with her clothes off. It was, I thought, incredibly childish.

It had nothing to do with what I felt, lately, when I heard Sotur sing. That was entirely different. It had nothing to do with bodies. It was my soul that listened and was filled with pain and glory and unspeakable yearning....

Late that summer Yaven and Torm came to Vente with the Father, and the division between Family and slaves was again drawn deep by the presence of the Family men. I went out one day seeking solitude. Among the forested hills south of the farmhouse I found a beautiful oak grove in the fold of two hills. A clear stream ran down through it, and there was a strange little structure of rock halfway up the slope: a shrine, certainly, but to what god I did not know. I told Sallo about it, and she wanted to see it. So one afternoon I took her and Ris and Tib there. Tib saw nothing to interest him in the place; he was restless, and soon roamed off back to the farm. Ris and Sallo felt as I did that there was some presence or blessing in the grove, the glade, the ruined altar. They settled down in the thin shade of the old oaks, near the small, quick-running creek, on what had once been a lawn around the shrine. Each of them had her drop-spindle and a sack of cloudy wool, for they were at the age now when women were to be seen doing women's work wherever they were. That they could run off with me, unguarded, not even asking permission, was part of the miraculous ease of life at Vente. Anywhere else, two house-slave girls of fourteen would not have been allowed to leave the house at all. But they were good girls; they took their work with them; and the Mother trusted them as she trusted the benevolence of the place. So we sat on the thin grass of the slope in the hot August shade, feeling the cool breath of the running water, and were silent for a long time, at peace, in freedom.

"I wonder if it was an altar to Mé," Ris said.

Sallo shook her head. "It's not the right shape," she said.

"Who, then?"

"Maybe some god that only lived here."

"An oak-tree god," I said.

"That would be Iene. No," Sallo said, with unusual certainty, "it isn't Iene. It was a god that was here. This place's god. Its spirit."

"What should we leave as an offering?" Ris asked, half serious, half joking.

"I don't know," Sallo said. "We'll find out."

Ris spun a while, the motion of her arm and hand graceful and hypnotic. Ris was not as pretty as Sallo, but calm and charming in her ripening womanhood, with a splendid mane of glossy black hair, and a dreamy look in her long eyes. She heaved a quiet sigh and said, "I don't ever want to leave here."

She would be given in a couple of years, probably to young Odiran Edir, possibly to the heir of Herramand—wherever the interests and allegiances and debts of Arca indicated. We all knew that. The slave girls had been brought up to be given. Ris trusted her House to give her where she would be valued and well treated. She had no dread and a good deal of lively curiosity about where and to whom she would be sent. I'd heard her and Sallo talking about it. Sallo would not be given away from our House; she was destined for Yaven, that was equally well known. But at Arcamand daughters of the Family were not married off early, and slave girls were not given at thirteen or fourteen even if they were physically mature. Iemmer repeated the Mother's words to our girls—"A woman is healthier and lives longer if she has had time to grow into her womanhood, and does not bear children while she is still a child." And Everra quoted Trudec in approval: "Let a maiden remain a maiden until she be full grown and have wisdom, for the worship of a virgin daughter is most pleasing to her Ancestors." And Sem the hostler said, "You don't breed a yearling filly, do you?"

So Ris wasn't speaking in imminent concern about having to leave home and learn how a gift-girl was treated at Edirmand or Herramand, but only in the knowledge that within a few years she'd be sent into a new life, and seldom if ever see us, and almost certainly never know any such freedom as this again.

Her unprotesting melancholy touched Sallo and me, safe as we were in knowing we would always live with our own Family and people.

"What would you do, Ris," my sister asked, looking across the stream into the warm, shadowy depths of the woods, "if you were set free?"

"They don't set girls free," Ris said, practical and accurate. "Only men who do something heroic. Like that tiresome slave who saved his master's treasure in the *Fables*."

"But there are countries where there aren't any slaves. If you lived there you'd *be* free. Everybody is."

"But I'd be a foreigner," Ris said with a laugh. "How do I know what I'd do? Crazy foreign things!"

"Well, but pretend. If you did get set free, here, in Etra."

Ris set herself to think about it. "If I was a freed-woman, I could get married. So I could keep my own babies... But I'd have to look after them myself whether

I wanted to or not, wouldn't I? I don't know. I don't
know any freedwomen. I don't know what it's like.
What would you do?"

"I don't know," Sallo said. "I don't know why I think
about it. But I do."

"It would be nice to be married," Ris said after a
while, thoughtfully. "So that you *knew*." I did not know
what she meant.

"Oh, yes!" Sallo said, heartfelt.

"But you *do* know, Sal. Yaven-dí wouldn't ever pass
you around."

"No, he wouldn't," Sallo said, and there was a tenderness in her voice, as always when she spoke of Yaven,
and a proud embarrassment.

I understood now that Ris had meant a master's
power to give away the girl he'd been given, or lend her
out to other men, or send her to the women's quarters
to nurse other women's babies, whatever he pleased—
a power she had no part in but must simply submit to.
Thinking about that made me feel extremely lucky to
be a man. So in turn I was a little embarrassed when
Sallo asked me, "What would you do, Gav?"

"If I was set free?"

She nodded, looking at me with that same loving

tenderness and pride but no embarrassment, only a little teasing.

I thought a while and said, "Well, I'd like to travel. I'd like to go to Mesun, where the University is. And I'd like to see Pagadi. And maybe the ruins of Sentas. And cities you read about, like Resva of the Towers, and Ansul the Beautiful, with four canals and fifteen bridges…"

"And then?"

"Then I'd come back to Arcamand with a lot of new books! Teacher-dí won't even talk about getting any new books. 'Oldest is safest,'" I mouthed froggily, imitating Everra being pompous. Ris and Sallo giggled. And that was all our conversation on a freedom we could not imagine.

Nor did we leave any offering to the spirit of that place, unless remembrance is a kind of offering.

The following summer, our stay at the farm was cut short by rumors of war.

We arrived there as usual, with the cousins from Herramand, and on the first evening all nine of us went out to Sentas Hill expecting to find it in ruins again. But though the winter rains had damaged the moat and earthworks, the walls and towers stood, and had even been built higher in places. Some of the farm children must have taken it over and made it their own refuge or play fortress. Umo and Uter were indignant, feeling our Sentas had been invaded, polluted, but Astano said, "Maybe it will always be here, now."

Oco and Umo were the only ones who worked much that summer at cleaning out the moat and strengthening the earthworks and palisade. Astano and Sotur were kept with the women much of the time, and the rest of us dispersed on our own pursuits. Tib and I swam and fished; Sallo and I went back to the oak-grove shrine when she could get away from the house, with Ris or by ourselves. And I made an unexpected friend.

I had been giving the little girls a hand at bracing up the palisade at Sentas and was coming home through the vineyard in the heat of the day, crickets shrilling and cicadas rasping far and near in the trance of light and heat. A vineyard worker was coming towards me down another row. I glimpsed him now and then between the high vines, on which the grape clusters were just beginning to swell. As we passed each other he stopped and said, "Dí." It was how the country people spoke to a master, not by name, merely with the honorific.

Surprised, I stopped and peered at him around the long-armed vine. I recognised him, Comy, the boy who had led the jenny when we climbed to the summit of the hills, and who had sung that evening. He looked much older. I would have taken him for a grown man. He had a sparse stubble of beard and his face was hard and bony. I said his name.

He was clearly surprised and gratified that I knew him. He stood silent a while and then said, "Hope it was all right what we did at the rock place."

"It was fine," I said.

"It was some of Meriv's fellows knocked it down last year."

"It's all right. It's just a game." I didn't know what to say to this grim fellow. His accent was hard for me to understand. I could smell his stale sweat though we were four or five feet apart. He was barefoot and his dark calloused feet stood in the earth like the vine roots.

There was a long silence, and I was about to say goodbye and go on when Comy said, "I can show you a good fishing place."

I'd done a lot of fishing that summer. Tib and I heard that there were streams where the farm people caught salmon-trout, though we'd never caught any. I said something to show my interest, and Comy said, "At the rock fort this evening," and went striding on down between the vines.

Though I was dubious about the whole venture, I went back to Sentas late in the afternoon, telling myself that if Comy didn't turn up I could do a little more work for Oco and Umo. But I saw him coming through the vineyard not long after I got there. I went down and joined him and we went in silence up the creek at the hill's foot till it joined a larger stream, and then along that for a half mile or so on a thread of a path through willows and alders and laurels, till at the foot of a hill the water came down into deep basins where it flowed full and still among great smooth boulders. We each had our rudimentary fishing gear. In silence we baited our lines and chose a boulder to stand on and cast out into the dark pools. It was a warm, still evening in the long days of the year, not yet sunset for an hour or so. The light filtered through the trees in soft slanting shafts. Tiny flies dimpled the water's surface and flitted in the darkness under the banks. Within a minute a fish rose to my line, and I brought it in by instinct or accident—a splendid rosy-spotted creature weighing three or four pounds. I hardly knew what to do with such a catch. I saw Comy's grin. "Beginner's luck," he said, throwing out his line again.

As we stood there, casting and now and then catching, I felt a liking and gratitude to the silent youth who stood there on the rocks over the water, thin, rawboned, enigmatic. I didn't know why he reached out to me across the ignorance and enmity that kept the farm people and the city people apart, or how he knew that we could make friends despite the enormous difference of our knowledge and experience. But we did; we said almost nothing, but in our silence there was trust.

When the ruddy light had died away among the trees, we gathered up our catch. He had a net pouch, and I put my fish into it, the first grand big one and two smaller ones, along with the two he'd caught, one salmon-trout and one thin fierce-mouthed fish, a pikelet maybe. I followed him down the invisible path through the dusky woods and out at last into the vineyard. It was almost dark by then even under the open sky. When we got to the road I said, "Thanks, Comy."

He nodded, and stopped to give me my fish.

"Keep them."

He hesitated.

"I can't cook them."

He shrugged, and his smile flashed in the dusk. He muttered thanks and made off, vanishing almost at once in the twilight among the high vines with their reaching arms.

After that I went fishing with Comy several times, always at a different place. It was a little unnerving to realise that he always knew where I was, when he was free to find me and ask, almost wordlessly, if I wanted to go fishing that evening. I never brought Tib, never even told him of my expeditions with Comy; I felt that I had no right to. If Comy wanted Tib along he would have asked him. I did tell Sallo about Comy, because I had no secrets from her. She liked hearing about him. When I puzzled at his choosing me for a companion and taking me to his prized fishing pools, she said, "Well, he's lonely, probably, and he likes you."

"How would he know he liked me?"

"Seeing you that day we climbed the hills. And they see more of us than we do of them, I'm sure...He could tell he could trust you."

"It's sort of like knowing a wolf," I said.

"I wish we could go to their village," my sister said. "It seems so strange that we can't. Like they really were wild animals or something. Some of the women who come up to the farmhouse are relatives of the house people. They seem nice enough, only it's hard to understand what they say."

This put it into my head to ask Comy if I could go home with him sometime, for I too had always been curious about those dark houses down in the valley, even if our orchard wars and the ambush on the road had put us at odds with the farm people. So the next time Comy and I came up from the river in the twilight, I said, "I'll go on with you." We had a really good catch that night, our prize a monster salmon-trout as long as my forearm. Carrying it made a kind of excuse. He said nothing, and after a while I said, "Will they mind?"

I think he had as much trouble figuring out what the words I used meant as I did with his dialect. He pondered, and finally shrugged. We went on into the village. Smoke was rising from the chimneys of the longhouses and the cabins and there were strong smells of cooking. Dark figures passed us in the rutted, dusty street that rambled among the houses, and dogs barked insistently. Comy turned aside not to a longhouse as I had expected but to one of the shambling cabins, built up on short poles to keep them from the winter mud. A man was sitting out on the wooden steps that led up to the door. I had seen him working in the vineyards. He and Comy greeted each other with a kind of grunt and the man said, "Who's that?"

"From the House," Comy said.

"Hey," the man said, startled, stiffening, ready to get up. I think he thought Comy had brought one of the Family boys here, and was terrified. Comy said something that identified me as a house slave and calmed the man down. He stared at me in silence. I felt extremely uncomfortable, but having come this far didn't want to back out. I said, "May I come in?"

Comy hesitated and gave his hunching shrug. He led me into the house. It was completely dark inside except for the dim glow of a fire under heavy ashes in the hearth. There were people—women, an old man, some children—dark bulks crowded in the heavy air that smelled of human bodies and dogs and food and wood and earth and smoke. Comy took the big fish from me and gave it and our other catch to a woman whom I could see only as a bulky shadow and the flash of an eye. He and she said a word or two, and she turned to me: "D'you want to eat with us then, dí?" Her voice seemed unfriendly, even sneering, yet she waited for an answer.

"No, ma-ío, I have to get home, thank you," I said.

"It's a grand fish," she said, holding up the big one.

"Thanks, Comy," I said, backing out. "Luck and Ennu bless the house!" And I made off, intimidated and appalled and glad to get away, yet also glad I had gone so far. At least I had a little to tell Sallo.

She guessed that it was a family in the cabin, that the man on the steps may have been Comy's father; she had gathered from talk among the farmhouse women that though of course there was no marriage, these country people commonly lived with their spouse and children, or sometimes spouses and children. It was all to the good of the farm if the slaves bred up more slaves who knew the work and the land and nothing else, whose whole life was in that dark village by the stream.

"I wish I could meet Comy again," Sallo said.

The next time he found me, I said, "Do you know the old altar in the oak grove?"

He nodded; of course he did; Comy knew every rock and tree and stream and field on the Vente farm and for miles around it.

"Meet us there this evening," I said. "Instead of fishing."

"Who's us?"

"My sister."

He thought about it, gave his shrug-nod, and went off.

Sallo and I were there an hour or so before sunset. She sat with her spinning, the cloudy mass of fine-carded wool endlessly turning under her fingers to a grey-brown, even, endless thread. Comy appeared silently, coming up the little streambed among the willow shrubs. She greeted him, and he nodded and sat down at some distance from us. She asked him if he was a vineyarder and he said yes, and told us a little about the work, haltingly. "Do you still sing, Comy?" she asked, and he shrugged and nodded.

"Will you?"

As before, on the hilltop, he made no reply and was silent for a long time; then he sang, that same strange, high, soft singing that seemed to have no source or center, as if it did not come from a human throat but hung in the air like the song of insects, wordless but sad beyond all words.

I planned to bring Sotur to the oak grove, maybe to hear Comy sing, maybe just to sit there with Sallo and me in the peace of the place. I could imagine what it would be like when Sotur was there, how she would go look at the altar and maybe know what god it belonged to, how she would go down to the little stream and maybe wade in it a bit to get cool, how she and Sallo would sit side by side, spinning and talking softly, laughing sometimes. I decided it would be best if Sallo asked her to come. Lately I wanted very much to talk to Sotur but for some reason found it harder and harder to do so. And I put off asking Sallo to ask Sotur to come with us to the oak grove, I don't know why, maybe because I had such pleasure in thinking about it, imagining it...and then it was too late.

Sotur's brothers and Torm came riding from Etra all in haste and full of alarms and orders: We must pack up tonight and leave the farm first thing in the morning; marauders from Votus had crossed the Morr and burned the vineyards and orchards of Merto, a village not ten miles south of Vente. They could be here at any moment. Torm was in his element, striding about, brusque and warlike. He ordered that the girls of the Family sleep in the house, and we few who stayed outdoors got little sleep, for Torm kept pacing past us and around the house, keeping watch. Very early, before sunrise, the Father himself rode in; he had been kept at civic duties until midnight, but his worry for us had not let him wait in the city.

The morning was bright and hot. The farmhouse

people worked hard with us to get everything packed and loaded, and called goodbye to us mournfully as the procession set off at last down the long hill road. The slaves at work in the fields glanced up as we passed, unspeaking. I looked for Comy, but saw no one I knew. The people of the farm would have to wait there, defenseless, in hope that the soldiers sent out from Etra would intercept the marauders. The Father had reassured them that a large force had gone out and would by now be between Merto and Vente, driving the Votusans back to the river.

It was hot already and dusty on the road. Torm, riding a nervous, foaming, sweating horse, harried the drivers with his shouts to speed up, move on, hurry! The Father, jogging along beside the Mother's chariot, said nothing to Torm to calm him down. The Father had always been firm and stern with Yaven, but he seemed increasingly reluctant to chide Torm or even restrain him. Sallo and I talked about it as we walked. I thought he was afraid of sending Torm into one of his fury fits. Sallo nodded, but added, "Yaven isn't like his father. Torm is. At least in looks. He walks just like him now. Just like Twinny does."

That was pretty harsh talk for gentle Sallo, but she'd always disliked both Torm and Hoby. We shut up abruptly when we realised that Sotur-ío had come up with us on foot and might have heard us discussing our Father and his sons. Sotur said nothing, just walked along steadily with us, her face closed and frowning. I think she hadn't obtained permission to get down and walk, certainly not to walk with the slaves, but had escaped from the Family, as she'd often done before. All she said to us, after we had walked a long way together in silence, was, "Oh, Sallo, Gav…the summers are over." And I saw tears in her eyes.

◆ 5 ◆

The raiders were driven back to the river, where our soldiers cornered them; not many got back to Votus.

But we didn't return to Vente that summer, nor the next. Incursions and alarms were constant: from Votus, from Osc, and finally from a far more powerful enemy, Casicar.

As I look back on them, those years of alarms and battles were not unhappy ones. The threat and presence of war lent tension and the gleam of excitement to ordinary matters. Perhaps men rely on war, like politics, to give them a sense of importance they lack without it;

and the possibility of violence and destruction sheds a glamour on the household life which they otherwise hold in contempt. Women, I think, not needing the self-importance and not sharing the contempt, often fail to understand the virtue and necessity of warfare; but they may be caught in the glamour, and they love the beauty of courage.

Yaven was now an officer in the army of Etra. His regiment under the command of General Forre was mostly west and south of the city, fending off incursions from Osc and Morva. Fighting was sporadic, with long quiet spells while the enemy regrouped, and during these periods Yaven was often able to come home.

For his twentieth birthday, his mother gave him my sister Sallo, who was now about sixteen. The gift of a maiden "from the Mother's hands" was not made lightly, but with due formality; and it was a happy occasion, for Sallo loved Yaven with all her heart and asked only to love and serve him and him alone. He couldn't have resisted such generous tenderness if he'd wanted to, but she was what he wanted, too. Eventually of course he'd have to marry a woman of his own class, but that was years off, and didn't matter now. He and Sallo were a blissful couple, their delight in each other so clear and lively it shed pleasure around them as a candle sheds light. When he was in the city and off duty he spent the days with his fellow officers and other young men, but every night he came home to Sallo. When he went off to his regiment she wept bitterly, and grieved and worried till he came riding home, tall and handsome and laughing, shouting, "Where's my Sallo?"—and she came running out of the silk rooms to meet him, shy and afire with joy and pride and love, like any young soldier's bride.

When I was thirteen I was exiled at last from the women's rooms and sent across the court. I'd always dreaded going to the barrack, but it wasn't as bad as I'd feared, though I grievously missed the nook where Sallo and I had always slept and talked before we slept. Tib, who'd been sent across the year before, made a show of protecting me, but it wasn't needed; the big fellows didn't persecute me. They were hard on some of the young boys, but evidently I'd paid my dues that night at the well, and earned their respect by my silence. They called me Marshy or Beaky, but nothing worse, and most of them simply left me alone.

During the day I saw little of any of them, since my work was now entirely in the schoolroom and library with Everra. Oco and a little boy called Pepa had taken

Sallo's and my place as sweepers. My task now was to get learning and to assist Everra in schooling the little ones. There was a new flock in the schoolroom, as Sotur's nieces and nephews became old enough to learn their letters, along with several new slave children we had bought or traded for. Sallo, as a gift-girl, was exempt from all heavy or dirty work; she was expected only to do a modest amount of spinning or weaving, and otherwise nothing except to keep herself fresh and pretty for Yaven. She was in fact very bored when he was off with the army. She was used to active work, and found the company of the other gift-girls and the ladies' maids tedious and stifling. She never said so, not being given to complaint, but whenever she could she got away from the silk rooms and came back to the schoolroom to continue her reading or help Everra and me with the young pupils. And often she and I met in the library, where we could talk, just the two of us alone. She confided in me as she always had done, and relied on me and knew I relied on her. Our companionship was the joy of my life. My sister was my other soul. Only with her was I wholly free and at peace. Only to her could I ever speak the entire truth.

I have said nothing this long time about what I called "remembering," those visions or waking dreams I had as a young child. They came to me still, though less often. My unbroken habit of not speaking of them to anyone but Sallo seems even now to make it hard to tell about them.

At Vente I scarcely ever had a memory of that kind, but when we came back to Arcamand, every now and then, usually when I was alone reading, or near falling asleep, or waking from sleep, I would see the blue hill over the shining water and the reeds and feel the slight unsteady motion of the boat. Or I'd watch the snow fall on the roofs of Etra (for they could be truly memories as well as foreseeings). Or I'd be in the graveyard by the river, or in the square watching the men fighting in the street, or in the high, dark room where the man turned his fine, sorrowful face to me and said my name.

Only rarely now did I have a new vision, remembering something I had not remembered before. Several times I remembered climbing a steep hill of a city I did not know; it was raining, and the streets between high dark houses were gloomy and strange, but there was some light shining in me or on me, as if I bore an invisible lamp—I can't describe it better than that.

Once, the winter Sallo was given to Yaven, I saw a terrible figure, a naked man as thin and black as a mummified corpse, dancing. His head was too large, with blank bright eyes and a red hole for a mouth. I saw him from below, as if I were lying down in some dark place. I hoped not to have that vision again. Several times I remembered being in a cave with a low stone roof, faint light falling strangely on the rocks of the cave floor. And there were brief scenes, glimpses, too quick to hold and recall clearly, though when (as sometimes happened) I met the place or person in daily life, I knew that I'd been there before, or seen that face. Many people have this experience from time to time, but can't say how it is that they seem to be remembering something which is happening for the first time. For me it was a little different, since I could remember, in the moment the event occurred, when and where I had remembered it before it occurred.

After it actually happened, my memory of it was like any memory, and I could summon it at will, which I couldn't do with the visions of things that hadn't happened yet. So with the snowfall, I had my memory of the event, and my memory of having seen it in a vision before it happened, and also, now and then, the vision itself, involuntary and immediate. One snowfall, three memories.

Part of the pleasure I had in being with my sister was that I could tell her about these strange visions or rememberings, and talk over with her what they might be or mean, and so weaken the horror that clung to some of them. And she could tell me about doings among the Family.

Now that Yaven and Astano were done with their schooling and Torm had been excused from it in order to study military arts, I saw only the young children of the Family, and Sotur. She still came to study with Everra, and often to the schoolroom or the library to read. Often enough she and Sallo and I were all together and fell to talking as easily, almost, as we had used to do under the stars at the Vente farm. But never so freely. We were no longer children, and had to be conscious of our status. And I was sorely confused by my feelings for Sotur, which were a mixture of chaste adoration, which I indulged, and passionate sexual desire, which, when I recognised what it was, I feared and denied.

Desire was forbidden. Chaste adoration was allowed, but I was too tongue-tied to express it, except in very bad poems, which I never showed her. In any case, Sotur didn't want either desire or adoration. She wanted our old friendship. She was lonely.

Her closest friend had always been Astano, and Astano was now being groomed for courtship and marriage. There was talk (so Sallo told me) of betrothing Astano to Corric Beltomo Runda, the son of the richest and most powerful Senator of Etra, a man to whom our Father Altan Arca owed a good deal of his own power and influence. Sallo heard a lot of gossip of this kind in the silk rooms. She brought whatever she heard to me and we talked it over. Corric Runda, they said, had never done any military service; his particular friends were a group of young, rich freedmen and minor nobles who led a wild life; he was said to be handsome but inclined to fat. We wondered how our gentle, gallant Astano felt about Corric Runda, and whether she wanted to be betrothed to him, and how far the Father and Mother would be swayed by what she wanted.

As for Sotur, their orphaned niece, her wishes in marriage wouldn't count for much. She'd be married to make the most advantageous connection. It was the lot of almost all girls of the Families; not that different from the slave girls. Sometimes the thought of my grave, sweet-voiced Sotur being handed off to some uncaring man drove me to burning, helpless rage, to the point where I thought I longed for it to happen—so that she'd be gone from the House, and I wouldn't have to see her daily, and be ashamed that I was only a slave and only fourteen years old and only able to write my stupid poems and yearn and yearn to touch her and never be able to touch her…

Sallo knew how I felt, of course; if I'd wanted to hide anything from Sallo I couldn't have. She knew that I kept, folded tight in a tiny pouch on a cord about my neck, a note Sotur had written me a year ago when I had a fever—*Get well soon dear Gavir, it is as dull as dust without you.* Sallo grieved for my impossible longing. She fretted over the injustice that allowed her love full satisfaction and utterly forbade it to mine, even in dream. Of course there were stories of love affairs between noblewomen and slaves, but they were all sad and shameful, ending in mutilation or death for the man, and for the woman maybe not death, these days, but horrible public shame and degradation. Sallo tried to make sense of these hard laws, to understand them as protecting us, and she convinced both me and herself that in fact they did protect us; but she didn't try to pretend that they were just. *Justice is in the hands of the gods,* an old poet wrote, *mortal hands hold only mercy and the sword.* I told her that line, and she liked it, and repeated it. I think it made her think of Yaven, her kind-hearted, beloved hero who held both mercy and a sword.

Romantic love and desire was my torment. Sallo was my solace, and so was my work.

Everra had finally given me free run of the library of Arcamand, which till then I had never entered, even when I was a sweeper boy and went all over the house. Its door was on the corridor past the domed shrine of the Ancestors. When I first entered it, I felt the fear of crossing a sacred threshold almost as I might have done if I had transgressed and gone among the Ancestors. It was a small room, well lighted by high windows of clear glass. There were over two hundred books on its shelves, all carefully arranged and dusted by Everra. The room smelled of books, that subtle smell which to some is stuffy and to others intoxicating, and it was silent. No one ever came down that corridor except to sweep it or to enter the library, and no one entered the library except Everra, Sotur, Sallo, and me.

The girls were allowed because Sotur had asked our teacher to allow her and Sallo the privilege, and Everra couldn't refuse her anything. Sotur was the only older child of the Family pursuing her reading or studies, for neither Yaven nor Astano was free to do what they liked any more. She told Everra that he had given her and Sallo the soul's hunger for books and thoughts, and must not deprive them now that Sallo was starving among the inanities of the silk rooms and she among the pomposities of merchants and the illiteracy of politicians. So, with the permission of the Father and Mother, and with many cautions about indiscriminate reading, he gave them each a key.

It was hard for me to admit it to myself, and I never talked about it with Sallo or Sotur, but the long-desired library was a disappointment. I already knew more than half the books in it, and the ones I didn't know, that looked so mysterious and treasurable sitting on the shelves in their dark leather covers or scroll boxes, mostly turned out to be dull—annals of law, compendia, endless epic poems by mediocre poets. They had all been there for at least fifty years, sometimes much longer. Everra was proud of the fact. "No modern trash for Arcamand," he said. I was willing to believe him that most modern writing was trash, on the evidence that so much old writing was trash; but I didn't put it that way to him.

Still, the library became dear to me as a place to be with Sallo, with Sotur, and by myself. It was a place of peace, where I could give myself to the poets I treasured, and the great historians, and my own dreams of adding something to literature.

My poems to Sotur, written with my heart's blood, were stiff and stupid. I knew I was no poet, though I loved both poetry and history—the arts that brought some clarity, some hope of meaning, to human emotions and the senseless, cruel record of human wars and governments. History would be my art. I knew I had a lot to learn, but learning was a delight to me. I had grand plans of books I would write. My life's work, I decided, would be to combine the annals of the various City States into one grand history; thus, incidentally, I would become a grand and famous historian. I made outlines of such a synthesis, ignorant, overambitious, full of errors, but not entirely foolish.

My great fear was that someone had already written my history of the City States and that I didn't know it, because Everra wouldn't buy any new books.

One morning in early spring he sent me across town to Belmand, a household known as ours was for its books and learning. I liked going there. The teacher, Mimen, a younger man than Everra, was his closest friend. They were always exchanging books and manuscripts, often with me as messenger. I was delighted to be excused from hearing little children drone out their alphabet, to get out of the house into the sunlight of morning. I took the long way round, through the sycamore grove where Torm used to drill us, south along the streets under the city walls, loitering along and enjoying my freedom all the way. At Belmand, Mimen made me welcome. He liked me, and had often talked to me about the works of some modern writers, reciting me poetry by Rettaca, Caspro, and others, whose names Everra wouldn't even say. Mimen never lent me their books, knowing Everra had forbidden me to read them. This day we talked a little, but only of the rumor of war with Morva. Both Yaven and a son of the Bel Family were with the army there. Mimen had to return to his schoolroom, so he gave me an armload of books, and I set off home.

I went directly across town this time, because the books were heavy. I was just crossing Long Street when I heard shouting. Looking down the street towards the River Gate I saw smoke—a house afire—or more than one house, for the clouds of smoke billowed up higher every moment. People now were rushing past me across the square behind the Forefathers' Shrine, some running from the fire, some towards it; those who ran towards it were city guards, and as they ran they drew their swords. I stood and saw, as I had seen before, a troop of soldiers coming up Long Street, mounted and afoot, under a green banner. The soldiers and the city guards met and fought with a shouting and clashing of arms. I could not move until I saw the riderless horse break from that knot and muddle of fighting men and gallop up the street straight at me, lathered with white sweat streaked red, blood running from where its eye should be. The horse screamed, and then I could move.

I dodged and ran across the square, between the Shrine and the Senate House, by the back streets, to Arcamand. I burst into the slaves' door shouting, "Invasion! Enemy soldiers inside the city!"

It was news to the household, for Arcamand is set apart by the quiet squares and broad streets of its neighborhood. There was great panic and dismay as the word spread. Elsewhere in Etra word of the incursion had got about much faster, and probably by the time Ennumer had stopped shrieking, the city guards and off-duty soldiers and citizens had driven the invaders back out the River Gate.

Cavalrymen from a troop quartered near the Cattle Market went in pursuit of them and caught a few stragglers east of the bridge, but the main body of the enemy got away. None of our soldiers had been killed, though several had been wounded. No damage had been done except the firing of several thatch-roofed storage sheds near the Gate; but the shock to the city was tremendous. How had troops from Casicar been able to approach Etra in broad daylight, let alone ride right in through the River Gate? Was this impudent foray merely the signal of a full-scale assault from Casicar, for which we were utterly unprepared? The incredulous shame, the rage, and the fear we all felt that first day were uncontrollable. I saw the Father, Altan Arca, weep as he spoke to Torm, giving orders for the defense of the house before he left for an emergency meeting of the Senate.

My heart swelled with the wish to help my Family, my people, to be useful, to stand against the enemies of Etra. I helped collect all the children in the dormitory with Iemmer, and then waited in the schoolroom for orders as to what we house people could do. I wanted very much to be with Sallo, but she was shut up in the silk rooms, where male slaves could not come. Everra, grey and shaken, sat reading in silence; I paced up and down the room. There was a long, strange silence in the great house. Hours passed.

Torm came by the door of the schoolroom and seeing me, stopped. "What are you doing here?"

"Waiting to know how we may be of use, Torm-dí,"
Everra said, getting up hastily.

Torm shouted to someone, "Two more here," then
strode on without a word to Everra.

Two young men came in and told us to follow
them. They were wearing swords and so must be
noblemen, though we did not know them. They took
us across the back court to the barrack. The barrack
doors had a great outside bolt across them, which I
had never seen closed before. The two young men slid
it aside and ordered us in. We heard the bolt slam to
behind us.

All the male slaves of Arcamand were there, locked
up in the barrack. Even the body servants of the Father,
who slept in his anteroom, were there, even the stablemen and Sem the head hostler, who lived and slept in
the mews over the stables. It was terribly crowded, for
with their various duties day and night not more than
half the men would normally be in the barrack, and
then only to change clothes or sleep. There were not
nearly enough bunks for this crowd, hardly room even
to sit down. Many were afoot, talking, excited and disturbed. It was quite dark, because not only were the

doors locked but the windows had been shuttered. The close air stank of sweat and bedding.

My teacher stood bewildered just inside the doors. I got him to come with me to his room, a little cubicle partitioned off from the main dormitory; there were four such cubicles reserved for the older and most highly favored slaves. Three stablemen were sitting on Everra's cot, but Sem ordered them off—"That's the Teacher's room, you stinking sons of horse dung! Get out of there!"

I thanked Sem, for Everra seemed almost stunned, unable to speak. I got him to sit down on his cot, and he was finally able to tell me that he was all right. I left him there and went to listen to what the other men were saying. When we first came in I heard angry voices, indignant protests, but these died down as some of the older men told the younger ones that this was nothing unusual, they weren't being punished; it simply was the rule when there was threat of an attack on the city: all male slaves were locked away—"Out of danger," said old Fell.

"Out of danger!" said a valet. "What if the enemy gets in again and sets fires? We'll roast here like pies in an oven!"

"Shut your fool trap," somebody told him.

"Who's looking after our horses?" said a stable hand.

"Why can't they trust us? What did we ever do but work for 'em?"

"Why should they trust us when they treat us like this?"

"I want to know who's looking after our horses."

It went on like that, on and off, all day. Some of the younger boys were my pupils. They tended to gather around me, out of habit I suppose. In the desperation of boredom I said at last, "Come on, we might as well do our lesson. Pepa! Start off *The Bridge on the Nisas!*" They'd been learning that fine singsong ballad, and they liked it. Pepa, a good student, was too shy to start reciting among all these grown men, but I started off—"'Beneath the walls of Etra'—come on, Pepa!" He joined in, and pretty soon the boys were passing the stanzas around, one to the next, just as if we were in the schoolroom. Ralli piped out bravely in his thin little voice,

Are we then men of Morva
To flee before the foe,
Or shall we fight for Etra
Like our fathers long ago?

And I realised that around us the men had fallen silent and were listening. Some remembered their own schooling, others were hearing the words, the story, for the first time. And they heard it without irony, simply stirred by the events and the call to patriotic courage. When one of the boys faltered, a couple of men picked up the verse which they'd learned long ago in Everra's schoolroom or maybe from the teacher before him, and passed it round to the next boy. At the rousing climax there was a cheer, and congratulations to the boys, and the first laughter we'd heard all day. "Good stuff, that," said Sem. "Let's have some more!" I saw Everra standing at the entrance to his cubicle, looking frail and grey, but listening.

We said them another of Ferrio's ballads, and they liked it well enough—almost all of them were listening by now—but *The Bridge on the Nisas* remained the favorite by far. "Let's have that Bridge again," some man would say, and get a boy to start off, "'Beneath the walls of Etra…'" By the end of the day in the barrack many of them had learned the whole thing, with the quickness of memory that we often lose with literacy, and could roar it out in unison.

Sometimes they added verses that would have made Ferrio's hair stand on end. They got scolded by other men—"Hey, keep it decent, there's kids here."

And they begged pardon of Everra, for whom most of them had an ungrudging, protective respect. The teacher was one of them and yet not one of them: a slave of value, a learned man, who knew more than most nobles knew. They were proud of him. As order began to be established in the crowded barrack, certain men came to the fore—Sem and Metter chief among them—as the keepers of order and the decision makers. Everra was consulted, but mostly set apart and looked after. And I was fortunate in being his disciple, since I got to sleep on the floor of his cubicle, not in the terrible crowding of the main room and the stink of the walled privies behind it.

The worst thing about those days, for most of us, was being kept in ignorance of what was going on, the city's fate, our fate. Food was prepared and brought to us by women slaves from the kitchen. The women were received, twice daily, when the bolt was shot back and the doors briefly opened, with roars of greeting and indecent proposals, and assailed with questions—Are we fighting? Did Casicar attack? Are they in the city? and so on—to most of which they had no answers, though they had plenty of hearsay. Then the women were herded back to the house, and while we ate, the men would chew over those scraps and rumors along with the bread and meat, and try to work out some sense from them. They generally agreed that there had been fighting outside the walls, probably at the River Gate, and that the attackers had not broken into the city, but had not yet been driven off entirely.

And when, on the fourth day, we were at last released, that proved to be the case. Troops in training, hastily brought up from south of the city, had joined the cavalry troop that had been nearby, and beat back the attackers. The cavalry was now pursuing the Casicarans across country. The city guard had been able to retire within the walls and man them against forays. Casicar had brought no siege engines, counting on a surprise mass assault on the gate to get them into the city. If one of their captains, hungry for glory, hadn't led his troop to make that premature raid, we would have had little or no warning, and the city might have been taken and burnt.

And we locked in the barrack…But there was no use thinking about that. We'd been released, and the joy of release was tremendous, it made up for everything.

All of us who could ran out that night to cheer the first troops returning across the Nisas. My sister sneaked out of the silk rooms to meet me and, dressed as a boy, went with me to the River Gate to cheer. It was a crazy thing to do, for a gift-girl who went out in the streets could be horribly punished; but there was a sense of joyous license that night, and we rode on the flood of it. We cheered the troops with all our heart and soul. Among them, in the wild torchlight, we saw Torm, marching along with his odd gait, swinging his arms, short and grim and soldierly. Sallo looked down at once to hide her face, for it wouldn't do if Torm saw his brother's gift-girl out on the loose. She and I slipped back to Arcamand after that, laughing and breathless, through the quiet dark streets and courts of our dear city.

The next day we heard—from Sallo, who heard it from the Mother herself—that Yaven's regiment was to be brought back to guard the city. Sallo was alight with joy. "He's coming, he's coming! I don't care what happens so long as he's here!" she said.

But that was the last good news we had for a while.

Knowing Etra's armies were occupied with truce breakers from Morva and Osc, Casicar had sent that first wave of soldiers to make a lightning assault and take the city by surprise if they could. Repelled, they fell back at once, but only to the front lines of a whole army marching through the hills from Casicar, the great city on the Morr.

Etra was now fast filling up with farmers and country people fleeing from the invaders, some in panic, empty-handed, others bringing all they could in wagons and barrows and driving their cattle before them. But on the third day after our night of rejoicing, the gates were shut. Etra was surrounded by an enemy army.

From the walls we saw them methodically setting up camp, dragging up timbers, digging earthworks as their defense against our soldiers' attack. They had come prepared for a long siege. They set up ornate tents for their officers, their wagon trains were loaded high with grain and fodder, they made great pens for the cattle and sheep they'd taken from farms along the way and would slaughter as they needed. We saw another city growing around ours, a city of swords.

We were sure at first that our armies in the south would sweep in and save us. That hope died hard. Weeks passed before we saw the first Etran troops come to harry the Casicarans and raid their ditch-and-wall defenses. We cheered them from the walls, and shot fire missiles into the tent-city to distract the enemy, but our men always had to fall back. They were small troops, outnumbered ten or twenty to one. Where were the strong regiments that had gone to drive the Morvans and Oscans back to their own lands? What had happened in the south? Dire rumors ran through the city. There was no way to counter them, since we were cut off from all news.

On the first morning of the siege the Senate sent a deputation to the tower above the River Gate to call out for a parley, demanding the reasons for this unprovoked and undeclared attack. The Casicaran generals refused to make any answer, allowing their soldiers to shout and jeer at the Senators. One of the Senators was Altan Arca. I saw him when he came home, dark with fury and humiliation.

The next day the Senate named one of its members, Canoc Ereco Bahar, as Dictator, an ancient title revived in emergencies for a temporary supreme commander. New rules and ordinances immediately began to govern our lives. Strict control of food went into effect: supplies were gathered from all households into the great market warehouses and shared out with ritual punctuality and exactness; hoarders were hanged in the square before the Shrine of the Forefathers. All male citizens over twelve and under eighty years of age were conscripted into defense forces commanded by the city guard. As for slaves, when the siege began, many houses locked up all their male slaves again. The Father of Arcamand merely restricted us to the house and its grounds at night, keeping a strict curfew; and the same policy was soon ordered by the Dictator. Obviously male slaves were needed to do the work of the city, and were worse than useless if shut up like calves being fattened. Bahar decreed that though slaves remained their masters' property, they were also at the disposal of the City of Etra during the emergency. He and the other Senators could order work parties from any house to join the civic workforce in the city barrack. A slave ordered to a work party lived there for the duration of the job, under the command of the veteran General Haster.

I was sent there for the first time in June, about two months into the siege. I was glad to go, to be of use to my city, my people. The schoolroom seemed to me shameful in its peaceable detachment from daily fears and concerns. I longed to get away from the little children and join the men. I was in high spirits, as were most of us at Arcamand and in the city as a whole. We had survived the first shock and terror and found we could live under stern conditions, on a minimum of food, among endless alarms, trapped by an enemy bent on destroying us by sword or fire or starvation. We could not only live, we could live well, in hope and comradeship.

Sallo came to see me the evening before I left for the civic barrack. She was several months pregnant, her eyes bright, her brown skin radiant, almost luminous. Though of course we had received no word of Yaven, she had made up her mind that if he came to any harm she would know it. She was certain that all was well with him. "You remember things," she said to me, smiling, hugging me as we sat side by side on the school bench, as we had when we were children. "You remembered the start of this war, the first raid, didn't you? You saw it. I don't see things. But I know things. And I know I know them. Like Gammy always said: We Marsh people, we have our powers..." She laughed and rocked me sideways, bumping me with her hip.

"Oh, Sal," I said, "did you ever think you'd like to go there, to the Marshes, to see where we came from?"

"No," she said, laughing again. "I just want to be here, with Yaven-dí home, and no siege, and lots to eat!...But you, maybe they'll let you travel, when the

siege is over, when you're a scholar—they'll let you go
buy books, like Mimen did, he went to Pagadi, didn't
he? You can travel all over the Western Shore, you can
go to the Marshes…And everybody there will have a
big nose just like yours." She stroked my nose. "Like
storks. My Beaky. You'll see!"

Sotur also came by before I left. I was tongue-tied
with her. She put a small leather purse in my hand: "It
might be useful. We'll be free soon, Gavir!" she said,
smiling.

The freeing of the city meant freedom to all of us
in Arcamand, even if we were slaves.

I found a different mood in the civic barrack. I
found a very different life there. I soon understood how
childishly foolish my eagerness to go there had been.
Nothing in my life in Arcamand had prepared me for
the heavy work and the brutal life of a civic slave. The
gang I was put in had the job of taking down an old
storage building and carrying the building stones to
the West Gate for use in repairs to the tower and wall.
The stones were massive, weighing a half ton or so. The
work required skills which nobody in the group had
and tools which we had to improvise. We worked from
dawn till night. We lived on the same rations we had received at Arcamand, which were adequate for that life,

not for this one. Our gang boss, Cot, was a man whose only qualifications were great strength and indifference to pain. Cot's chief, Haster's assistant for this division of the slaves, was Hoby.

Hoby was the first person I saw when I came to the civic barrack. He had grown powerfully muscular. His head was shaven, which made his likeness to the Father and Torm less apparent. But there was the scar that split his eyebrow, and his old truculent look. I was about to speak to him when he looked at me directly, a stare of contemptuous hatred, and turned away.

He never spoke to me for the two months I lived in the civic barrack. It was he who put me on the rock gang, as we were called. He made my life hard in other ways, which he had the power to do. The other men saw that, and some mistreated me in order to curry favor with Hoby, while others did what they could to protect me from him. They asked me what "the Chief" had against me, and I answered that I didn't know, except that he blamed me for his scar.

Haster demanded that we bank any money we had with him, for there were men in the barrack who'd kill you for a penny if they knew you had it. I hated to part with the ten bronze eagles in the leather purse, Sotur's gift, and the only money of my own I had ever had.

Haster was honest, by his lights, keeping a fifth of whatever he held for you, but doling out the rest in small change on demand. There was a thriving black market in food, which I'd known nothing about at Arcamand, and I soon learned where to go to get cracked grain or dried meat to fill my empty belly, and which extortioner gave you the best value for your pennies.

My money gave out before my time was up, and the last half month on the rock gang was the worst. I don't remember it very clearly, partly because hunger and exhaustion put me in a condition where the visions, the rememberings, came on me more and more often, so that sometimes I went from one to another, from the place of the silky blue waters to a stinking bed where I lay gazing up at a roof of dark rock just above my face, then I was standing at a window looking at a white mountain across a shining strait, and then all at once I was back straining to hoist or haul great stones in the summer heat. It was often the fiery sting of Cot's whip on my ribs that brought me back. "Wake up, you staring fool!" he'd shout, and I'd try to understand where I was and what I should be doing, while my workmates cursed me for slacking, letting them down, sometimes putting them in danger. I learned later that Cot had asked Hoby to take me off his crew weeks before. Hoby refused. At last Cot went over his head to Haster, who said, "He's useless, send him home."

When I was released, it took me an hour to cross the city. I had to sit down at every corner and in every square to catch my breath and gather strength and try to push away the rememberings, the voices and strange lights and faces that filled my head. Through the branches of a forest I saw the fountain and the broad facade of Arcamand across the sunlit square. Through the darkness of a reeking cave I crossed the square, and went round to the slaves' door, and knocked. Ennumer opened the door. "We haven't anything to give you," she said sharply. I couldn't speak. She recognised me and burst into tears.

I was taken to the infirmary and put to bed. Old Remen rubbed comfrey salve on my whip cuts and gave me catnip tea; my sister came to hug me, stroke my hair, croon and cry and tease me and sit beside the bed. I remembered how the Mother had come when I was there before, and the memory was so clear it was like the rememberings. I spoke to her, thanking her. "I'm so glad to be home!" I said.

"Of course you are. Now go to sleep," Sallo said in her husky soft voice. "And when you wake up you'll still be home, dear Beaky, dear Gav!" And so I slept.

As soon as I recovered—and rest and food, though the food was in woefully short supply by now, were all I needed—I went back to the schoolroom and took up my duties with Everra as if I'd never been away.

When in August I was called to another civic work crew, Everra was so distressed that he went to the Father and protested. He came back to me and said, "The House of Arca is blessed indeed, Gavir. It cares for its children even in the days of war and famine. The Father explained to me that you won't be under Haster's command, nor live in that barrack. The men you'll work with are all educated slaves. The task is to move the sacred prophecies and annals of the Ancients from the old repository under the west wall to the vaults of the Shrine of the Forefathers, where they'll be safe from fire and water and can be hidden in case of invasion. The College of Priests of the Shrine needs literate and intelligent slaves for the task, which must be done with due precaution and in accordance with the rituals of the Ancestors. It will take care, but will not be heavy work. It is an honor to our House that you've been chosen." He clearly took it as an honor to himself, too, and was, I think, a little envious of me, longing to see those ancient documents with his own eyes.

I was glad enough to quit my schoolroom duties for a while, though apprehensive, especially about food. By now we all thought all the time about food. Arcamand had no hoarded supplies, and the city supply of everything but grain was now almost exhausted. The Father and Mother set an example of patient abstinence, and by rigorous supervision of the kitchens whatever food the household got was at least shared out with justice among us all. I dreaded going back to favoritism, unfairness, and bitter rivalry over rations, the cheating and sharp dealing of the black marketeers. But I went as ordered to the slave quarters of the College of the Priests of the Forefathers' Shrine, and when the first meal I had there was a rich chicken broth with succulent barley, such as I hadn't tasted for months, I knew I was in luck.

The half dozen slaves of the Shrine were all older men, so the priests had asked for assistants from Houses such as Arca, Erre, and Bel, where some slaves were educated. Mimen, Everra's friend from Belmand, was there, and I was very glad to see him. He had brought three younger men with him, his students. The men from Erremand, both in their forties, were called Tadder and Ienter. I had heard Everra speak of them with grudging, suspicious admiration—"very learned men," he said, "very learned, but not sound, not sound." I knew he meant they read "the moderns"—books written in the last century or two. I was right. When we went to the dormitory that night—and it was crowded, with thirteen men sleeping where six had slept, but warm, well lighted, and as comfortable as one could hope—the first thing I saw by one bedside was a copy of the *Cosmologies* of Orrec Caspro. Everra had spoken of this poem once or twice the way a doctor might speak of a ghastly, deadly, infectious disease.

Tadder, a dry-faced man with keen eyes under heavy black brows, saw my glance. "Have you read it, laddy?" he asked. He had a northern accent, and some unfamiliar turns of speech.

I shook my head.

"Take it then," said Tadder, and held it out to me. "Have a look!"

I didn't know what to do. I couldn't help glancing at Mimen, as if he might report me to Everra for even looking at the book.

"Everra hasn't let him read the new poets, you know," Mimen said to Tadder. "Or anybody since Trudec. Is Caspro a bit much to start with?"

"Not at all," said the northerner. "What are you,

laddy, fourteen, fifteen? The very age to follow Caspro to glory. Here, d'ye know his song, then?" And he sang out in a fine, pure tenor, "'As in the dark of winter night—'"

"Hey, hey there," said the other man from Erremand, Ienter, "don't get us in hot water the first night, brother!"

"Is that Caspro's hymn, then?" asked the priests' senior slave, a soft-spoken old man with an unassuming air of authority. "I have never heard it sung."

"Well, there's places one gets hanged for singing it, Reba-dí," Ienter said with a smile.

"Not here," Reba said. "Go on, please. I'd like to hear it."

Tadder and Ienter exchanged glances, and then Tadder sang—

As in the dark of winter night
The eyes seek dawn,
As in the bonds of bitter cold
The heart craves sun,
So blinded and so bound, the soul
Cries out to thee:
Be our light, our fire, our life,
          Liberty!

The beauty of his voice and the sweet, sudden leap of the tune on that last word brought tears into my eyes.

Ienter saw it and said, "Ah, look what you've done to the boy, Tadder. Corrupted him with a single verse!"

Mimen laughed. "Everra will never forgive me," he said.

"Sing it again, Tadder-dí," one of Mimen's students asked, with a glance at Reba for permission; Reba nodded; and this time several voices joined in the singing. And I realised then that I'd heard the tune, fragments of it, in the civic barrack, now and then, whistled, a few notes, like a signal.

"Enough," the senior slave said in his quiet voice, "we don't want to wake our masters."

"Oh, no, surely not," said Tadder. "We don't want to do that."

✦ 6 ✦

Working with those men was as pleasant as working on the rock gang had been miserable. The labor was heavy at times, lifting and carrying massive chests and strongboxes full of documents, but we used intelligence to plan the work instead of rushing at it with impatient brutality, and we were patient with one another, too. The work was shared fairly, and rather than whipping and shouted orders there was joking and conversation—sometimes about the ancient scrolls and records we were handling, sometimes about the siege, the latest attack or fire, or anything under the sun. It was an education in itself to work with these men. I knew that. But I was deeply troubled by much they said.

While we were with Reba and the others our talk was harmless, but most of the day the priests and their slaves were busy with their ritual duties at the Shrine and the Senate, and having seen he could trust us to do the work with scrupulous care, Reba left us unsupervised. So while we were in the old repository under the west wall, figuring out what we had to deal with, how to move the decaying boxes and fragile scrolls without damaging them, we were on our own, seven slaves in an ancient, thick-walled temple, nobody to hear us. There Mimen, Tadder, and Ienter talked as I had never heard men talk. Now I understood why Everra spoke of the modern writers as evil influences. My companions were always quoting Denios, Caspro, Rettaca, and other "new poets" and philosophers I'd never heard of, and everything they quoted, though much of the poetry was beautiful beyond any I knew, seemed to be critical, destructive, full of fierce emotions—pain, anger, dissatisfied longing.

It confused me very much. The rock gang were brutal men but they would never question their place in the system, and would think it childish to ask why one man should have power and another none. As if fate and the gods cared for our questions and opinions, as if all the great structure of society the Ancestors had left us could be changed at a whim! My companions here, more refined in their manners than many nobles, and honest and mild in daily life, were in their talk and thought shamelessly disloyal to their Houses and to Etra itself, our city under siege. They talked of their masters disrespectfully, contemptuous of their faults. They had no pride in the soldiers of their House. They speculated about the morals even of the Senators. Tadder and Ienter thought it possible that some Senators, secretly in league with Casicar, had deliberately sent most of the army south so that Casicar could take Etra.

I listened to days of this kind of talk without saying anything, but protest and anger grew in me. When Tadder, who was not even an Etran but came from north of Asion, began to talk about the fall of our city not as a disaster but as an opportunity, I couldn't stand it any longer. I burst out at him. I don't know what I said—I raged at him as faithless, traitorous, ready to destroy our city from within even as the enemy besieged the walls.

The other young men, Mimen's students, began to pour indignation and mockery onto me, but Tadder stopped them. "Gavir," he said, "I'm sorry to have offended you. I respect your loyalty. I ask you to consider that I too am loyal, though not to the House that bought me or the city that uses me. My loyalty is to my own people, my own kind. And however I may talk, never think that I'd urge any slave to rebel! I know where that leads."

Taken aback by his apology and his earnestness, embarrassed by my own outburst, I subsided. We went on with our work. For a while Mimen's students shunned and snubbed me, but the older men treated me just as before. The next day, when Ienter and I were taking a coffer to the Shrine in a little handcart we had devised to carry the fragile relics, he briefly told me Tadder's history. Born free in a northern village, he had been captured as a boy by raiders and sold to a household in the great city of Asion, where he was educated. When he was twenty, there had been a slave revolt in Asion. It was savagely repressed: hundreds of men and women slaves had been slaughtered, and every suspect branded— "You've seen his arms," Ienter said.

I had seen the terrible ridged scars, and thought they were from a fire, an accident.

"When he says his own people," Ienter told me, "he

doesn't mean a tribe or a town or a household. He means you and me."

It made little sense to me, for I couldn't yet conceive of a community greater than the walls of Etra, but I accepted it as a fact.

Mimen's students continued to ignore me most of the time, but without malice. I was much younger than the youngest of them, in their eyes a half-educated boy. At least they trusted me not to betray them by reporting seditious conversations, for they talked freely in my presence. And though I was shocked by much they said, and silently despised them as hypocrites who feigned loyalty to masters they hated, I found myself listening, just as I had listened, disgusted, repelled, but fascinated, to the sexual talk of some of the men in the barrack at home.

Anso, the eldest of Mimen's students, liked to tell about the "Barnavites," a band of escaped slaves living somewhere in the great forests northeast of Etra. Under the leadership of a man named Barna, a man of immense stature and strength, they had formed a state of their own—a republic, in which all men were equal, all free. Each man had a vote, and could be elected to the government, and diselected too, if he misgoverned. All work was done by all, and all goods and game shared in common. They lived by hunting and fishing and by raiding rich people's chariots and the traders' convoys that went to and from Asion. Villagers and farmers in the whole region supported them and refused to betray them to the governments of Casicar and Asion; for the Barnavites generously shared their loot and bounty with their neighbors in those lonely districts, who, if not slaves, were bondsmen or freedmen living in dire poverty.

Anso drew a lively picture of the Barnavites' life in the forests, answerable to no master or senator or king, bound only by freely given allegiance to their community. He knew stories of their daring attacks on guarded wagon convoys on the roads and merchant ships on the Rassy, and the clever disguises they used to go into towns, even into Casicar and Asion, to trade their loot for things they needed in the market. They never killed but in self-defense, Anso said, or, if a man came upon their hidden realm deep in the forest, then he must either pledge his life to live as a free man with them, or die. They never took from the poor, and even from rich farms took only the harvest, never the seed grain. And the women of the farms and villages didn't fear them, for a woman was welcome among them only if she joined them of her own free will.

Tadder read a book or left the room when Anso got launched on these stories. Once or twice he burst out, calling the Barnavites a mere band of thieving runaways. His scorn for them made me wonder if they had something to do with the slave revolt for which he and other slaves in Asion had suffered. Ienter derided the stories more mildly as impossible romances. I agreed with him, for the idea that a band of slaves could live as if they were masters, turning the age-old, sacred order upside down, could only be a daydream; but still I liked to hear these idylls of forest liberty.

For the words liberty, freedom, had come to have a presence, a radiance in my mind, dominating it, like the great, bright stars I used to see on summer nights in Vente, and which I often looked up to see, fainter and farther, from the dark city. We were at leisure, evenings in the dormitory, and the priests allowed us oil for our lamps. I read Denios' *Transformations*, which Tadder lent me, and that was a great discovery to me. It was like that dream I had had of finding rooms in a house that I had not known were there, where I was made welcome among wonders, and greeted by a golden animal.

Denios—the greatest of poets, all my companions said—had been born a slave. In his poems he used the word liberty with a tenderness, a reverence, that made me think of my sister when she spoke of her beloved. And Mimen had a battered little pocket manuscript of Caspro's *Cosmologies*, which he said went with him everywhere; he encouraged me to read it. I found the poem disturbing and strange and understood very little of it, but sometimes a line would take me by the heart, the way his song had, that first night.

I was allowed to run across the city to see my sister for an hour. It was hot September weather. Sallo did not look very well, her body and legs swollen with her pregnancy, her face drawn and tired. She hugged me and asked all about the priests and the other slaves and our work, and I talked the whole time, and then had to run back to the Shrine.

A few days later Everra sent word to me that Sallo's child had been born at seven months and had lived only an hour.

We could not bury in the slave cemetery by the river, for it was outside the walls. During the siege, the bodies of slaves who died were burned in the fire towers, as if they were citizens. Their ashes mingled with those of free men in the waters of the Ash Brook, which rose by the fire towers and ran out through a narrow pipe under the walls to join the Nisas, and then the Morr, and then the sea.

I stood in the autumn dawn at the fire towers by the brook with a few of the people of Arcamand. Sallo was not well enough yet to come to the baby's funeral, but Iemmer said she was in no danger. I was allowed to go see her after a few days. She was thin and tired-looking, and she wept when she hugged me. She said, in her soft tired voice, "If he'd lived, you know, they'd have traded him as soon as they could. If they could. I heard that one House traded a slave baby for a pound of meal. Nobody wants a new mouth in a siege. I think he knew it, Gav. Nobody really wanted him to be alive. Not even me. What…" She didn't finish her question, but opened her hands in a small, desolate gesture that said, What could he have been to me or I to him?

I was shocked at how my people at Arcamand looked. They were all bone-thin, with the same weary look Sallo had—the siege face. Visiting the schoolroom I found my young pupils pitifully skinny and listless. Children are the first to die in famine. We at the Shrine were eating twice as well as most people in the city.

Sallo was delighted to see my good health, and wanted me to tell her about the food we got, the priests' fishpond, their carefully guarded flock of chickens that gave us eggs and now and then a bit of meat or a soup, their garden of holy herbs which included a good many lay vegetables, the gifts of grain to the Ancestors which fed the descendants of the Ancestors....I was ashamed to talk about it, but she said, "I love to hear about it! Do the priests have olives? Oh, I miss olives more than anything!" So I told her we had olives sometimes, though in fact I hadn't tasted one for months.

I saw Sotur just before I left. She too looked listless, her beautiful hair gone dry and dull. She greeted me gently and I said, without knowing I was going to say it, "Sotur-ío, will you give me a quarter-bronze? I want to buy Sallo some olives."

"Oh, Gav, there haven't been any olives for months," she said.

"I know where to get them."

She looked at me with big eyes. After a moment she nodded. She went off and came back with a coin, which she pressed into my hand. "I wish there was more I could do," she said. So she made my first begging an easy thing.

For a quarter-bronze, which would have bought a pound of them last year, the black marketer gave me ten wizened olives. I ran back with them to Arcamand and gave them to Iemmer for Sallo, who was in the silk rooms. I was long overdue getting back to the College of Priests, but Reba didn't say anything, perhaps because he saw I was in tears.

Reba was a gentle man with a serene mind. Sometimes he talked a little with me, telling me about the worship of the Ancestors in the Shrine, which was carried out as much by the priests' slaves as by the priests. He made me feel the dignity of that life and the peaceful beauty of the ever-repeated round of rites and prayers, on which the welfare, the very being, of the city depended. I think he saw the possibility that I might be given by my House to the College, and it flattered me that he wanted me. I could imagine living there as a priest of the Shrine. But I didn't want to live anywhere but Arcamand, near my sister, or do anything but what I had been brought up all my life to do—to learn so that I could teach the children of my House.

We were drawing near the end of our job. The ancient documents had been moved to the vaults under the Forefathers' Shrine, and all we had to do now was sort and store them—work which in fact could be drawn out almost indefinitely, for many of these old scrolls and annals were unidentified, and ought to be read and labeled and listed, as well as cleaned, preserved from insects, and given proper storage. Our Houses weren't eager to have us back, we were only extra mouths in a famine; and the priests and their slaves were glad to have us do the work. In fact, they couldn't have done it without us. I'd been surprised to discover that all seven of us, even I, were much better educated than the priests of the College. They knew the ancestral rites, but very little history or anything else, not even the history of the rites. We were finding all kinds of interesting documents, lives of great men of Etra from the earliest days, prophecies, records of civil and foreign wars and alliances with other cities—all of which fascinated me, drawing me back to my dream of writing a history of all the City States. I was content to be burrowing among the old scrolls and parchments down in the silent vaults, under the silent, dying city.

"What a comfort the past is," Mimen said, "when the future offers none."

Burning the bodies of those who died of starvation went on night and day now down by the Ash Brook.

The smoke of the pyres rose and mixed with the mists of autumn and made a pall over the roofs. Sometimes the smell was the smell of burnt roasting meat and my mouth would water with hunger and sick revulsion.

Outside the north walls the enemy was preparing a huge earthen ramp on which they could bring their siege engines right up to the parapet. The city guardsmen threw paving stones down among the workers, but they swarmed like ants, and their archers shot at any man who showed himself along the walls. Our archers saved those arrows pulled from dying men, and made their own from any tree within the walls, even the old sycamores.

Unrest ran through the Senate and was shouted in the squares by orators: Why had Etra been so unprepared for attack—without weapons stockpiled, without sufficient food stored, her armies far away? Were there traitors among the Senators—lovers of Casicar? Men said the Senate refused to open the gates because they wanted Etra to starve, to die, before it was surrendered. To some this was noble and courageous, to others a vile betrayal. Rumors of unfair distribution of food now ran wild, true or not. Black marketers whose supplies ran out were murdered on the suspicion of withholding food. A merchant's house was attacked and torn down by a mob who believed he was hoarding. They found nothing but a half barrel of dried figs hidden in the slaves' barrack. There were constant stories of grain being hidden under the Senate House… under the Shrine of the Forefathers…That came too close to home. The priests of the College went in terror for their fishpond, their garden, their poultry, their lives. They begged for guards to be set around the Shrine, and ten men were put on duty. They couldn't have done much if a mob had stormed the Shrine, but its sanctity still defended it, and us.

It was mid-October. Life hung in a kind of dead lull which we all felt preceded the end. Within a few days, either the assault on the north wall would begin and would be successful, or a mob out of control would open one of the gates, trying to escape before the slaughter and the burning. Or, conceivably, the Senate would vote to surrender the city in hopes of avoiding total destruction.

And then the thing we had lost all hope of happened.

At daybreak, fog and smoke hanging heavy in the streets, over the enemy camp, along the Nisas, there came a sound of alarms, shouting, bugles signaling, the neighing of horses, the clash of arms. The armies of Etra had come home at last.

All morning we heard the noise of battle outside the walls, and those allowed on the walls and roofs could watch it. We slaves were locked into the compound of the Shrine, and could only beg for news from those who ran past the gates. Late in the morning a great troop of city guards marched through the square, stopping before the Shrine for the blessing of the Ancestors. They were all afoot—every horse in the city had been slaughtered for food long since—and there was a poor, lank look about them, their arms, their clothes, their gaunt faces, as if they were beggars pretending to be soldiers, or were the ghosts of soldiers. But the Ancestors blessed them through the priests' voices, and they marched on down Long Street to the River Gate. They marched in silence, no sound but the rhythmic clink of their weapons. Then for the first time in six months the gate was flung open, and the Etran guard burst forth in a sortie, surprising the besiegers from the rear as they faced our armies. This much we heard as people shouted word from roof to roof, and then we heard a great roar and shouts of victory. "We've got the bridge!" the watchers shouted. "Etra has taken the bridge!"

The rest of the day, though there were alarms and setbacks, was a long turn of the tide, the Casicarans giving way under Etran assaults, trying to regroup, getting knocked apart again, seeking ways to retreat and finding them blocked, until by evening the whole besieging army had become a horde of scattered men running for their lives through all the country between Etra and the Morr and the farmlands across the Nisas, chased by our mounted troops, hunted, cut down—the pig hunt, it was called later. Outside the walls, corpses were strewn thick over the earthworks and through the ravaged camp, thousands of dead men, many already naked, stripped of arms and clothing by our soldiers. The Nisas was dammed in places by dead bodies.

We were released after sunset. I went up on the parapet by the North Gate and saw the live men moving among the corpses, heaving them about like dead sheep to get at their armor and weapons, sometimes slashing a throat if the man seemed not certainly dead. Soon a call went out for slaves to bring the Etran dead into the city to our pyres by the Ash Brook. We seven were sent on that duty, and worked all night by moonlight and torchlight carrying corpses. It was an unearthly business. What I chiefly remember of it was that each time Anso and I, working together, laid a body down in the burning-grounds, I thought of Sallo's baby, Yaven's son, my nephew, who had lived an hour in the starving city. And each time I asked Ennu to guide, not the soldier, but that tiny, unmade soul, into the fields of darkness and the fields of light.

Many of the bodies we carried were those of city guards. They had paid a high cost for their brave foray.

All that night there was a kind of feeble riot, as both citizens and slaves poured out the open gates to plunder the food stores of the Casicaran army, and the Etran soldiers posted to guard them gave way before the pleas and the press of starving people, many of whom they knew. Some soldiers even brought up supply wagons to bring grain into the city. People fought over the supplies, mobbing the grain carts. Order was established only when daylight came, and then only by the use of violence—whips, cudgels, swords. In the morning light I saw the horror on the soldiers' faces as they looked at their people, the men and women of their city, swarming over a rack of sheep carcasses like maggots on a dead rat.

Slaves were ordered to their owner's house by noon, on pain of death. So I left the Shrine of the Forefathers with only time to thank old Reba and to accept from Mimen his little handwritten copy of Caspro's poem.

"Don't let Everra see it," he said with his wry smile, and not knowing how to thank him I only stammered, "No, no, I won't..."

It was the first book I'd ever owned. It was the first thing I'd ever owned. I called what I wore my clothes, the desk I used in the schoolroom I called my desk, but in fact they were not mine, they were the property of the House of Arca, as I was. But this book, this was mine.

◆ ◆ ◆

WHEN YAVEN CAME HOME he greeted the Father and Mother with suitable affection and decorum and headed straight for the silk rooms. It was wonderful to see how Sallo bloomed and shone, now that he was back. Yaven wasn't as thin as most city people were, but he'd been through hard times too, and was weathered and toughened and tired. He told us about the campaign, me and Sallo and Sotur and Astano and Oco, all back in the schoolroom with Everra, like the old days.... The forces of Morva had been reinforced by an army from Gallec, the Votusans and Oscans had joined them; Etra's army had been hard put to withstand attackers on so many fronts. There had been, Yaven thought, some mistakes, some confusion in command, but no betrayal. The Etrans could not come to the relief of their city till they defeated the enemies who would have followed them right to the walls. Then they came as fast as they could. They crossed the Morr at night, making a boat bridge, so as to take the besieging army by surprise from the east, the unexpected direction.

"But we had no real idea how hard it was for you here," he said. "I still can't imagine what it was like…" Astano showed him a piece of "famine bread" she had kept: a brownish wafer like a chip of wood, made from a little barley or wheat meal, sawdust, earth, and salt. "We had plenty of salt," she said. "All we needed was something to put it on."

Yaven smiled, but the grim lines were set in his face. "We'll make Casicar pay for this," he said.

"Oh," said Sotur, "pay… Are we merchants, then?"

"No, little cousin. We're soldiers."

"And the wives of soldiers, and the lovers and mothers and sisters and cousins of soldiers… And what is it Casicar will pay us?"

"It's how it is," Yaven said gently. His hand was on Sallo's hand, as they sat side by side on the schoolroom bench.

Everra spoke of the honor of the city, the insult to the power of the Ancestors, the vengeance due. Yaven listened to him with us, but said nothing more of such matters. Presently he asked me about my time at the Shrine, and the ancient documents that we had been rescuing. As I was telling him, I saw in his absorbed face the face of the boy who loved the epics and the ballads, who had led us to build Sentas on those summer afternoons. It came into my head to wonder what Yaven would make of the "new poets." Maybe someday, when he was Father of Arcamand and I was the teacher in this classroom, I would give him *The Transformations* to read and he would discover that new world...but I couldn't quite imagine it. Still, the thought moved me to tell him how we'd recited *The Bridge on the Nisas* in the barrack, early in the siege, how all the men had roared it out together—"Beneath the walls of Etra"— We ended up, all of us in the schoolroom, reciting the ballads, with Yaven the lead voice; and some of my skinny little pupils crept in to listen, round-eyed and wondering at the tall soldier laughing as he declaimed,

"Then fled the Morvan soldiers, the men of Morva ran…"

"Again and again," Sotur whispered. "And back and forth." She was not saying the poems with us. She looked wretched and bewildered. She saw me gazing at her with concern, and turned her head sharply away.

Those autumn weeks after the siege we enjoyed what may be the sweetest of all pleasures: relief from incessant, intense strain and fear. That relief, that release, is freedom made manifest. It lets the heart soar. A mood of lenience and kindness filled Arcamand. People were grateful to one another that they had survived together. They could laugh together, and they did.

Early in the winter, Torm came back to the House to live. He had been in the city all through the siege, but not at Arcamand. The Dictator had levied a special troop of cadets, soldiers invalided home, and veterans as an auxiliary to the city guard, doing sentry duty, manning the walls and gates, and serving as firemen and civic police. These men had done good service in defense and fighting fires and had at first been popular heroes, but their increasing role in punishing black marketers, hoarders, and suspected traitors had led people to fear their investigations and accuse them of using their power arbitrarily. They had been disbanded a few days after liberation, when the Dictator resigned, restoring full power to the Senate.

Torm was seventeen now but looked much older, carrying himself and behaving like a grown man, grim, self-contained, and silent.

He brought Hoby back to Arcamand with him. As his own reward for service, he had requested that Hoby be released from the civic workforce to serve as his bodyguard. Like Metter, the Father's bodyguard, Hoby slept outside his master's door. Though he still shaved his head, and was a bigger man than Torm, their resemblance was clear to see.

The occasion of Torm's return was Astano's betrothal ceremony. The Mother had not approved her marriage with Corric Beltomo Runda, but instead had chosen for her a relative of that House through the female line, Renin Beltomo Tarc. Tarcmand was an ancient though not a wealthy House, and Renin a promising young Senator; he was a good-looking fellow and a pleasant talker, though, according to Sallo, our principal informant, he didn't know anything—"not even Trudec! Maybe he knows politics."

Sotur said nothing about the betrothal to us. We saw little of her. It seemed she hadn't felt the release from fear as we did. She hadn't regained her weight and looks as we all were doing. She still had the siege face. When I found her in the library at the table with a book, she would greet me kindly but wouldn't talk much and very soon would slip away. My ache of desire for her was gone, turned to an ache of pity, with a tinge of impatience—why must she go on moping in these good days of freedom?

Everra was to deliver an address at the betrothal ceremony. He spent days getting all his quotations from the classics ready. In the benign mood of that autumn, I felt it mean and dishonorable to hide from my old teacher what I'd learned from Mimen and the others at the Shrine. I told him I'd read Denios and that Mimen had given me his copy of Caspro's *Cosmologies*. My teacher shook his head gravely, but didn't go into a tirade. That encouraged me to ask him how Denios' poems could corrupt a reader, since they were noble in both language and meaning.

"Discontent," Everra answered. "Noble words to teach you how to be unhappy. Such poets refuse the gifts of the Ancestors. Their work is a bottomless pit. Once you remove the firm foundation of belief on which all our lives are built, there is nothing. Only words! Gorgeous, empty words. You can't live on words,

Gavir. Only belief gives life and peace. All morality is founded upon belief."

I tried to say what I thought I had glimpsed in Denios, a morality larger than the one we knew, but my ideas were mere gropings, and Everra demolished them with his certainty. "He teaches nothing but rebellion against what must be—refusal of truth. Young men like to play with rebellion, to play at disbelief. I know that. But you'll tire of that sick folly as you grow older, and come back to belief, the one foundation of the moral law."

It was a relief to hear the old certainties again. And he hadn't told me to stop reading Caspro. I did not read often in the *Cosmologies*, for it was difficult and seemed remote and strange to me; but sometimes lines from it or from Denios would come into my mind, unfolding their meaning or their beauty, as a beech leaf unfurls in spring.

I thought of one of those lines when I stood with all the household to watch Astano, wearing robes of white and silver, cross the great atrium to meet and welcome her husband-to-be: *She is a ship on a flowing of bright waters...*

Everra made his speech, bristling with classical quotations, so that everyone could be impressed by the learning of the House of Arca. The Mother of the House of Arca said the words that gave her daughter to the House of Tarc. The Mother of that House came forward to receive our Astano as the future Mother of Tarcmand. Then my little pupils sang a wedding song Sotur had rehearsed with them for weeks. And so it was done. Lyre players and drummers in the gallery tuned up, and the wellborn went to the great rooms to feast and dance. We house people had a feast too, and our own music and dancing in the back courtyard. It was cold and a little rainy, but we were ready to dance—and always ready to feast again.

Betrothed in winter, Astano was married on the day of the spring equinox. A month later Yaven was called back to his regiment.

Etra was mounting an invasion of Casicar. Votus, which had been part of the alliance with Morva against us, had come over to our side, fearing the power of Casicar and seeing a chance to cripple it while it was weakened by defeat. Etrans and Votusans together would invade and take or besiege the city of Casicar— a great city, sometimes our enemy, sometimes our ally. *Again and again, back and forth*, Sotur had said.

I saw Sallo the day Yaven left. She had been allowed to go down to the River Gate to see him and his troops march out to war amid the wild cheering of the people. She was not tearful. She had the same certain hope she had had for him all through the siege. "I think Luck listens to him," she said, with a smile, but seriously. "In battle, I mean. In war. Not here."

"Not here? What do you mean, Sal?"

We were in the library alone and could talk freely. Yet she hesitated for a long time. Finally she looked up at me and seeing I really had no idea what she meant, she said, "The Father was glad to see him go."

I protested.

"No, listen, truly, Gav!" She spoke very low, sitting close to me. "The Father hates Yaven-dí. He does! He's jealous. Yaven will inherit Altan Arca's power. His House. His seat in the Senate. And he's beautiful, and tall, and kind, like his mother—he's a Galleco, not an Arca. His father can't bear to look at him, he's so jealous of him. I've seen it! A hundred times!— Why do you think it's Yaven, the elder son, the heir, who gets sent off again to war? While the younger son, who should be the soldier, who's had all the fancy training to be a soldier, stays safe at home? With his *bodyguard*! The cowardly, pompous little adder!"

I had never in my life heard my good-natured,

tender-hearted sister speak with such hatred. I was appalled, wordless.

"Torm will be groomed for the Senate, you'll see," she said. "Altan Arca hopes Yaven will be—will be killed—" Her soft, passionate voice broke on that word, and she gripped my hand hard. "He *hopes* it," she repeated, in a whisper.

I wanted to refuse and refute everything she said, but still no words came to me.

Sotur came into the library. She stopped, seeing us, as if to withdraw. Sallo looked up at her and said in a plaintive whisper, "Oh, Sotur-ío!"—and Sotur came to her and took her in her arms, a thing I had never seen that reticent, shy, proud girl do with anyone. The two clung to each other as if trying to reassure each other and unable to. I sat in dumb wonder. I tried to believe that they were consoling each other for losing Yaven, but I knew it wasn't that. It wasn't grief I saw, or love. It was fear.

And when Sotur's eyes met mine, over my sister's head, there was a fierce indignation in her look, which softened gradually. Whatever enemy she had been seeing in me, she saw me again at last.

She said, "Oh, Gavir! If you could get Everra to ask

for Sallo to help him teach the little ones—something—anything to get her out of the silk rooms! I know, you can't, he can't...I know! I asked for her as my maid. I asked the Mother—for my nameday present—just while Yaven is away—may I have Sallo? And she said no, it was not possible. I have never asked for anything. Oh, Sallo, Sallo—you must get sick! You must starve again! Get thin and ugly, like me!"

I didn't understand.

Sotur couldn't comprehend my incomprehension. Sallo did. She kissed Sotur's cheek and turned to me and hugged me, saying, "Don't worry, Gav. It'll be all right, you'll see!"

And she went off, back to the chambers of the wellborn and the silk rooms, and I went back to the slave barrack, puzzled and worried, but always coming back to the belief, the sure belief, that the Father and Mother and Ancestors of our House would not let anything go really wrong.

PART TWO

◆ 7 ◆

I am lying in the dark in a strange, strong-smelling bed. Not far above my face is a ceiling, a low vault of raw black rock. Beside me lies something warm, pressing heavily against my leg. It raises its head, a long, grey head, grim black lips, dark eyes that gaze across me: a dog, a wolf? I remembered this many times, remembered waking up with the dog or wolf pressed close beside me, lying among rank-smelling furs in the dark place with a rock ceiling, a cave it must be. I remember it now. I am lying there now. The dog gives a whining groan and gets up, steps over me. Someone speaks to it, then comes and crouches beside me and speaks to me, but I don't understand what he says. I don't know who he is, who I am. I can't lift my head. I can't lift my hand. I am weak, empty, nothing. I remember nothing.

I will tell you what happened in the order it happened, as historians do, but there is deep untruth in doing so. I did not live my life as history is written. My mind used to leap ahead, remembering what had not yet come to pass; now, what was past was lost to me. What I tell you now, it took me a long time to find again. Memory hid from me and buried itself in darkness, as I lay buried in that dark place, that cave.

It was early in the morning, in the first warmth of spring. The open inner courtyards of Arcamand were cheerful in the sunlight.

"Where's Sallo? Oh, Sallo and Ris both went off with Torm-dí, Gav."

"With Torm-dí?"

"Yes. He took them off to the Hot Wells. Last night, pretty late."

Falli was talking to me. Falli was the gate guard to the silk rooms. She sat in the western court with her spinning, a heavy, slow-spoken woman who had long ago been one of the Father's gift-girls. She made a reverence whenever she spoke of the Father or the Mother or any of the Family or any other wellborn family. She worshipped them as gods. People used to laugh at her for it—"Falli thinks they're already Ancestors," Iemmer said. Falli was a foolish woman. What foolish thing had she just said, bobbing her head when she said "Torm-dí"—that Torm had taken Ris and my sister to the Hot Wells?

The Hot Wells belonged to Corric Runda, son of the Senator Granoc Runda, the wealthiest and most powerful man in the government of Etra. Corric had wanted to marry our Astano, and failed, but seemingly he held no grudge; lately he'd become Torm's friend or patron. Torm was always with him and his circle of young, rich men. Young, rich men could live the high life, now that Etra was free and prosperous again— endless feasts, women, drinking parties that ended up as riots in the city streets...A strange friendship for Torm, it seemed to some of us, with his stiff grim ways and his warrior's training, but Corric had taken a fancy to him, insisted on having him; and the Father approved of the friendship, encouraging it as a good thing for the Family, for the Arca interest with the House of Runda. Young men would be young men, there would be women and drinking and so on, there was no harm in it, nothing would go really wrong.

Tib, a prentice cook now, followed Hoby about like a dog when Hoby was at Arcamand. And Tib told us the stories Hoby told him. Corric and his friends liked to get Torm drunk because he went crazy when he was drunk and would do anything they dared him to do— fence with three men at once, fight a bear, tear off his clothes and dance naked on the Senate steps till he fell down in a foaming fit. They thought Torm was wonderful, Hoby said, they all admired him. To some of us it sounded as if they used him as a clown, for entertainment, like the dwarfs Corric kept as wrestlers, or his half-witted, one-eyed, giant bodyguard Hurn. But it wasn't like that at all, according to Hoby as related by Tib. Hoby said that Corric Runda took lessons in swordfighting from Torm, treating him as a master of the art. He said all Corric's friends respected Torm. They feared his great strength. They liked him to run wild because then everybody feared him and them.

"Torm-dí is young," Everra said. "Let him have his fling while he's young. He'll be the wiser for it when he's older. The Father knows that. He had his wild days too."

The Runda estate called the Hot Wells was a mile or so from Etra in the rich grainlands west of the city. The Senator built a grand new house there and gave it to his son Corric. Hoby told Tib all about it and Tib told us: the luxurious chambers, the silk rooms full of women, the courts full of flowers, and the wonderful bathing pool in a back court—the water came up from a hot spring and was always the temperature of blood, but it was transparent blue-green, and peacocks spread their plumage beside it on pavements of green and purple marble...Hoby had been there many times as Torm's bodyguard. All these young noblemen had bodyguards, it was the fashion; Corric had three be-sides the giant, Torm had bought a second one recently. The bodyguards were invited to share the women in the silk rooms at the Hot Wells, to take their pick of the food and the women, after their masters, of course. Hoby had swum in the warm pool. He told Tib all about the pool, about the women, about the food— minced livers of capon, the tongues of unborn lambs.

So when Falli said to me that Torm had taken Ris and Sallo to the Hot Wells, though my mind seemed blank as if I'd run into a stone wall and been stunned, I went after a little while to the kitchens and looked for Tib. I thought he might know something from Hoby. I don't know what I thought he might know. He knew nothing. When I told him what Falli had said, he looked taken aback for a moment, dismayed. Then he said,

"There are a lot of women there, the Rundas keep dozens of slave women there. Torm just took the girls there to have a good time."

I don't know what I answered, but it made Tib go sullen and defensive. "Look, Gav, maybe you're teacher's pet and all, but remember, after all, Sal and Ris are gift-girls."

"They weren't given to Torm," I said. I spoke slowly, because my mind was still blank and slow. "Ris is a virgin. Sallo was given to Yaven. Torm can't take them out of the house. He can't have taken them there. The Mother would never allow it."

Tib shrugged. "Maybe Falli got the story mixed up," he said, and turned away to his work.

I went to Iemmer and told her what Falli said. I repeated what I'd said to Tib—that it could not be: the Mother would not allow it.

Iemmer, who like so many people since the siege now looked much older than she was, said nothing at all for a while. Then only a great "Ah," and shook her head, again and again.

"Oh, this is— This is not good," she said. "I hope, I hope Falli is wrong. She must be. How could she let him take off the girls without permission? I'll speak with her. And with other women in the silk rooms. Oh, Sallo!" She had always loved my sister best of all the girls. "No, it can't be," she said with more energy. "Of course you're right, Mother Falimer-ío wouldn't allow it. Never. Yaven-dí's Sallo! And little Ris! No, no, no. That suet-headed Falli has got something mixed up. I'll go get this straight right now."

I was used to trusting Iemmer, who generally did get things straight. I went off to the schoolroom and put my young pupils through their drills and recitations. I kept my mind from thinking until the morning was over. I went to the refectory. People were talking, a group of them, men and women. "No," Tan was saying, "I put the horses in myself. He took them off in the closed car, with Hoby and that lout he bought from the Rundas in with them, and himself driving the horses."

"Well, if the Mother let them go, there's no harm in it," Ennumer said in her high vague voice.

"Of course the Mother let them go!" said another woman, but Tan, who was second hostler now, shook his head and said, "They were bundled up like a lot of washing in sacks. I didn't know who they were, even, till Sallo pokes out her head and tries to shout out something. Then Hoby pushes her back into the car like a sack of meal and bang goes the door and off they go at a gallop."

"A prank, like," one of the older men said.

"A prank that'll get Sonny-dí and Twinny into some trouble with Daddy-dí, maybe!" Tan said savagely. He saw me then. His dark eyes locked on mine. "Gav," he said. "You know anything about it? Did Sallo talk to you?"

I shook my head. I couldn't speak.

"Ah, it'll be all right," Tan said, after a moment. "A prank, like uncle said. A damn fool stupid joke. They'll be back this evening."

I stood there with the others, but it was as if everything and everyone moved away from me and I stood alone in a place where there was nothing and no one. I moved through the halls and courts of Arcamand with an emptiness around me. Voices came to me from a distance.

The emptiness closed in and became dark, a low rough roof of black stone, a cave.

"I know things," Sallo said to me. "And I know I know them. We Marsh people, we have our powers!" And she laughed. Her bright eyes shone.

I knew she was dead before they sent for me, before

Everra told me. They thought it proper that Everra should be the one to tell me.

An accident, last night, in the pool at the Hot Wells. A sad accident, a terrible thing, Everra said, tears in his eyes.

"An accident," I said.

He said Sallo had been drowned—had drowned, he corrected himself—had drowned, as the young men, who had drunk too much and gone past all decency, were playing with the girls in the pool.

"The pool of warm water," I said, "where there are peacocks on the marble."

Yes, my teacher said, looking up at me with tear-wet eyes. He seemed to me to have a sly, cringing expression, as if he was ashamed of himself for doing something he should not have done but would not confess, like a schoolboy.

"Ris is home," he said, "with the women in the silk rooms. She is in a lamentable state, poor girl. Not injured, but…It was madness, madness. We know that Torm-dí has always—has always had this frenzy that comes upon him—but to take the girls out of the house! To take them there, among those men! Madness, madness. Oh the shame, the shame, the pity of it, oh, my poor Gavir," and my teacher bowed his grey head before me, hiding his wet eyes and cringing face. "And what will Yaven-dí say!" he cried.

I went through the halls, past the room of the Ancestors, to the library, and sat there a while alone. The emptiness was around me, the silence. I asked Sallo to come to me, but no one came. "Sister," I said aloud, but I could not hear my voice.

Then I thought, and it was perfectly clear to me, that if she had been drowned she would be lying on the floor of the pool of green water warm as blood. If she was not there, where was she? She could not be there, so she could not have been drowned.

I went looking for her. I went to the silk rooms, to the western court. I said to women I met there, "I'm looking for my sister."

I had forgotten who the women were, the people that took me to her, but I knew her.

She was lying among white cloths that covered her up. Her face, which was all I could see, was not rosy brown but greyish, with a dark bruise across one cheek. Her eyes were closed, and she looked small and tired. I knelt beside her, and they let me be there.

I remember that they came and said, "The Mother

has sent for you, Gavir," as if this was a solemn, important thing. I kissed Sallo and told her I'd be back soon. I went with them.

They took me through the familiar corridors to the Mother's apartments, which I knew only from outside; Sallo was allowed in to sweep the Mother's rooms, but not I; I only swept the hallways there. She was waiting for me, tall in her long robes, the Mother of Arcamand. "We are so sorry, so sorry, Gavir, for your sister's death," she said in her beautiful voice. "Such a tragic accident. Such a sweet girl. I do not know how I am ever to tell my son Yaven. It will be a bitter grief to him. I know you loved your sister. I loved her too. I hope the knowledge of that will be some comfort to you. And this." She put into my hands a small heavy pouch of silk. "I will send my own women to her funeral," she said, gazing earnestly at me. "Our hearts are broken for our sweet Sallo."

I reverenced her and stood there. The people came and took me away again.

They would not take me back to Sallo. I never saw her face again, so I had to remember it greyish, bruised, and tired. I didn't want to remember it that way, so I turned away from the memory, I forgot it.

They took me back to my teacher, but he did not want me nor I him. As soon as I saw him, words broke out of me—"Will they punish Torm? Will they punish him?"

Everra started back as if afraid of me. "Be calm, Gavir, be calm," he said placatingly.

"Will they punish him?"

"For the death of a slave girl?"

Around his words silence spread out. Silence enlarged around me, wider and deeper. I was in a pool, at the bottom of a pool, not of water but of silence and emptiness, and it went on to the end of the world. I could not breathe the air, but I breathed that emptiness.

Everra was talking. I saw his mouth open and shut. His eyes glistened. An old grey-haired man opening and shutting his mouth. I turned away.

There was a wall across my mind. On the other side of the wall was what I couldn't remember because it hadn't happened. I had never been able to forget, but now I could. I could forget days, nights, weeks. I could forget people. I could forget everything I'd lost, because I'd never had it.

But I remember the burial ground when I stand there, very early the next morning, just as day lightens the sky. I remember it because I've remembered it before.

When we buried old Gammy, when we buried little Miv, I remember standing there in the green rain of the willows, just outside the walls, by the river, and wondering who we were burying on this other morning.

It must be someone important, for all the Mother's personal serving women are there in their white mourning garments, hiding their faces in their long shawls, and the body is wrapped in beautiful white silk, and Iemmer is weeping aloud. She can't say the prayer to Ennu-Mé. When she tries to, she makes a shrieking wail that tears a horrible, raw hole in the silence, so that now other women, weeping too, have gone to her to hold and console her.

I stand near the water and watch how it eats at the riverbank, lapping and gnawing at the earth, undercutting the bank, eating away at it so that the grass overhangs it, the white roots of the grass dangling down into the air above the water. If you looked in the earth of the bank you'd find white bones thin as roots, bones of little children buried there where the water would come and eat their graves.

A woman stood not far from me, not with the other women. A long, ragged shawl was pulled over her head and hid her face, but she looked at me once. It was Sotur. I know that. I remember, for a little while.

When she and the other women were gone, there were some people around me, men, and I asked them if I could stay there in the cemetery. One of them was Tan, the stableman, who was kind to me when we were boys. He was kind to me then. He put his hand on my shoulder. "You'll be back in a bit, then?"

I nodded.

His lips were pinched together to keep from trembling. He said, "She was the sweetest girl I ever knew, Gav."

He went off with the others. There was nobody in the cemetery now. They had put the green sod back over the grave as well as they could so that it hardly showed among all the other graves, but it didn't matter, since the river would wash all the graves away and there would be nothing left but a few white rags twisting in the current going to the sea. I walked away from the grave, upstream along the Nisas, under the willows.

The way narrowed to a path between the city wall and the river, and then I was at the River Gate. I waited for the market traffic coming into the city across the bridge to pass, heavy wagons drawn by white oxen, little carts pulled by a donkey or by a slave. At last there was a space among them so I could cross the roadway. I went on up the west bank of the Nisas. The path was pleasant, wandering nearer and farther from the river-bank, passing the small gardens that thrifty freemen planted and tended. Some old men were already in their plots, hoeing, weeding, enjoying the mild spring morning, the cloudy sunrise. I walked on into the silence, the empty world. I walked under a low ceiling of raw black rock into the dark.

◆ ◆ ◆

THERE IS MUCH I will never remember of the days after that day. When at last I learned forgetting, I learned it very quickly and all too well. What fragments I can find of those days may be memories or may not, they may be the other kind of remembering that I do, of times that have not come and places I have not yet been. I lived where I was and where I was not, all those days, all that time, a month, two months. I wasn't walking away from Arcamand, because there was nothing behind me but a wall, and I'd forgotten most of what lay on the other side of it. There was nothing ahead of me at all.

I walked. Who walked with me? Ennu, who guides

us in death? or Luck, who is deaf in the ear you pray to? The way took me. If there was a path I followed it, if there was a bridge I crossed it, if there was a village and I smelled food and was hungry, I went and bought food. In my pocket, ever since it was given to me, I had carried the little silk purse as full and heavy with money as a heart is full and heavy with blood. Six silver pieces, eight eagles, twenty half-bronzes, nine quarter-bronzes. I counted them first as I sat by the Nisas, hidden among flowering shrubs and high grass. In the villages I spent only the quarter-bronzes. Even they were more than many people could change. Villagers and farmers gave me extra food when they could not give me pennies. Few people grudged me food, and some would rather give it than sell it to me. I wore white, the white of mourning, and I spoke as educated men of the city speak, and when they said, "Where are you going, dí?" I said, "I am going to bury my sister."

"Poor boy," I heard women say. Sometimes little children ran after me shouting, "Crazy! Crazy!" but they never came close to me.

I wasn't robbed by the poor people I went among because I had no thought of being robbed, no fear of it. If I had been robbed it wouldn't have mattered to me at

all. When you have nothing to pray for, that's when
Luck hears you.

If Arcamand had sought their runaway slave then,
they would have found me easily enough. I didn't hide.
Anyone along the Nisas could have put them on my
trail. Probably at Arcamand they said to one another
that Gavir had drowned himself that morning at the
slave cemetery after the others left, that he had taken a
heavy stone in his arms and walked out into the river.
Instead I took the Mother's silken purse heavy with
money because it was in my pocket, and walked out
into the empty world because it didn't occur to me to
take a stone and walk into the river. It didn't matter
where I walked. The ways were all the same. There was
only one way I could not go, and that was back.

I crossed the Nisas somewhere. The little roads between villages took me round and about, one direction
then another. One day I saw the heads of high, round,
green hills ahead of me. I had wandered onto the Ventine Road. If I kept on it that road would take me up
into the hills, to the farm, to Sentas. Those names and
places came to me out of the forgetting. I remembered
Sentas, the farm, I remembered someone who lived
there: the farm slave Comy.

I sat down in the shade of an oak and ate some bread someone had given me. Thinking was a slow business for me then, it took a long time. Comy had been a friend. I thought I could go up to the farm and stay there. All the house slaves knew me, they'd treat me well. Comy would fish with me.

Maybe the farm had been burned to the ground when Casicar invaded, the orchards hacked down, the vines torn out.

Maybe I could live in Sentas, as if it were a real place.

All the slow, stupid thoughts went by and I got up and turned my back on the road to Vente. I walked between two fields on a lane that went northeast.

The lane took me to a road, narrow and rutted, with very few people on it. It kept going, leading away from things I remembered and wanted to forget, and I kept going on it. There was a town where I bought food in the market, enough for several days, and bought a rough brown blanket I could use for a bed at night. Later there was a desolate village where the dogs came out and barked and kept me from stopping there. But there was nothing to stop for.

After that village the road dwindled to a footpath.

No crops were planted on the rolling hills. Sheep grazed, scattered out on the slopes, and their tall grey guard dog would stand up and watch me as I passed. Trees grew thick in the dales between the hills. I slept in those groves, drinking from the small streams that ran down among them. When I had no more food, for a while I looked for something to eat. It was too early for anything but a few tiny strawberries, and I did not know what to look for. I gave up looking and went on walking up the path between the hills. Hunger is painful. There was a thought in my head, not a memory, only a thought, that while I ate so well with the priests of the Shrine, there was someone who had not had enough to eat, so that the baby starved in her womb, and so now it was my turn to go hungry. It was only fair.

The distance I walked each day got shorter. I sat down often in the hot sunshine among the wild grasses. The flowering grasses were beautiful in their diversity. I would watch the little flies and bees in the air, or remember what had happened or not happened, as if it were all one dream. The day would pass, the sun would pass on its great path across the sky, before I got up and trudged on looking for a place to sleep. I lost the path one day and after that followed nothing but the folds of the hills.

I was going slowly down a slope to find the stream at the bottom in the early twilight, feeling my legs shake under me, when something came rushing at me from behind and I felt my breath go out of me as the trees whirled around in a burst of light.

Some time after that I was lying in a strange, strong-smelling bed of furs. Not far above my face was a ceiling, a low vault of raw black rock. It was almost dark. Beside me something warm pressed against my leg, a big animal. It raised its head, a dog's long, grey, heavy head, grim black lips, dark eyes that gazed across me. It made a whining groan and got up and stepped over my legs. Someone spoke to it, then came and crouched down beside me. He spoke to me but I didn't understand for a long time. I stared at him in the weak light that seemed to glance and reflect off the black rocks on the floor of the cave. I could see the whites of his eyes clearly, and the grey-black hair that stuck out in shaggy clumps around his dark face. He smelled stronger than the dirty, half-cured furs of the bed. He brought me water in a cup made of bark, and helped me drink, for I couldn't lift my head.

Most of the time I lay in the low cave room, I had no memories of any other place or time. I was there, only there. I was alone, except when the dog was with me, lying by my left leg. Sometimes it raised its head and stared into the dark air. It never looked into my face. When the man came stooping into the room, the dog stood up and went to him, putting its long nose into his hand, and then went out. Later it would come back with him or by itself, step over me, turn round once, and lie down by my leg. Its name was Guard.

The man's name was Cuga or Cuha. Sometimes he said one, sometimes the other. He talked strangely, deep in his throat, as if something obstructed his voice, which came out as if through rocks. When he came, he would sit down by me, give me fresh water, and offer me food: usually thin strips of smoke-dried meat or fish, sometimes a few berries as they came ripe. He never gave me much at a time. "What were you doing then, starving?" he said. He talked a good deal when he was with me, and often I heard him in the other part of the cave talking to himself or to the dog, the same low gargling broken stream of words never waiting for an answer. To me he said, "What did you want to go starving for anyhow? There's food. Food where you find it.

What brought you up here? I thought you was from Derram. I thought they was after me again. I followed you, you know. I followed you and watched. I can watch all day. I told Guard, Lay low. You got up and I thought you was going on, but then you come straight down here, straight to my door, what am I to do, man? I'm behind you, I got my stick in hand, and so I hit you on the head, whack!" and he pantomimed a tremendous blow and laughed, showing his brown, wide-spaced teeth. "You never knew I was there, did you? I killed him, I thought, I killed him. You went down like a dead branch, there you was, I killed him. So much for Derram! So then I take a look and it's a kid. Sampa, Sampa, I gone and killed a kid! No, not dead. Didn't even break his fool egg head. But he's down like a dead branch. A kid. I picked you up with one hand like a fawn. I'm strong, you know. They all know that. They don't come here. What did you come here for, boy? What brought you? What was you starving for? Lying there with ten thousand moneys in your purse! Bronzes, silvers, the faces of gods! Rich as King Cumbelo! What was you starving for? What sort of place is this to come with all those moneys? You going to buy deer from Lady Iene? Are you crazy, boy?" He nodded. "You are, you are."

Then he chuckled and said, "So am I, boy. Crazy Cuga." He chuckled again and gave me a sliver of sweet fibrous meat, bitter with smoke and ash. I slowly chewed at it, my mouth full of the juices of hunger.

That was all there was for a while, my hunger, the vivid taste of the food he doled out to me, his broken voice talking, the black rock roof above my face, the reek of smoke and fur, the dog pressed against my leg. Then I could sit up. Then I could crawl to the entrance of the rock chamber, and discover that it was the innermost, lowest one of several such chambers in the cave which Cuga had made his house. Slowly I explored them. In some you could stand up, at least in the center, and the largest room was quite spacious, though its floor was a jumble of big stones. The black rock of the cave was porous and cracked, and light came through cracks and crevices from above, making a smoky dimness. When I first went out, the sunlight blinded me with great dazzling bursts of red and gold, and the air smelled sweet as honey.

From outside the cave, even at its very entrance, you could not see it, only a massive slant of rocks like a dry waterfall all overgrown with creepers and fern.

Cuga's possessions were the deerskins and rabbit furs he had crudely cured; some bark cups; some spoons and other implements he had whittled of alderwood; a roll of fine sinew; and his treasures—a metal box half full of dirty salt crystals, a tinderbox for fire making, and two horn-handled hunter's knives of good steel, which he kept sharp on a fine-grained river pebble. Of these treasures he was fiercely jealous, suspicious of me, hiding them from me. I never knew where he kept the salt. The first time he had to bring out one of the knives where I could see it, he flourished it at me snarling and said in his choked voice, "Don't touch it, don't touch it, or by the Destroyer I'll cut out your heart with it."

"I won't touch it," I said.

"It'll turn and cut your throat of itself if you do."

"I never will."

"You're a liar," he said. "Liars, men are liars." Sometimes he would say a thing like that over and over, and would say nothing else all day: *Men are liars, men are liars…Keep away, keep out! Keep away, keep out!…*At other times his talk was sane enough.

I had little to say, and that seemed to suit him. He talked to me as he did to the dog, recounting his daily expeditions through the woods to his rabbit snares and fishing holes and berry patches, everything he had

caught or seen or smelled or heard. I listened just as the
dog did to these long tales, intently, not interrupting.

"You're a runaway," he said to me one evening as we
sat out looking up through the leaves at the heavy,
bright stars of August. "House slave, brought up soft.
You run away. You think I'm a slave, don't you? Oh no.
Oh no. You want runaways? You go on north, go on to
the forest, that's where they are. I got nothing to do
with them. Liars, thieves. I'm a free man. I was born
free. I don't want to mix with them. Nor the farmers.
Nor the townsfolk, Sampa destroy them, liars, cheats,
thieves. All of them liars, cheats, thieves."

"How do you know I'm a slave?" I asked.

"What else could you be?" he said with his dark grin
and quick, canny look.

I didn't know.

"I come here to be free of them, all of them," Cuga
said. "They call me the wild man, the hermit, they're
afraid of me. They leave me be. Cuga the hermit! They
keep away. They keep out."

I said, "You're the Master of Cugamand."

He sat for a while in silence and then he broke out
in his choked, chuckling laugh, and slapped his thigh
with his big, heavy hand. He was a big man, and very

strong, though he must have been fifty or more. "Say it again," he said.

"You're the Master of Cugamand."

"That I am! That I am! This is my domain and I'm the master here! By the Destroyer, that's the truth. I met a man that speaks truth! By the Destroyer! A man that speaks truth! He come here and how do I welcome him? Smash his head in with a stick! How's that for a greeting? Welcome to Cugamand!" And he laughed for a long time. He would be silent and then laugh again, and then again. At last he looked over at me through the grey starlight and said, "You're a free man here. Trust me."

I said, "I trust you."

Cuga lived in filth and never bathed, and his carelessly tanned hides and furs stank and rotted; but he was meticulous in preserving and storing food. He smoke-dried the meat of all the larger animals he caught—rabbits, hares, the occasional fawn—and hung it from the roof of the fireplace room of the cave. He set snares for the little creatures of the grasslands too, wood rats, even harvest mice, and those he broiled on the fire and ate fresh. His snares were wonderfully clever and his patience endless, but he had no luck with his hooks and lines and seldom caught a fish big enough to be worth smoking. I could help him there. The sinew that was all he had for lines softened in the water; I pulled out some of the linen warp threads from the end of my brown blanket, and using them with the fine bone hooks he carved, I caught some big perch and bass as well as the little brown trout that swarmed in the pools of the stream. He showed me how to dry and smoke the fish. Aside from that I was of little use to him. He did not want me with him on his expeditions. Often he ignored me entirely all day long, lost in his muttered repetitions, but when he ate he always shared his food with me and with Guard.

I never asked him why he'd taken me in and kept me alive. It didn't occur to me as a question. I never asked him any questions but one. I asked where Guard came from.

"Sheepdog bitch," he said. "Had her litter up over there east on the rocky slopes. I seen the pups playing. Thought they was wolves, went over there with my knife to dig 'em out and cut their throats. I just got to the den and the bitch come round the hill, and she was going to go for me, but I says hey now, hey there, mother, I'll kill a wolf but never hurt a dog, will I? And she shows her teeth"—he showed his brown teeth in a grinning snarl—"and goes into the den. And so I go back and back, and we get to know each other, and she brings the pups out, and I watch 'em play. And this one and I got on. So he come away with me. I go back there sometimes. She's got a litter there now."

He never asked me any questions at all.

If he had, I would have had no answers. When I found myself remembering anything, I turned away from it to whatever was under my eyes and in my hands and lived in that only. I had none of the rememberings, the visions I used to have. If I dreamed in sleep, I did not remember the dreams when I woke.

The light in the mornings was more golden, the days ending sooner, the nights growing cool. The Master of Cugamand, sitting across a small fire from me in the hearth room of his cave, slid a whole troutlet off the stick into his mouth, chewed a while, swallowed, wiped his hands on his naked, dirt-caked chest, and said, "Cold here in winter. You'd be dead of it."

I said nothing. He knew what he was talking about. "You go on."

After a long time I said, "Nowhere to go, Cuga."

"Oh yes. Oh yes. The woods, that's where you go." He nodded towards the north. "The woods. Daneran. The big forest. No end to it they say. And no slave takers there. Oh no. No slave takers. Just the men of the woods. That's where to go."

"No roof," I said, and put another bit of bark on the fire.

"Oh yes. Oh yes. They live soft there. Roofs and walls and all. Beds and coats and all. They know me, I know them. We don't trouble each other. They know me. They keep away." He scowled and went off into one of his mutterings, *Keep away, keep out*...

Next morning he shook me awake early. On the flat stone in front of the cave entrance he had set out my brown blanket, the silk purse swollen with money, a filthy fur cape he had given me a while ago, and a packet of dried meat. "Come on," he said.

I stood still. His face went watchful and grim.

"Keep this for me," I said, holding out the silk purse.

He chewed his lip.

"Don't want to be killed for it, eh?" he said finally, and I nodded.

"Maybe," he said. "Maybe they would. Thieves, cheats...I don't want this stuff. Where'd I keep it from thieves?"

"In your salt box," I said.

He glared. "Where's that?" he snapped, fiercely suspicious.

I shrugged again. "I don't know. I never found it. Nobody could."

That made him laugh, slowly, opening his mouth wide. "I know," he said. "I know! All right."

The heavy, stained, discolored purse was swallowed up in his big hand. He went back into the cave with it and was gone some while. He came out and nodded at me. "Come on," he said. And he set off at his loping walk that seemed slow but ate up the miles.

I was fit again, and could keep up with him all day, though by evening I was weary and footsore.

At the last stream we came to he told me to drink deep. We crossed it, climbed a long slope, and halted on the top of the hill, the last of the hills. From it the land fell slowly away into vast forest, treetops going on and on into blue dimness, no end to them. The sun had not set, but the shadows were long.

Cuga was busy immediately; he gathered wood and built a fire, a large one, using green wood, not dry. The smoke went curling up into the clear sky. "All right," he said. "They'll come." And he turned to go back as we had come.

"Wait," I said.

He stopped, impatient. "Just wait," he said. "They'll be here."

"I'll come back, Cuga."

He shook his head angrily and went off, striding through the dry grass, holding his body in a slight crouch. In a minute he was out of sight through the trees under the crest of the hill. Over the dark treetops the sunset flamed.

I slept alone by the fire on the hilltop that night, wrapped in my blanket and the fur cape. The smoky stink of the fur was pleasant to me. I had been healed in that stink.

I waked again and again in the night. Once I built up the fire, as a signal, not for warmth. Towards morning I dreamed: I was sleeping in Sentas, in the fortress of dreams. The others were there with me. I heard their soft voices murmuring in the dark. One of the girls laughed...I woke and remembered the dream. I clung to it, trying to stay in it. But I was thirsty, thirst had waked me. Telling myself I'd go look for water at the foot of the hill as soon as it was light, I lay waiting for the light.

We never slept in Sentas, I thought. We always slept out near the farmhouse, under the trees. We always saw the stars through the leaves. We talked about going out to Sentas to sleep but we never did.

❖ 8 ❖

Four of them were around me before I saw one of them. I was barely awake. I had sat up, on the open hillside by the dead fire, alone. They were around me, without movement, out of the grass, out of the dim grey air of early dawn. I looked from one to the next and sat still.

They were armed, not like soldiers but with short bows and long knives. Two carried five-foot staffs. They looked grim.

One of them finally spoke in a soft, hoarse voice, almost a whisper. "Fire out?"

I nodded.

He went and kicked at the few half-burnt sticks left, trampled them carefully, felt them with his hands. I got up to help him bury the cold cinders.

"Come on then," he said. I bundled up my blanket and the last scraps of dried meat to carry. I wore the cape of rabbit and squirrel skins for warmth.

"Stinks," said one of the men.

"Reeks," said another. "Bad as old Cuga."

"He brought me here," I said.

"Cuga?"

"You was with him?"

"All summer."

One stared, one spat, one shrugged; the fourth, the one who had spoken first, motioned with his head and led us down the long hill towards the forest.

I knelt to drink from the stream at the foot of the hill. The hoarse-voiced leader nudged me with his staff while I was still drinking thirstily. "That's enough, you'll be pissing all day," he said. I scrambled up and followed them across the stream and under the dark eaves of the trees.

He led us all the way. We moved hastily through the woods, often at a trot, until mid-morning, when we stopped in a small clearing. It smelled of stale blood. A pack of vultures flapped up heavily on great black wings from some remnants of guts and skulls. The carcasses of three deer had been butchered and hung, glittering with flies, high from a tree limb. The men brought them down and divided and roped them so each of us could carry a load of meat, and we set off again, but now at an easier pace. I was tormented with thirst and by the flies that kept swarming around us and our burdens. The load I carried was not well balanced, and my feet, sore from the long walk yesterday, blistered in my old shoes. The trail we followed was very slight and winding, seldom visible more than a few paces ahead among the big, dark trees, and often made difficult by tree roots. When we came at last to a stream crossing I went right down again on hands and knees to drink.

The leader turned back to stir me up, saying, "Come on! You can drink when we get there!" But one of the other men was down with his face in the water too, and looked up to say, "Ah, let him drink, Brigin." The leader said nothing then, but waited for us.

The water bathed my feet with wonderful coolness as we waded across the stream, but then as we went on the blisters grew worse, my wet shoes rubbing them, and I was hobbling with pain by the time we came to the forest camp. We cast down our burdens of venison in an open shed, and I could stand up straight at last and look around.

If I'd come there from where I used to live, it wouldn't have looked like anything at all—a few low huts, a few men, in a meadow where alders grew by a small stream, dark forest all around. But I came there from the lonesome wilderness. The sight of the buildings was strange and impressive to me, and the presence of other people even stranger and more frightening.

Nobody paid any attention to me. I got up my courage and went to the stream under the alders, drank my fill at last, then took off my shoes and put my raw, burning, bloody feet in the water. It was warm in the meadow, the autumn sun still pouring into it. Presently I took off my clothes and got into the water entirely. I washed myself, then I washed my clothes as well as I could. They had been white. White clothing is worn by a girl in her betrothal ceremony, and by the dead, and by those who go to bury the dead. There was no telling what color my clothes had been. They were brown and grey, rag-color. I did not think about their whiteness. I laid them on the grass to dry and got back in the stream and put my head under water to wash my hair. When I came up I couldn't see, for my hair hung down over my eyes, it had grown so long. It was filthy and matted and I washed it again and again. When I came up from the last dip and scrubbing, a man was sitting beside my clothes on the stream bank, watching me.

"It's an improvement," he said.

He was the one who'd told the leader to let me drink.

He was short and brown, with high, ruddy cheekbones and narrow, dark eyes; his hair was cut short to his head. He had an accent, a way of talking that came from somewhere else.

I came up out of the water, dried myself as well as I could with the old brown blanket, and pulled on my wet tunic, seeking modesty, though there seemed to be only men around, and also seeking warmth. The sun had left the clearing though the sky was still bright. I shivered. But I didn't want to put the filthy fur cape on my hard-won cleanness.

"Hey," he said, "hang on." He went off and came back with a tunic and some kind of garment I did not recognise. "They're dry, anyhow," he said, handing them to me.

I shucked off my limp wet tunic and put on the one he gave me. It was brown linen, much worn, soft, long-sleeved. It felt warm and pleasant on my skin. I held up the other piece of clothing he had brought. It was black and made of some heavy, dense material; it must be a cape, I thought. I tried to put it on over my shoulders. I could not get it to fit.

The man watched me for a little while and then he lay back on the stream bank and began to laugh. He laughed till his eyes disappeared entirely and his face turned dark red. He curled up over his knees and laughed till you could tell it hurt him, and though it wasn't a noisy laugh, some men heard and came over and looked at him and looked at me, and some of them began laughing too.

"Oh," he said at last, wiping his eyes and sitting up. "Oh. That did me good. That's a kilt, young 'un. You wear it—" and he began to laugh again, and doubled up, and wheezed, and finally said, "You wear it on the other end."

I looked at the thing, and saw it had a waistband, like trousers.

"I'll do without," I said. "If you don't mind."

"No," he said, wheezing. "I don't mind. Give it back, then."

"Why would the kid want one of your fool skirts, Chamry?" one of the onlookers said. "Here, kid, I'll get you something decent." He came back with a pair of breeches that fit me well enough, though loosely. When

I had them on he said, "Keep 'em, they're too tight for my belly. So you came in with Brigin and them today? Joining up, are you? What'll we call you?"

"Gavir Arca," I said.

The man who had given me the kilt said, "That's your name."

I looked at him, not understanding.

"Do you want to use it?" he asked.

I had done so little thinking for so long, my mind would not move quickly at all; it needed a lot of time. I said at last, "Gav."

"Gav it is," said the man who had given me the kilt. "I'm Chamry Bern of Bernmant, and I use my name, for I'm so far from where I came that no one can track me by name or fame or any game."

"He's from where the men wear skirts and the women piss standing," said one of the onlookers, and got some laughter from the others.

"Lowlanders," said Chamry Bern, of them, not to them. "They know no better. Come on, you, Gav. You'd better take the oath, if that's what you came for, and get your share of dinner. I saw you carrying in your share of it and more."

The god Luck is deaf in one ear, they say, the ear we pray to; he can't hear our prayers. What he hears, what he listens to, nobody knows. Denios the poet said he hears the wheels of the stars' great chariots turning on the roads of heaven. I know that while I was sunk far beneath any thought of prayer, with no hope, no trust in anything, no desire, Luck was always with me. I lived, though I took no care to survive. I came to no harm among strangers. I carried money and was not robbed. When I was alone and on the verge of death, an old mad hermit beat me back to life. And now Luck had sent me to these men, and one of them was Chamry Bern.

Chamry went and whacked on a crowbar hung from a post of the largest hut. The signal brought men to gather around the porch of the hut. "Newcomer," he said. "Gav is his name. He says he's been living with Cuga the Ogre, which would explain the smell that came with him. And after a bath in our river he seeks to join our company. Right, Gav?"

I nodded. I was intimidated by being the center of what seemed to me a great crowd of men—twenty or more—all looking me over. Most of them were young and had a trim, fit, hard look, like Brigin, the man who'd led me here, though there were several grey or bald heads and a couple of slack bellies.

"Do you know who we are?" one of the bald heads demanded.

I took a deep breath. "Are you the Barnavites?"

That caused some scowling and some laughter. "Some of us used to be," the man said, "maybe. And what do you know of Barna's lot, boy?"

I was younger than they were, but I didn't like being called kid and boy all the time. It put my back up.

"I heard stories. That they lived in the forest as free men, neither masters or slaves, sharing fairly all they had."

"Well put," said Chamry. "All in a nutshell." Several men looked pleased and nodded.

"Well enough, well enough," the bald man said, keeping up his dignity. Another man came up close to me; he looked very much like Brigin, and as I learned later they were brothers. His face was hard and handsome, his eyes clear and cold. He looked me over. "If you live with us you'll learn what fair sharing means," he said. "It means what we do, you do. It's one for all with us. If you think you can do whatever you like, you won't last here. If you don't share, you don't eat. If you're careless and bring danger on us, you're dead. We have rules. You'll take an oath to live with us and keep our rules. And if you break that oath, we'll hunt you down surer than any slave taker."

Their faces were grim; they all nodded at what he said.

"You think you can keep that oath?"

"I can try," I said.

"Try's not good enough."

"I'll keep your oath," I said, my temper roused by his bullying.

"We'll see," he said, turning away. "Get the stuff, Modla."

The bald man and Brigin brought out of the hut a knife, a clay bowl, a deer antler, and some meal. I will not tell the ceremony, for those who go through it are sworn to secrecy, nor can I tell the words of the oath I took. They all swore that oath again with me. The rites and the oath-speaking brought them all together in fellow feeling, and when all was done and spoken several of them came to pound my back and tell me I'd borne the initiation well, and was a brave fellow, and welcome among them.

Chamry Bern had come forward as my sponsor, and a young man called Venne as my hunting mate. They sat on either side of me at the celebration that followed. Meat had already been roasting on spits, but they added more to make a feast of it, and night had fallen by the time we sat to eat—on the ground, or on stumps and crude stools, around the red, dancing fires. I had no knife. Venne took me in to a chest of weapons and told me to choose one. I took a light, keen blade in a leather sheath. With it I cut myself a chunk out of a sizzling, dripping, blackened, sweet-smelling haunch and sat down with it and ate like a starved animal. Somebody brought me a metal cup and poured something into it—beer or mead—sour and somewhat foamy. The men laughed louder as they drank, and shouted, and laughed again. My heart warmed to their good fellowship—the friendship of the Forest Brothers. For that was the name they called themselves, and had given me, since I was one of them.

All around the firelit clearing was the night forest, utter darkness under the trees, high leaf crowns grey in the starlight for miles and miles.

◆ ◆ ◆

IF CHAMRY BERN hadn't taken a liking to me and if Venne hadn't taken me as his hunting partner I would have had a worse time of it that fall and winter than I did. As it was, I was often at the limit of my endurance. I'd lived wild with Cuga, but he'd looked after me, sheltered me, fed me, and that was in summer, too, when it's easy to live wild. Here my city softness, my lack of physical strength, my ignorance of the skills of survival, were nearly the death of me. Brigin and his brother Eter and several other men had been farm slaves, used to a hard life, tough, fearless, and resourceful, and to them I was a dead loss, a burden. Other men in the group, town-bred, had some patience with my wretched incompetence, and gave and taught me what I needed to get by. As with Cuga, my knack at fishing gave me a way to show I could try at least to be useful. I showed no promise at all in hunting, though Venne took me with him conscientiously and tried to train me with the short bow and in all the silent skills of the hunter.

Venne was twenty or so; at fifteen he had run away from a vicious master in a town of the region of Casicar, and made his way to the forest—for everybody in Casicar, he said, knew about the Forest Brothers, and all the slaves dreamed of joining them. He enjoyed the life in the woods, seemed fully at home in it, and was one of the best hunters of our band; but I soon learned that he was restless. He didn't get on with Brigin and Eter. "Playing the masters," he said drily. And after a while, "And they won't have women with us...Well, Barna's men have women, right? I think of joining them."

"Think again," said Chamry, sewing a soft upper to

a shoe sole; he was our tanner and cobbler, and made pretty good shoes and sandals for us of elk hide. "You'll be running back to us begging us to save you. You think Brigin's bossy? Never was a man could match a woman for giving orders. Men are by nature slaves to women, and women are by nature the masters of men. Hello woman, goodbye freedom!"

"Maybe," Venne said. "But there's other things comes with her."

They were good friends, and included me in their friendship and their conversation. Many of the men of the band seemed to have little use for language, using a grunt or a gesture, or sitting stolid and mute as animals. The silence of the slave had gone so deep in them they could not break it. Chamry on the other hand was a man of words; he loved to talk and listen and tell stories, rhyming and chiming them in a kind of half poetry, and was ready to discuss anything with anybody.

I soon knew his history, or as much of it as he saw fit to tell, and as near or far from the truth as suited him. He came from the Uplands, he said, a region far north and east of the City States. I'd never heard of it and asked him if it was farther than Urdile, and he said yes, far beyond Urdile, beyond even Bendraman. I knew the name of Bendraman only from the ancient tale *Chamhan*.

"The Uplands are beyond the beyond," he said, "north of the moon and east of the dawn. A desolation of hill and bog and rock and cliff, and rising over it all a huge vast mountain with a beard of clouds, the Carrantages. Nobody deserves to live in the Uplands but sheep. It's starving land, freezing land, winter forever, a gleam of sunlight once a year. It's all cut up into little small domains, farms they'd call them here and poor sorry farms at that, but in the Uplands they're domains, and each has a master, the brantor, and each brantor has an evil power in him. Witches they are, every one. How'd you like that for a master? A man who could move his hand and say a word and turn you inside out with your guts on the ground and your eyes staring into the inside of your brain? Or a man who could look at you and you'd never think a thought of your own again, but only what he put into your head?"

He liked to go on about these awful powers, the gifts he called them, of the Upland witches, his tales growing ever taller. I asked him once, if he'd had a master, what his master's power was. That silenced him for a minute. He looked at me with his bright narrow eyes. "You wouldn't think it much of a power, maybe," he said. "Nothing to see. He could weaken the bones in a body. It took a while. But if he cast his power on you, in a month you'd be weak and weary, in half a year your legs would bend under you like grass, in a year you'd be dead. You don't want to cross a man who could do that. Oh, you lowlanders think you know what it is to have a master! In the Uplands we don't even say slave. The brantor's people, we say. He may be kin to half of 'em, his servants, his serfs—his people. But they're more slaves to him than ever the slave of the worst master down here!"

"I don't know about that," said Venne. "A whip and a couple of big dogs can do about as well as a spell of magic to destroy a man." Venne bore terrible scars on his legs and back and scalp, and one ear had been half torn off his head.

"No, no, it's the fear," Chamry said. "It's the awful fear. You didn't fear the men that beat you and the dogs that bit you, once you'd run clear away from 'em, did you? But I tell you, I ran a hundred miles away from the Uplands and my master, and still I cringed when I felt his thought turn on me. And I felt it! The strength went out of my legs and arms. I couldn't hold my back up straight. His power was on me! All I could do was go on, go on, go on, till there was mountains and rivers and miles between me and his hand and eye and cruel power. When I crossed the great river, the Trond, I grew stronger. When I crossed the second great river, the Sally, I was safe at last. The power can cross a wide water once but not twice. So a wise woman told me. But I crossed yet another to be sure! I'll never go back north, never. You don't know what it is to be a slave, you lowlanders!"

Yet Chamry talked often of the Uplands and the farm where he had been born, and all through his railing at it as a poor, unhappy, wretched place I heard his yearning homesickness. He made of it a vivid picture in my mind, the great barren moorlands and cloudy peaks, the bogs from which at dawn a thousand wild white cranes would rise at once, the stone-walled, slate-roofed farm huddled under the bare curve of a brown hill. As he told about it, I could see it almost as clearly as if I remembered it myself.

And that put me in mind of my own power, or whatever it was, of remembering what was yet to happen. I remembered that I had had such a power, once. But when I thought about that, I began to remember places I didn't want to remember. Memories made my body hunch up in pain and my mind go blank in fear. I pushed them away, turned away from them. Remembering would kill me. Forgetting kept me alive.

The Forest Brothers were all men who had escaped,

run away from something unendurable. They were like me. They had no past. Learning how to get through this rough life, how to endure never being dry or warm or clean, to eat only half-raw, half-burnt venison, I might have gone on with them as I had with Cuga, not thinking beyond the present hour and what was around me. And much of the time I did.

But there were times when winter storms kept us in our drafty, smoky cabins, and Chamry, Venne, and some of the other men gathered to talk in the half dark by the smoldering hearth, and then I began to hear their stories of where they came from, how they'd lived, the masters they'd escaped from, their memories of suffering and of pleasure.

Sometimes into my thoughts would come a clear image of a place: a big room full of women and children; a fountain in a city square; a sunny courtyard surrounded by arches, under which women sat spinning… When I saw such a place I gave it no name, and my mind turned away from it hastily. I never joined the others' talk about the world outside the forest, and did not like to hear it.

Late one afternoon the six or seven tired, dirty, hungry men around the crude hearth in our cabin had run out of anything to talk about. We all sat in a dumb discouragement. It had been raining a cold hard rain almost ceaselessly for four days and nights. Under the cloud that pressed down on the dark forest trees it seemed night all day long. Fog and darkness tangled in the wet, heavy boughs. To go out to get logs for the fire from the dwindling woodpile was to be wet through at once, and indeed some of us went out naked, since skin dries quicker than cloth and leather. One of our mates, Bulec, had a wretched cough that shook him about like a rat in a dog's mouth. Even Chamry had run out of jokes and tall tales. In that cold, dreary place I was thinking of summer, of the heat and light of summer on the open hills, somewhere. And a cadence came into my mind, a beat, and the words with it, and without any intention I said the words aloud.

> As in the dark of winter night
> The eyes seek dawn,
> As in the bonds of bitter cold
> The heart craves sun,
> So blinded and so bound, the soul
> Cries out to thee:
> Be our light, our fire, our life,
>   Liberty!

"Ah," Chamry said out of a silence that followed the words, "I've heard that. Heard it sung. There's a tune to it."

I sought the tune, and little by little it came to me, with the sound of the beautiful voice that had sung it. I have no singing voice, but I sang it.

"That's fine," Venne said softly.

Bulec coughed and said, "Speak some more such."

"Do that," Chamry said.

I looked into my mind for more remembered words to speak to them. Nothing came for a while. What I found at last was a line of writing. I read it: "'Wearing the white of mourning, the maiden mounted the high steps...'" I said it aloud, and in a moment the line led me on to the next, and that to the next. So I told them the part of Garro's poem in which the prophetess Yurno confronts the enemy hero Rurec. Standing on the walls of Sentas, a girl in mourning, Yurno calls down to the man who killed her warrior father. She tells Rurec how he will die: "Beware of the hills of Trebs," she says, "for you will be ambushed in the hills. You will run away and hide in the bushes, but they will kill you as you try to crawl away without being seen. They will drag your naked body to the town and display it, sprawled face down, so all can see that the wounds are in your back. Your corpse will not be burned with prayers to the Ancestors as befits a hero, but buried where they bury slaves and dogs." Enraged at her prophecy, Rurec shouts, "And this is how *you* will die, lying sorceress!" and hurls his heavy lance at her. All see it pass through her body just below the breast and fly out, trailing blood, behind her—but she stands on the battlement in her white robes, unharmed. Her brother the warrior Alira picks up the lance and hands it up to her, and she tosses it down to Rurec, not hurling it, but end over end, lightly, contemptuously. "When you're running away and hiding, you'll want this," she says, "great hero of Pagadi."

As I spoke the words of the poem, in that cold smoky hut in the half dark with the noise of the rain loud on the low roof, I saw them written in some pupil's labored handwriting in the copybook I held as I stood in the schoolroom in Arcamand. "Read the passage, Gavir," my teacher said, and I read the words aloud.

A silence followed.

"Eh, that's a fool," Bacoc said, "thro'n a lance at a witch, don't he know, can't kill a witch but with fire!"

Bacoc was a man of fifty by the look of him, though it's hard to tell the age of men who have lived their life half starved and under the whip; maybe he was thirty.

"That's a good bit of story," Chamry said. "There's more? Is there a name to it?"

I said, "It's called *The Siege and Fall of Sentas*. There's more."

"Let's have it," said Chamry, and the others all agreed.

For a time I could not recall the opening lines of the poem; then, as if I had the old copybook in my hand, there they were and I spoke them—

> To the councils and senate of Sentas they came, the
>   envoys in armor,
> With their swords in their hands, arrogant, striding
>   into the chamber
> Where the lords of the city sat to give judgment...

It was night, true night, when I finished saying the first book of the poem. Our fire had burned down to embers on the rough hearth, but nobody in the circle of men had moved to build it up; nobody had moved at all for an hour.

"They're going to lose that city of theirs," Bulec said in the dark, in the soft drumming of the rain.

"They should be able to hold out. The others come too far from home. Like Casicar did, trying to take Etra last year," said Taffa. It was the most I'd ever heard him say. Venne had told me Taffa had been not a slave but a freeman of a small city-state, conscripted into their army; during a battle he had escaped and made his way to the forest. Sad-faced and aloof, he seldom said anything, but now he was arguing almost volubly: "Stretched out their forces too far, see, Pagadi has, attacking. If they don't take the town by assault quick, they'll starve come winter."

And they all got into the discussion, all talking exactly as if the siege of Sentas was taking place right now, right here. As if we were living in Sentas.

Of them all Chamry was the only one who understood that what I had told them was "a poem," a thing made by a maker, a work of art, part history of long ago, part invention. It was, to them, an event; it was happening as they heard it. They wanted it to go on happening. If I'd been able to, they'd have kept me telling it to them night and day. But after my voice gave out that first evening, I lay in my wooden bunk thinking about what had been given back to me: the power of words. I had time then to think and to plan how and when to use that power—how to go on with the poem, to keep them from exhausting both it and me. I ended by telling it for an hour or two every night, after we ate, for the winter nights were endless and something to make them pass was welcome to all.

Word got about, and within a night or two most of the men of the band were crowded into our hut for "telling the war," and for the long passionate discussions and arguments about tactics and motives and morals that followed.

There were times I couldn't fully recall the lines as Garro wrote them, but the story was clear in my mind, so I filled in these gaps with tags of the poetry and my own narrative, until I came again to a passage that I had by memory or could "see" written, and could fall back into the harsh rhythm of the lines. My companions didn't seem to notice the difference between my prose and Garro's poetry. They listened closest when I was speaking the poetry—but those were also often the most vivid passages of action and suffering.

When we came again in the course of the tale to the passage I'd recited first, Yurno's prophecy from the battlements, Bacoc caught his breath; and when Rurec "in a fury uplifts his heavy lance," Bacoc cried out, "Don't throw it, man! It's no good!" The others shouted at him to pipe down, but he was indignant: "Don't he know it's no good? He thro'n it before!"

I was at first merely bemused by my own capacity to recall the poetry and their capacity to listen to it. They didn't say much to me about it, but it made a difference in the way I was treated, my standing among them. I had something they wanted, and they respected me for that. Since I gave it freely, their respect was ungrudging. "Hey, haven't you got a fatter rib than that for the kid? He's got to work tonight, telling the war..."

But every up's a down, as Chamry said. Brigin and his brother and the men closest to them, their cabin mates, looked in at one time or another on the recital, listened a while standing near the doorway, then left in silence. They said nothing to me, but I heard from others that they said men who listened to fools' tales were worse fools than those who told them. And Brigin said that a man willing to hear a boy yammer booktalk half the night was no fit Forest Brother.

Booktalk! Why did Brigin say it in that contemptuous tone? There were no books in the forest. There had been no books in Brigin's life. Why did he sneer at them?

Any of these men might well be jealous of a knowledge that had been jealously kept from them. A farm slave who tried to learn to read could have his eyes put out or be whipped to death. Books were dangerous, and a slave had every excuse to fear them. But fear is one thing, contempt another.

I resented their sneers as mean-spirited, for I couldn't see anything unworthy of manhood in the tale I was telling. How was a tale of warfare and heroism weakening the men who listened to it so hungrily every night? Didn't it draw us together in real brotherhood, when after the telling we listened to one another argue the rights and wrongs of the generals' tactics and the warriors' exploits? To sit stupid, mute, night after night under the rain like cattle, bored to mindlessness—was that what made us men?

Eter said something one morning, knowing he was within my hearing, about great idle fools listening to a boy tell lies. I was fed up. I was about to confront him with what I've just said, when my wrist was caught in an iron grip and a deft foot nearly tripped me.

I broke free and shouted, "What d'you think you're doing?" to Chamry Bern, who apologised for his clumsiness while renewing his grip on my wrist. "Oh keep your trap shut, Gav!" he whispered desperately, hauling me away from the group of men around Eter. "Don't you see he's baiting you?"

"He's insulting all of us!"

"And who's to stop him? You?"

Chamry had got me around behind the woodpiles now, away from the others, and seeing I was now arguing with him, not challenging Eter, he let go my wrist.

"But why— Why—"

"Why don't they love you for having a power they don't have?"

I didn't know what to say.

"And they've got the hard hand, you know, though you've got the soft voice. Oh, Gav. Don't be smarter than your masters. It costs."

In his face now was the sadness I had seen in the face of every one of these men, the mark of the harrow. They had all started with very little, and lost most of that.

"They're not my masters," I said furiously. "We're free men here!"

"Well," Chamry said, "in some ways."

✦ 9 ✦

Eter and Brigin, if they resented my sudden popularity, must have seen that any attempt to break up the evening gathering might rouse real opposition. They contented themselves with sneers at me, and at Chamry and Venne as my mates, but let the other men alone. So I and my fierce audience went on through all *The Siege and Fall of Sentas*, as the dark winter slowly turned towards spring. We came to the end of it just about the time of the equinox.

It was hard for some of the men to comprehend that it was over, and why it had to be over. Sentas had fallen, the walls and the great gates were torn down, the citadel burnt to the ground, the men of the city slaughtered, the women and children taken as slaves, and the hero Rurec had set off triumphant with his army and loot to Pagadi—and so, what happened next?

"Is he going to go by the hills of Trebs now?" Bacoc wanted to know. "After what the witch said?"

"Sure enough he'll go by Trebs, if not this day then another," said Chamry. "A man can't keep from going where the seer's eye saw him go."

"Well, why don't Gav tell it, then?"

"The story stops at the fall of the city, Bacoc," I said.

"What—like they all died? But it's only some of 'em dead!"

Chamry tried to explain the nature of a story to him, but he remained dissatisfied; and they were all melancholy. "Ah, it's going to be dull!" said Taffa. "I'll miss that sword fighting. It's a horrible thing when you're in it, but it's grand to hear about."

Chamry grinned. "You could say that of most things in life, maybe."

"Are there more tales like that, Gav?" somebody asked.

"There are a lot of tales," I said, cautiously. I wasn't eager to start another epic. I felt myself becoming the prisoner of my audience.

"You could tell the one we had all right over," said one man, and several agreed enthusiastically.

"Next winter," I said. "When the nights are long again."

They treated my verdict as if it were a priest's rule of ritual, accepting it without dispute.

But Bulec said wistfully, "I wish there was short tales for the short nights." He had listened to the epic with almost painful attention, muffling his cough as well as he could; to the battle scenes he preferred the descriptions of the rooms in the palaces, the touching domestic passages, the love story of Alira and Ruoco. I liked Bulec, and it was painful to see him, a young man, getting sicker and weaker day by day even as the weather brightened and grew warm. I couldn't withstand his plea.

"Oh, there's some short tales," I said. "I'll tell you one." And I thought first to say *The Bridge on the Nisas*, but I could not. Those words, though they were clear in my mind, bore some weight in them that I could not lift. I could not speak them.

So I put myself in the schoolroom in my mind, and opened a copybook, and there was one of Hodis Baderi's fables, "The Man Who Ate the Moon." I told it to them word for word.

They listened as intently as ever. The fable got a mixed reception. Some of them laughed and shouted,

"Ah, that's the best yet! That beats all!"—but others thought it silly stuff, "foolery," Taffa said.

"Ah, but there's a lesson in it," said Chamry, who had listened to the tale with delight. They got to arguing whether the man who ate the moon was a liar or not. They never asked me to settle or even enter these discussions. I was, as it were, their book. I provided the text. Judgment on the text was up to them. I heard as keen moral arguments from them as I was ever to hear from learned men.

After that they often got a fable or a poem out of me in the evening, but their demand was not so urgent now that we no longer had to cower in our huts from the rain and could live outdoors and be active. Hunting and snaring and fishing went on apace, for we'd lived very thin at the end of winter and beginning of spring. We craved not only meat but the wild onions and other herbs that some of the men knew how to find in the forest. I always missed the grain porridge that had been much of our diet in the city, but there was nothing like that here.

"I heard the Forest Brothers stole grain from rich farmers," I said once to Chamry, as we grubbed for wild horseradish.

"They do, those who can," he said.

"Who's that?"

"Barna's lot, up north there."

The name rang strangely in my head, bringing around it a whole set of fleeting images of young men talking in a crowded, warm dormitory, the face of an old priest...but I ignored such images. Words were what I could remember safely.

"So there really is a man called Barna?"

"Oh, yes. Though you needn't mention him around Brigin."

I wheedled for more, and Chamry never could resist telling a story. So I found that, as I had suspected, our band was a splinter from a larger group, with which they weren't on good terms. Barna was the chief of that group. Eter and Brigin had rebelled against his leadership and brought a few men here to the southern part of the forest—the most remote from any settlements and so the safest for runaway slaves, but also the poorest in resources except, as Chamry said, cattle with antlers.

"Up there, they bag the real thing," he said. "Fat bullocks. Sheep! Ah! what wouldn't I give to taste mutton! I hate sheep from the pit of my heart, wily, woolly, wicked brutes. But when one of 'em lies down and turns into roast mutton, I could swallow him whole."

"Do Barna's men raise the cattle and sheep?"

"Mostly they let other folk do that for them. And then pick out a few choice ones. There's those who'd call it thieving, but that's too delicate and legal a word. Tithing, we called it. We tithed the farmers' flocks."

"So you lived there, with Barna's band?"

"A while. Lived well, too." Chamry sat back on his haunches and looked at me. "That's where you should be, you know. Not here, with this lot of hard rocks and knotheads." He knocked the dirt off a horseradish root, wiped it on his shirt, and bit into it. "You and Venne. You should be off. He'll be welcome for his hunting, you for your golden tongue..." He chewed raw horseradish a while, wincing and his eyes watering. "All your tongue will do here is talk you into trouble."

"Would you come with us?"

He spat out fiber and wiped his mouth. "By the Stone, but that's hot! I don't know. I came away with Brigin and them because they were my mates. And I was restless...I don't know."

He was a restless man. It wasn't hard for Venne and me to coax him into coming with us, when we made up our minds to go. And we did that soon.

Brigin and Eter, feeling dissatisfaction among us,

tried to repress it with ever harsher demands and commands. Eter told Bulec, who was deathly ill by now, that if he didn't go out hunting for meat for the camp pot, he'd get nothing to eat from it. Eter may have just been bullying, or may have believed his threat would work; some men who live hard and in good health can't believe sickness or weakness is anything but laziness, a sham. At any rate Bulec was scared or shamed into insisting that a hunting party take him along. He got a little way out of camp with them and collapsed, vomiting blood. When they carried him back, Venne confronted Eter, shouting that he'd killed Bulec like any slave driver. Venne rushed off in his distress and rage. He found me fishing at a pool up the stream. "We were going to find Bulec a place he could sit down and wait for us, soon as we got clear away from camp, but he couldn't even walk that far. He's dying. I can't stay here, Gav. I can't take their orders! They think they're masters and us their slaves. I want to kill that damned Eter! I've got to get out."

"Let's talk to Chamry," I said. We did; he counseled at first that we wait, but when he saw how dangerous Venne's anger was, he agreed to go that night.

We ate with the others. Nobody talked. Bulec lay fighting for breath in one of the cabins. I could still hear the slow, gasping drag of his breath in the darkness before dawn when Venne, Chamry, and I stole out of camp with what little we considered ours by right: the clothes we wore, a blanket apiece, our knives, Venne's bow and arrows, my fishing hooks and rabbit snares, Chamry's cobbler's toolkit, and a packet of smoked meat.

It was a couple of months after the equinox, late May, perhaps; a sweet dark night, a slow misty dawn, a morning of birdsong. It was good to be going free, leaving the rivalries and brutalities of the camp behind. I walked all day lightly, lighthearted, wondering why we'd borne Eter and Brigin's bullying so long. But at evening, as we sat fireless, lying low in case they pursued us, my heart went down low too. I kept thinking of Bulec, and of others: Taffa, who, being a deserter, had also deserted the wife and children he loved and could never go back to them; Bacoc, the simple heart, who didn't even know the name of the village where he'd been born a slave—"the village" was all he knew…They had been kind to me. And we had sworn a vow together.

"What's the trouble, Gav?" said Chamry.

"I feel like I'm running out on them," I said.

"They could run, too, if they liked," Venne said, so promptly that I knew he'd been thinking along the same lines, justifying our desertion to himself.

"Bulec can't," I said.

"He's gone farther than we've gone, by now," Chamry said. "Never fret for him. He's home…You're too loyal, Gav, it's a fault in you. Don't look back. Touch and go, it's best."

That seemed strange to me; what did he mean? I never looked back. I had nothing to be loyal to, nothing to hold on to. I went where my luck took me. I was like a wisp of cloth twisting and drifting in a river.

Next day we came to a part of the great forest I'd never been to. We were outside our territory from here on. The trees were evergreens, fir and hemlock. They made impenetrable walls and mazes of their fallen trunks and the young trees that sprouted out of them. We had to travel along the streambeds, and that was hard going, scrambling through water, over rocks, and around rapids, in the half darkness of the huge trees overhead. Chamry kept saying we'd be out of it soon, and we did come out of it at last late on the second day, following a stream up to its spring on an open, grassy hillside. As we sat luxuriating in the soft grass and the clear twilight, a line of deer came walking past not twenty feet away downhill; they glanced at us unconcerned and walked on quietly, one after the other, flicking their big ears to and fro. Venne quietly took up his bow and fitted an arrow. There was no sound but the twang of the bowstring, like the sound of a big beetle's wings. The last deer in line started, went down on its knees, and then lay down, all in that peaceful silence. The others never turned, but walked on into the woods.

"Ah, why'd I do that," Venne said. "Now we've got to clean it."

But that was soon done, and we were glad to have fresh meat that night and for the next day. As we sat, well fed, by the coals of our fire, Chamry said, "If this was the Uplands I'd have said you called those deer."

"Called 'em?"

"It's a gift—calling animals to come. A brantor goes out hunting, well, he takes a caller with him, if he hasn't the gift himself. Boar, or elk, or deer, whatever they're after, they'll come to the caller."

"I can't do that," Venne said after a while in his low voice. "But I can see how it might be. If I know the land, I know pretty much, most times, where the deer are. As they know where I am. And if they're afraid, I'll never see them. But if they're not afraid, they'll come. They show themselves—'Here I am, you wanted me.' They give themselves. A man who doesn't know that has no business hunting. He's only a butcher."

We went on for two days more through rolling,

open woods before we came to a good-sized stream. "Across that is Barna's country," said Chamry. "And we'd best stay on the path and make noise, let them know we're here, lest they think we're sneaking in to spy." So we came crashing into Barna's lands like a herd of wild pigs, as Venne said. We came on a path and followed it, still talking loudly. Soon enough there was a shout to halt and hold still. We did that. Two men came striding down the path to meet us. One was tall and thin, one was short and broad-bellied.

"Do you know where you are?" said the short one, false-jovial, not quite menacing. The tall one held his crossbow loaded, though not aimed.

"In the Heart of the Forest," said Chamry. "Seeking a welcome, Toma. You don't remember me?"

"Well, by the Destroyer! The bad penny always turns up!" Toma came forward to take Chamry by one shoulder and shake him back and forth with aggressive welcome. "You Upland rat," he said. "You vermin. Crawled off at night you did, with Brigin and that lot. What did you want to go with them for?"

"It was a mistake, Toma," said Chamry, getting his footing so Toma could go on shaking him. "Call it a mistake and forgive it, eh?"

"Why not? Won't be the last thing I forgive you, Chamry Bern." He let him go at last. "What have you brought with you there? Baby rats, are they?"

"All I took away with me was those pigheads Brigin and his brother," Chamry said, "and what I'm bringing back with me is two pearls, pearls set in gold for the ears of Barna. Venne, here, who can drop a deer at a thousand paces, and Gav, here, who can tell tales and poetry to make you weep one moment and laugh the next. Take us into the Heart of the Forest, Toma!"

So we went on a mile or so through the forest of oak and alder, and came to that strange place.

The Heart of the Forest was a town, with kitchen gardens and barns and byres and corrals outside the palisade walls, and inside them houses and halls, streets and squares—all of wood. Towns and cities were built of stone and brick, I thought; only barns for cattle and huts for slaves were built of wood. But this was a city of wood. It was swarming with people, men, and women too, and children—everywhere, in the gardens, in the streets. I looked at the women and children with wonder. I looked at the cross-beamed, gable-roofed houses with awe. I looked at the broad central square full of people and stopped, scared. Venne was walking right next to me, pressed up against my shoulder for courage. "I never saw nothing like this, Gav," he said hoarsely. We followed as close behind Chamry as two little kids behind the she-goat.

Chamry himself was looking about with some amazement. "It wasn't half this size when I left," he said. "Look how they've built!"

"You're in luck," said Toma, our fat guide. "There's himself."

Coming across the square towards us was a big, bearded man. Very tall, broad-chested, ample in girth, with dark reddish curly hair and a beard that covered all his cheeks and chin and chest, with large, clear eyes, and a singularly upright, buoyant walk, as if he were borne up a little above the ground—as soon as you saw him you knew he was, as Toma said, himself. He was looking at us with a pleasant, keen curiosity.

"Barna!" Chamry said. "Will you have me back, if I bring you a couple of choice recruits?" Chamry did not quite reverence Barna, but his posture was respectful, despite his jaunty tone. "I'm Chamry Bern of Bernmant, who made the mistake of going off south a few years back."

"The Uplander," Barna said, and smiled. He had

a broad white smile that flashed in his beard, and a magnificently deep voice. "Oh, you're welcome back for yourself, man. We're free to come and free to go here!" He took Chamry's hand and shook it. "And the lads?"

Chamry introduced us, with a few words about our talents. Barna patted Venne's shoulder and told him a hunter was always welcome in the Heart of the Forest; at me he looked intently for a minute, and said, "Come see me later today, Gav, if you will. Toma, you'll find them quarters? Good, good, good! Welcome to freedom, lads!" And he strode on, a head taller than anyone else.

Chamry was beaming. "By the Stone!" he said. "Never a hard word, but welcome back and all's forgiven! That's a great man, with a great heart in him!"

We found lodgings in a barrack that seemed luxurious after our ill-built, smoky huts in the forest camp, and ate at the commons, which was open all day to all comers. There Chamry got his heart's desire: they'd roasted a couple of sheep, and he ate roast mutton till his eyes gleamed with satisfaction above his cheeks shining with mutton fat. After that he took me to Barna's house, which loomed over the central square, but did not go in with me. "I won't press my luck," he said. "He asked you to come, not me. Sing him that song of yours, 'Liberty,' eh? That'll win him."

So I went in, trying to act as if I wasn't daunted, and said to the people that Barna had asked me to come. They were all men, but I heard women's voices farther in the house. That sound, the sound of women's voices in other rooms of a great house, made my mind stir strangely. I wanted to stop and listen. There was a voice I wanted to hear.

But I had to follow the men who took me to a hall with a big hearth, though there was no fire in it now. There Barna was sitting in a chair big enough for him, a regular throne, talking and laughing with both men and women. The women wore beautiful clothes, of such colors as I had not seen for months and months except in a flower or the dawn sky. You will laugh, but it was the colors I stared at, not the women. Some of the men were well dressed, too, and it was pleasant to see men clean, in handsome clothing, talking and laughing aloud. It was familiar.

"Come here, lad," said Barna in his deep, grand voice. "Gav, is it? Are you from Casicar, Gav, or Asion?"

Now, in Brigin's camp you never asked a man where

he was from. Among runaway slaves, deserters, and wanted thieves, the question wasn't well received. Chamry was the only one of us who often talked freely about where he'd run from, and that was because he was so far away from it. Not long ago we'd heard of raids into the forest, slave takers looking for runaways. For all of us it was better to have no past at all, which just suited me. I was so taken aback by Barna's question that I answered it stiffly and uneasily, sounding even to myself as if I were lying. "I'm from Etra."

"Etra, is it? Well, I know a city man when I see one. I was born in Asion myself, a slave son of slaves. As you see, I've brought the city into the forest. What's the good of freedom if you're poor, hungry, dirty, and cold? That's no freedom worth having! If a man wants to live by the bow or by the work of his hands, let him take his choice, but here in our realm no man will live in slavery or in want. That's the beginning and the end of the Law of Barna. Right?" he asked the people around him, laughing, and they shouted back, "Right!"

The energy and goodwill of the man, his pure enjoyment in being, were irresistible. He embraced us all in his warmth and strength. He was keen, too; his clear eyes saw quick and deep. He looked at me and said,

"You were a house slave, and pretty well treated, right? So was I. What were you trained to do in the great house for your masters?"

"I was educated to teach the children of the house." I spoke slowly. It was like reading a story in my mind. I was talking about somebody else.

Barna leaned forward, intensely interested. "Educated!" he said. "Writing, reading—all such?"

"Yes."

"Chamry said you were a singer?"

"A speaker," I said.

"A speaker. What do you speak?"

"Anything I've read," I said, not as a boast, but because it was true.

"What have you read?"

"The historians, the philosophers, the poets."

"A learned man. By the Deaf One! A learned man! A scholar! Lord Luck has sent me the man I wanted, the man I lacked!" Barna stared at me with amazed delight, then got up from his huge chair, came to me, and took me into a bear hug. My face was mashed into his curling beard. He squeezed the breath out of me, then held me out at arm's length.

"You will live here," he said. "Right? Give him a

room, Diero! And tonight, will you speak for us tonight? Will you say us a piece of your learning, Gav-dí the Scholar? Eh?"

I said I would.

"There's no books for you here," he said almost anxiously, still holding me by the shoulders. "Everything else a man might need we have, but books—books aren't what most of my men would bring here with them, they're ignorant letterless louts, and books are very heavy matters—" He laughed, throwing back his head. "Ah, but now, from now on, we'll remedy that. We'll see to it. Tonight, then!"

He let me go. A woman in delicate black and violet robes took me by the hand and led me off. I thought her old, over forty surely, and she had a grave face, and did not smile; but her manner and her voice were gentle, and her dress beautiful, and it was amazing how differently she moved, and walked, and spoke, from how men did. She took me to a loft room, apologising for its being upstairs and small. I stammered something about staying with my mates in the barrack. She said, "You can live there, of course, if you wish, but Barna hopes you will honor his house." I was unable to disappoint this elegant, fragile person. It seemed everybody was taking my learning very much on trust, but I couldn't say that.

She left me in the little loft room. It had a small, square window, a bed with a mattress and bedding, a table and chair, an oil lamp. It looked like heaven to me. I did go back to the barrack, but Chamry and Venne had both gone out. I told a man who was lounging on his bunk there to tell them that I'd be staying at Barna's house. He looked at me at first disbelieving, then with a knowing smirk.

"Living high, eh?" he said.

I put what little gear I had with Chamry's, for I wouldn't need fish hooks or my filthy old blanket; but I wore my sheathed knife on my belt, having seen that most men here did. I went back to Barna's house. I could look at it better now that I was not so overawed. Its facade on the central square was wide and high, with mighty beams and deep gables; it was built of wood, and there was no glass in the small-paned windows, but it was an impressive house.

I sat on the bed in my room—my own room!—and let bewildered excitement flood through me. I was very nervous about reciting to this genial, willful, unpredictable giant and his crowd of people. I felt I must prove myself at once and beyond doubt to be the scholar he wanted me to be. That was a strange thing to be called on to do. Coming out of the silence I'd lived in so long, the silence of the forest, the mute forgetfulness... But I had recited all *Sentas* to my companions in the silence, hadn't I? I had called on it, and it came to me. It was mine, it was in me. I remembered all I had learned in the schoolroom with—

I came too near the wall. My mind went numb. Blank, empty.

I lay back and dozed, I think, till the light was growing reddish in the small, deep-framed window. I got up and combed my hair as well as I could with my fingers and tied it back again with an end of fishing line, for it hadn't been cut for a year. That was all I could do to make myself elegant. I went down the stairs and to the great hall, where thirty or forty people were gathered, chattering like a flock of starlings.

I was made welcome, and the grave, sweet-mannered woman in black and violet, Diero, gave me a cup of wine, which I drank thirstily. It made my head spin. I didn't have the courage to keep her from refilling the cup, but I did have the wits not to drink any more. I looked at the cup, thin silver chased with a pattern of

olive leaves, as beautiful as anything in...as anything I
had seen. I wondered if there were silversmiths in the
Heart of the Forest, and where the silver came from.
Then Barna loomed over me, his grand voice rumbling.
He put his arm round my shoulders. He took me in
front of the people, called for silence, told his guests he
had a treat for them, and nodded at me with a smile.

I wished I had a lyre, as strolling tellers did, to set
the tone and mood of their recitation. I had to start off
into silence, which is hard. But I had been trained well.
Stand straight, Gavir, keep your hands still, bring your
voice up from your belly, out from your chest...

I spoke them the old poem *The Sea-Farers of Asion*.
It had come into my head tonight because Barna said
he was from that city. And I hoped it might suit the
company I was in. It is the tale of a ship carrying treasure up the coast from Ansul to Asion. The ship is
boarded by pirates, who kill the officers and order the
slaves at the oars to row to Sova Island, the pirates'
haven. The oarsmen obey, but in the night they plot
an uprising, unfasten their chains, and kill the pirates.
Then they row the ship with all its treasure on to the
port of Asion, where the Lords of the City welcome
them as heroes and reward them with a share of the
treasure and their freedom. The poem has a swing to it

like the sea waves, and I saw my audience in their fine
clothes following the story with open eyes and mouths,
just like my ragged brothers in the smoky hut. I was
borne up on the words and on their attention. We were
all there in the ship in the great grey sea.

So it ended, and after the little silence that comes
then, Barna rose up with a roar—"Set them free! By
Sampa the Maker and Destroyer, they set them free!
Now there's a tale I like!" He gave me one of his bear
hugs and held me off by the shoulders as his way was,
saying, "Though I doubt that it's a true history. Gratitude to a lot of galley slaves? Not likely! Here, I'll tell
you a better ending for it, Scholar: They never sailed
back to Asion at all, but sailed south, far south, back
to Ansul where the money came from, and there they
shared it out and lived on it the rest of their lives, free
men and rich!—How's that?—But it's good poetry,
grand poetry well spoken!" He clapped me on the back
and took me around introducing me to the others, men
and women, who praised me and spoke kindly. I drank
off my wine and my head went round again. It was very
pleasant, but at last I was glad to get away, go up to my
loft in amazement at all that had happened this long
day, fall onto my soft bed, and sleep.

So began my life in the Heart of the Forest and my

acquaintance with its founder and presiding spirit. All I could think was that Luck was with me still, and since I didn't know what to ask him for, he'd given me what I needed.

Barna's welcome to me hadn't been just jovial bluster; there was a bit of that in most of what he said and did, but under it was a driving purpose. He had wanted men of learning in his city of the free, and had none.

He took me into his confidence very quickly. Like me, he'd grown up a slave in a great house where the masters and some of the slaves were educated and there were books to be read. More than that, scholars who came to Asion visited and talked with the learned men of the house; poets stayed there, and the philosopher Denneter lived there for a year. All this had fascinated and impressed the boy, and he in turn had impressed his masters and the visitors with his quickness at learning, especially philosophy. Denneter made much of him, wanted to make a disciple of him; he was to be Denneter's student and go traveling with him through the world.

But when he was fifteen, the slaves in the great civic barracks of Asion rebelled. They broke into the armory of the city guard, used the armory as a fortress, and killed the guards and others who tried to assault them.

They declared themselves free men, demanded that the city recognise them as such, and called on all slaves to join them. Many house slaves did, and for several days Asion was in a state of panic and confusion. A regiment of Asion's army was sent into the city, the armory was besieged and taken, and the rebels slaughtered. Almost all male slaves were suspect after that. Many were branded to mark them indelibly as unfree. Barna, a boy of fifteen, had escaped branding, but there was no more talk of philosophy and travel. He was drafted to refill the civic barracks, sent to hard labor.

"And so all my education stopped then and there. Not a book have I held in my hands since that day. But I had those few years of learning, and hearing truly wise men talk, and knowing that there's a life of the mind that's far above anything else in the world. And so I knew what was missing here. I could make my city of free men, but what's the good of freedom to the ignorant? What's freedom itself but the power of the mind to learn what it needs and think what it likes? Ah, even if your body's chained, if you have the thoughts of the philosophers and the words of the poets in your head, you can be free of your chains, and walk among the great!"

His praise of learning moved me deeply. I had been

living among people so poor that knowledge of any-thing much beyond their poverty had no meaning to them, and so they judged it useless. I had accepted their judgment, because I had accepted their poverty. There had been a long time when I'd never thought of the words of the makers; and when they came back to me, at Brigin's camp, it seemed a miraculous gift that had nothing to do with my will or intention. Having been so poor, so ignorant myself, I had no heart to say that ignorance cannot judge knowledge.

But here was a man who had proved his intelligence, energy, and courage, raising himself out of poverty and slavery to a kind of kingship, and bringing a whole people with him into independence; and he set knowl-edge, learning, and poetry above even such achieve-ments. I was ashamed of my weakness, and rejoiced in his strength.

Admiring Barna more as I came to know him, I wanted to be of use to him. But for the time being it seemed all he wanted of me was to be a kind of dis-ciple, going about the city with him and listening to his thoughts—which I was happy to do—and then, in the evening, to recite whatever poetry or tales I wished to his guests and household. I suggested teaching some of his companions to read, but there were no books, he said, to teach from, and though I offered to, he wouldn't let me waste my time writing out copybooks. Books would be looked for and brought here, he said, and men of education would be found to assist me, and then we'd have a regular school, where all could learn who wanted.

Meanwhile some of Barna's people coaxed me to teach them, young women who lived in his house seeking a new entertainment; and with his permission I held a little class in writing and reading for a few of them. Barna laughed at me and the girls. "Don't let 'em fool you, Scholar. They're not after literature! They just want to sit next to a bit of pretty boy-flesh." He and his men companions teased the girls about turning into bookworms, and they soon gave it up. Diero was the only one who came more than a few times.

Diero was a beautiful woman, gracious and gentle. She had been trained from girlhood as a "butterfly woman." The "butterflies" of Asion—an ancient city famous for its ceremony, its luxury, and its women—were schooled in a science of pleasure far more refined and elaborate than anything known in the City States.

But, as Diero herself told me, reading wasn't one of

the arts taught to the "butterflies." She listened with yearning intensity to the poetry I spoke, and had a great, timid curiosity about it. I encouraged her to let me teach her to write her letters and spell out words. She was humble, self-distrustful, but quick to learn, and her pleasure in learning was a pleasure to me. Barna looked on our lessons with genial amusement.

His older companions, all of whom had been with him for years, were very much his men. They had brought from their years of slavery a habit of accepting orders and not competing to lead, which made them easy company. They treated me as a boy, not a rival to them, telling me what I needed to know and occasionally giving me a warning. Barna would give you the coat off his back, they told me, but if he thinks you're poaching his girls, look out! They told me Diero had come with Barna from Asion when he first broke free and had been his mistress for many years. She wasn't that now, but she was the woman of Barna's House, and a man who didn't treat Diero with affectionate respect wouldn't be welcome there.

Barna explained to me one day as we sat up on the watchtower of the Heart of the Forest that men and women should be free to love one another with no hypocritical bonds of promised faithfulness to chain them together. That sounded good to me. All I knew of marriage was that it was for the masters, not for my kind, so I'd thought little about it one way or the other. But Barna thought about such things, and came to conclusions, and had them enacted in the Heart of the Forest. He had ideas about children, too, that they should be entirely free, never punished, allowed to run about as they pleased and find out for themselves what best suited them to do. This seemed admirable to me. All his ideas did.

I was a good listener, sometimes putting a question, but mostly content to follow the endless inventions and generous vistas of his mind. As he said, he thought best out loud. He soon claimed me as a necessity to him: "Where's Gav-dí? Where's the Scholar? I need to think!"

I lived at Barna's house, but I went to see Chamry often. He had joined the cobblers' guild, where he lived snug and complained of nothing but the scarcity of women and roast mutton. "They've got to send the tithing boys out for roasting mutton!" he said.

Venne had soon found that as a hunter he'd have to spend most of his time away off in the woods just as he'd done for Brigin, since all the game near the Heart of the Forest had long since been hunted out. Hunting was not what fed the town these days. One of the groups of "tithing boys" asked him to come with them as a guard when they found what a good shot he was with the short bow, and he joined them. He first went out on the road with them about a month after we came to the Heart of the Forest.

The tithers or raiders went out from our wooden city to meet drovers and wagons on the roads outside the forest. Their goal was to bring back flocks and herds, loaded wagons, drivers and horses, thus increasing our stock of food, vehicles, animals, and men—if the men were willing to join the Brotherhood. If they weren't, Barna told me, they were left blindfolded with their hands tied, to wander in hope the next passerby would untie them. He laughed his mighty laugh when he told me that some of the drivers had been robbed so often by the Forest Brothers that they meekly stuck their hands out to be tied.

There were also the "netmen" who went singly or in pairs into Asion itself, sometimes to bargain in the market for things we needed, but sometimes as thieves to steal from the houses of the rich and the coffers of wealthy shrines. No money was used among us, but the Brotherhood wanted cash to buy things the raiders could not steal—including the goodwill of towns near the forest, and the silence of colluding merchants in the cities. Barna liked to boast that he sat on a fortune that the great merchants of Asion might envy. Where the gold and silver was kept I never knew. Bronze and copper coins were to be had for the asking by anyone going into a town to buy goods.

Barna and his assistants knew who left the Heart of the Forest. Not many did, and only tried and trusted men. As Barna put it, one fool blabbing in an alehouse might bring the army of Asion down on us. The narrow, intricate woodland paths that led to and from the gate were closely guarded and often changed and obliterated, so that the tracks of wagons or herds of cattle couldn't easily lead anyone to the wooden city. I remembered the sentries we had met, the challenge and the loaded crossbow. We all knew that if a trail guard saw anyone going away from the gate without permission, he was not to challenge, but to shoot.

They asked Venne to be a trail guard, but he didn't like the idea of having to shoot a man in the back. Raiding wagon trains or rustling cattle suited him better, and being a raider gave a man great prestige among the Brothers. Barna himself said the raiders and the "justicers" who policed the town were the most valuable members of the community. And every man in the Heart of the Forest should follow his own heart in choosing what he did. So Venne went off cheerily with a band of young men, promising Chamry he'd come back with "a flock of sheep, or failing that, a batch of women."

In fact there weren't many women in the Heart of the Forest, and every one of them was jealously guarded by a man or group of men. Those you saw in the streets and gardens seemed all to be pregnant or dragging a gaggle of infants with them, or else they were mere bowed backs sweeping, spinning, digging, milking, like old women slaves anywhere. There were more young women in Barna's house than anywhere else, the prettiest girls in the town, and the merriest. They dressed in fine clothes the raiders brought in. If they could sing or dance or play the lyre, that was welcome, but they weren't expected to do any work. They were, Barna said, "to be all a woman should be—free, and beautiful, and kind."

He loved to have them about him, and they all flirted and flattered and teased him assiduously. He joked and played with them, but his serious talk was always with men.

As time went on, and he kept me his almost constant companion, I felt the honor and the burden of his trust. I tried to be worthy of it. I continued to recite in the evening in his great hall for all who wanted to hear; and because of that and because Barna had me with him so often, most people treated me with respect, though it was often begrudged or puzzled or patronising, since I was after all still a boy. And some of them saw me, I know, as a kind of learned halfwit. They sensed that there was something lacking in me, that for all the endless words at my command, my knowledge of the world was slight and shallow, like a child's.

I knew that too, but I could not think about it or why it should be so. I turned away from such thoughts, and went about with Barna, following him, needing him. His great fullness of being filled my emptiness.

I wasn't the only one who felt that. Barna was the heart of the Heart of the Forest. His vision, his decision, was always the point of reference for the others, his will was their fulcrum. He didn't maintain this mastery by intimidation but through the superiority of his energy and intelligence and the tremendous generosity of his nature: he was simply there before the others, seeing what must be done and how to do it, drawing them to act with him through his passion, activity, and goodwill. He loved people, loved to be among them, with them, he believed in brotherhood with all his heart and soul.

I knew his dreams by now, for he told them to me as we went about the city, he directing, encouraging, and participating in work, I as his listening shadow.

I couldn't always share his love for the Forest Brothers, and wondered how he could keep any patience at all with some of them. Lodging, food, all the necessities of life were shared as fairly as possible, but it had to be rough justice, and one room will always be bigger than another, one serving of pie will have more raisins than another. The first response of many of the men to any perceived inequity was to accuse another man of hogging, and fight their grudge out with fists or knives. Most of them had been farm or hard-labor slaves, brutalised from childhood, used to getting what little they got by grabbing for it and fighting to keep it. Barna had lived that life too and understood them. He kept the rules very simple and very strict, and his justicers enforced them implacably. But still there were murders now and then, and brawls every night. Our few healers, bonesetters, and tooth pullers worked hard. The ale made by our brewery was kept weak at Barna's orders, but men could get drunk on it if they had a weak head or drank all night. And when they weren't drunk and quarreling they were complaining of unfairness, injustice, or the work they were allotted; they wanted less of it, or to do a different kind of work, or to work with one group of mates not another, and so on endlessly. All these complaints ended up with Barna.

"Men have to learn how to be free," he said to me. "Being a slave is easy. To be a free man you have to use your head, you have to give here and take there, you have to give your orders to yourself. They'll learn, Gav, they'll learn!" But even his large good nature was exasperated by the demands on him to settle petty jealousies, and he could be angered by the backbiting and rivalry of the men closest to him, his justicers and the men of his household—our government, in fact, though they had no titles.

He had no title himself, he was simply Barna.

He chose his men, and they chose others to assist them, always with his approval. Election by popular vote was an idea which he knew little about. I was able to tell him that some of the City States had at one time or another been republics or even democracies, although of course only freeborn men of property had the vote. I remembered what I had read of the state and city of Ansul, far to the south, which was governed by officials elected by the entire people, and had no slavery, until they were themselves enslaved by a warlike people from the eastern deserts. And the great country of Urdile, north of Bendile, did not permit any form of bondage; like Ansul, they considered both men and women to be citizens; and every citizen had the vote, electing governing consuls for two years and senators for six. I could tell Barna of these different polities, and he listened with interest, and added elements from them to his plans for the ultimate government of the Free State in the forest.

Such plans were his favorite topic when he was in his good mood. When the bickering and brawling and backbiting and the innumerable, interminable details of provisioning and guard duty and building and everything else that he took responsibility for wore him out and put him in a darker mood, he talked of revolution—the Uprising.

"In Asion there are three slaves, or four, for every free man. All over Bendile, the men who work the farms are slaves. If they could see who they are—that nothing can be done without them! If they could see how many they are! If they could realise their strength, and hold together! The Armory Rebellion, back twenty-five years ago, was just an outburst. No plan, no real leaders. Weapons, but no decisions. Nowhere to go. They couldn't hold together. What I'm planning here is going to be entirely different. There are two essential elements. First, weapons—the weapons we're stockpiling here, now. We'll be met with violence, and we must be able to meet it with insuperable strength. —And then, union. We must act as one. The Uprising must happen everywhere at once. In the city, in the countryside, the towns and villages, the farms. A network of men, in touch with one another, ready, informed, with weapons at hand, each knowing when and how to act—so that when the first torch is lighted the whole country will go up in flames. The fire of freedom! What's that song of yours? 'Be our fire…Liberty!'"

His talk of the Uprising disturbed and fascinated me. Without really understanding what was at stake, I liked to hear him make his plans, and would ask him for details. He'd catch fire then and talk with great passion. He said, "You bring me back to my heart, Gav.

Trying to keep things running here has been eating me up. I've been looking only at what's to be done next and forgetting why we're doing it. I came here to build a stronghold where men and arms could be gathered, a center from which men would go back, a network of men in the northern City States and Bendile, working to get all the slaves in Asion with us, and in Casicar, and the countryside. To get them ready for the Uprising, so that when it comes there'll be nowhere for the masters to fall back to. They'll bring out their armies, but who will the armies attack—with the masters held hostage in their own houses and farms, and the city itself in the hands of slaves? In every house in the city, the masters will be penned up in the barrack, the way they penned us in when there was threat of war, right?—but now it's the masters locked up while the slaves run the household, as of course they always did, and keep the markets going, and govern the city. In the towns and the countryside, the same thing, the masters locked up tight, the slaves taking over, doing the work they always did, the only difference is they give the orders…So the army comes to attack, but if they attack, the first to die will be the hostages, the masters, squealing for mercy, *Don't let them slaughter us! Don't attack, don't attack!* The general thinks, ah, they're nothing but slaves with pitchforks and kitchen knives, they'll run as soon as we move in, and he sends in a troop to take the farm. They're cut to pieces by slaves armed with swords and crossbows, fighting from ambush, trained men fighting on their own ground. They take no prisoners. And they bring out one of the squealing masters, the Father maybe, where the soldiers can see, and say: *You attacked: he dies*, and slice off his head. *Attack again, more of them die.* And this will be going on all over the country—every farm, village, town, and Asion itself—the great Uprising! And it won't end until the masters buy their liberty with every penny they have, and everything they own. Then they can come outside and learn out how the common folk live."

He threw his head back and laughed, merrier than I'd seen him in days. "Oh, you do me good, Gav!" he said.

The picture he drew was fantastic yet terribly vivid, compelling my belief. "But how will you reach the farm slaves, the city house slaves?" I asked, trying to sound practical, knowledgeable.

"That's the strategy: exactly. To reach into the houses, into the barracks and the slave villages, send men to talk to them—catch them in our net! Show them what they can do and how to do it. Let them ask questions. Get them to figure it out for themselves, make their own plans—so long as they know they must wait for our signal. It'll take time to do that, to spread the net, set up the plan all through the city and the countryside. And yet it can't be too slow in building, because if it goes on too long, word will leak out, fools will begin to blab, and the masters will get jumpy—*What's all this talk in the barrack? What are they whispering in the kitchen? What's that blacksmith making there?*— And then the great advantage of surprise is lost. Timing is everything."

It was only a tale to me, his Uprising. In his mind it was to take place in the future, a great revenge, a rectification of the past. But in my mind there was no past.

I had nothing left but words—the poems that sang themselves in my head, the stories and histories I could bring before my mind's eye and read. I did not look up from the words to what had been around them. When I looked away from them I was back in the vivid intensity of the moment, now, here, with nothing behind it, no shadows, no memories. The words came when I needed them. They came to me from nowhere. My name was a word. Etra was a word. That was all; they had no meaning, no history. Liberty was a word in a poem. A beautiful word, and beauty was all the meaning it had.

Always sketching out his plans and dreams of the future, Barna never asked me about my past. Instead, one day, he told me about it. He'd been talking about the Uprising, and perhaps I'd answered without much enthusiasm, for my own sense of emptiness sometimes made it hard for me to respond convincingly. He was quick to see such moods.

"You did the right thing, you know, Gav," he said, looking at me with his clear eyes. "I know what you're thinking about. Back there in the city…You think, 'What a fool I was! To run off and starve, to live in a forest with ignorant men, to slave harder than I ever did in my masters' house! Is that freedom? Wasn't I freer there, talking with learned men, reading the books of the poets, sleeping soft and waking warm? Wasn't I happier there?' —But you weren't. You weren't happy, Gav. You knew it in your heart, and that's why you ran off. The hand of the master was always on you."

He sighed and looked into the fire for a little; it was autumn, a chill in the air. I listened to him as I listened to him tell all his tales, without argument or question.

"I know how it was, Gav. You were a slave in a great

house, a rich house, in the city, with kind masters who had you educated. Oh, I know that! And you thought you should be happy, because you had the power to learn, read, teach—become a wise man, a learned man. They let you have that. They allowed it to you. Oh yes! But though you were given the power *to do* certain things, you had no power *over* anyone or anything. That was theirs. The masters. Your owners. And whether you knew it or not, in every bone of your body and fiber of your mind you felt that hand of the master holding you, controlling you, pressing down on you. Any power you had, on those terms, was worthless. Because it was nothing but their power acting through you. Using you... They let you pretend it was yours. You filched a bit of freedom, a scrap of liberty, from your masters, and pretended it was yours and was enough to keep you happy. Right? But you were growing into a man. And for a man, Gav, there is no happiness but in his own freedom. His freedom to do what he wills to do. And so your will sought its full liberty. As mine did, long ago."

He reached out and clapped me on the knee. "Don't look so sad," he said, his white grin flashing in his curly beard. "You know you did the right thing! Be glad of it, as I am!"

I tried to tell him that I was glad of it.

He had to go see about affairs, and left me musing by the fire. What he said was true. It was the truth.

But not my truth.

Turning away from his tale, I looked back for the first time in—how long? I looked across the wall I'd built to keep me from remembering. I looked and saw the truth: I had been a slave in a great house, a rich house, in the city, obedient to my masters, owning no freedom but what they allowed me. And I had been happy.

In the house of my slavery I had known a love so dear to me that I could not bear to think about it, because when I lost it, I lost everything.

All my life had been built on trust, and that trust had been betrayed by the Family of Arcamand.

Arcamand: with the name, with the word, everything I had forgotten, had refused to remember, came back and was mine again, and with it all the unspeakable pain I had denied.

I sat there by the fire, turned away from the room, bent over, my hands clenched on my knees. Someone came near and stood near me at the hearth to warm herself: Diero, a gentle presence in a long shawl of fine pale wool.

"Gav," she said very quietly, "what is it?"

I tried to answer her and broke into a sob. I hid my face in my arms and wept aloud.

Diero sat down beside me on the stone hearth seat. She put her arms around me and held me while I cried.

"Tell me, tell me," she said at last.

"My sister. She was my sister," I said.

And that word brought the sobbing again, so hard I could not take breath.

She held me and rocked me a while, until I could lift my head and wipe my nose and face. Then she said again, "Tell me."

"She was always there," I said.

And so one way and another, weeping, in broken sentences and out of order, I told her about Sallo, about our life, about her death.

The wall of forgetting was down. I was able to think, to speak, to remember. I was free. Freedom was unspeakable anguish.

In that first terrible hour I came back again and again to Sallo's death, to how she died, why she died— all the questions I had refused to ask.

"The Mother knew—she had to know about it," I said. "Maybe Torm took Sallo and Ris out of the silk rooms without asking, without permission, it sounds as if that's what he did. But the other women there would know it—they'd go to the Mother and tell her—*Torm-dí took Ris and Sallo off, Mother—they didn't want to go, they were crying— Did you tell him he could take them? Will you send after them?*— And she didn't. She did nothing! Maybe the Father said not to interfere. He always favored Torm. Sallo said that, she said he hated Yaven and favored Torm. But the Mother—she knew—she knew where Torm and Hoby were taking them, to that place, those men, men who used girls like animals, who— She knew that. Ris was a virgin. And the Mother had given Sallo to Yaven herself. And yet she let the other son take her and give her to— How did they kill her? Did she try to fight them? She couldn't have. All those men. They raped her, they tortured her, that's what they wanted girls for, to hear them scream—to torture and kill them, drown them— When Sallo was dead. After I saw her. I saw her dead. The Mother sent for me. She called her 'our sweet Sallo.' She gave me—she gave me money—for my sister—"

A sound came out of my throat then, not a sob but a hoarse howl. Diero held me close. She said nothing.

I was silent at last. I was mortally tired.

"They betrayed our trust," I said.

I felt Diero nod. She sat beside me, her hand on mine.

"That's what it is," she said, almost inaudibly. "Do you keep the trust, or not. To Barna it's all power. But it's not. It's trust."

"They had the power to betray it," I said bitterly.

"Even slaves have that power," she said in her gentle voice.

◆ 10 ◆

For days after that I kept to my room. Diero told Barna I was ill. I was sick indeed with the grief and anger that I hadn't been able to feel all the uncounted months since I walked away from the graveyard by the Nisas. I had run away then, body and soul. Now at last I'd turned around and stopped running. But I had a long, long way to go back.

I could not go back to Arcamand in my body, though I thought often and often of doing so. But I had run away from Sallo, from all my memory of her, and I had to return to her and let her return to me. I could no longer deny her, my love, my sister, my ghost.

To grieve for her brought me relief, but never for long. Always the pure sorrow became choked thick with anger, bitter blame, self-blame, unforgiving hatred. With Sallo they all came back to me, those faces, voices, bodies I had kept away from me so long, hiding them behind the wall. Often I could not think of Sallo at all but only of Torm, his thick body and lurching walk; of the Mother and the Father of Arca; or of Hoby. Hoby who had pushed Sallo into the chariot while she was crying out for help. Hoby the bastard son of the Father, full of rancorous envy, hating me and Sallo above all. Hoby who had nearly drowned me once. They might have let— At that pool— It might have been Hoby who—

I crouched on the floor of my room, stuffing the folds of a cloak into my mouth so that no one could hear me scream.

Diero came up to my room once or twice a day, and though I couldn't bear to have anyone else see me as I was, she brought me no shame, but even a little dignity. There was in her a bleak, gentle, unmoved calm, which I could share while she was with me. I loved her for that, and was grateful to her.

She made me eat a little and look after myself. She was able to make me think, sometimes, that I had come to this despair in order to find a way through it, a way back to life.

When at last I went downstairs again, it was with her to give me courage.

Barna, having been told I'd had a fever, treated me kindly, and told me I mustn't recite again till I was perfectly well. So though my days were again mostly spent with him, often in the winter evenings I'd go to Diero's peaceful rooms and sit and talk with her alone. I looked forward to those hours and cherished them afterwards, thinking of her greeting and her smile and her soft movements, which were professional and mannered like those of an actor or dancer, and yet which expressed her true nature. I knew she welcomed my visits and our quiet talk. Diero and I loved each other, though she never held me in her arms but that once, by the great hearth, when she let me cry.

People joked about us, a little, carefully, looking at Barna to be sure he didn't take offense. He seemed if anything amused by the idea that his old mistress was consoling his young scholar. He made no jokes or allusions about it, an unusual delicacy in him; but then he always treated Diero with respect. She herself did not care what people thought or said.

As for me, if Barna thought she and I were lovers,

it kept him from suspecting me of "poaching" his girls. Though they were so pretty and apparently so available as to drive a boy my age crazy, their availability was a sham, a trap, as men of the household had warned me early on. If he gives you one of the girls, they said, take her, but only for the night, and don't try sneaking off with any of his favorites! And as they knew me better and came to trust my discretion, they told me dire stories about Barna's jealousy. Finding a man with a girl he himself wanted, he had snapped the man's wrists like sticks, they said, and driven him out into the forest to starve.

I didn't entirely believe such tales. The men themselves might be a bit jealous of me, after all, and not sorry to scare me off the girls. Young as I was, some of the girls were even younger; and some of them were cautiously flirtatious, praising and petting me as their "Scholar-dí," begging me prettily to make my recital a love story "and make us cry, Gav, break our hearts!" For after a while I became their entertainer again. The words had come back to me.

During the first time of agony, when I regained all that I had cut out of my memory, all I could remember was Sallo, and Sallo's death, and all my life in Arcamand and Etra. For many days afterwards, I believed that that was all I ever would remember. I didn't want to remember anything I'd learned there, in the house of the murderers. All my treasure of history and verse and stories was stained with their crime. I didn't want to know what they'd taught me. I wanted nothing they had given me, nothing that belonged to the masters. I tried to push it all away from me, forget it, as I had forgotten them.

But that was foolish, and I knew it in my heart. Gradually the healing took place, seeming as it always does that it wasn't taking place. Little by little I let all I'd learned return to me, and it was not stained, not spoiled. It didn't belong to the masters, it wasn't theirs: it was mine. It was all I ever really had owned. So I stopped the effort to forget, and all my book learning came back to me with the clarity and completeness some people find uncanny, though the gift isn't that rare. Once again I could go into the schoolroom or the library of Arcamand in my mind, and open a book, and read it. Standing before the people in the high wooden hall, I could open my mouth and speak the first lines of a poem or a tale, and the rest would follow of itself, the poetry saying and singing itself through me, the story renewing itself in itself as a river runs.

Most of the people there believed that I was improvising, that I was the maker, the poet, incomprehensibly inspired to spout hexameters forever. There wasn't much point in arguing with them about it. People generally know better than the workman how the work is done, and tell him; and he might as well keep his opinions to himself.

There was little else in the way of entertainment in the Heart of the Forest. Some of the girls and a few men could play or sing. They and I always had a benevolent audience. Barna sat in his great chair, stroking his great curly beard, intent, delighted. Some who had little interest in the tales or the poetry attended either to win favor with Barna or simply because they wanted to be with him and share his pleasure.

And he still took me with him, talking about his plans. So talking and listening, and having leisure time and comfort in which to think—for thinking goes much quicker when one is warm, dry, and not hungry—I spent the end of that winter working through all I'd recovered when I came back at last to my Sallo and could grieve for her, and know my loss, and look at what my life had been and what it might have been.

It was still hard for me to think at all of the Mother and Father of Arca. My mind would not come to any clarity concerning them. But I thought often of Yaven. I thought he would not have betrayed our trust. I wondered if when he came home, he had exacted vengeance, useless as it might be. Surely he would not forgive Torm and Hoby, however long he must withhold punishment. Yaven was a man of honor, and he had loved Sallo.

But Yaven might be dead, killed at the siege of Casicar. That war had been as much a disaster for Etra, so people said, as the siege of Etra had been for Casicar. Torm might now be the heir of Arca. That was a thought my mind still flinched away from.

I could think of Sotur only with piercing grief and pain. She had kept faith with us as best she could. Alone there, what had become of her? She would be, she probably had been, married off into some other household—one where there was no Everra, no library of books, no friendship, no escape.

Again and again I thought of that night when Sallo and I were talking in the library, and Sotur came in, and they tried to tell me why they were afraid. They had clung to each other, loving, helpless.

And I hadn't understood.

It was not only the Family who had betrayed them. I had betrayed them. Not in acts: what could I have done? But I should have understood. I had been unwilling to see. I had blinded my eyes with belief. I had believed that the rule of the master and the obedience of the slave were a mutual and sacred trust. I had believed that justice could exist in a society founded on injustice.

Belief in the lie is the life of the lie. That line from Caspro's book came back to me, and cut like a razor.

Honor can exist anywhere, love can exist anywhere, but justice can exist only among people who found their relationships upon it.

Now, I thought, I understood Barna's plans for the Uprising, now they made sense to me. All that ancient evil ordained by the Ancestors, that prison tower of mastery and slavery, was to be uprooted and thrown down, replaced by justice and liberty. The dream would be made real. And Luck had brought me here to the place where that great change would begin, the home and center of the liberty to come.

I wanted to be one of those who made it real. I began to dream of going to Asion. Many of the Forest Brothers were from that city, a great city with a large population of freemen and freedmen, merchants and artisans, into which a fugitive slave could mix without being questioned or suspected. Barna's netmen went back and forth often, passing as traders, merchants, cattle buyers, slaves sent on commission by farmers, and so on. I wanted to join them. There were educated people in Asion, both nobles and freemen, people to whom I could present myself as a freeman seeking work copying or reciting or teaching. And so doing I could do Barna's work, laying the foundation of the Uprising among the slaves I would meet there.

Barna absolutely forbade it. "I want you here," he said. "I need you, Scholar!"

"You need me more there," I said.

He shook his head. "Too dangerous. One day they ask, where did you get your learning? And what'll you say?"

I'd already thought that out. "That I went to school in Mesun, where the University is, and came down to Asion because there are too many scholars in Urdile, and the pay's better in Bendile."

"There'd be scholars there from the University who'd say no, that boy was never there."

"Hundreds of people go to the colleges. They can't all know one another."

I argued hard, but he shook his big curly head, and his laugh changed to a grimmer look. "Listen, Gav, I tell you a learned man stands out. And you're already famous. The lads talk as they go about, you know, winning folk in the villages and towns to come here to join us. They boast of you. We've got a fellow, they say, that can speak any tale or poem that was ever made! And only a boy yet, a wonder of the world! Well, you can't go to Asion with a name like that hanging about you."

I stared at him. "My name? Do they say my name?"

"They say the name you gave us," he said, untroubled.

Of course he, and everyone else but Chamry Bern, assumed that "Gav" was a false name. Nobody here, not even Barna, used the name he'd had as a slave.

As Barna saw my expression, his changed. "Oh, by the Destroyer," he said. "You kept the name you had in Etra?"

I nodded.

"Well," he said after a minute, "if you ever do leave, take a new one! But that's all the more reason for me to say stay here! Your old masters may have sent word around that their clever slave boy they'd spent so much money educating ran off. They hate to let a runaway escape. It gripes them to the soul. We're a good way from Etra here, but you never know."

I'd never given a thought to pursuit. When I left the graveyard and walked up the Nisas, it was a death. I had walked away from everything, into nothing, going nowhere. I had no fear, then, because I had no desire.

As I began to live again, here, I still had no fear. I'd gone so far in my own mind that it never occurred to me that anyone from the old life would follow me.

"They think I'm dead," I said at last. "They think I drowned myself that morning."

"Why would they think that?"

I was silent.

I hadn't told Barna anything about my life. I'd never spoken of it to anyone but Diero.

"You left some clothing on the riverbank, eh?" he said. "Well, they might have fallen for that old trick. But you were a valuable property. If your owners think you might be alive, they'll have their ears open. It's been only a year or two, right? Don't ever think you're safe—except here! And you might tell the lads you came from Pagadi or Piram, so that they don't say Etra if they speak of you, eh?"

"I will," I said, humbled.

Had there been no end to my stupidity? No limit to the patience Luck had had with me?

But I did repeat my request to go into Asion. Barna said, "You're a free man, Gav. I give you no orders! But I tell you, it's not time yet for you to go. You wouldn't be safe. Your being in Asion now could endanger others there, and the whole scheme of the Uprising. When the time comes for you to go there, I'll tell you. Before then, if you go, you go against my heart."

I couldn't argue with that.

In early spring a couple of newcomers arrived, runaways from a household in Asion, who came hidden in a goods wagon driven by netmen. They brought with them, stolen from their masters' house, a good sum of money and a long box. "What's this stuff?" asked one of Barna's men who opened the box, holding up a scroll so that it slipped from the rod and unrolled at his feet. "Cloth, is it?"

"It's what I asked for, man," said Barna. "It's a book. Now take care with it!" He had indeed requested his netmen to bring books. Nobody had brought any until now, most of our recruits—and recruiters—being illiterate and having no idea where to look for books or even, like this fellow, what a book looked like.

The new pair of runaways were educated, one trained in accounting, the other in recitation. The books were a motley lot, some scrolls, some paged and bound; but all could be useful for teaching, and one was a treasure to me—a little, elegantly printed copy of Caspro's *Cosmologies*, replacing the manuscript copy that Mimen had given me, for which I had grieved, once I began to remember what I had lost and left at Arcamand.

The new recruits were, as Barna said, a good catch: the accountant assisted him in record keeping, and the reciter could tell fables and Bendili epics by the hour, giving me a vacation.

I looked forward to talking to these educated men, but that didn't go well. The accountant knew only figures and calculations, while the reciter, Pulter, made it clear that he was older and more accomplished than I was, and that my pretensions to scholarship didn't qualify me to converse with a truly learned man. It galled him that most of our people liked my recitations better than his, though he soon had a following. I'd been taught to let the words do the work, while he performed in alternate shouts and whispers, with long pauses, dramatic intonations, and quavering tremolos of emotion.

The copy of the *Cosmologies* was his, but he had no interest in reading Caspro, saying all the modern poets were obscure and perverse. He gave me the book, and for that alone I would have forgiven him all his snubs and all his quavers. I found the poem difficult, but kept going back to it. Sometimes I read from it to Diero, quiet afternoons in her room.

Her friendship was like nothing else in my life. Only with her could I speak of my life at Arcamand. When I was with her I felt no wish for revenge, no desire to overturn the social order, no rage at the poor dead impotent Ancestors. I knew what I had lost, and could remember what I had had. Though Diero had never been in Etra, she was my link to it. She hadn't known Sallo, but she brought Sallo to me, and so eased my heart.

Like most slaves, Diero had been casually mothered and had no brother or sister that she knew; the two children she had borne when she was young were sold as infants. The craving for family relationship was deep in her, as it was in all of us. Barna knew that and called on it to form and strengthen his Brotherhood.

I was unusual in having had so close a bond to a sister: my loss was specific, my craving acute. It was as an older sister that I loved Diero, while to her I was a younger brother or a son, and also, perhaps, the one man she ever knew who did not want to be her master.

She loved to hear me tell about Sallo and the others at Arcamand, and our days at the farm; she was curious about the customs of Etra, and also about my origin. The great marshes where the Rassy rises lie not far south of Asion, and she had known me at once for what I was, one of the Marshmen, dark-skinned, short and slight, with thick black hair and a high-bridged nose. The Rassiu, she called the Marsh people. They came into Asion, she said, to trade at a certain monthly market; they brought herbs and medicines that were in high demand, and fine basketry and cloth they wove of reeds, to trade for pottery and metalware. They came under an ancient religious truce which protected them from slave takers. They were respected as freemen, and some of them had even settled in one quarter of the city. She was shocked to learn that Etra raided the marshes for slaves. "The Rassiu are a sacred people," she said. "They have a covenant with the Lord of the Waters. Your city will suffer for enslaving them, I think."

Some of the young women of Barna's house treated Diero with servility, fawning, as if she had the kind of power they'd known in woman slave owners. Others were trustfully respectful; others ignored her as they did all old women. She treated them all alike—kind, mild, yielding, with a dignity that set her apart. I think she was very lonely among them. Once I saw her talking with one of the younger girls, letting the girl talk and weep for home, as she had done for me.

There were no children in Barna's house. When a girl got pregnant she moved to one of the houses where other women lived in the town and had her baby there;

she kept it or gave it away as she chose. If she wanted to bring the baby up, that was fine, but if she wanted to come back and live the free life at Barna's house, she couldn't bring it with her. "This is where we get 'em, not where we keep 'em!" Barna said, to a shout of approval from his men.

Soon after Pulter and the accountant arrived, a new girl was brought to the household, with a little sister from whom she refused to be parted. Very beautiful, fifteen or sixteen years old, Irad had been taken from a village west of the forest. Barna was immediately smitten with her and made his claim on her clear to the other men. Whether she was already experienced with men or simply had no defenses, she submitted to everything with no pretense of resistance, until they told her she must let her little sister be taken away. Then she turned into a lion. I didn't see the scene, but the other men told me about it. "If you touch her I'll kill you," she said, whipping out a thin, long, unexpected knife from the seam of her embroidered trousers, and glaring round at Barna and all of them.

Barna began to reason with her, explaining the rules of the household, and assuring her that the child would be well cared for. Irad stood silent, her knife held ready.

At this point, Diero interfered. She came forward

and stood beside the sisters, putting her hand on the little girl's head as she cowered against Irad. She asked Barna if the girls were slaves. I can imagine her mild, unemphatic voice asking the question.

He of course proclaimed that they were free women in the City of Freedom.

"So, if they like, both of them can stay with me," said Diero.

The men who first told me the story thought that Diero had at last become jealous, Irad being so young and so beautiful. They laughed about it. "The old vixen has a tooth or two left!" one of them said.

I didn't think it was jealousy that moved her. Diero was without envy or possessiveness. What had made her intervene this time?

She got her way, to the extent that she went off with the child that night to her rooms. Barna of course took Irad with him for the night. But whenever he didn't call for her, Irad stayed with little Melle in Diero's rooms.

When the women of Barna's house were all together, I was often daunted by the sheer power of their youthful femininity. I got my revenge as a male by feeling contempt for them. They were healthy, plump, mindless, content to lounge about the house all day trying on the latest stolen finery and chattering about nothing. If one or another of them went off to have a baby, it made no difference—there was no end of them, others just as young and pretty would arrive with the next convoy of raiders.

Now it occurred to me to wonder about this endless supply of girls. Were they all runaways? Did they all ask to come here? Were they all seeking freedom?

Yes, of course they were. They were escaping from masters who forced sex on them.

Was Barna's house any better than whatever they'd escaped from?

Yes, of course it was. Here, they weren't raped, they weren't beaten. They were well fed, well clothed, idle.

Exactly like the women in the silk rooms at Arcamand.

I cringe, remembering how I cringed when that thought first came to me. I am ashamed now as I was then.

I thought I was keeping and cherishing Sallo in my memory, but I had forgotten her again, refused to see her, refused to see what her life and her death had shown me. I had run away again.

I had a hard time making myself go see Diero, then. For several nights I went into town to talk with Venne and Chamry and their friends. When I finally did visit

Diero's rooms, my shame kept me tongue-tied. Besides, the little girl was there. "Of course Irad is usually with Barna at night," Diero said, "but then I get to sleep with Melle. And we tell stories, don't we, Melle?"

The child nodded vigorously. She was about six years old, dark, and extremely small. She sat next to Diero and stared at me. When I looked back, she blinked, but went on staring. "Are you Cly?" she asked.

"No. I'm Gav."

"Cly came to the village," the child said. "He looked like a crow too."

"My sister used to call me Beaky," I said.

After a minute she looked down at last. She smiled. "Beaky-beaky," she murmured.

"Her village is near the Marshes," Diero said. "Maybe Cly came from there. Melle looks a bit like a Rassiu herself. Look, Gav, what Melle did this morning." She showed me a scrap of the thin, stiffly sized canvas that we used for writing lessons, since we had almost no paper. On it a few letters were written in a large uncertain script.

"T, M, O, D," I read out. "You wrote that, Melle?"

"I did like Diero-ío did," the child said. She jumped up and brought me Diero's scroll copybook, unrolled to the last few lines of poetry. "I just copied the big ones."

"That's very good," I said.

"That one is wobbly," Melle said, examining the D critically.

"She could learn so much more from you than I can teach her," said Diero. She seldom expressed any wish, and when she did it was so gentle and indirect I often missed it. I caught it this time.

"It's wobbly, but I can read it quite well," I said to Melle. "It says D. D is how you start writing Diero's name. Would you like to see how to do the rest of it?"

The little girl said nothing, but leapt up again and fetched the inkstand and the writing brush. I thanked her and carried them over to the table. I found a clean scrap of canvas and wrote out DIERO in big letters, pulled up a stool for Melle to perch on, and gave her the brush.

She did a pretty good job of copying, and was praised. "I can do it better," she said, and crouched over the table to copy again, eyebrows drawn tight together, brush held tight in the sparrow-claw hand, pink tongue clamped tight between the teeth.

Again Diero had given me back something I had lost when I left Arcamand. Her eyes were bright as she watched us.

After that I came by her apartment nearly every day

to read with her and to teach little Melle her letters. Often the child's sister was there. Irad was very shy with me at first, and I with her; she was so beautiful, so un-guarded, and so clearly Barna's property. But Diero al-ways stayed with us, protecting us both. Melle adored Diero and soon attached herself passionately to me too. She'd rush at me when I came into the room, crying, "Beaky! Beaky's here!" and strangle me with hugging when I picked her up. That made Irad begin to trust me, and talking and playing with the child put us at ease. Melle was serious, funny, and very intelligent. In Irad's fiercely protective love for her there was an ele-ment of admiration, almost awe. She would say, "Ennu sent me to look after Melle."

They each wore a tiny figure of Ennu-Mé, a crudely modeled clay cat's head, on a cord around the neck.

It wasn't hard for me to persuade Irad that learning how to read and write along with Melle was a good idea, and so she joined in the lessons. Like Diero, she was doubtful and hesitant in learning. Melle was not, and it was touching to see the little sister coaching the big one.

Lessons with the other girls in the house had never got further than half the alphabet; they always lost in-terest or were called away. The pleasure of teaching

Melle made me think I might gather some of the young children of the town into a class. I tried, but couldn't make it work. The women wouldn't trust their girls to any man; the children were needed to go into the fields with their mother, or look after their baby brother; or they were simply unable to sit still long enough to learn a lesson, and their parents had no idea why they should do so. I needed Barna's backing, his authority.

I approached him with the proposal of establishing a school, a place set aside, with regular hours. I'd teach reading and writing. To flatter his sense of superiority to me, Pulter would be asked to recite and lecture on literature. The accountant might teach a little practical arithmetic. Barna listened, nodded, and approved heartily, but when I began to suggest the place I thought suitable, he had reasons why it would not do. Finally he said, clapping me on the shoulder, "Put it off till next year, Scholar. Things are too busy now, people just can't spare the time."

"Children of six or seven can spare the time," I said.

"Kiddies that age don't want to be locked up in a classroom! They need to be running about and playing, free as birds!"

"But they aren't free as birds," I said. "They're

drudging at field work with their mothers, or lugging their baby sisters and brothers around. When are they going to learn anything else?"

"We'll see that they do. I'll talk about this with you again!" And he was off to see about the new additions to the granaries. He was indeed endlessly busy and I made allowance for it, but I was disappointed.

I made up for it to myself by offering to give talks in the room I'd hoped to use as a schoolroom. I told people I'd tell some of the history of the City States and Bendile and other lands of the Western Shore, evenings, if they wanted to come listen. I got an audience of nine or ten grown men; women didn't go in the streets at night. My hearers mostly came just to hear stories, but a couple of them took a shrewd interest in the variety of customs and beliefs, laughing heartily at outlandish ways of doing and thinking, and ready to talk about whys and wherefores. But they'd worked hard all day, and when I went on long I'd see half my audience asleep. If I were ever to educate the Forest Brothers, I'd have to catch them younger.

My failure to start a school left me all the more time to be with Diero and Melle, and I was happier with them than anywhere else. I still went about with Barna, but his interest was all in immediate projects, the new buildings and planned expansion of the community kitchens. The Heart of the Forest was rapidly becoming more prosperous as the herds and gardens thrived and the raiders brought in goods. When I talked with the netmen who went into Asion, over the weak beer in the beer house Chamry frequented, they spoke only about stealing and trading. It seemed to me they were sent out mostly to get luxuries.

Venne was back from a long trip with his group, and he and some of his mates often joined us at the beer house. He liked his work. It was exciting, and he hadn't had to shoot anybody, he said. I asked him if people outside the forest knew who they were. Over towards Piram, where he had been, he said the villagers called the raiders "Barna's boys." They were willing to barter with them, but were wary, always urging them to go on to the next town and "skin the merchants."

I asked Venne if the raiders ever talked to people about the Uprising. He'd never heard of it at all. "A revolt? Slaves? How could slaves fight? We'd have to be like an army, to do that, seems like." His ignorance made me think that only certain men were entrusted with the risky task of spreading the plans for the Uprising; but I didn't know who they were.

I asked the raiders if slaves in the villages or on the farms often asked to join them. They said sometimes a boy wanted to run off with them, but they usually wouldn't take him, for not even cattle theft roused such vengeful pursuit as slave stealing. But they all had stories about slaves who'd escaped and followed them on their own. Most of them had been such runaways themselves. "See, we knew we couldn't get into Barna's town without we went with Barna's boys," said a young man from a village on the Rassy. "And I do keep an eye out for fellows like I was."

"And that's how you get the girls you bring in too?" I asked.

That brought on laughter and a babble of stories and descriptions. Some girls were runaways, I gathered, but the raiders had to be careful about accepting them, "because they'll be followed, like as not, and not know how to hide their tracks, and likely they're with child"—and another man broke in, "It's only the pregnant and the ugly ones and maimed and harelips that tries to join us. The ones we want are kept shut up close."

"So how do you get them to join you?" I asked.

More laughter. "Same way we get the cattle and sheep to join us," said Venne's leader, a short, rather pudgy man, who Venne told me was a fine hunter and scout. "Round 'em up and drive 'em!"

"But don't touch, don't touch," said another man, "at least not the prettiest one or two. Barna likes 'em fresh."

They went on telling stories. The men who had taken Irad and Melle were there, and one of them told the tale, rather boastfully, since everybody knew Irad was Barna's favorite. "They was just out at the edge of the village, the two of 'em, in the fields, and Ater and I come by on horseback. I took one look and give Ater the wink and hopped off and grabbed the beauty, but she fought like a she-bear, I tell you. She was trying to get her hand to that knife of hers, now I know it, and lucky she didn't, or she'd have had my guts out. And the little one was jabbing at my legs with the little sharp spade she had, cutting 'em to ribbons, so Ater had to come pull her off, and he was going to toss her aside, but the two of 'em hung on to each other so tight, so I said take both the damn little bitches then, and we tied 'em up together and put 'em up in front of me on my big mare. They screeched the whole time, but we was just far enough from the houses nobody heard. That was a lucky haul, by Sampa! I doubt they missed those girls till nightfall, and by then we was halfway to the forest."

"I wouldn't want a woman that fought like that, with a knife and all," said Ater, a big, slow man. "I like 'em soft."

The conversation wandered off, as it often did in the beer house, into comparing kinds of women. Only one of the eight men around our table had a woman of his own, and he was teased remorselessly about what she did while he was off raiding. The others were talking more about what they wanted than what they had. The Heart of the Forest was still a city of men. An army camp, Barna sometimes said. The comparison was apt in many ways.

But if we were soldiers, what war were we fighting?

"He's gone off broody again," Venne said, and clucked like a hen. I realised somebody had made a joke about me and I'd missed it. They laughed, good-natured laughter. I was the Scholar, the bookish boy, and they liked me to play my absent-minded role.

I went back to Barna's house. I was to give a recital that evening. Barna was there, as always, in his big chair, but he had Irad sitting on his lap, and he fondled her as he listened to me tell a tale from the *Chamhan*.

Though he sometimes caressed his girls in public, he had always done it jokingly, calling a group of them to come around him and "keep me warm on a winter night," and inviting some of his men to "help themselves." But that was after feasting and drinking, not during a recitation. Everyone knew he was besotted by Irad, calling her to his bedroom every night, ignoring all his earlier favorites. But this crass display in public was a new thing.

Irad held perfectly still, submitting to his increasingly intimate caresses, her face blank.

I stopped before the end of the chapter. The words had dried up. I'd lost the thread of the story, and so had many of my hearers. I stood silent a minute, then bowed and stepped down.

"That's not the end, is it?" said Barna in his big voice.

I said, "No. But it seemed enough tonight. Maybe Dorremer would play for us?"

"Finish the tale!" Barna said.

But other people had begun to move about and talk, and several seconded my call for music, and Dorremer came forward with her lyre as she often did after Pulter or I recited. So it passed off, and I made my escape. I went to Diero's rooms, not my own. I was troubled and wanted to talk with her.

Melle was asleep in the bedroom. Diero was in her sitting room without any light but the moon's. It was a sweet clear night of early summer. The forest birds they called nightbells were singing away off among the trees, calling and answering, and sometimes a little owl wailed sweetly. Diero's door was open. I went in and greeted her, and we sat without talking for a while. I wanted to tell her about Barna's behavior, but I didn't want to spoil her serenity, which always quietened me. She said at last, "You're sad tonight, Gav."

I heard someone run lightly up the stairs. Irad came in. Her hair was loose and she was panting for breath. "Don't say I'm here!" she whispered, and ran out again.

Diero stood up. She was like a willow, black and silver in the moonlight. She took up the flint and steel and struck a light. The little oil lamp bloomed yellow, changing all the shadows in the room and leaving the moon's cold radiance out in the sky. I didn't want to lose our quiet mood, and was about to ask Diero, petulantly, why Irad was playing hide-and-seek. But there was the noise of heavier feet on the staircase, and now Barna stood in the doorway. His face was almost black, swollen, in the tangled mass of his hair and beard. "Where is the bitch?" he shouted. "Is she here?"

Diero looked down. Trained in submissiveness all her life, she was unable to answer him with anything but a shrinking silence. And I too shrank from the big man blind with rage.

He pushed past us, flung open the bedroom door, looked around in the bedroom, and came out again, staring at me. "You! You're after her! That's why Diero keeps her here!" He rushed at me like a great, red boar charging, his arm upraised to strike me. Diero came between us crying out his name. He knocked her aside with one hand. He seized me by the shoulders and lifted and shook me as Hoby used to do, slapped my head left and right, and threw me down.

I don't know what happened in the next minute or two. When I could sit up and see through the dazzling blackness that pulsed in my eyes, I saw Diero huddled on the floor. Barna was gone.

I managed to get to my hands and knees, then get up. I looked into the bedroom. No one was there but a tiny shadow cowering against the wall by one of the beds.

I said, "Don't be afraid, Melle, it's all right." I found it difficult to talk. My mouth was filling with blood and a couple of teeth were loose on the right side. "Diero will be here in a moment," I said.

I went back to Diero. She had sat up. The lamp was still burning. In its weak pool of light I could see that the soft skin of her cheek was bruised. I could not bear to see that. I knelt down by her.

"He found her," she whispered. "She hid in your room. He went straight there. Gav, what will you do?" She took my hand. Her hand was cold.

I shook my head, which made it ring and spin again. I kept swallowing blood.

"What will he do to her?" I said.

She shrugged.

"He's angry—he could kill her—"

"He'll hurt her. He doesn't kill women. Gav. You can't stay here."

I thought she meant this room.

"You must go. Leave! She went to your room. She didn't know where to hide. Oh, poor child. Oh, Gav! I have loved you so much!" She put her face down on my hand, weeping silently for a moment, then raised her head again. "We'll be all right. We're not men, we don't matter. But you have to go."

"I'll take you," I said. "And them—Irad and Melle—"

"No, no, no," she whispered. "Gav, he'll kill you. Go now. Now! The girls and I are safe." She got up, pulling herself up by the table, and stood shakily a minute; then she went into the bedroom. I heard her soft voice talking to the child. She came out carrying her. Melle clung to her, hiding her face.

"Melle-sweet, you must say goodbye to Gav."

The child turned and held out her arms, and I took her and held her tight. "It will be all right, Melle," I said. "Do your lessons with Diero. Promise? And help Irad with them. Then you'll both be wise." I didn't know what I was saying. I was in tears. I kissed the child and set her down. I took Diero's hand and held it against my mouth a moment, and went out.

I went to my room, belted on my knife, put on my coat, and put the small copy of the *Cosmologies* in the pocket. I looked around the little room with its one high window, the only room of my own I'd ever had.

I left Barna's house by the back way and went round through the streets to the cobblers' barrack. In the great wash of moonlight the city of wood was a city of silver-blue, shadowed, silent, beautiful.

PART THREE

◆ 11 ◆

Chamry roused up quickly when I sat down on his bunk. I told him I wanted to stay with him a while, as there'd been a misunderstanding at Barna's house. "What do you mean?" he said. He got the story out of me, though I didn't want to say much. "That girl? She was in your room? Oh by the Stone! You get clear out, clear away, tonight!"

I argued. It had merely been a misunderstanding. Barna had been drunk. But Chamry was out of bed, rummaging under the bunk. "Where's that stuff you left, your fishing gear and all— There. Knew it was here. All right. Take this stuff of yours and go to the gate. Tell the watch that you want to be at the trout pool before sunrise, it's the best fishing just at sunrise—"

"The best fishing's at sunset," I said.

He looked at me with pained disgust. Then his look sharpened. He touched my cheek. "Got a whack, did you? Lucky he didn't kill you right there. If he sees you again he will. He turns on men like that. Over women. Or somebody trying to shake his power. I've seen it. Saw him kill a man. Strangled him and broke his neck with his bare hands. You take this stuff. Here's your old blanket, take it too. Go to the gate."

I stood there blank as a post.

"Oh, I'll go with you," he said crossly. And he did walk me, hastily and by the back streets, towards the city gate, talking with me all the way, telling me what to say to the watchmen, and what to do when I was in the woods. "Don't go by the paths! Don't take any path. They're all guarded, one time or another. I wish— Yes! that's it, he can take you— Come on, this way!" He changed course, turning off on the street where Venne lived with his raiding group. He left me standing in the black shadow of the barrack and went in. I stood there looking at the silver-blue roofs, which danced a little to the throbbing in my head. Chamry came out again, with Venne. "It's hunting you're going," he said, "not fishing. Come on!"

Venne was carrying a couple of bows and had his quiver on his back. "Sorry you're in trouble, Gav," he said mildly.

I tried to explain that I wasn't in trouble, Barna had just been drunk, and all this panic was unnecessary. Chamry said, "Don't listen to him. Got his brains knocked loose. Just take him to where he can get clear away."

"I can do that," Venne said. "If they'll let us out the gate."

"Leave that to me," said Chamry. And indeed he talked us out the city gate with no trouble. Chatting with the guards, he made sure at once that Barna hadn't sent out anybody after me. The guards knew all of us, and let us go with nothing but a warning to be back by sunset. "Oh, I'll be back in no time," said Chamry. "I don't set out on hunting trips at midnight! I'm just seeing these idiots off."

He went with us till we were past the gardens and at the forest's edge. "What'll I tell them when I come back?" Venne asked.

"You lost him. At the river. Looked for him all day. He fell in, or maybe he ran off.— Think it'll do?"

Venne nodded.

"It's thin," Chamry said judiciously, "pretty thin. But I'll say I'd heard Gav talking about running off to Asion. So, he tricked you into taking him out hunting, and then gave you the slip. You'll be all right."

Venne nodded again, unworried.

Chamry turned to me. "Gav," he said, "you've been nothing but a burden and trouble to me ever since you turned up and tried to wear my kilt on your head. You dragged me back here, and now you're running out on me. Well, have a good run. Go west."

He looked for confirmation to Venne, who nodded.

"And stay out of the Uplands," Chamry said. He put his arms round me in a hard embrace, turned away, and was gone in the darkness under the trees.

Unwillingly, I followed Venne, who set off without hesitation on a path I could scarcely make out at all. The flashes of moonlight through the branches and trunks of the trees dazzled and bewildered me. I kept stumbling. Venne realised that I was having trouble and slowed down. "Fetched you a whack, eh?" he said. "Dizzy?"

I was a little dizzy, but I said it would wear off, and we went on. I was still sure that everybody had gone into a foolish panic, urging me into running away from a mere misunderstanding that could all be explained in the morning. I'd seen Barna in a rage before. His anger was mindless, brutal while it lasted, but it didn't last, it blew over like a thunderstorm. I planned that at dawn I'd tell Venne I was turning around and going back.

But as we went on at an easy pace in the cool night air and silence, my head gradually cleared. What had happened in Barna's house began to come back to me; I began to see it again. I saw Barna fondling the motionless, expressionless girl while men and women watched. I saw the terror in Irad's face when she ran to us to hide from him, and the madness in his face. I saw the dark red bruise on Diero's cheek.

Venne halted on the rocky, steep bank of a small stream to drink. I washed my face. My right ear and both cheeks were sore and swollen. A little owl wailed away off in the woods. The moon had just set.

"Let's wait here till there's a bit of light," Venne said in his low voice, and we sat there in silence. He dozed. I wet my hand and laid the cool of it against my swollen ear and temples again and again. I looked into the darkness. I cannot say how my mind moved in that darkness, but as the trees and their leaves and the rocks of the stream bank and the movement of the water began mysteriously to take on being in the grey dim beginning of the light, I knew, with a certainty beyond decision, that I could not go back to Barna's house.

The only emotion I felt was shame. For him, for myself. Again I had trusted, and again I had betrayed and been betrayed.

Venne sat up and rubbed his eyes.

"I'll go on," I said. "You don't have to come farther."

"Well," he said, "my story is you gave me the slip, so I've got to spend all day pretending to look for you. And I want to get you on far enough they won't catch you."

"They won't be looking for me."

"Can't be sure of that."

"Barna won't want me back."

"He might want to finish knocking your brains out." Venne stood up and stretched. I looked up at him with a melancholy fondness, the slender, scarred, soft-voiced hunter who had always been a kind companion. I wished I could be certain he would not get into trouble with Barna for abetting my escape.

"I'll go on west," I said. "You circle round and come back from the north, so if they do send out after me you can send them off the wrong way. Go on now so you have time to do that."

He insisted on coming with me till he could get me on a path that would take me out of the Daneran Forest, to the west road. "I've seen you going in circles in the woods!" he said. And he gave me many instructions: not to light a fire till I was clear out of the woods, to remember that at this time of the year the sun set well south of west, and so on. He fretted that I had no food with me. As we went along, on no path at all but through fairly open oak woods, he kept looking at every hump and hillock in the ground, and eventually pounced on a heap of brush and trashwood, tore it open, and laid bare a wood rat's granary: a couple of handfuls of little wild walnuts and acorns. "Acorns'll give you the pip, but better than nothing," he said. "And over by the west road there's a big stand of sweet chestnuts. You might find some still on the trees. Keep an eye out. Once you're out of the forest, you'll have to beg or steal. But you've done that before, eh?"

We came at last to the path he was looking for, a clear wood road that curved right off to the west. There I insisted that he turn back. It was late morning already. I was going to shake his hand, but he embraced me, hard, as Chamry had done. He muttered, "Luck go with you, Gav. I won't forget you. Or your stories. Luck go with you!"

He turned away, and in a moment was gone among the shadows of the trees.

That was a bleak moment.

At this time yesterday I'd been at the food handout in Barna's house with a cheerful group of men and women, looking forward to reciting for Barna in the evening…Barna's scholar. Barna's pet…

I sat down on the edge of the wood road and took stock of what I had. Shoes, trousers, shirt, and coat; the old ragged evil-smelling brown wool blanket, my fishing gear, a pocket full of nuts stolen from a wood rat, a good knife, and Caspro's *Cosmologies*.

And all my life in Arcamand, and in the forest. Every book I had read, every person I had known, every mistake I had made—I brought that with me, this time. I will not run away from it, I said to myself. Never again. It comes with me. All of it.

And where should I take it?

The only answer I had was the road I was on. It would lead me to the Marshes. To where Sallo and I had been born. To the only people in the world I might

belong to. I'll bring you back your stolen children, or
one of them anyway, I said in my mind to the people of
the Marshes, trying to be jaunty and resolute. I got up
and set out walking west.

◆ ◆ ◆

WHEN I WENT UP the riverbank away from Etra, I
was a boy dressed in white mourning, going alone, a
strange sight in itself; and people could tell that I was
not in my right mind. That had protected me. The mad
are holy. Now, walking along this lonely forest road, I
was two years older and looked and dressed like what I
was: a runaway. If I met people, my only protection
from suspicion or from slave takers was in my own wits,
and from Luck, who might be getting tired of looking
after me.

The road would bring me out on the west side of
the Daneran Forest, and going on west or southwest I'd
come to the Marshes. I didn't know what villages might
be on my way; I was sure there were no towns of any
size. I had seen the country where I now was, from far
off, long ago, in the golden evening light, from the summit of the Ventine Hills. It had looked very empty. I
remembered the great blurred shadow of the forest

eastward, and the level, open lands stretching north. Sallo and I had gazed for a long time. Sotur asked us if we could remember the Marshes, and I spoke of my memory of the water and the reeds and the blue hill far off, but Sallo said we'd both been too young to remember anything. So that memory must be the other kind I used to have, a memory of what had not happened yet.

It had been a long time since I had such a vision. When I left Etra I left my past behind me, and with it, the future. For a long time I'd lived in the moment only—until this past winter, with Diero, when I finally had the courage to look back, and take back again the gift and burden of all I'd lost. But the other, the visions and glimpses of time to come, it seemed I'd lost forever.

Maybe it was living among the trees, I thought as I walked along the forest road. The infinite trunks and tangling, shadowing branches of the forest kept the eye from seeing far ahead in space or in time. Out in the open, in the level lands, between the blue water and blue sky, maybe I'd be able to look forward again, to see far. Hadn't Sallo told me long ago, sitting close beside me on the schoolroom bench, that that was a power I had from our people?

"Don't talk about it," says her small, soft voice, warm in my ear. "Gavir, listen, truly, you mustn't talk about it to anybody."

And I never had. Not among our captors, our masters in Arcamand, who had no such powers, who feared them and would not understand. Not among the escaped slaves in the forest, for there I had had no visions of the future, only Barna's dreams and plans of revolution and liberation. But if I could go among my own people, a free people, without masters or slaves, maybe I'd find others with such powers, and they could teach me how to bring back those visions, and learn the use of them.

Such thoughts buoyed my spirits. I was in fact glad to be alone again at last. It seemed to me now that all the year I was with Barna, his great, jovial voice had filled my head, controlling my thoughts, ruling my judgment. The power of his being was in itself like a spell, leaving me only corners of my own being, where I hid in shadow. Now, as I walked away from him, my mind could range freely back over all my time in the Heart of the Forest, and with Brigin's band, and before that, with Cuga, the old mad hermit who had saved the mad boy from death by starvation....But that thought brought me sharply back to the present moment. I hadn't eaten since last night. My stomach was beginning to call for dinner, and a pocket full of walnuts wasn't going to take me far. I decided I wouldn't eat any until I reached the end of the forest. There I'd have a wood-rat banquet and decide what to do next.

It was still only mid-afternoon when the road came out through a thin stand of alders to meet another, larger road that ran north and south. There were cart ruts on it left from the last rains, many sheep tracks, and some horseshoe tracks, though it lay empty as far as I could see. Across it was open country, scrubby and nondescript, with a few stands of trees.

I sat down behind a screen of bushes and solemnly cracked and ate ten of my walnuts. That left me twenty-two, and nine acorns, which I kept only as a last resort. I got up, faced left, and walked boldly down the road.

My mind was busy with what I might tell any carter or drover or horseman who overtook me. I decided the one thing I had that might show me as something more than a runaway slave boy was the little book I carried in my pouch. I was a scholar's slave, sent from Asion to carry this book to a scholar in Etra, who was ill and wished to read it before he died, and had begged his friend in Asion to send it to him, with a boy who could read it to him, for his eyes were failing. . . . I worked on the story diligently for miles. I was so lost in it I didn't even see the farm cart that turned from a side track into the road a little way behind me until the jingle of harness and the clop-clop of big hoofs woke me up. The horse's enormous, mild-eyed face was practically looking over my shoulder.

"Howp," said the driver, a squat man with a wide face, looking me over with no expression at all on his face.

I mumbled some kind of greeting.

"Hop up," the man said more distinctly. "Good ways yet to the crossroads."

I scrambled up onto the seat. He studied me some more. His eyes were remarkably small, like seeds in his big loaf of a face.

"You'll be going to Shecha," he said, as an inarguable fact.

I agreed with him. It seemed the best thing to do.

"Don't see you folk much on the road no more," the driver said. And at that I realised that he had taken me for—that he had recognised me as—one of the Marsh people. I didn't need my complicated story. I wasn't a runaway, but a native.

It was just as well. This fellow might not have known what a book was.

All the slow miles to the crossroads, through the late afternoon and the immense gold-and-purple sunset, he told me a tale about a farmer and his uncle and some hogs and a piece of land beside Rat Water and an injustice that had been done. I never understood any of it, but I could nod and grunt at the right moments, which was what he wanted. "Always like talking with you folk," he said when he dropped me off at the crossroads. "Keep your counsel, you do. There's Shecha road."

I thanked him and set off into the dusk. The side road led off southwest. If Shecha was a place of the Marsh people, I might as well go there.

After a while I stopped and cracked all the rest of the walnuts between two stones, and ate them one by one as I went on, for my hunger had grown painful.

Evening was darkening when I saw a glimmer of lights ahead. As I came closer, the shining of water reflected the last light in the sky. I came through a cow pasture to a tiny village on the shore of a lake. The houses were built up on stilts, and some stood right out over the water at the end of piers; there were boats docked, which I could not make out clearly. I was very tired and very hungry and the yellow glimmer of a lighted window was beautiful in the late dusk. I went to that house, climbed the wooden stairs to the narrow porch, and looked in the open door. It seemed to be an inn or beer house, windowless, with a low counter, but no furniture at all. Four or five men sat on a rug on the floor with clay cups in their hands. They all looked at me and then looked away so as not to stare.

"Well, come in, boy," one said. They were dark-skinned, slight, short men, all of them. A woman behind the counter turned around, and I saw old Gammy, the piercing bright dark eyes, the eagle nose. "Where d'you come from?" she said.

"The forest." My voice came out as a hoarse whisper. Nobody said anything. "I'm looking for my people."

"Who are they then?" the woman asked. "Come in!" I came in, looking hangdog, no doubt. She slapped something on a plate and shoved it across the counter towards me.

"I don't have money," I said.

"Eat it," she said crossly. I took the plate and sat

down with it on a seat by the unlighted hearth. It was
a kind of cold fish fritter, I think, quite a large one, but
it was gone before I knew what it was.

"Who's your people, then?"

"I don't know."

"Makes it a bit hard to find 'em," one of the men
suggested. They kept looking at me, not with a steady
stare or with hostility, but covertly studying the new
thing that had come their way. The instant disappear-
ance of the fritter had caused some silent amusement.

"Around here?" another man asked, rubbing his bald
head.

"I don't know. We were stolen—my sister and I.
Slave raiders from Etra. South of here, maybe."

"When was that?" the innkeeper asked in her sharp
voice.

"Fourteen or fifteen years ago."

"He's a runaway slave, is he?" the oldest of the men
murmured to the one next to him, uneasy.

"So you was a little tad," said the innkeeper, filling a
clay cup with something and bringing it to me. "What
name had you?"

"Gavir. My sister was Sallo."

"No more than that?"

I shook my head.

"How'd you chance to be in the forest?" the bald man asked, mildly enough, but it was a hard question and he knew it.

I hesitated a little and said, "I was lost."

To my surprise, they accepted that as an answer, at least for the moment. I drank the cup of milk the woman had given me. It tasted sweet as honey.

"What other names do you remember?" the woman asked.

I shook my head. "I was one or two years old."

"And your sister?"

"She was a year or two older."

"And she's a slave in Etra?" She pronounced it "Ettera."

"She's dead." I looked around at them, the dark, alert faces. "They killed her," I said. "That's why I ran away."

"Ah, ah," said the bald man. "Ah, well...And how long ago was that?"

"Two years ago."

He nodded, exchanging glances with a couple of the others.

"Here, give the boy something better than cow piss, Bia," said the oldest man, who had a toothless grin and looked a little simple. "I'll stand him a beer."

"Milk's what he needs," said the innkeeper, pouring my cup full again. "If that was beer he'd be flat on his face."

"Thank you, ma-ío," I said, and drank the milk down gratefully.

The honorific, I think, made her give a rasp of a laugh. "City tongue, but you're a Rassiu," she observed.

"So they're not on your trail, so far as you know," the bald man asked me. "Your city masters, down there."

"I think they think I drowned," I said.

He nodded.

My weariness, the food filling my hunger, their wary kindness and cautious acceptance of me as what I was—and maybe my having to say that Sallo had been killed—it all worked on me to bring tears into my eyes. I stared at the ashes in the hearth as if a fire was burning there, trying to hide my weakness.

"Looks like a southerner," one of the men murmured, and another, "I knew a Sallo Evo Danaha down at Crane Levels."

"Gavir and Sallo are Sidoyu names," the bald man said. "I'm off to bed, Bia. I'll set off before dawn. Pack us up a dinner, eh? Come along south with me if you like, Gavir."

The woman sent me upstairs after him to the common sleeping room of the inn. I lay down in my old blanket on a cot and fell asleep like a rock dropping into black water.

The bald man shook me awake in the dark. "Coming?" he said, and I struggled up and got my gear and followed him. I had no idea where he was going or why or how, only that he was going south, and his invitation was my guidance.

A tiny oil lamp burned in the room downstairs. The innkeeper, who stood behind the counter as if she had stood there all night long, handed him a large packet wrapped in something like oiled silk, took his quarter-bronze, and said, "Go with Mé, Ammeda."

"With Mé," he said. I followed him out into the dark and down to the waterside. He went to a boat, which looked immense to me, tied up to a pier. He untied the rope and dropped down into the boat as casually as stepping down a stair. I clambered in more cautiously, but in a hurry, as it was already drifting from the pier. I crouched in the back end of the boat, and he came and went past me doing mysterious things in the dark. The gold spark of the inn doorway was already far behind us over the black water and fainter than the reflections of the stars. He had raised a sail on the short mast in the middle of the boat, not much of a sail, but it took the slight wind and we moved steadily on. I began to get used to the strange sensation of walking while floating, and by the time there was some light in the sky I could move around well enough, if I hung on to things.

The boat was narrow and quite long, decked, with a low rope rail all round; the whole middle of it was a long, low house.

"Do you live on the boat?" I asked Ammeda, who had sat down in the stern by the tiller and was gazing off over the water at the growing light in the east.

He nodded and said something like "Ao." After a while he remarked, "You fish."

"I have some gear."

"Saw that. Give it a try."

I was glad to be of use. I got out my hooks and lines and the light pole that Chamry had taught me how to make in fitted sections. Ammeda offered no bait, and I had nothing but my acorns. I stuck the wormiest one on the barb of a hook, feeling foolish, and sat with my legs over the side trailing the line. To my surprise, I got a bite within a minute, and pulled up a handsome reddish fish.

Ammeda gutted, split, and boned the fish with a wicked, delicate knife, sprinkled something from his pouch on it, and offered me half. I'd never eaten raw fish, but ate it without hesitation. It was delicate and sweet, and the spice he'd put on it was ground horse-radish. The hot taste took me back to the forest, a year ago, digging horseradish roots with Chamry Bern.

My other acorns wouldn't stay on the hook. Ammeda had kept the fish guts on a leaf of what looked like paper. He gave them to me as bait. I caught two more of the reddish fish, and we ate them the same way.

"They eat their kind," he said. "Like men."

"Looks like they'll eat anything," I said. "Like me."

Always when I'm hungry, I crave the grain porridge of Arcamand, thick and nutty, seasoned with oil and dried olives, and I did then; but I was feeling very much better with a pound or two of fish in my belly. The sun had come up and was warming my back deliciously. Small waves slipped by the sides of the boat. Ahead of us and all around us was bright water, dotted here and there with low islands of reeds. I lay back on the deck and fell asleep.

We sailed all that day down the long lake. The next day, as its shores drew together, we entered a maze of channels between high reeds and rushes, lanes of blue-silver water widening and narrowing between walls of pale green and dun, endlessly repeated, endlessly the same. I asked Ammeda how he knew his way and he said, "The birds tell me."

Hundreds of small birds flitted about above the rushes; ducks and geese flew overhead, and tall silver-grey herons and smaller white cranes stalked the margins of the reed islets. To some of these Ammeda spoke as if in salutation, saying the word or name *Hassa*.

He asked me no more about myself than he had the first night, and he told me nothing about himself. He was not unfriendly, but he was deeply silent.

The sun shone clear all day, the waning moon at night. I watched the summer stars, the stars I'd watched at the Vente farm, rise and slide across the vault of the dark. I fished, or sat in the sunlight and gazed at the ever-differing sameness of channels and reed beds, the blue water and the blue sky. Ammeda steered the boat. I went into the house and found it almost filled with cargo, mostly stacks and bundles of large sheets of a paperlike substance, some thin, some thick, but very tough. Ammeda told me it was reedcloth, made from beaten reeds, and used for everything from dishes and clothing to house walls. He carried it from the southern and western marshes, where it was made, to other parts, where people would pay or barter for it. Barter had filled his house with oddments—pots and pans, sandals, some pretty woven belts and cloaks, clay jugs of oil, and a large supply of ground horseradish. I gathered that he used or traded these things as he pleased. He kept his money—quarter- and half-bronzes and a few silver bits—in a brass bowl in the corner of the structure, with no effort to conceal it. This, and the behavior of the people at the inn at Shecha, gave me an idea that the people of the Marsh were singularly unsuspicious or unafraid, either of strangers or of one another.

I knew, I knew all too well, that I was prone to put too much trust in people. I wondered if the fault was inborn, a characteristic, like my dark skin and hawk nose. Overtrustful, I had let myself be betrayed, and so had betrayed others. Maybe I had come to the right place at last, among people like me, who would meet trust with trust.

There was time for my mind to wander among such thoughts and hopes in the long days of sunlight on the water, and to think back, too. Whenever I thought of my year in the Heart of the Forest, I heard Barna's voice, his deep, resonant voice, ringing out, talking and talk-ing…and the silence of the marshes, the silence of my companion, were a blessing, a release.

The last evening of my journey with Ammeda, I'd fished all day and had a fine catch ready. He lighted and tended a fire of charcoal in a big ceramic pot with a grill over the top of it set out on the deck in the lee of the house. Seeing me watching him, he said, "You know I have no village." I had no idea what he meant or why he said it, and merely nodded, waiting for more; but he said no more. He spattered the fish with oil and a few grains of salt and broiled them. They were succulent. After we ate he brought out a pottery jug and two tiny cups and poured us what he called ricegrass wine, clear and very strong. We sat in the stern. The boat was mov-ing slowly down a wide channel. He did nothing to catch the wind, but only touched the tiller now and then to keep the course. A clear blue-green-bronze dusk lay over the water and the reeds. We saw the eve-ning star tremble like a drop of water low in the west.

"The Sidoyu," Ammeda said. "They live near the border. Slave takers come through there. Could be that's where you come from. Stay if you like. Look around. I'll be back through in a couple of months." After a pause he added, "Been wanting a fisherman."

I realised that he was saying in his laconic way that if I wanted to rejoin him then, I was welcome.

Next morning at sunrise we were again in open water. After an hour or two we approached a solid shore where some trees grew and little stilted houses stood up over the banks. I heard children shouting. A small mob of them were on the pier to meet the boat. "Women's village," Ammeda said. I saw that the adults following the children were all women, dark, thin-limbed, in brief tunics, with short curling hair like Sallo's hair—and I saw Sallo's eyes, I saw her face, glimpses, flashes of her everywhere among them. It was strange, troubling, to see these strangers, these sisters all about me.

As soon as we tied up at the pier, the women were scrambling over the boat, peering at what Ammeda had to offer, feeling the reedcloths, sniffing the oil jars, chattering away to him and to one another. They didn't speak to me, but a boy of ten or so came up, stood in front of me with his feet apart, and said importantly, "Who are you, stranger?"

I said, with a rush of absurd hope of being instantly recognised, "My name is Gavir."

The boy waited a moment and then asked rather pompously, as if offended, "Gavir—?"

It seemed I needed more names than I had.

"Your clan!" the boy demanded.

A woman came and pulled him away without ceremony. Ammeda said to her and an older woman with her, "He was taken as a slave. Maybe from the Sidoyu."

"Ah," the older woman said. Turning sideways to me, not looking at me, but unmistakably speaking to me, she asked, "When were you taken?"

"About fifteen years ago," I said, the foolish hope rising in me again.

She thought, shrugged, and said, "Not from here. You don't know your clan?"

"No. There were two of us. My sister Sallo and I."

"Sallo is my name," the woman said in an indifferent voice. "Sallo Issidu Assa."

"I am seeking my people, my name, ma-ío," I said.

I saw the sidelong, flashing glance of her eye, though she stayed turned half from me. "Try Ferusi," she said. "The soldiers used to take people from down there."

"How will I come to Ferusi?"

"Overland," Ammeda said. "Walk south. You can swim the channels."

While I turned to get my gear together, he talked with Sallo Issidu Assa. He told me to wait for her while she went into the village. She came back with a reed-cloth packet and laid it on the deck beside me. "Food," she said in the same indifferent tone, her face turned from me.

I thanked her and stowed the packet in my old blanket, which I had washed out and dried on the journey through the marshes, and which served as a backpack. I turned to Ammeda to thank him again, and he said, "With Mé."

"With Mé," I said.

I started to hop off the pier onto the ground, but a couple of women called out a sharp warning, and the officious boy came rushing to block my way. "Women's ground, women's ground!" he shouted. I looked about not knowing where to go. Ammeda pointed me to the right, where I made out a path marked with stones and clamshells right at the edge of the water. "Men go that way," he said. So I went that way.

Within a very short distance the path led me to another village. I was uneasy about approaching it, but nobody shouted at me to keep away, and I went in among the little houses. An old man was sunning himself on the porch of his house, which seemed to be built of heavy reedcloth mats hung on a wooden frame. "With Mé, young fellow," he said.

I returned the greeting and asked him, "Is there a road south from here, ba-dí?"

"Badí, badí, what's badí? I am Rova Issidu Meni. Where do you come from, with your badí-badí? I'm not your father. Who is your father?"

He was more teasing than aggressive. I had the feeling he knew the salutation I had used perfectly well, but didn't want to admit it. His hair was white and his face had a thousand wrinkles.

"I'm looking for my father. And my mother. And my name."

"Ha! Well!" He looked me over. "Why d'you want to go south?"

"To find the Ferusi."

"Ach! They're a queer lot. I wouldn't go there. Go there if you like. The path goes through the pasture." And he settled back down, stretching his little, black, bony legs, like crane's legs, out in the sun.

No one else seemed to be in the village; I could see fishing boats out on the water. I found the path leading inland through the pasture and set off south to find my people.

◆ 12 ◆

It was a two days' walk to Ferusi. The path meandered a great deal but tended always south, as well as I could tell by having the sun on my left in the morning and on my right at sunset. There were many channels through the grasslands and willow meads to wade or swim, holding my pack and shoes up out of the water on a stick, but it was easy walking otherwise, and my supply of dried fish cakes and salted cheese lasted me well enough. From time to time I saw the smoke of a cabin or a village off to one side or another and a side path leading to it, but the main way kept on, and I kept on it. So late on the second day the path turning left along the sandy shore of a great lake led me to a village—pastures with a few cows, a few willows, a few little houses up on stilts, a few boats at the piers. Everything in the Marshes repeated itself with a slightly varied sameness, an extreme simplicity.

There were no children around the village, and I saw a man spreading out a fishing net, so I walked on between the houses and called to him, "Is this Ferusi?"

He laid the net down carefully and came towards me. "This is East Lake Village of Ferusi," he said.

He listened gravely as I told him the quest I was on. He was thirty or so, the tallest man I'd seen among the Rassiu, and his eyes were grey; I knew later that he was the son of a Marsh woman raped by an Etran soldier. When I told him my name he said his, Rava Attiu Sidoy, and courteously invited me to his house and table. "The fishermen are coming back now," he said, "and we'll go to the fish-mat. Come with us and you can ask your question of the women. It's the women who will know."

Boats were coming in to the piers and unloading their catch, a dozen or more light boats with small sails that made me think of moth wings. The village began to come alive with the voices of men, and dogs, too. Dogs came leaping out of the boats to prance ashore through shallow water, slender black dogs with tight-curled coats and large bright eyes. The manners of these dogs were quite formal: they greeted one another with a single bark, each investigated the other's other end while tail-wagging vigorously, one of them bowed and the other accepted the bow, and then they parted, each following its master. One of the dogs carried a large dead bird, a swan perhaps; it went through no ceremonies with other dogs but trotted off importantly along the beach westward with its bird. And quite soon all the men followed it, carrying their catch in nets and baskets. Rava brought me along with them. Around a grassy headland, in a little cove, we came to the women's village of East Lake.

A number of women were waiting in a meadow at a large sheet of reedcloth spread out on the ground. A lot of children ran about the edges, but were careful not to set a foot on the cloth. Pots and reedcloth boxes full of cooked food were set out as if at a market. The men set down and displayed their catch on the cloth in the same way, and the dog laid the bird down and stood back wagging its tail. There was a lot of talking and joking, but it was unmistakably a formal occasion, a ceremony, and when a man came forward to take a box or pot of food, or a woman to pick up a net bag of fish, they said a ritual phrase of thanks. An old woman pounced on the swan, shouting, "Kora's arrow!" and that brought on more joking and teasing. The women seemed to know exactly which catch went to which woman; the men did a little more discussing over who got what, but the women mostly made it clear, and when two young men had an argument over a box of fritters a woman settled it by nodding at one of the rivals. The one who didn't get them went off sulkily. When everything had been picked up, Rava brought me forward and said to the women in general, "This man came to the village today, looking for his people. He was taken to Ettera by the soldiers as a young child. He knows his name only as Gavir. People in the north thought he might be a Sidoyu."

At that all the women came forward to stare at me, and a sharp-eyed, sharp-nosed, dark-skinned woman of forty or so asked, "How many years ago?"

"About fifteen, ma-ío," I said. "I was taken with my older sister Sallo."

An old woman cried out—"Tano's children!"

"Sallo and Gavir!" said a woman with a baby in her arms, and the old woman carrying the dead swan by its large black feet pushed up close to study me and said, "Yes. Her children, Tano's children. Ennu-Amba, Ennu-Mé!"

"Tano went for blackfern, down the Long Channel," one of the women said to me. "She and the children. They didn't come back. Nobody found the boat."

"Some said she drowned," another woman said, and another, "I always said it was the slave takers," and the older women pressed forward still closer to look at me, looking in me for the woman they had known. The young women stood back, eyeing me in a different way.

The dark woman who had spoken to me first had said nothing and had not come forward. The old woman with the swan went and talked to her, and then the dark one came close enough to say to me, "Tano Aytano Sidoy was my younger sister. I am Gegemer Aytano Sidoy." Her face was grim and she spoke harshly.

I was daunted, but after a minute I said, "Will you tell me my name, Aunt?"

"Gavir Aytana Sidoy," she said, almost impatiently. "Did your mother—your sister—come back with you?"

"I never knew my mother. We were slaves in Etra. They killed my sister two years ago. I left and went to the Daneran Forest." I spoke briefly and said "left," not "escaped" or "ran away," because I needed to speak like a man, not like a runaway child, to this woman with her crow's face and crow's eyes.

She looked at me briefly, intensely, but did not meet my gaze. She said at last, "The Aytanu men will look after you," and turned away.

The other women clearly wanted to keep looking at me and talking about me, but they followed my aunt's lead. The men were beginning to straggle back to their village. So I turned and followed them.

Rava and a couple of older men were having a discussion. I couldn't follow all they said; the Sidoyu dialect was strange to my ears and contained a lot of words I didn't know. They seemed to be talking about where I belonged, and finally one of them turned back and said to me, "Come."

I followed him to his cabin, which was wood-framed, with a wooden floor, and walls and roof of reedcloth. It had no door or windows, since you could open up a whole side of it by raising any of the walls. Having put away the box and clay pot of food which he'd got from the women, the man raised the wall that faced the lake and tied it up on posts so that it extended the roof, shading that part of the deck from the hot late-afternoon sunlight. There he sat down on a thick reedcloth mat and set to work on a half-made fish hook of clamshell. Not looking up at me, he gestured to the house and said, "Take what you like."

I felt intrusive and out of place, and did not want to take anything at all. I did not understand these people. If I was truly a lost child of the village, was this all the welcome they had for me? I was bitterly disappointed, but I wasn't going to show any disappointment, any weakness to these coldhearted strangers. I would keep my dignity, and act as standoffish as they did. I was a city man, an educated man; they were barbarians, lost in their marshes. I told myself that I'd come a long way to get here and might as well stay the night at least. Long enough to decide where else I might go, in a world where evidently I belonged nowhere.

I found another mat and sat down on the outer edge of the deck. My feet dangled a couple of inches above the mud of the lakeshore. After a while I said, "May I know the name of my host?"

"Metter Aytana Sidoy," he said. His voice was very soft.

"Would you be my father?"

"I would be the younger brother of that one, your aunt," he said.

The way he spoke, keeping his face down, made me suspect that he was not so much unfriendly as very shy. Since he didn't look at me, I felt I shouldn't stare too much at him, but from the corner of my eye I could tell he didn't look much like the crow woman, my aunt, or like me.

"And of my mother?"

He nodded. One deep nod.

At that I had to look round at him. Metter was younger than Gegemer by a good deal, and not so dark and sharp-faced; in fact he looked something like Sallo, round-cheeked, with clear brown skin. Maybe that was what my mother Tano had looked like.

He would have been about the age I was now when his sister disappeared with her two little children.

After a long time I said, "Uncle."

He said, "Ao."

"Am I to live here?"

"Ao."

"With you?"

"Ao."

"I will have to learn how to live here. I don't know how you live."

"Anh," he said.

I would soon be familiar with these grunted or murmured responses: *ao* for yes, *eng* for no, and *anh* for anything between yes and no, but having the general meaning: I heard what you said.

Another voice made itself heard: *mao!* A small black cat appeared from a heap of something in the darkness of the hut, came across the deck, and sat down beside me, decorously curling its tail round its front paws. Presently I gave its back a tentative stroke. It leaned up into my hand, so I continued stroking it. It and I gazed out across the lake. A couple of the black fishing-dogs ran past on the lakeshore; the cat ignored them. My uncle Metter was, I noticed, looking at the cat instead of bending industriously over his work. His face had relaxed.

"Prut's a good mouser," my uncle said.

I kneaded the nape of the cat's neck. Prut purred.

After a while Metter said, "Mice are thick this year."

I scratched behind Prut's ears and wondered if I should tell my uncle that for one summer of my life I had eaten mice as a major part of my diet. It seemed unwise. Nobody had yet asked me anything about where I came from.

No one in Ferusi ever would. I had been in "Ettera"— where the slave takers came from, the robbing, raping, murdering, child-stealing soldiers. That was all they needed to know. I'd been elsewhere. They didn't want to know about elsewhere. Not many people do.

It wasn't easy for me to ask them about Ferusi, not that they didn't know all about it or didn't want to talk about it, but because it was their entire universe and was therefore taken for granted. They could not understand the kind of questions I asked. How could anybody not know the name of the lake? Why would anybody ask why men and women lived separately— surely no one could think they should live shamelessly in the same village, the same house? How could anybody possibly be ignorant of the evening worship or the words to say when giving or receiving food? How could a man not know how to cut reedgrass or a woman not know how to pound it to make reedcloth? I soon learned that I was more ignorant here than I'd been even my first winter in the forest, for there was a lot more to be ignorant of. City people might say that the Sidoyu were simple people, living a simple life; but I think only a life as solitary, poor, and crude as Cuga's could be called simple, and even so the word belies it. In the villages of the Sidoyu existence was full, rich, elaborate, a tapestry of demanding relationships, choices, obligations, and rules. To live as a Sidoy was as complex and subtle a business as to live as an Etran; to live rightly as either was, perhaps, equally difficult.

My uncle Metter had taken me into his house without any show of welcome, certainly, but without the least reluctance; he was quite ready to be fond of his long-lost nephew. He was a mild, modest, gentle man, embedded contentedly in the village network of duties and habits and relations like a bee in a hive or a swallow in a colony of mud nests. He wasn't very highly considered by the other men, but didn't mind, not being restless or rivalrous. He had several wives, and that did earn him respect, though any relationship with women was of course set apart from the rest of a man's life....But if I try to tell what I learned about living as a Sidoy as I learned it—slowly, in fragments, by guesswork—my story will go on and on. I must explain what I can while I get on with what happened.

What happened was that I ate a good supper of cold fish cakes and ricegrass wine with my uncle, his cat Prut, and his dog Minki, a kind old bitch who showed up just in time for her supper. She put her greying muzzle on my palm very politely. I watched my uncle dance and speak a brief worship to the Lord of the Waters on the deck of his hut in the twilight, as other men were doing on the decks of their huts in the twilight, and then he unrolled a bed mat for himself and helped me lay out the sitting mats as my bed. The cat went mousing underneath the hut, and the dog curled up on her master's mat as soon as he unrolled it. We lay down, said good night, and went to sleep while the last gleam of daylight was fading from the water of the lake.

Before sunrise the men of the village went out on the lake, one or two of them to a boat, with a dog or two. Metter told me that this was the season for great numbers of a fish called tuta to come into the lake from the seaward channels, and they hoped this morning might begin the run. If so, I gathered they'd be working hard for a month or so in both villages, the men catching fish and the women drying them. I asked if I could come with him and begin to learn how they fished. He was the sort of man who finds it impossible to say no. He hemmed and mumbled. Somebody was coming that I should talk to, was all I could understand.

"Is it my father who is coming?" I asked.

"Your father? Metter Sodia, you mean? Oh, he went north after Tano was lost," Metter said rather vaguely. I tried to ask but all he would say was, "Nobody ever heard about him again."

He got away as soon as he could and left me alone in the village—with the cats. Every house had its black cat, or several of them. When the men and dogs were gone, the cats ruled, lying about on the decks, wandering over the roofs, having hissing matches between houses, bringing kittens out to play in the sun. I sat and watched cats, and though the kittens made me laugh, I felt my heart very heavy. I knew now that Metter meant no unkindness. But I had come home to my people, and they were utterly strange to me, and I a stranger to them.

I could see the fishing boats away off on the lake, the tiny wings of the sails on the silken blue water.

A boat was coming towards the village. It was a big canoe, several men paddling hard. The canoe slid up to the muddy shore, the men leapt out, drew it up farther, and then came directly to me. Their faces were painted, I thought, then saw it was tattooing: all had many lines drawn from temple to jaw, and an older man's whole forehead to the eyebrows was covered with vertical black lines, as was the top of his nose, so that he looked like a heron with a head dark above and light below. They walked with stately dignity. One of them carried a stick with a great plume of white egret feathers on top of it.

They halted in front of the deck of Metter's cabin and the older man said, "Gavir Aytana Sidoy."

I stood up and reverenced them.

The older man made a long statement which I did not understand a word of. They waited a moment, and then he said to the man with the stick, "He hasn't had any of the training."

They conferred for a while, and the man with the stick turned to me. "You will come with us for your initiation," he said. I must have looked blank. "We are the elders of your clan, the Aytanu Sidoyu," he said. "Only we can make you a man, so that you can do a man's work. You've had no training, but do your best, and we'll show you what to do."

"You can't stay as you are," the older man said. "Not among us. An uninitiated man is a danger to his village and a disgrace to his clan. The claw of Ennu-Amba is against him and the herds of Sua flee from him. So. Come." He turned away.

I stepped down from the deck among them, and the man with the stick touched my head with the egret plume. He didn't smile, but I felt his good will. The others were cold, stern, formal. They closed in round me and we went to the canoe, got in, pushed off. "Lie down," Egret Plume murmured to me. I lay down between the rowers' feet, and could see nothing but the bottom of the canoe. It too was made of reedcloth, I realised, heavy strips laminated across and across and stiffened with a translucent varnish till it was smooth and hard as metal.

Out in mid-lake the rowers lifted their paddles. The canoe hung in the silence of the water. In that silence, a man began to chant. Again the words were completely incomprehensible. I think now that they may have been in Aritan, the ancient language of our people, preserved over the centuries in the ritual of the Marsh dwellers, but I don't know. The chanting went on a long time, sometimes one voice, sometimes several, while I lay still as a corpse. I was half in a trance when Egret Plume whispered to me, "Can you swim?" I nodded. "Come up on the other side," he whispered. And then I was being picked up by several men as if I were indeed a corpse, swung high up into the air, and thrown right out of the boat headfirst.

It was all so sudden that I didn't know what had happened. Coming up and shaking the water out of my eyes, I saw the side of the canoe looming above me. "Come up on the other side," he'd said—so I dived right down and swam under the huge shadow of the canoe, coming up again gasping just outside its shadow in the water. There I trod water and stared at the canoe full of men. Egret Plume was shaking his feathered stick and shouting "Hiyi! Hiyi!" He reversed the stick and held out the plain end to me. I grabbed it and he hauled me in to the side of the canoe, where several hands pulled me aboard. The instant I sat up, something was jammed down over my head—a wooden box? I couldn't move my head inside it, and it came right down onto my shoulders. I could see nothing but the gleam of light from below my chin. Egret Plume was shouting "Hiyi!" again and there was some laughter and congratulation among the others. Whatever had happened apparently had happened the right way. I sat on a thwart with my head in a box and did not try to make sense out of anything.

I've told this much of the initiation because it isn't secret; anybody can see it. The fishermen out on the lake had gathered near the war canoe to watch. But once I had the box on my head, we steered straight for the village where the secret rites were held.

Ferusi was five villages: the one where I was born, East Lake, and four others strung out within a few miles along the shores of Lake Feru. They took me for initiation to South Shore, the largest village, where the sacred things were kept. The big canoes were called war canoes not because the Marsh people ever fought a war either against others or among themselves, but because men like to think of themselves as warriors, and only men paddled the big canoes. The box on my head was a mask. While I wore the mask I was called the Child of Ennu. To the Rassiu the cat goddess Ennu-Mé is also Ennu-Amba, the black lion of the Marshes. I can't tell more of the rites of initiation, but when they were all done I had a fine black line tattooed from the hair above my temple down to my jaw, one on each side. I am so dark-skinned the lines are hard to see. Once I was initiated and came back to East Lake, I realised that all the men had such lines down the side of their face, and most had two or more.

And when I was initiated and came back to East Lake, I was one of them.

I was an odd one, to be sure, since I was so ignorant. But the men of my village let me know they thought I wasn't totally stupid, probably because I showed promise as a fisherman.

I was treated much as the other boys were. Normally, a boy came over from the women's village after his initiation at about thirteen and lived with an older

male relative for some years—his mother's brother, or
an older brother, occasionally his father. Fatherhood
was much less important than relation through the
mother's family, one's clan.

Here in the men's village, boys learned the men's
trades: fishing and boat building, bird hunting, planting
and harvesting ricegrass, cutting reeds. The women
kept poultry and cattle, gardened, made reedcloth, and
preserved and cooked food. Boys older than seven or
eight living in the women's village weren't expected or
even allowed to do women's work, so they came over to
the men's village lazy, ignorant, useless, and good for
nothing, or so the men never got tired of telling them.
Boys weren't beaten—I never saw a Rassiu strike another person, or dog, or cat—but they were scolded
and nagged and ordered about and criticized relent-
lessly until they had learned a craft or two. Then they
had their second initiation, and could move into a hut
of their own choice, alone or with friends. The second
initiation wasn't permitted until the older men agreed
that the boy had fully mastered at least one skill. Sometimes, they told me, a boy, refusing his second initiation,
chose to return to the women's village and live there as
a woman the rest of his life.

My uncle had several wives. Some Rassiu women had several husbands. The marriage ceremony consisted of the two people announcing, "We are married," at the daily food exchange. Scattered along between the two half villages were some little reedcloth huts, just big enough for a cot or mat, which were used by men and women who wanted to sleep together. They made their assignation at the food exchange or at a private meeting in the paths or fields. If a couple decided to marry, the man built a marriage hut, and his wife or wives came to it whenever they agreed or arranged to. I once asked my uncle as he left in the evening which wife he was going to, and he smiled shyly and said, "Oh, they decide that."

As I watched the young people flirting and courting, I saw that marriage had a good deal to do with skill in fishing and skill in cooking, for a husband gives the fish to the wife, who cooks it for him. That daily food exchange of raw for cooked was called "the fishmat." The women, with their poultry and dairying and gardening, actually produced a good deal more of our food than the men did by fishing, but their butter and cheese and eggs and vegetables were all taken for granted, while everybody made a fuss over what the men provided.

I understood now why Ammeda had seemed ashamed when he cooked the fish I'd caught. Village men never cooked. Boys and unmarried men had to bargain or wheedle for their dinners, or take whatever was left on the fish-mat. My uncle's taste in wives and cooks was excellent. I ate well while I lived with him.

I spent the year after my initiation as an Aytan Sidoy of the Rassiu learning how to do what the men of my people did: fish, plant and harvest ricegrass, and cut and store reeds. I was unhandy with a bow and arrow, so I wasn't asked to go out in the boat to shoot wild fowl, as boys often were. I became my uncle's net thrower. While we dragged the net, I fished with the rod and line. My knack for this was recognised at once and won me approval. Often we took a boy along to shoot, and it was the joy of old Minki's life to leap into the water after the duck or goose when he brought one down, fetch it back to the boat, and carry it proudly ashore, wagging her tail. She always gave her birds to my uncle's oldest wife Pumo, and Pumo thanked her gravely.

Planting and harvesting ricegrass is the easiest job on earth, I think. You go out in autumn in a boat on the silky blue water over at the north end of the lake where the rice islets are close together, and pole slowly down the tiny channels, tossing handfuls of small, dark, sweet-smelling grain in showers to right and left as you go. Then in late spring you go back, bend the tall grasses down into the boat from right and left, and knock the new seeds off the stems into the boat with a little wooden rake till the boat's half full of it. I know the women sniggered at the fuss the men made about planting and harvesting ricegrass, as if there were any skill to it; but they always received our bags of rice with praise and honor at the fish-mat exchange. "I'll stuff you a goose with it!" they said. And it tasted almost as good as Etran grain porridge.

As for reed cutting, that was hard work. We did a great deal of it, in late autumn and early winter, when the weather was often grey and cold or raining. Once I got used to standing all day in water two or three feet deep, and to the angle of the curved scythe and the triple rhythm of cutting and gathering and handing—for you must gather the reeds together before they separate and drift off on the water, and hand the long, heavy bundle up into the boat—I liked it well enough. The young fellows I went out with were good companions, rivalrous about their own prowess as cutters, but kind to me as a novice, and full of jokes and gossip and songs that they shouted across the great reed beds in the rainy wind. Not many of the older men went reed cutting; the rheumatism they had got from doing it as young men kept them from it now.

It was a dull life, I suppose, but it was what I needed. It gave me time to mend. It gave me time to think, and to grow up at my own pace.

Late winter was a pleasant, lazy time. The reeds had been cut and handed over to the women to make into reedcloth, and there wasn't much for the men to do unless they were boat makers. Nothing bothered me but the damp, foggy cold: our only heat was from a tiny charcoal fire in a ceramic pot. It made a very small sphere of warmth in the hut. If the sun was shining, I went to the shore and watched the boat makers at their work, a refined and exacting skill. Their boats are the finest art of the Rassiu. A war canoe is like a true line of poetry, there is nothing to it that is not necessary, it is purely beautiful. So when I wasn't huddled over the fire pot dreaming, I watched the boat grow. And I made myself a good set of rods and lines and hooks, and fished if it wasn't raining hard, and talked to my friends among the young people.

Though women didn't set foot in the men's village or men in the women's village, we had, after all, the rest of the world to meet in. Men and women got to talking at the fish-mat, and out on the lake from boat to boat—for the women fished too, especially for eels—and in the grasslands inland from the villages. My luck in fishing helped me make friends among the girls, eager to trade their cooked food for my catch. They teased me and flirted mildly and were happy to walk along the lakeshore or an inland path, a few of them with a few of us young men. Real pairing off was forbidden until the second initiation. Boys who broke that law were exiled from their village for life. So we young people stayed together as a group. My favorite among the girls was Tisso Betu, called Cricket for her pinched little face and skinny body; she was bright and kind and loved to laugh, and she tried to answer my questions instead of staring at me and saying, "But Gavir, everybody knows that!"

One of the questions I asked Tisso was whether anybody ever told stories. Rainy days and winter evenings were long and dull, and I kept an ear out for any tales or songs, but subjects of talk among the boys and men were limited and repetitive: the day's events, plans for the next day, food, women, rarely a little news from a man from another village met out on the lake or in the grasslands. I would have liked to entertain them and myself with a tale, as I had Brigin's band and Barna's people. But no one here did anything like that at all. I knew that foreign ways, attempts to change how things were done, weren't welcomed by the Marsh people, so I didn't ask. But with Tisso I wasn't so afraid of putting a foot wrong, and I asked her if nobody told stories or sang story-songs. She laughed. "We do," she said.

"Women?"

"Ao."

"Men don't?"

"Eng." She giggled.

"Why not?"

She didn't know. And when I asked her to tell me one of the stories I might have heard if I'd been a little boy growing up in the women's village, it shocked her. "Oh, Gavir, I can't," she said.

"And I can't tell you any of the stories I learned?"

"Eng, eng, eng," she murmured. No, no, no.

I wanted to talk to my aunt Gegemer, who could tell me about my mother. But she still held aloof from me. I didn't know why. I asked the girls about her. They shied away from my questions. Gegemer Aytano was, I gathered, a powerful and not entirely beloved woman in the village. At last, on a winter day when Tisso Betu and I were walking in the pastures behind the rest of the group, I asked her why my aunt didn't want anything to do with me.

"Well, she's an ambamer," Tisso said. The word means marsh-lion's daughter, but I had to ask what that meant.

Tisso thought about it. "It means she can see through the world. And hear voices from far away."

She looked at me to see if I knew what she was talking about. I nodded a little uncertainly.

"Gegemer hears dead people talking, sometimes. Or people who aren't born yet. In the old women's house, when they do the singing, Ennu-Amba Herself comes into her, and then she can walk all across the world and see what's happened and what's going to happen. You know, some of us do some of that kind of seeing and hearing while we're children, but we don't understand it. But if Amba makes a girl her daughter, then she goes on seeing and hearing all her life. It makes her kind of strange, you know." Tisso pondered for a while. "She has to try to tell people what she saw. The men won't even listen. They say only men can have the power of seeing and an ambamer is just a crazy woman. But Mother says that Gegemer Aytano saw the poison tide, when the people who eat shellfish in the Western Marshes got sick and died, a long time before it happened, when she was just a child.... And she knows when people in the village are going to die. That makes people afraid of her. Maybe it makes her afraid of them.... But sometimes she knows when a girl's going to have a baby, too. I mean, even before she is. She said, 'I saw your child laugh, Yenni,' and Yenni cried and cried, she was so happy, because she wanted a child and she'd never got one. And a year later she did."

All this gave me a great deal to think about. But it still didn't answer my question. "I don't know why my aunt doesn't like me," I said.

"I'll tell you what Mother told me, if you won't say anything to any of the other men," Tisso said earnestly. I promised silence, and she told me. "Gegemer tried and tried to see what had happened to her sister Tano and her babies. For years she tried. They had singings for her that went on and on. She even took the drugs, and an ambamer shouldn't take the drugs. But Amba wouldn't let her see her sister or the children. And then—then you came walking into the village, and still she didn't see you. She didn't see who you were, until you said your name. Then everyone saw. She was ashamed. She thinks she did something wrong. She thinks Amba is punishing her because she let Tano go alone so far south. She thinks it was her fault the soldiers raped Tano and sold you and your sister. And she thinks you know this."

I was about to protest, but Tisso forestalled me: "Your soul knows it—not your mind. It doesn't matter what your mind doesn't know, if your soul knows. So you are a reproach to Gegemer. You darken her heart."

After a while I said, "That darkens my heart."

"I know," Tisso said sadly.

It was strange how Tisso made me think of Sotur. Utterly different in everything, they were alike in their quickness to feel pity, to understand grief, and not to say too much about it.

I gave up the idea of trying to approach my aunt through her armor of guilt. I longed to learn more about her powers, and Tisso's saying, "Some of us do that kind of seeing when we're children," had intrigued me. But the limits drawn around men's knowledge and women's knowledge were nearly as clear as the line separating the half villages. Tisso was uneasy about having said so much to me, and I could not press her further. None of the other girls would let me ask about "sacred stuff" at all: they hooted like owls or yattered like king-fishers to drown me out—half alarmed at my trans-gression and half laughing at me for being, as they said, such a tadpole.

I was reluctant to ask the boys my age what they knew about these powers of seeing. I was different enough already, and talking about such things would only estrange me further. My uncle left all mysteries alone, seeking comfort only where it was easy to find. I didn't know any of the older men well. Rava was the kindest, but he was an elder, an initiator of his clan, and spent much of his time in South Shore. There was only one man I thought might welcome my questions. Peroc was old, his thick hair quite white, his face seamed and drawn; he was crippled with rheumatism, and lived, I think, in pain. His arthritic hands were not good for much, but he laboriously knotted and mended fishing nets, and though he was slow at the work it was always done perfectly. He lived by himself in a tiny house with a couple of cats. He spoke little, but had a gentle man-ner. He was often too lame to go to the fish-mat. Tisso's mother sent food for him, and I offered to take it to him. It became a regular thing that she'd give it to me and I'd take it and set it down on the old man's deck and say, "From Lali Betu, Uncle Peroc." We young men called all the old men uncle.

He'd be sitting in the sun if there was any sun, working at a net, or just gazing over the grasslands, humming. He'd thank me, and as soon as I turned away, the soft humming would begin again. Soon half-comprehensible words would enter into the tune, strange song words about the marsh lion, the lords of the fish, the heron king.... They were the only serious songs I had heard in Ferusi, the only ones that hinted at a story behind them. One day I put down his reed box of food and said, "From Lali Betu, Uncle Peroc," and he thanked me, but I did not turn away; I stood by his deck and said, "Can I ask about the songs you sing, Uncle?"

He glanced up at me and back at his work, then laid the net down and looked at me steadily. "After the second initiation," he said.

That was what I'd been afraid of. There was no arguing with the rules of the sacred. I said, "Anh." But he saw I had a second question, and waited for it.

"Are all the stories sacred?"

He gazed at me a minute, thinking, and finally nodded. "Ao."

"So I may not listen to you sing?"

"Eng," he said, the soft negative. "Later. When you've been to the king's palace." He looked at me with sympathy. "You'll learn the songs there, as I did."

"The heron king?"

He nodded, but murmured, "Eng, eng," with a gesture to prevent my asking more. "Later," he said. "Soon."

"There are no stories that are not sacred?"

"Those the women and children tell. They are not fit for men."

"But there are tales of heroes—like Hamneda, the great hero who wandered all the length of the Western Shore—"

Peroc gazed at me a while and shook his head. "He did not come here to the Marshes," he said. And he bent to his work again.

So all my tales and poems remained closed up in my head, silent, as my copy of Caspro's poem lay closed and wrapped in reedcloth in my uncle's house, the only book in all Ferusi, unread.

◆ ◆ ◆

I WAS FISHING by myself one day in spring; my uncle had gone netting with another man. Old Minki jumped into the boat as a matter of course and sat in the prow like a curly-eared figurehead. I put up the little sail and let the wind carry us slowly up the lake. I didn't net but fished with the rod and line for ritta, a small bottom fish, sweet and succulent. The ritta were lazy and so was I. I gave up after a while and just sat in the boat, drifting. All around me was the silken blue water, and in the distance a few reed islands, and beyond them the low green shore, and far in the distance a blue hill…

So I had come round to the earliest and oldest of all my rememberings or visions, and was in the memory, the vision itself.

Remembering that, I began all at once to remember other things.

I remembered the streets of cities, the lights of houses crowded over a canal, the dark cobblestones of a steep street in the winter wind—there was the fountain in front of Arcamand and there was a tower over a harbor full of ships and there was a tall house with red rain-beaten walls—all in a rush and tumult of images, dozens of visions all crowded into one another and then sliding away, ungraspable, gone, leaving nothing but the blue sky and water, the low green shore and the distant hill, where I had been, where I had been all my life and was now again, this once, in this one moment.

The visions lessened, faded. Minki looked round, towards home. I sailed slowly back to the village. People were already gathering for the fish-mat. I had only a couple of little ritta to offer, but Tisso and her mother always had something cooked for me. I took my portion and Peroc's and went back to the men's village, to Peroc's house, where he sat mending a fine net. I set his portion down and said, "From Lali Betu. May I ask you a question, Uncle?"

"Anh."

"All my life I've seen through the world. I've remembered what I had never yet seen, and been where I've never yet been." He had raised his face and was looking at me gravely. I went on, "Is this a power of our people—of the Rassiu? Is it a gift or a curse? Are there any people here who will tell me what my visions are?"

"Yes," he said. "In South Shore. I think you should go there."

He got up laboriously and stepped down off his deck. He came with me to Metter's cabin. My uncle was sitting eating his dinner, with Minki on one side thumping her tail on the deck and Prut on the other with his tail wrapped round his paws. My uncle greeted Peroc and offered him his dinner to share.

"Gavir Aytana in kindness brought me food from the fish-mat," the old man said. He spoke very formally. "It is well known that there have been great seers in your clan, Metter Aytana. Is this not so?"

"Ao," my uncle said, staring.

"It may be that Gavir Aytana has the power. It would be well that the keepers of the sacred things be told this."

"Anh," my uncle said, staring at me now.

"Your net will be ready tomorrow," the old man said in a different tone of voice, and turned to limp back to his cabin.

I sat down near my uncle and began to eat my own dinner. Tisso's mother had made excellent fish cakes rolled up in lettuce leaves with a drop of hot pepper sauce.

"I suppose I'd better go to South Shore," my uncle said. "Or should I talk to Gegemer first, I wonder. But she's...I suppose I should just go. I don't know."

"May I go with you?"

Minki thumped her tail.

"That might be good," my uncle said, with relief.

So next day we sailed to South Shore Village, where I'd been initiated. Metter seemed to have no idea what to do once we got there, so I led off to the Big House, where the sacred things were stored and initiations were held. It was the biggest house I'd seen in the Marshes, with walls of rigid lacquered reed such as they built the war canoes of, and a high reed-bundle roof. The fenced court in front of it was bare earth, with a small pool and a great old weeping willow tree beside it. The building was very dark inside, and awesome with the memories of the initiation rites; we did not dare enter, or even speak. We waited by the pool until a man came into the court. I had been about to suggest that we find some members of our clan, the Aytanu, and ask them for advice or assistance, but my uncle went over to the man and began at once to tell him that he was here with his nephew who had the power of seeing visions. The man was one-eyed and had a rake-broom in his hand; he had evidently come to sweep the courtyard. I tried to prevent Metter from babbling to somebody who appeared to be the janitor, but he babbled on. The man nodded, and looked more and more important. At last he said, "I will tell my cousin Dorod Aytana, the seerman of Reed Isles, and he perhaps will find if your nephew is suitable for training. Ennu-Amba has guided your steps to this place. Go with Mé!"

"With Mé," Metter said gratefully. "Come along,

Gavir. It's all settled." He couldn't wait to get away from that big house with its dark open doorway. We went straight back to the docks and got into our boat, which Minki had been guarding by lying curled up asleep in the stern, and sailed home.

I didn't put much credit in the one-eyed man's boasts. I thought that if I wanted to find out anything about my visions, I'd have to do it myself.

So I got up my courage and, at the fish-mat that evening, I approached my aunt Gegemer. I'd traded a good catch of ritta with Kora for a goose he'd shot, a fine fat bird which I cleaned and plucked carefully. I had seen men who were courting women make such an offering, and so I offered it to Gegemer. "I need advice and guidance, Aunt," I said, more bluntly than I had intended. She was a formidable woman, hard to speak to.

At first she didn't answer or take the goose from me. I could feel her recoil, her wish to refuse. But she put out her hand at last for the gift and gestured with her head to the gardens, outside which men and women often met to talk. We walked there in silence. I arranged in my mind what I'd say, at least to start with, and when she stopped by a row of old dwarf cherry trees and faced me, I said it.

"I know you're a woman of power, Aunt. I know you see through the world sometimes, and walk with Ennu-Amba."

To my great surprise she laughed, a surprised, scornful laugh. "Hah! I never thought to hear that from a man!" she said.

That took me aback, and I hesitated, but managed to go on with what I'd planned to say. "I am a very ignorant person," I said, "but I have two kinds of power, I think. I can remember very clearly what I've heard and seen. And I can remember, sometimes, what I have not yet heard and seen." There I stopped. I waited for her to speak.

She turned away a little and rested her hand on the gnarled, scaly trunk of a little tree. "And what can I do for a man of power?" she asked at last, with the same hostile scorn.

"You can tell me what the visions are. How to use them, how to understand them. Where I was, in the city, in the forest, no one had this power. I thought, if I could come back to my people, maybe they'd tell me what I need to know. But I think no one here can, or will, except you."

She turned quite away from me at that and was silent for a long time. At last she turned round and faced me. "I could have taught you, Gavir, if you'd been here as a child in our village," she said, and I saw she was holding her mouth tight to keep it from quivering. "It's too late now. Too late. A woman can't teach a man anything. Wherever you've lived, you must have learned that!"

I said nothing, but she must have seen my protest in my face, and that she had hurt me.

"What can I say to you, sister's son? You come by your gifts truly. Tano could tell any tale she'd heard once, and repeat words she'd heard years before. And I have walked with the lion, as you say—for all the good it's done me. To bring back the past in memory is a great power. To remember what hasn't yet come to pass is a great power too. What's the use of it, you ask me? I don't know. I've never known. Maybe the men know, who look down on women's visions as meaningless foolishness. Ask them! I can't tell you. I can only say, hold to the other power, the one your mother Tano had, for it won't drive you crazy."

She would not look at me steadily. Her glance was fierce and black as a crow's. I heard how like my own voice hers was.

"What's the good of remembering all the stories I ever heard, if men aren't allowed to tell stories or hear them?" I said, my thwarted anger rising to meet hers.

"No good," she said. "You should have been a woman, Gavir Aytana. Then one of your powers might have brought you good."

"But I'm not a woman, Gegemer Aytano," I said bitterly.

She looked round at me again and her expression changed. "No," she said. "Nor quite a man yet. But well on the way." She paused, and drew a deep breath, and finally said, "I'll give you what advice I can, though I think you won't take it. So long as you remember yourself, you're safe. When you begin to remember farther, you begin to lose yourself—you begin to be lost. Don't lose yourself, Tano Aytano's son. Hold to yourself. Remember yourself. No one told me to do that. No one but me will tell you to do it. So, take your risks. And if I ever see you when I walk with the lion, I'll tell you what I see. That's the only gift I might have to give you. In return for this," and she swung the dead goose by its webbed red feet, and scowled, and walked away.

◆ ◆ ◆

A LITTLE LATER in the spring, when the weather was getting very warm, I came back one afternoon with Minki and my uncle from fishing and found two strangers sitting on the deck. One of them was tall and heavyset for a Rassiu, dressed in a long narrow robe of fine reedcloth bleached almost white; I thought he must be some kind of priest or official. The other man was shy and silent. The man in the robe introduced himself as Dorod Aytana, and named off a litany of our clan relationship. Metter scurried off with our catch to the fish-mat, since Dorod said it was me they came to talk to, and he was glad to get away from strangers. When he had gone, Dorod said to me, smiling but with authority, "You came to South Shore seeking me."

"It may be that I didn't know it," I said, a fairly common phrase among the Marsh people, who avoid direct negatives and unnecessary commitments.

"You have not seen me in vision?"

"I believe I have not," I said humbly.

"Our ways have been coming closer for a long time now," Dorod said. He had a deep, soft voice and an impressive manner. "I know that you were brought up among foreigners and have only been in Ferusi for a year. Our kinsman at the Big House in South Shore sent to tell me that you had come at last. You seek a teacher; you have found him. I seek a seer; I have found him. Come with me to my village, Reed Isles, and we will begin your training. For it is late, very late. You should have been learning the way of the visions for years now. But we will make up for lost time—for time is never lost, is it? We will bring you into your power, maybe within a year or two, if you give all your soul to it. Your second initiation then will not be as a mere fisherman or reed cutter, but as a seer of your clan. There is no seer of the Aytanu now. Not for many years. You have been long wanted, long awaited, Gavir Aytana!"

Of all he said, it was those last words that went to my heart. Who had ever waited for me to come? A stolen child, a slave, a runaway, a kind of ghost to my own people, a stranger everywhere else—who wanted or would wait for me?

"I'll come with you," I said.

❖ 13 ❖

Reed Isles was the westernmost, the smallest, and the poorest of the five villages of Ferusi. Its houses were scattered on the isles and inlets of a bay in the southwest corner of Ferusi Lake. Dorod lived with his meek and silent cousin Temec in a hut on a muddy, reed-surrounded peninsula. There were fewer women than men in the village, and the women seemed indifferent and aloof. There were forty or so people, but only four marriage huts. The fish-mat was not the sociable, pleasurable event it was in East Lake.

I didn't get to know anyone in this village well but Dorod. He kept me busy and away from the others. I missed the easy, lazy companionship of fishing with my uncle or with the young men, talking with Tisso and other girls, watching the boat builders, cutting reeds, planting ricegrass, the slow day rhythm that I had lived in for a year now, often bored into a kind of trance, but never unhappy.

I went out fishing daily here, and we often kept half the catch for ourselves, for the women provided few vegetables, little meal, no fruit. I certainly would have been willing to fry up our catch or make fish cakes with the coarse meal the women ground, but for a village man to cook would turn society inside out and upside down and make me an outcast from my people forever. As it was, Dorod and I ate a good deal of fish raw, as I'd done with Ammeda, but we didn't have any horse-radish to give it a kick. Nobody here shot birds; they were forbidden in this village as sacred creatures—hassa—wild goose, duck, swan, and heron. Little fresh-water clams, delicious and very common here, were a staple of the local diet, but they became poisonous at rare, unpredictable intervals; Dorod forbade himself and me to eat them.

Temec told me that Dorod's previous novice, a child, had died of the shellfish poisoning three years ago.

Dorod and I did not get on well. My heart is not naturally rebellious, and I wanted very much to learn what he could teach me about my power, but I'd learned to distrust my own trustfulness. Dorod demanded absolute trust. He gave me arbitrary orders and expected silent obedience. I questioned the reason for each act. He refused to answer. I refused to obey.

This went on for a half month or so. One morning he instructed me to spend the entire day kneeling in the hut with my eyes shut, saying the word *erru*. Two days earlier I had done just that. I told him I couldn't kneel that long again, my knees were still too painful from the last time. He said, "You must do as I say," and went off.

I'd had enough. I made up my mind to walk back round the lake to East Lake Village.

He came back into the hut and found me knotting up the little bundle of my belongings in the old brown blanket, which my uncle's cat Prut had nearly worn to shreds by kneading it with his claws before he went to sleep on it.

"Gavir, you cannot go," he said, and I said, "What can I learn if you keep me in ignorance?"

"The seerman is the guide. It is his burden and task to carry the mystery for the seer."

He spoke, as he often did, pompously, but I felt he believed what he said.

"Not this seer," I said. "I need to know what I'm doing and why I should do it. You want blind obedience. Why should a seer be blind?"

"The seer of visions must be guided," Dorod said. "How can he guide himself? He gets lost among the visions. He doesn't know whether he lives now or years ago or in years to come! You yourself, though you've barely begun to travel in time, have felt that. No one can walk that path by himself, unguided."

"My aunt Gegemer—"

"An ambamer!" Dorod said. "Women, babbling nonsense, screeching and screaming, seeing useless glimpses of things they don't understand. Phoh! A seer is trained and guided, he serves his clan and people, he is a man of value. I can make you a man of value. I know the secrets, the techniques, the sacred ways. Without a seerman a seer is no better than a woman!"

"Well, maybe I am no better than a woman," I said. "But I'm not a child. You treat me as a child."

New ideas came hard to Dorod, as perhaps they do to most villagers and tribesmen, but he could listen, he could think, and he was extremely, almost unnaturally, sensitive to mood and hint. What I said struck him hard.

He said nothing for a while and finally asked, "How old are you, Gavir?"

"About seventeen."

"Seers are trained young. Ubec, whom I was training, was only twelve when he died. And I took him when he was seven." He spoke slowly, thinking as he spoke. "You are an initiated man. A child can be trained to obey in all things."

"I was well trained in trust and obedience," I said with some bitterness. "As a child. Now I want to know what I'm to put my trust in, and what power I'm obeying."

Again he listened to what I said, and thought before he spoke. "The power of your soul to see truth," he said at last—"that is what both the seer and seerman must follow."

"Since I'm not a child, why can't I learn to do it by myself?"

"But who would read your visions?" he said with blank surprise.

"Read them?" I said as blankly.

"I must learn to read the truth in what you see, so

that I can tell people of it. That's my task as your seer-man! How can a seer do that for himself?" He saw that I was as perplexed as he was. "Do you know what it is you see, Gavir? Do you know the people, the place, the time, the meaning of the vision?"

"Only after they come to pass," I admitted. "But how can *you* know?"

"That is my power! You are the eyes of our people, but I am your voice! The seer is not given the gift of reading what he sees. That is for the man trained in the ways of the myriad channels, who knows the roots of the reeds, where Amba walks, where Sua passes, where Hassa flies. You will learn to see and to tell me what you see. To you the visions are mysteries—is that not so? You can tell me only what you see. But I, looking with the eyes of Amba, looking deep within, I will under-stand the mysteries, and learn to speak the meaning of what is seen, and so give guidance to our people. You need me as I need you. And our kinfolk and all the clans of Ferusi need us both."

"How do you know how to...read my visions?" I hesitated on the word "read," which was not one I had ever heard before in the Marshes, and which clearly did not have the meaning I knew.

Dorod gave a kind of laugh. "How do you know how to see them?" he asked. He looked at me now with a less lofty expression, almost companionably. "Why does a man have one power and not another? You can't teach me to see visions. I can teach you how to see them, but not how to read them, because that is my power, not yours. I tell you, we need each other."

"You can teach me how to see visions?"

"What do you think I've been trying to do?"

"I don't know! You never say. You say fast every third day, never go barefoot, don't sleep with my head to the south, kneel till my knees break—a hundred rules and do's and don'ts, but what for?"

"You fast to keep your spirit pure and light, so it can travel easily."

"But I'm not getting enough to eat between fasts. My spirit is so pure and light that it thinks about nothing except food. What good is that?" He frowned, and in fact looked a little ashamed. I pressed my advantage: "I don't mind fasting, but I won't starve. Why do I have to wear shoes?"

"To keep your feet from contact with the earth, which draws the spirit down."

"Superstition," I said. He looked blank. I said, "I've

had visions both shod and barefoot. I don't need to learn obedience. I've had that lesson. I want to understand my power, and to learn how to use it."

Dorod bowed his head in silence. After a long time he answered me, gravely, without patronising impatience or pompousness, "If you will do as I tell you to do, Gavir, I will try to tell you why seers do these things. Perhaps it is true that such knowledge befits your mind as an initiated man."

I was proud of myself for standing up to him, and pleased with myself for earning some respect from him. I put my things back on the shelf by my cot and stayed on with him in his lonely, rather dirty hut.

I saw well enough that Dorod did indeed need me, since his child pupil, when he died, had taken Dorod's position as seerman with him. But if he'd teach me what he knew, it was a fair bargain, I thought.

It was hard for him to abandon his position as master, to answer my questions, to explain to me why I must do this or that. He was not an ill-natured man, and I think sometimes he found it a pleasure to have, instead of a pupil-slave, a student and companion; but still he never told me anything unless I asked him.

All that he could or would teach me of the songs

and the ritual stories I learned quickly. I was at last learning a little of the gods and spirits, the songs and tales of the Rassiu, coming a little closer to the heart of the Marshes.

The gift of memorising hadn't deserted me, for all that I hadn't used it in a long time. So in that way I came along much faster than he had expected. He laughed once and said, of a ritual story I had just repeated to him, "I spent a month trying to hammer that into Ubec's head, and he never got it half right! You learned it in one saying."

"That is half my power, and all my training when I was a slave," I said.

But my power of vision seemed to resist his efforts to bring it forth and train it. I stayed with him a month and another month, and still had no more of those seeings I used to call remembering. I was impatient; he seemed untroubled.

The central practice of his teaching he called waiting for the lion. It was to sit and breathe quietly and bring my thoughts away from all that was around me into a silence within myself: a very difficult thing to do. My knees began to get used to it at last, but it seemed my mind never would.

And he wanted me to tell him every vision I had ever had. This was very hard for me at first. Sallo sat beside me and whispered to me, "Don't talk about it, Gav!" All my life I had obeyed her. Now I was to disobey her to serve the wishes of this strange man. I resisted confiding in Dorod, and yet only he could teach me what I needed to know. I forced myself to speak, haltingly and incompletely describing what I had seen. His patience was inexhaustible: little by little he drew from me everything I could tell him of each "remembering"—the snowfall in Etra, the assault of the Casicaran troop, the cities I walked in, the man in the room with the books, the cave, the terrible dancing figure (which I had seen again when I was initiated), even the first and simplest of them all, the blue water and the reeds. He wanted to hear the visions over and over. "Tell me again," he would say. "You are in a boat."

"What is there to tell? I see the Marshes. Just as they are. Just as I saw them when I was a baby, before I was stolen, no doubt. Blue water, green reeds, a blue hill way off there…"

"To the west?"

"No, south."

How did I know the hill was in the south?

He listened with the same intentness every time,

often asking a question but never making any com-ment. Many words I used evidently meant nothing to him, as when I was trying to describe the cities I saw, or the room full of books where the man turned to me and said my name. Dorod had never seen a city. He used the word "read" but could not read; he had never seen a book. I took my small book, the *Cosmologies,* out of its silky reedcloth wrappings to show him what the word meant. He glanced at it but was not interested. He did not ask for realities or for meanings, only for the closest, most detailed description I could give him of what I had seen in vision. What he made of all I told him I never knew, because he never said.

I wondered about other seers and seermen. I asked Dorod who the other seers of Ferusi were. He told me two names, one in South Shore, one in Middle Village. I asked if I could talk to one of these men. He looked at me, curious: "Why?"

"To talk with him—to find out if it's like it is for me—"

He shook his head. "They wouldn't talk to you. They speak of their visions only to their seerman."

I insisted a little. He said, "Gavir, these are holy men. They live in seclusion, alone with their visions. Only their seerman talks with them. They don't come out among people. Even if you were fully a seer your-self you wouldn't be allowed to see them."

"Is that how I am to be—secluded, shut away, liv-ing among my visions?"

The idea was horrible to me, and I think Dorod felt my horror.

He hesitated and said, "You are different. You began differently. I cannot say how you will live."

"Maybe I'll never have any more visions. Maybe I came back to the beginning there out on the lake, and the beginning was the end."

"You're afraid," Dorod said, with unusual gentle-ness. "It's hard to know the lion is walking towards you. Don't be afraid. I will be with you."

"Not there," I said.

"Yes, even there. Go wait for the lion on the deck now."

I obeyed, listlessly, kneeling on the little deck of the hut over the mud and stones of the end of the penin-sula, looking out at the lake under a calm grey sky. I breathed as he had taught me and tried to keep my thoughts from drifting. Presently I was aware that a black lioness was walking across the ground behind me, but I did not turn round. Whatever it was I had been afraid of, my fear had gone. There were flowers in the narrow garden where I sat. I walked up a cobbled street at night in rain, and saw the rain blown against a high red wall over the street in the faint light from a window across the way. I was in the sunlit courtyard of a house I knew, my house, and a young girl came to greet me, smiling; it gave me great joy to see her face. I stood in a river, the current pushing me nearly off my feet, and on my shoulders was a heavy burden, so heavy I could barely stand up as the water pushed at me, and the sand under my feet slipped and slid. I staggered and took a step forward. I was kneeling on the deck of the hut in Reed Isles. It was evening. A last flight of wild duck passed across the reddish cloud cover where the sun had set.

Dorod's hand was on my shoulder. "Come in," he said in a low voice. "You've made a long journey."

He was silent and gentle with me that night. He asked nothing about what I had seen. He made sure I ate well, and sent me to sleep.

Over the next days I told him my visions, little by little, and over and over. He knew how to draw from me things I would not have thought to tell, things I didn't even know I'd seen until he made me recall the vision again, closer, seeking details, as if studying a picture. In this I felt my two kinds of memory come together into one.

And several times during those days I "journeyed," as he put it, again. It was as if a door stood open that I could go through, not at will, but at the lion's will.

"I don't see how my visions can be of use or guidance to our clan," I said to Dorod one evening. "They're always of other places, other times—almost nothing of the Marshes. What use can they be here?"

We were out fishing. Our contributions to the fishmat had been rather poor lately, and what the women gave us had been correspondingly meager. We had thrown out the net and were drifting a while before we began to pull it in.

"You are still making the journeys of a child," Dorod said.

"What do you mean?"

"The child sees only with his own eyes. He sees what is before him—places he will come to. As he learns to journey as a man, he learns to see more widely. He learns to see what other eyes may see, he sees where others will come. He goes where he will never himself go in his body. All the world, all places, all times are open to the great seer. He walks with Amba and flies with Hassa. He journeys with the Lord of the Waters." He said all this quite matter-of-factly. He looked round at me with a quick, shrewd glance. "Untaught, begin-

ning so late, you see as a child sees. I can teach you how
to make the greater journeys. But only if you trust me."

"Do I distrust you?"

"Yes," he said calmly.

My aunt had said something to me about remembering myself but going no further. I could have found
her words in my memory if I looked for them, but I did
not look for them. Dorod was right: if I was to learn
from him I must do it his way.

We pulled in our net. We were in luck. We brought
two big carp to the fish-mat. I found carp a bony,
muddy fish, but the women of Reed Isles were fond of
it, and we were given a good dinner that night.

After we'd eaten it, I asked Dorod, "How will you
teach me to see beyond the child's visions?"

He didn't answer for a long time. "You must be
ready," he said at last.

"What will make me ready?"

"Obedience and trust."

"Do I disobey you?"

"Only in your heart."

"How do you know that?"

He looked at me with something like scorn or pity,
and said nothing.

"What must I do, then? How do I prove I trust you?"

"Obedience."

"Tell me what to do and I'll do it."

I did not like this battle of wills, I did not want it, but it was what he wanted. And having got what he wanted, he changed his tone. He spoke very seriously. "You need not go on, Gavir," he said. "It is a hard way, the seer's way. Hard and fearful. I will always be with you, but you are the one who makes the journey. I can guide you to the beginning of the way, but after that I can only follow. It is your will that dares, your eye that sees. If you wish not to make the greater journeys, so be it. I will not force you—I cannot. If you want, leave me tomorrow, go back to East Lake. Your child-visions will return sometimes, but they will soon begin to fade; you will lose them, lose the power. Then you can live as an ordinary man. If that is what you want."

Much taken aback, confused, challenged, I said, "No. I told you, I want to know my power."

"You will know it," he said with a quiet exultation.

From that night on he was both gentler with me and even more exacting. I was determined to obey him without question, to find if I could, indeed, learn to know my power. He asked me again to fast every third day. He controlled my diet very strictly, allowing me no milk or grain, but adding certain foods that he said were sacred: the eggs of duck and other wild fowl, a root called shardissu, and eda, a small fungus that sprang up in the willow groves inland—all eaten raw. He spent a great deal of time obtaining these foods. The shardissu and eda were vile-tasting and left me sick and dizzy, but I had to eat only tiny quantities of each.

After some days of this diet, and many hours of kneeling daily, I began to feel a lightness of body and mind, a sense of floating free. As I knelt on the deck of the hut I would say the word "hassa, hassa," over and over, and feel myself lifted on the wings of the wild goose, the swan.

I knelt on the deck and saw all the Marshes beneath me, and the cloud shadows drifting over them. I saw villages on the shores of lakes, and fishing boats out on the water. I saw the faces of children, of women, of men. I crossed a great river with a burden on my shoulders, borne down, heavy laden, and threw off the burden and found my wings again, the heron's wings. I flew and flew…and landed sick and cold and stiff, my knees afire with pain, my head dull, my belly aching, on the deck of Dorod's house.

He helped me up. He brought me in by the tiny fire

in the clay pot, for winter was coming on. He comforted me and praised me. He fed me translucent slices of raw fish and vegetables, beaten egg, a bit of sickening shardissu, a draft of water to take the evil taste out of my mouth. "She gave me milk," I said, remembering the woman in the inn when I first came to the Marshes, longing for the taste of milk. All my memories were with me all night. I lay in Dorod's hut as I sat beside my sister in the schoolroom of Arcamand while the storm destroyed the village called Herru, tearing the roofs and reedcloth walls from the posts in utter darkness full of screaming voices and the howl of wind....

I was very sick, vomiting again and again, lying on my belly on the deck vomiting into the mud below, writhing with the pain in my stomach and lungs. Dorod knelt by me, his hand on my back, telling me it was all right, it would be over soon and I could sleep. I slept and my dreams were visions. I woke and remembered what I had never known. He asked me to tell him all I had seen, and I tried, but even as I told him new visions came to me and he and the hut were gone, I was gone, lost among people and places I would never know and could never remember. And then I would be lying in the dark hut, sick and aching and dizzy, hardly able to sit up. He would come and give me water and make me eat a little, talk to me and try to make me talk. "You are a brave man, my Gavir, you will be a great seer," he told me, and I clung to him, the only face that was not a dream or vision or memory, the only actual face, the only hand I could hold, my guide and savior, my false guide, my betrayer.

There came another face among the dreams and visions. I knew her. I knew her voice. But did I not know all the faces, all the voices? I remembered everything, everything. Cuga stooped over me. Hoby came at me down the corridor. But she was there, I knew her, and I spoke her name: "Gegemer."

Her crow's face was grim, her crow's eyes black and sharp. "Nephew," she said. "I told you that if I saw you in vision I'd tell you of it. You remember that."

I remembered everything. She had told me that before. All this had happened before. I was remembering it because it had happened a hundred times, like everything else. I was lying down because I was too tired from journeying to sit up. Dorod was sitting cross-legged near me. The hut was dark and cramped. My aunt was not in the hut, it was a man's hut and she was a woman: she knelt in the doorway, she must stop at the threshold. She looked at me and spoke to me in her harsh voice.

"I saw you cross a river, carrying a child. Do you understand me, Gavir Aytana? I saw the way you are to go. If you look, you'll see it. It is the second river you must cross. If you can cross it, you'll be safe. Across the first river is danger for you. Across the second, safety. Across the first river, death will follow you. Across the second river, you will follow life. Do you understand me? Do you hear me, my sister's son?"

"Take me with you," I whispered. "Take me with you!"

I felt Dorod move forward to come between us.

"You've given him eda," my aunt said to Dorod. "What else have you poisoned him with?"

I managed to sit up, and stand. I staggered to the doorway, though Dorod got up to stop me. "Take me with you," I cried out to my aunt. She caught the hand I reached out to her and pulled me out of the house. I could barely stay afoot. She put her arm around me.

"Wasn't one boy enough to kill?" she said to Dorod, savage as the crow that attacks the nest-robbing hawk. "Give me what is his from your hut and let him go with me, or I'll shame you before the elders of Aytanu and the women of your own village so your shame will never be forgotten!"

"He will be a great seer," Dorod said, shivering with rage, but not moving from the doorway of the hut. "A man of power. Let him stay with me. I won't give him the eda again."

"Gavir," she said, "choose."

I did not know what they were saying, but I said to her, "Take me with you."

"Give me what is his," she said to Dorod.

Dorod turned away. He came back to the doorway presently with my knife, my fishing gear, the book wrapped in reedcloth, the ragged blanket. He set them down on the decking in front of the doorway. He was sobbing aloud, tears running down his face. "May evil follow you, evil woman," he cried. "Filth! You know nothing. You have no business with sacred things. You defile all you touch. Filth! Filth! You have polluted my house."

She said nothing, but helped me pick up my things, helped me get down from the deck and walk out the small pier where she had tied her boat, a woman's boat, light as a leaf. I clambered down into it, trembling, and crouched in it. All the time I heard Dorod's voice cursing Gegemer with the foul words men use for women. As she cast off the rope he cried out, howling in rage and grief—"Gavir! Gavir!"

I huddled down with my head in my arms, hiding from him. It was silent then. We were out on the water. It was raining a little. I was too sick and weak and cold to lift my head. I lay huddled against the thwart. The visions came around me, swarming, faces, voices, places, cities, hills, roads, skies, and I began again to journey on and journey on.

◆ ◆ ◆

FOR GEGEMER TO COME to Dorod's house and stand at his very threshold had been an act of transgression barely justified by the urgency of her message to me. She could not bring me into the women's village of East Lake; she could not enter the men's village herself. She took me to an unused marriage hut between the villages, made the bed up for me, and left me there, coming to look after me a couple of times a day—a common enough arrangement when a man fell ill and a wife or sister wanted to nurse or visit him.

So I lay in the tiny, flimsy hut, the wind flapping the reedcloth walls, the rain beating on them and dripping between the reed bundles of the roof. I shivered and raved or lay in stupor. I don't know how long I had stayed with Dorod, or how long my recovery took, but it was summer when I went with him, and when I began to come to myself, be myself again, it was early spring. I was so thin and wasted my arms looked like reed stems. When I tried to walk I panted and got dizzy. It took me a long time to get my appetite back.

My aunt told me something about the drugs Dorod had given me. She spoke of them with hatred, with spite. "I took eda," she said. "I was determined to know where your mother went. I listened to what the seer-men told me, the wise men in the Big House, may they choke on their words, may they eat mud and drown in quicksand. Take eda, they said, and your mind will be free, you will fly where you will! The mind flies, yes, but the belly pays, and the mind too. Fool that I was, I never saw your mother, but I was sick for a month, two months, from a single mouthful. How much did he give you, how often? And bile root, shardissu—that makes you dizzy and your heart beats too hard, and your breath comes short—I never took it, but I know it. I know what men do to each other and call it sacred medicine!" She hissed like a cat. "Fools," she said. "Men. Women. All of us."

I was sitting in the doorway of the hut and she nearby on a wicker seat she'd brought with her; the women made such light, folding seats of cane and carried them to sit in, anywhere outdoors. The ground was still wet from recent rain, but the sky was pale radiant blue, and there was a new warmth to the sun.

My aunt and I were at ease with each other. I knew she had saved my life, and so did she. I think that knowledge softened her self-reproach for having let my mother go to her death. Gegemer was harsh, hard, with a bitter temper, but her care of me in my illness had been patient, even tender. Often she and I didn't understand each other, but it didn't matter; there was an understanding beneath words, a likeness of mind beneath all differences. One thing we both knew without ever saying: that when I was well enough, I would leave the Marshes.

I was in no hurry, but she was. She had seen me going north with death pursuing me. I must go. I must cross the second river to be safe. I must go as soon as I could. She said that to me at last.

"No matter when I go," I said, "death will pursue me."

"Eng, eng, eng," she said, shaking her head fiercely, frowning. "If you put off going too long, death will be waiting for you!"

"Then I'll stay here," I said, half joking. "Why should I leave my kin and clan and go running after death? I like my people here. I like to fish…"

I was teasing her, of course, and she knew it and didn't really mind, but she had seen what she had seen and I had not. She couldn't make light of it.

And among all the meaningless, endless swarming of visions that I lived with while I was with Dorod and when I was first back in East Lake, there was one that I remembered with particular exactness and clarity. I am waist deep in a river that tugs at my legs and feet, trying to pull me with its current, and on my back is a heavy weight that constantly unbalances me. I take a step forward, directly towards the riverbank, but it is wrong—I know it at once—the sand is unstable, there is no footing there. I cannot see where to go, through the rush and swirl of the water, but I take a step to the right, and another, and then on that way, as if following some path under the water, one step after the other, against all the force of the current—and that is all. I see no more.

This remembering, this vision, came back to me again as I began to recover my health. It was, I think, the last of the visions of my illness. I told it to Gegemer when she came the next day. She winced and shuddered as I told her.

"It is the same river," she murmured.

I shivered too when she said that.

"I saw you there," she said. "It is a child you carry, riding on your back." After a long time she said, "You will be safe, sister's son. You will be safe." Her voice was low and rough, and she spoke with so much yearning that I took her words not as prophecy but only as her desire.

I had been a fool indeed to go off with Dorod, poor Dorod who had waited for me and wanted me only for his own sake, to make him important among his people, a seerman, a dealer in destiny, a person of power. I had turned my back on Gegemer, who even if she hardly knew it had truly waited for me, truly wanted me, not to make her great, but for love's sake.

I was well enough to go back to my uncle's house by April, though not well enough yet to go any farther. The last day I stayed at the marriage hut, my aunt came by for no reason but to say goodbye. We sat in front of the house in the sunlight, and I said, "Mother's sister, may I tell you of my sister?"

"Sallo," she said in a whisper. The name of a child of two or three, a lost child.

"She was my guardian and defender. She was always brave," I said. "She couldn't remember the Marshes, she didn't know anything about our people, but she knew we had powers the others didn't have. She told me never to tell them, the others, of my visions. She was wise. She was beautiful—there isn't a girl in the village as beautiful as Sallo was. Or as kind, and loving, and true-hearted." And seeing how intently my aunt listened, I talked on, trying to tell her what Sallo had looked like, how she had spoken, what she had been to me. It did not take very long. It is hard to say what a person is. And Sallo's life had been too short to make much of a story. She had not lived as long even as I had lived now.

When I fell silent, partly because I could not speak for the tears I wanted to cry, Gegemer said, "Your sister was like my sister." And she laid her dark hand on my dark hand for one moment.

So once more I gathered up my little bundle, blanket, gear, knife, book, and walked back to the men's village, to my uncle's house. Metter welcomed me with calm kindness. Prut came to meet me waving his tail, and as soon as I put my old blanket on my cot he jumped up onto it and began to knead it industriously, purring like a windmill. But there was no courteous greeting from old Minki. She had died in the winter, Metter told me sadly. And old Peroc, too, had died, alone in his house. Metter had gone one morning to give him a net to mend, and found him sitting bent over by his cold fire pot, his work in his cold hands.

"There's a litter of puppies in Rava's house," Metter said after a while. "We might go look them over tomorrow."

We did that, and chose a fine, upstanding, bright-eyed puppy whose black coat curled as tight as lamb's wool. Metter named her Bo, and took her out fishing that same day. Just as he pushed off she leapt into the water and began paddling along beside the boat. He fished her out and spoke to her severely, while she wagged her tail in joyful unrepentance. I wanted to be with them, but I wasn't strong enough to go out fishing yet; just the walk to Rava's house had left me out of breath and shaky. I sat down on the deck in the sunshine and watched the little moth-wing sail of Metter's boat grow smaller and smaller on the silky blue water of the lake. It was good to be here. This house, I thought, was probably as near home as I'd ever come.

But it wasn't my home. I didn't want to live my life here. That was clear to me now. I had been born with two gifts, two powers. One of them belonged here; it was a power the Marsh people knew, knew how to train and use. But my training in it had failed, whether through my teacher's ignorance and impatience, or because my power of vision was in fact not great, but only the gift, common enough here, of seeing, sometimes, a little way ahead. A child's gift, a wild gift, that could not be trained or counted on, and that would grow weaker as I grew older.

And my other power, though reliable, was utterly useless here. What good was a head full of stories and histories and poetry? The less a man of the Rassiu said, the more he was respected. Stories were for women and children. Songs were secrets, sung only at the terrifying sacred rites of initiation. These were not people of the word. They were people of the vision and the moment. All I had learned from books was wasted among them. Was I then to forget it all, betray my memory, and let my mind and spirit, too, dwindle away and grow weaker as I grew older?

The people who stole me from my people had stolen my people from me. I could never wholly be one of them.

To see that was to see that I must go on.

Where to go, then?

North, Gegemer said. She saw me going north. Across two great rivers. The Somulane and the Sensaly, those would be. Asion was north and west of the Somulane, in Bendile; the city of Mesun lay on the north bank of the Sensaly, in Urdile. There was a great university in Mesun. Scholars, poets lived there. The poet Orrec Caspro lived there.

I got up and went into the little house. Prut was working on my old blanket, his eyes half closed and his claws going in and out and in and out and his windmill running. I reached across him and took from the shelf the little reedcloth packet, brought it outside and sat down cross-legged with it. I thought of the hours, days, months I had spent on my knees on Dorod's deck, and swore in my heart that I'd never kneel again. I wished I had one of the women's legless wicker chairs, but men did not use women's things. Women used and did what there was to use and do, but men shunned and despised a great many things, such as wicker chairs and cooking and storytelling, depriving themselves of many skills and pleasures, in order to prove that they weren't women. Wouldn't it be better to prove it by doing, rather than by not doing?

Better for me, not for them. I was not one of them.

I sat cross-legged, then, and unwrapped the silky reedcloth from the book. And for the first time in how long—a year, two years?—I opened it. I opened the book where it opened, letting it choose the page, and read.

In the domain of the Lord of the Waters
the rushes grow, the green reeds grow.
  Hassa! hassa!
Swans fly over the waters, calling,
over the green reeds, the rushes.
  Hassa! hassa!
Grey herons fly over the marshes
and shadows pass under their wings.
Under the clouds pass shadows,
over the marshlands, over the islands
of reeds and ricegrass. Blessed
are the wings of the waterbirds,
blessed the realm of the Lord of the Waters,
the Lord of the Springs and Rivers.

I closed the book and closed my eyes, leaning back against the doorpost, letting the sunlight flow through my eyelids, through my bones. How did he know? How did he know what it was like here? How did he know the sacred name of the swan and heron? Was Orrec Caspro a Rassiu, a Marshman? Was he a seer?

I fell asleep with the murmur of the lines in my mind. I woke when Bo jumped into my lap and washed my face enthusiastically. Metter was just climbing up onto the deck. "What's that?" he said, looking with mild curiosity at the book.

"A box of words," I said. I held it up and showed it to him. He shook his head and said, "Anh, anh."

"Any ritta today?"

"No. Just perch and a pikelet. I need you to go out with me for ritta. Are you coming to the fish-mat?"

I went with him there, and talked with Tisso afterwards. I was glad to see her, and we talked for quite a while, sitting near the gardens. Later that evening, watching the sunset from the deck of our house, I knew with sudden sharp embarrassment and unease that Tisso was ready to fall in love with me, even though I hadn't yet had my second initiation, even though I still looked as if I was made of black sticks, and was a failed seer, a man of no accomplishments.

Metter was shaving. Men of the Marshes don't have much in the way of beards; my uncle shaved by pulling out random hairs with a clamshell as tweezers and a black bowl filled with water as a mirror. He clearly enjoyed the process. When he was done he handed me the clamshell. I was surprised, but when I felt my jaw and peered into the bowl I saw that I had sprouted some curly black beard hairs. I pulled them out one by one. It was, in fact, enjoyable. Almost all small daily acts here were enjoyable. I would miss the peacefulness of sitting here with my peaceful uncle. But I was now all the more sure that I must leave.

I could not go till I had my strength back, that was clear. So for the rest of the spring I kept to a steady regime. I stayed almost entirely in the men's village; I went to the fish-mat and spoke to people there, but did not go walking with the young men and women. When I walked to strengthen my legs and get my wind back, I went alone, miles along the lakeshore. I took up Peroc's craft of mending nets, which I could do sitting down, and though I was not very good at it, the nets I mended were better than nothing, and it gave me some usefulness to my village.

Before long I was able to go line-fishing with Metter and help him train Bo, though the little dog hardly needed training. Retrieving was bred into her brain and bone; the first time a fish, a big perch, took the hook off my line, Bo was into the water, under the water, and bobbed up with the struggling fish held delicately in her jaws, offering it to me, before I even knew I'd lost it.

Every morning and evening I sat out on the deck, under the lifted house wall if it was raining, and read a few pages in my book. Prut, who was getting older and lazier, often took this opportunity to sit on my lap. Then my uncle and I ended the day with the brief reverence-dance and words of praise to the Lord of the Waters, which I had learned when I first lived in the village; and we went to bed.

So the days passed. It was high summer, past the solstice. I didn't think about my need to leave the village. I had no needs. I was content.

My aunt came to me, stalking around the fish-mat, glaring like an angry crow. Little children scattered in fear before her. "Gavir!" she said. "Gavir, I saw a man. A man pursuing you. A man who is your death."

I stared at her.

"You must go, sister's son!"

PART FOUR

✦ 14 ✦

My aunt told everyone I was obeying her vision and would leave the day after tomorrow. When I went next day to the fish-mat for the last time, Tisso's mother was waiting to offer me a blanket woven of reed treated so that the fibers were fuzzy and made a thick, soft texture, warm as wool. "My daughter wove it," Lali Betu said, and I said, "I thank her for it and will think of you both when the nights are cold." Tisso hung back and did not try to speak to me. I said goodbye to the women and spoke briefly with my aunt. She did not want to talk, she wanted me to be gone, to get across the second river and be safe.

I left early the next morning before my uncle got up. The puppy was sleeping on his feet. Prut was curled up on my old blanket. I whispered, "Go with Mé," to them all and slipped out of the little house and away from my village. My heart was heavy in me.

I went overland, eastward. My aunt would have disapproved, wanting me to hurry straight to the north. I refused to let her fear drive me. I had no boat, and heading north on foot, I'd have to take a maze of a way through the Marshes, endless days of walking. I had no money with me and no means of earning it while I traveled.

But it was in my mind that I did have money. Blood money, guilt money, the payment for my sister's death. I had left it with Cuga, hidden in his cave. It would be enough to take me to Mesun, if I lived light, and I was used to living light. I knew the way that I'd walked with Chamry and Venne; I could keep east of the Heart of the Forest, so as not to run into Barna's guards, when I got that far north. The tricky part would be finding Cuga's cave, south of the Daneran Forest. I was sure my gift of memory would guide me when I came among the hills and valleys I had known that summer—if I could find them.

I had a backpack stuffed with wayfarer's food, dried

smoked fish, hard cheese, hard bread, dried fruit: the women at the fish-mat had offered me more food than I could ever use, the men of my village had come to Metter's hut to share with me their little hoards of travel supplies. I had no fear of going hungry for days to come. Besides the food and my new blanket, I carried as always my fishing gear, my knife, and the book, wrapped safe in waterproof reedcloth to protect it when I had to ford or swim. I was fit again, able to walk steadily all day and to enjoy it.

Within two days I came out of the Marshes into a rising, thinly wooded country. I kept bearing east now; as well as I could judge, I was not far north of the city of Casicar. I saw a few farmsteads in the distance, desolate-looking places. Cattle and sheep were scattered out in the valleys, not many of them. I passed orchards that had been burned, a ruined farmhouse. Armies had come through here, looting and laying waste, the endlessly warring armies of the City States.... There were no roads, only tracks, and I saw no people but an occasional herdsman or shepherd. We spoke or waved, and I went on.

The land continued to rise, and now I was in the hilly, broken, wild country I was looking for. The problem was finding the piece of it I wanted. I had no idea of the direction Cuga's cave lay from where I was now. The woods were thick enough that there was never an overview of the hills. All I could do was go forward, following my nose. As the sun began getting low and golden through the trees that day, I felt myself completely lost—walking at random. My plan was hopeless. I could wander in these hills till I became as weak and crazy as I had been when I first came into them. I sat down to eat a little and put some heart in myself, planning to go on as long as the light lasted before I found a sheltered place to sleep. As I sat down in a little clearing, my back against a young oak, I said with a sigh, "Oh, Ennu, guide me now."

I split a lump of hard bread with my knife, laid a thin slice of smoked fish on it, and ate it slowly, tasting salt and smoke and thinking of my village. I looked up at some movement and saw a black lion come into the clearing about twenty feet from me. It was a lioness, pacing with her head and her long tail low. She stopped and looked straight at me. I said, with no voice, "Ennu-Amba," naming her. She gazed a moment longer and then walked on. She vanished almost at once in the thickets.

After a while I finished my dinner. I wrapped up

the fish and put it carefully away in my pack. I licked my greasy fingers and wiped them on the deer fern amidst which I sat. My mouth was dry, and I drank from the little bottle of lacquered reedcloth I had re-filled at the last stream. I got up slowly. It seemed to me that I had only one way to go: that was to follow the lion. It did not seem a wise thing to do, but I was in a place where wisdom, maybe, was no use. I followed the lion.

Once I was through the thickets, the way she had gone appeared to be a faint path that went through open oak woods along the top of a long, winding hill, easy walking with fairly good visibility. I did not see the lion again. I went on steadily for a long time. The sun was striking level through the trees when I recognised where I was. Cuga had led me through this glade—past that enormous, ancient oak—when he took me to meet the Forest Brothers. We were in Cugamand, I thought, and then wondered why I had thought "we," not "I." All I had to do to reach the cave was turn off the lion's road and follow the way I knew, downward and to the right.

I stopped and thanked Ennu, then turned to the right and went down through woods I knew with in-creasing familiarity, until I came to the home stream and crossed it and stood before the rockslide that held and concealed the door of the cave. Sunset light was bright on the tops of the trees.

I started to say his name, but I knew with absolute certainty that he was not there. I said nothing. After a while I went in through the narrow entrance. My eyes found only darkness in the cave. The smell of smoke and badly cured fur, Cuga's reek, Cuga's stink, was there, but faint, a kind of echo of a smell. It was cold in that darkness. There was no light. I went back outside. The evening seemed marvelously bright and warm, and I remembered the blinding glory of daylight the first time I ever left the cave.

I put my pack down by the cave door and took my water bottle to fill it at the stream. I drank, and filled the bottle, and squatted there for a while; and as I watched the flow and movement of the water in the gathering twilight, I saw him on the bank of the stream.

Animals and the water and weather of a year or two years had not left very much of him: his skull, with the forehead broken in, and other bones, a couple of scraps of moldy fur clothing, and his leather belt.

I touched the skull where it lay, and stroked it a little, talking to Cuga. The light was failing fast and I was very tired. I did not want to sleep in the cave. I rolled up in my reedcloth blanket in a grassy bay of the great rock formation and slept deep and long.

In the morning I went into the cave, thinking to bury him there; but it was so cheerless that it seemed better to let him be where he was. I dug a small grave high enough above the stream to be out of the winter floods. I gathered his bones into it, and his belt, and one of his knives I found in the cave, and the metal box of salt that had been his greatest treasure. He'd kept it hidden all the time I was with him, and I was never to know where, for I found it lying out on the floor of the fireplace cave. There was still a little salt in the bottom of the box. In it also was one of his two prized knives, and the small, heavy bag of money that I had left with him and he had kept for me.

It was a relief to my heart to know that he hadn't been killed for the sake of that money. From the fact that he'd taken the things out and not put them away again, I imagined that maybe having been hurt or feeling ill, he'd wanted to look at his treasures. But when he knew he was dying, he left them and went to die outside, in the place he liked to sit beside the stream.

I covered the small grave over, smoothing the dirt

with my hands, and asked Ennu to guide him. I put the bag of money in the bottom of my pack without opening it. I said farewell and set off, back up the way that led north and east to the hill where I had first met the Forest Brothers.

Ever since I left East Lake I had felt very lonely. Solitude had always been a pleasure to me, but it had been a rare and relative solitude—almost always there had been others nearby, in reach. This was different, this aloneness. To have once again walked away from my own people, from all I knew—to know that wherever I went I would always be among strangers—no matter how I tried to tell myself it was freedom, it felt like desolation. That day I left Cugamand was the hardest of all. I plodded on and plodded on, finding the way without thinking about it. When I got to the top of the hill where Cuga had left me, it was time to stop. I stopped. I made no fire, for I didn't want to bring the Forest Brothers or anybody else. I had to go alone, and I would. But I lay there that night and grieved. I grieved for myself, and for Cuga. And I grieved for my people in East Lake, Tisso and Gegemer and my kind, lazy uncle—all of them. And for Chamry Bern, and Venne, and Diero, and even Barna, for I had loved Barna. And for my people of Arcamand, Sotur, Tib and Ris and little Oco, Astano, Yaven, my teacher Everra, and Sallo, my Sallo, lost—all of them lost to me. I was heavy with tears I could not cry, and my head ached. The great stars of summer slid slowly to the west. I slept at last.

I woke with dawn, the sky a transparent pink hill of light over the dark hill of earth. I was hungry and thirsty. I got up and made up my pack and went on down the hillside, and at the creek in the hollow, where Brigin had not let me drink my fill, I drank my fill. I was alone—so, then, I'd go alone, and live my life as I saw fit. I'd drink where I wanted to drink. I'd go to Mesun, where all men were free men, and where the University taught wisdom, and the poet Caspro lived.

I tried to sing his hymn to Liberty as I strode along, but I never could sing, and my voice in the silence and birdsong of the woods sounded like a young crow squawking. Instead, I let the words of his poems come into my head and come with me on my way, making a quieter music to keep me company.

Things change fast in a forest, trees fall, young trees shoot up, brambles grow across the path, but the way was always clear enough when I looked for it and let my memory tell me where I'd gone. I came to the clearing where we'd picked up the venison, and ate my midday dinner there. I wished I had some of that venison. My pack was getting all too light. I wondered if I should begin to veer eastward again, to come out of the Daneran Forest and try my luck at buying food in a village or a town. But I didn't want to do that yet. I'd stay in the forest, making a wide pass around Brigin's camp, if it was still there, taking the way Chamry had taken us till I got to a safe distance from Barna's city. Then I'd head northeast to find one of the villages outside the forest, on the Somulane, the first of the two great rivers I was to cross.

My plan went well until I was more or less east of Barna's city, following the Somulane as it took a northerly bend through the forested hills. I was pretty hungry, and there were backwaters of the river in which I could see trout swimming as plain as pigeons flying in the sky. It was too much for me. I stopped at a lovely pool, put my rod together, baited my hook with a caddis fly, and caught a good fish in no time. And a second one in not much more than no time. I was just casting my line again when somebody said, "Gav?"

I jumped, lost my bait, grabbed for my knife, and stared at the man who stood behind me. For a moment

I didn't know him, then I recognised Ater—one of the raiders who had caught Irad and Melle—they'd told the story in the beer house—he'd said he liked his women soft…A big, heavy man he had been then, but he was a big, gaunt man now. I stared at him in terror, but there was no threat in his gaze. He looked dully surprised.

"How'd you get here, Gav?" he said. "I thought you drowned, or went off. Before."

"Went off," I said.

"You coming back, then?"

I shook my head.

"Nothing much to come back to," he said.

He looked at my two fish. I knew how hunger looks at food.

"What do you mean, Ater?" I said when I began to realise what he'd said.

He turned his hands out in a helpless gesture. "Well," he said. "You know." I stared at him. He stared at me. "It's all burned down," he said.

"The city? The Heart of the Forest? Burned down?"

It was hard for him to understand that I didn't know about the event that loomed so immense in his life. It took me a while to get much sense out of him.

My first concern was that other men would be following him, that Barna's guards would be on me, take me captive, but he just kept saying, "No. Nobody's coming. They're all gone. Nobody's coming." He said, "I came over to that village we used to go to, see if there was some food there, but they burned it too."

"Who?"

"The soldiers."

"Casicar?"

"I guess so."

Getting information out of him was going to be a slow business. I said, "Is it safe to make a fire?"

He nodded.

"Make one, then, and put the fish on a stick and toast them. I've got a little bread here." I succeeded in landing another big trout while he made the fire. He could hardly wait to char the fish over the fire. He ate with desperate haste, cramming the hard bread into his mouth and chewing it painfully. "Ah," he said, "ah, that's good, thanks, Gav. Thanks."

I went back to fishing after we ate; when the trout jump at an empty hook it's a sin not to let them do it. While I fished he sat on the bank and told me what had happened to the Heart of the Forest. Much of the story I had to guess from his incoherent telling.

Etra and Casicar were allies now, in a Northern League against Votus, Morva, and smaller cities south of the Morr. A lot of farm slaves had been killed during the wars between Etra and Casicar, or had run away, and had to be replaced or recaptured. Towns all round the Daneran Forest had long been full of rumors of the great camp or city of runaway slaves, and the new allies decided to go in and find out what was there. They sent an army, a legion from each city, on a rapid march up between Daneran and the Marshes. Barna's people knew nothing about the attack until outpost guards came running into the city shouting the warning.

Barna gathered all the men who would stand with him to defend the Heart of the Forest. He ordered the women and children to scatter out in the woods. Many of the men ran with them. Any who hesitated or stayed to fight were soon trapped: the soldiers surrounded the walls and methodically set them afire, and then the whole city, hurling torches onto the roofs of the wooden buildings. Barna's men made a sortie against them but were outnumbered, cut down, slaughtered. The soldiers ringed the burning town and caught all who fled the holocaust, then ranged out and rounded up people hiding or trying to escape in the woods. They spent a couple of nights waiting till the fires burnt out so they could loot what was left. They found the treasury and divided that. They divided the prisoners, half for Etra, half for Casicar, and then marched back, driving the chained slaves along with the cattle and sheep.

There were tears on Ater's cheeks as he told me the story, but his voice remained dull and even. He'd been out with a raiding party when they saw the smoke of the burning city from miles away in the north. They had crept back a couple of days after the soldiers left.

"Barna...," I said, and Ater said, "They said the soldiers cut off his head and kicked it around like a ball."

It was very hard to ask about any of the others. When I did, Ater had no answers; often he seemed not even to know who I was talking about. Chamry? He shrugged. Venne? He didn't know. Diero? He didn't know. But evidently a number of people had escaped one way or another, and many of them had regathered in the ruined city, not knowing where else to go. Some of the grain supplies had remained hidden and untouched, and they had lived off them and what was left of the gardens. For how long? Again Ater was vague. I guessed that the raid and fire had been about half a year ago, perhaps in early winter.

"You're going back there now?" I asked him, and he nodded. "It's safer there," he said. "The soldiers been raiding everywhere. Taking slaves. I was at Ebbera, over there. Near as bad off as we are. No slaves left to work the fields."

"I'll come with you," I said. I had to know what had become of my friends.

I'd caught five more good-sized fish. I packed them up in leaves and we set off. We came to the Heart of the Forest in the late afternoon.

The city I had last seen silver-blue in moonlight was a waste of charred beams, shapeless mounds, ashfields. At one edge, near the gardens, people had made huts and shelters with salvaged lumber, much of it half burned. An old woman was weeding in the garden, bowed back, averted face. A couple of men sat in the doorways of their huts, their hands hanging between their knees. A dog barked at us, then whined and cowered away. A child sat on the dirt gazing listlessly at Ater and me. As we came near, it too cowered away from us.

I had come in order to ask about my friends, but I could not ask. I could only see Diero trapped in Barna's house as it burned, Chamry's corpse dumped in a common grave, Venne driven down the road in chains. I said to Ater, "I can't stay here." I gave him the packet of fish. "Share it with somebody," I said.

"Where you going then?" he asked in his blank way.
"North."

"Look out for slave takers," Ater said.

I was about to turn back the way we'd come, when something grabbed both my legs so hard and suddenly that I nearly lost my balance. It was a child, the child who'd stared and shrunk from us. "Beaky, Beaky, Beaky," she cried in a high thin voice like a bird. "Oh Beaky, oh Beaky."

I had to pry her hands loose from my legs, and then she gripped my hands with sparrow-claw fingers, looking up into my face, her face all dust and bone and tears.

"Melle?"

She pulled me to her. I picked her up. She weighed nothing, it was like picking up a ghost. She clung to me tightly, just as she used to when I came to Diero's room to teach her letters. She hid her face against my shoulder.

"Where does she live?" I asked Ater, who had stopped to stare at us. He pointed to a hut nearby. I started to carry her towards it.

"Don't go there," she whispered, "don't go there."

"Where do you live then, Melle?"

"Nowhere."

A man looked from the doorway of the hut that Ater had pointed out. I'd seen him working as a carpenter but had never known his name. He too had the dull look, the siege face.

"Where's the girl's sister?" I asked him.

He shrugged.

"Diero didn't—escape—did she?"

The man shrugged again, this time with a grinning sneer at the question. Gradually his look sharpened. He said, "You want that one?"

I stared at him.

"Half a bronze for the night," he said. "Or food, if you've got any." He stepped forward, trying to get a look at my backpack.

I went through a quick, complex set of thoughts. I said, "What I have I keep," and set straight off walking back the way I'd come. Melle clung to my neck, silent, her face hidden.

The man shouted after me and the dog, barking, set off other dogs in a chorus of barks and howls. I drew my knife, glancing back constantly. But nobody followed us.

When I'd walked a half mile or so I knew that my little ghost was a great deal more solid than I'd thought, and also that I'd better think what I was doing. Coming across the faint trace of a path, I went along it for some way, then turned aside. Behind a thicket of elderberries that screened us from the path, I set Melle down on her feet and sat down next to her to get my breath. She squatted down beside me. "Thank you for taking me away," she said in a thread of a voice.

She would be seven or eight years old now, I thought. She hadn't grown very much, and was so thin her joints looked like knobs. I got some dried fruit out of my pack and offered it to her. She ate it with a pitiful and terrible attempt not to be greedy. She held out a piece to me. I shook my head. "I ate a little while ago," I said. She devoured the fruit. I cut a piece of my rock-hard bread into little morsels and warned her to suck them to soften them before she chewed. She sat with bread in her mouth, and her dirty, bony face began to relax.

"Melle," I said, "I'm going north. Away. To a city called Mesun."

"Please, can I come with you," she whispered, her face tightening again, her eyes getting big, only daring one glance up at me.

"You don't want to stay there, at—"

"Oh no, please no." The same whisper. "Please no!"

"There's nobody there who…"

She shook her head again and again.

"No, no, no," she whispered.

I didn't know what to do. That is, there was only one thing I could do, but I didn't know how I was going to manage it.

"Are you pretty good at walking?"

"I can walk and walk," she said earnestly. She put another little lump of bread in her mouth, timidly, and sucked it as I had told her to do.

"Well," I said, "you'll have to."

"I will, I will. You won't have to carry me. I promise."

"That's good. We ought to walk on a way now, because I want to get back to the river before dark. And tomorrow we'll leave the forest. All right?"

"Yes!" she said, and her eyes shone. She stood right up.

She walked along bravely, but her legs were short, and she didn't have much strength in her little starved body. Fortunately we reached the Somulane again sooner than I expected, coming down an open glade to a long bend in the river. The fishing there wasn't like the wonderful pool farther upstream, but I did catch a trout and a couple of perch, enough for our supper. The grass was soft and the light fell sweetly through the trees across the water, turning it to bronze. "It's pretty here,"

Melle said. She fell asleep as soon as she had eaten. She lay in a little heap on the grass. My heart turned over at the sight of her fragility. How could I take this child with me? But how could I not take her?

Luck hears prayers only with his deaf ear, but I spoke to him, to the ear that hears the wheels of the chariots of the stars. I said, "You used to be with me, Lord, when I didn't know it. I hope you're with this child now, and not just fooling her." And I spoke in silence also to Ennu, thanking her and asking her to guide us. Then there was nothing to do but roll Melle up with me in my soft reedcloth blanket, and sleep.

We both woke as dawn was brightening. Melle went off by herself to the riverside, and when she came back she had managed to wash herself quite clean, and was shivering with wet and cold. I wrapped the blanket round her again while we ate a little breakfast. She was shy and solemn.

"Melle," I said, "your sister…"

She said in a strange, small, even voice, "We tried to hide. Back of the sheep pastures. The soldiers found us. They took Irad away. I don't remember."

I remembered Barna's raider telling how they had taken the two girls from their village, how Ater had been going to toss the little one aside, but they clung too tight together.... They hadn't been able to hold on to each other this time.

Melle's chin trembled. She looked down and chewed on her bit of hard bread but could not swallow. Neither of us could say anything more about Irad. After a long time I said, "Your village was over on the west side of the forest. Do you want to go back there?"

"To the village?" She looked up, and thought hard. "I can't remember it much," she said.

"But you had family there. Your mother—"

She shook her head. "We didn't have any mother. We belonged to Gan Buli. He hit us a lot. My sister..." She didn't finish.

Maybe Luck had been with Melle after all.

But never with Irad.

"All right, then you'll come with me," I said, in as matter-of-fact a tone as I could manage. "But listen. We'll be going on the roads, into villages, some of the time at least. Among people. I think it might be better if you were my little brother. Can you pretend to be a boy?"

"Of course," she said, interested in the idea. She thought about it. "I need a name. I can be Miv."

I almost said, "No!" but stopped myself. She should have the name she chose herself. Like Melle, it was a common name.

"All right, Miv," I said, with a little effort. "And I'm Avvi."

"Avvi," she repeated, and then murmured, "Avvi Beaky," with a tiny smile.

"And who we are is this: we aren't slaves, because there aren't any slaves in Urdile, where we live. I'm a student at the University in Mesun. I study with a great man there, who's waiting for us. I'm taking you there to be a student too. We come from just east of the Marshes."

She nodded. It all seemed perfectly convincing to her. But she was eight years old.

"What I hope is, we can mostly keep off the big roads and just go through the countryside. I have some money. We can buy food in villages and from farmers. But we have to look out for slave takers. Everywhere. If we don't meet any of them, we'll be all right."

"What is the great man in Mesun's name?" she asked. A good question. I wasn't prepared for it. Finally I said the only name of a great man in Mesun I knew: "Orrec Caspro."

She nodded.

There seemed to be one more thing on her mind. She finally said it. "I can't pee like a boy," she said.

"That's all right. Don't worry. I'll stand guard."

She nodded. We were ready to go. A short way downstream from the bend of the river it widened and shoaled out, and I said, "Let's cross here. Can you swim—Miv?"

"No."

"If it gets too deep I can carry you." We took off our shoes and tied them to my pack. I fastened a length of light rope around Melle's waist and my own, with a few feet of slack between us. We waded out into the river hand in hand. I thought of my vision of crossing a river, and wondered if soon I'd be carrying the child on my shoulders (which were still sore from carrying her yesterday). But this didn't at all look like the river I remembered. By picking a zigzag way on the high point of the shoals I was never more than waist deep, and could hold Melle up well enough, except in one place where the current ran fast and deep alongside an islet of gravel. There I told her to hold tight to the rope around my waist and keep her head up the best she could, and I waded in, swam the few yards to the gravel bar, and wallowed ashore. Melle went under only at the last moment, when she thought she could touch bottom and couldn't. She came up choking and sputtering.

After that we had only shallow waters to wade, and soon came to the far shore.

As we sat getting our breath, drying out, and putting on our shoes, I said, "We've crossed the first of the two great rivers we have to cross. This is the land of Bendile."

"The hero Hamneda had to swim across a river when he was wounded, didn't he?"

I can't say how much that touched me. It wasn't that she'd learned the story of Hamneda from me. It was that she thought of him, that he was familiar to her mind and heart as he was to mine. We had a common language, this child and I, a language I hadn't spoken with anyone else since I left my own childhood in Etra. I put my arm around her little thin shoulders, and she wriggled against me comfortably.

"Let's go find a village and buy some food," I said. "Hold on, though. Let me get some money out so I don't wave all of it in people's faces." I dug into my pack and brought out the heavy little silk pouch. A faint, smoky Cuga-reek still clung to it, or maybe it had just been close to the smoked fish from Ferusi. I untied the cord, opened the pouch, and stared. I remembered what it had held: bronzes, and four silver pieces. But along with the bronzes there were now nine silver pieces, four of the gold pieces from Pagadi called dictators, and a broad gold coin from Ansul.

My Cuga had been a thief as well as a runaway.

"I can't carry this!" I said. I looked at the money with horror. All I saw was the danger it posed us if anyone should get the slightest notion that we carried such a fortune. It was in my mind to simply dump the gold pieces out in the grass and gravel and leave them.

"Did somebody give it to you?"

I nodded, speechless.

"You can sew up money in clothes to hide it," Melle said, handling the dictators with admiring curiosity. "These are pretty, but the big one is the prettiest. Have you got a needle and thread?"

"Only fish hooks and fishing line."

"Well, maybe I can get some sewing things in a village. Maybe there'll be a pedlar on the road. I can sew."

"So can I," I said stupidly. "Well, all I can do now is put it back. I wish I hadn't found it."

"Is it a lot of money?"

I nodded.

She was still studying the coins. "C—I—City of P—A—C—something—"

"Pagadi," I said.

"Oh, the words go all the way round. State and City of Pagadi Year 8 something." Her head was bent over the coin just as it had used to bend over her reading in Barna's house, in the lamplight in Diero's room. She looked up and smiled at me as she handed it back. Her eyes were luminous.

I kept out a few quarter- and half-bronzes and hid the pouch away again. We walked on up along the river, for there was a clear path. After we had gone for an hour or more, Melle said, "Maybe when we get to the city where we're going we can find out where my sister is and buy her from the soldiers with the gold."

"Maybe we can," I said, my heart twisting again.

Presently I added in my anxiety, "But we can't talk about it. At all."

"I won't," she said. She never did.

◆   ◆   ◆

FOLLOWING THE RIVER as it took a sharp turn north we came that afternoon to a fair-sized town. I summoned up my courage to enter it. Melle seemed quite fearless, trusting in my strength and wisdom. We walked boldly into the marketplace and bought ourselves food. I bought a blanket for Melle which she could also wear as a poncho, and haggled for a little case containing a stout needle and a hank of linen thread. People wanted to talk with us, asking us where we were from and where we were bound. I told my story, and "student of the University" was mysterious enough to most people that they didn't know what further questions to ask. The plump, snaggletoothed woman who was demanding a quarter-bronze for the thread and needle looked at Melle with compassion and said, "I can see it must be a terrible hard life for a little fellow, studenting!"

"He was sick all last winter," I said.

"Was he then? What's your name, sonny boy?"

"Miv," Melle said calmly.

"I'm sure your brother takes good care of you and doesn't let you walk too far," the woman said. And perhaps because she'd seen that I wasn't going to pay such a price as she asked, or for a better reason, she went on, "And this is for you, to keep you safe on your journey— a gift, a gift, I wouldn't ask money of a child for the blessing of Ennu!" She held out a little figure of a cat, carved of dark wood, with a copper wire round its neck to hang it from as a pendant; there were several such little Ennu-Més on her tray. Melle looked up at me with big eyes. I remembered she and Irad had worn such figures on a necklace, though these were finer than what they'd had. I handed the woman her extortionate price and nodded to Melle to take the carving.

She clutched it in her hand and held her hand tight to the base of her throat.

I felt unexpectedly easy and safe in the marketplace. We were strangers among strangers, lost in a crowd, not isolated, solitary travelers in a wilderness. A booth was selling some kind of sweet fried cake that smelled delicious. "Let's have some of that," I said to Melle, and when we each had a hot cake in hand we sat down on the broad edge of a fountain in the shade to eat them. They were greasy and heavy, and Melle got through only about half of hers. I looked at her sidelong, seeing what the snaggletoothed woman had seen: that this was a very thin little child who looked on the point of exhaustion.

"Are you tired, Miv?" I said.

After a slight struggle with herself she hunched her shoulders and nodded.

"Let's stay at an inn. We won't often get a chance to, I expect. This is a nice town," I said, recklessly. "You got cold crossing the river. You walked a long way today. You deserve a real bed tonight."

She hunched up some more and looked down at her greasy cake. She showed it to me. "Can you eat it, Beaky?" she whispered.

"I can eat anything, Squeaky," I said, proving it. "Now come on. There was an inn back there just off the market square."

The innkeeper's wife took an interest in Melle—evidently my companion was a passport to people's sympathy. We were given a nice little room at the back of the house, with a wide, short bed. Melle climbed up on the bed at once and curled up. She still held her Ennu-Mé tight in her hand. She was wearing her new poncho and didn't want to take it off. "It keeps me warm," she said, but I saw she was shivering. I covered her over, and she fell asleep soon. I sat in the chair by the window. It was a long time since I'd sat in a chair, since I'd been in a great, solid house like this, very different from the huts in the Marshes with their walls of reed. I took my book out and read for a while. I knew the *Cosmologies* pretty well by heart, but just holding the book, letting my eyes follow the printed lines, was reassuring to me. I needed reassurance. I had no real idea what I was doing or where I was going, and now I'd taken on a charge who at best would slow me down very much. Maybe I could leave her in this town with somebody, I thought, and come back for her later. —Leave her? Come back from where? I looked over at her. She was sound asleep. I went out quietly to see about dinner.

I brought her back a bowl of chicken broth, and she roused up to drink it, but drank very little; she was feverish, I thought. I consulted with the innkeeper's wife, Ameno, who had the hearty, jolly manner of her trade, but underneath it seemed a quiet, serious woman. She came and looked at Melle and said she might have caught something or might just be very tired. She said, "Go on and have your supper. I'll keep the fire up, and look in at the child." She had persuaded Melle to let her have the little cat figure so she could put it on a necklace. Melle was watching her braid thread for the necklace, and dozing off again. I went to the common room and had an excellent supper of roast mutton, which made me think with affection and pain of Chamry Bern.

We stayed at the inn in Rami four nights. It didn't take Ameno long to let me know she knew Melle wasn't a boy, but she asked no questions—it was clear enough why a girl might want to travel as a boy—and dropped no hints to anyone else. Melle wasn't sick, but she'd been pretty near giving out. Three days of rest and good food and kind care did wonders for her. She sat in bed and carefully sewed our gold pieces into our clothing, and then slept again. I would have stayed on still longer to build her up for travel if it hadn't been for what I heard the fourth night at the inn.

Men of the town came in every evening for a glass of beer or cider and to chat with one another and with any guests at the inn who wanted to be sociable. They were a bit cautious and stiff with me at first because I was supposed to be a scholar and a city man, but seeing that I wasn't much more than a boy and spoke little and modestly, they soon ignored me in a friendly fashion. They talked about local affairs, of course, but the travelers among them made conversation about the wider world too, which was interesting to me who had been for so long in the forest and the Marshes, hearing nothing of the City States and Bendile.

Melle was sleeping sound after a good supper, and I came to sit at the common-room fire. Conversation had fallen on the "Barnavites." Everybody had a story about Barna's men who used to raid the roads and farms and market towns. Some were the old romantic tales I'd heard in Etra, but one man here confirmed them. He said that three years ago, raiders had taken half the flock he was driving to market, but they'd truly taken half his flock, counting them out "one for you, one for us," when they could as well have taken them all, and so, he said, he could only curse them with half a curse. I had the impression that his hearers half believed him, too.

Then they all had tales about Barna's city, how the slaves kept houses full of beautiful women, how they had so much stolen gold there that they used it for roofing, and when the soldiers burned the city molten gold ran in streams in the gutters. Everybody knew about Barna, the giant with flaming red hair, taller than any other man, who'd planned to attack Asion, make himself king of Bendile, and put the slaves to rule their fallen masters. There was some discussion of the fact that you never could trust a slave no matter how loyal he seemed, and several examples of slavish treachery were given.

"Well, here's a tale for you," said one of the guests of the inn, a wool buyer from eastern Bendile. "About a disloyal slave and a loyal one too. I just heard this one.

There was a slave boy from the Marshes who'd been the pride of his masters in the city of Etra. He could tell any tale or sing any song, no matter what, he knew them all. He was worth a hundred gold pieces to his masters. He defiled a daughter of the house and ran away, stealing a bag of gold with him. They sent out slave takers after him, but none found him, and some said he'd drowned. But the son of the house had a loyal slave who swore he'd find the boy and bring him back to Etra to take his punishment for shaming the house of his masters. So he got on the track, and after a while he heard word of a young runaway in Barna's city who was famous for his speaking and singing. Barna himself, having been a learned slave, set a great value on this boy. But before the soldiers came, the boy gave Barna the slip too, and vanished again. The slave is still hunting for him. I talked to a man who knows him, he calls him 'Three Eyebrows.' He's been to the Marshes, and to Casicar, and Piram, and says he'll hunt the runaway down if it takes him the rest of his life. Now there's a slave loyal to his masters, I say!"

The others expressed modified approval. I tried to imitate their judicious nods, while the heart in me was cold as a lump of ice. My pose of being a scholar, which

I hoped would save me from suspicion, now looked likely to bring it upon me. If only the man hadn't said the runaway was from the Marshes! My looks, the color of my skin, always drew some notice, anywhere outside the Marshes. And sure enough, a townsman eyed me over his beer and said, "You look to be from that side of the country. Do you know anything about this famous slave, then?"

I couldn't speak. I shook my head with as much indifference as I could pretend. More stories of escapes and slave takers followed. I sat through them, drank my cider, and told myself that I must not panic, that nobody had questioned my story, that having the child with me would avert suspicion. Tomorrow we'd set off again. It had been a mistake to stay anywhere for any length of time. But then, Melle could never have gone on if we hadn't rested here. It would be all right. We would come to the second river in only a few days, and cross it, and be free.

I spoke with Ameno that night, asking if she knew of any carters going north that might give us a lift. She told me where to go. Early in the morning I routed sleepy Melle out. Ameno sent us off with a packet of food and took the silver piece I offered her. "Luck be with you, go with Ennu," she said, and gave Melle a long, grave embrace. We went off through the foggy dawn to a yard on the far edge of town where carters met to make up their loads and sometimes find passengers, and there we found a ride as far as a place called Tertudi, which the carter said was halfway to the river. I had no clear map of this part of Bendile in my mind, and had to rely on what people told me, knowing only that the river was north of us, and Mesun across it and well to the east.

It took our carter's slow horses all day to get to Tertudi, a small, poor town with no inn. I didn't want to stay there and be noticed. I hoped to break any connection with the inn at Rami, to leave no traceable path behind us. We spoke to no one in Tertudi, but simply walked away from it for a couple of miles into the hayfields that surrounded it, and made ourselves a camp by a little stream for the night. Crickets sang all about us in the warm evening, near and far. Melle ate with a good appetite and said she wasn't tired. She wanted me to tell her a story she knew. That was her request: "Tell me a story I know." I told her the beginning of the *Chamhan*. She listened, intent, never moving, till at last she began to blink and yawn. She fell asleep curled up in her poncho, holding the little cat figure at the base of her throat.

I lay listening to the crickets and looking out for the first stars. I slipped into sleep peacefully, but woke in the dark. There was a man in the hayfield, standing watching us. I knew him, I knew his face, the scar that split his eyebrow. I tried to get up but I was paralyzed as I had been paralyzed by Dorod's drugs, I could not move and my heart pounded and pounded...It was deep night, the stars blazing. Most of the crickets had fallen silent but one still trilled nearby. No one was there. But I could not sleep again.

It grieved me that blind hate and rancor should be my last link to Arcamand. I could think now of the people of that house with gratitude for what they had given me—kindness, security, learning, love. I could never think that Sotur or Yaven had or would have betrayed my love. I was able to see, in part at least, why the Mother and Father had betrayed my trust. The master lives in the same trap as the slave, and may find it even harder to see beyond it. But Torm and his slave-double Hoby never wanted to look beyond it; they valued nothing but power, the most brutal control of other people. My escape, if he heard of it, would have rankled

Torm bitterly. As for Hoby, always seething with envious hatred, the knowledge that I was going about as a free man would goad him to rageful, vengeful pursuit. I had no doubt that he was on my trail. And I was deeply afraid of him. By myself I was no match for him, and now I had my little, helpless hostage with me. She would awaken all his cruelty. I knew that cruelty.

I roused Melle well before dawn and we set off. All I knew to do was walk, walk on, get away.

We walked all day through rolling, open country; we passed a couple of villages at a distance, and avoided the few farms with their barking dogs. Mostly it was grazing land, cattle scattered out across the grasslands. We met up with a cowboy who waited for us and walked his horse along with us to talk. Melle was afraid of him, shrinking away from him, and I was none too glad of his company. But he had no curiosity about where we came from or where we were going. He was lonesome and wanted somebody to talk to. He got off his horse and rambled along with us, talking all the way about his horse and his cattle and his masters and whatever came into his head. Melle gradually seemed to feel easier. When he offered her a ride she shrank away again, but she was much attracted by the friendly little horse, and finally she let me put her up in the saddle.

Our new friend had told us he was out to round up some of his master's cattle which had strayed from the main herd, but he seemed to be in no great hurry about it, and went on with us for miles, Melle sitting in the saddle, looking increasingly blissful, while he led the horse. When I asked about the river, we talked at cross-purposes for quite a while, he insisting that it was to the east, not the north; finally he said, "Oh you're talking of the Sally River! I only know the name of it. It's a long, long way, it's the edge of the world! Our Ambare flows to it, I guess, but I don't know how far. You'll be walking a long time. Better get horses!"

"If we go east, we'll come to your river?"

"Yes, but it's a good long ways too." He gave us complicated directions involving drovers' paths and cart roads, and then ended up saying, "Of course if you just cut across those hills ahead of us you'll be at the Ambare in no time."

"Well, maybe we'll head that way," I said, and he said, "I might as well go that way too. Those cattle might be over there."

That made me suspicious of him. So fear taints the mind. I walked along wondering if he had been watching for us, if he was leading us to a trap, and how to get rid of him, and at the same time certain that he was simply a lonely man happy to have company and pleased to please a child. As I grew silent he talked with Melle, who timidly asked him questions about the horse and its gear. Soon he was giving her a riding lesson, letting her hold the rein, telling her how to put Brownie into a trot. He was soft-voiced and easygoing with both the horse and the child. When he put out his hand to show her how to hold the rein, she pulled away from him in fear, and after that he never came very close to her, treating her with an innate tact. It was hard to distrust him. But I strode on weighed down with suspicion and worry. If it was so far to the Sensaly that this man thought it the end of the world, and if with Melle I could not walk more than ten miles a day, how long would it take us to get there? I felt that as we crept across these open plains we were exposed, visible to anybody looking for us.

Our companion's guidance so far was true: having crossed the low range of hills we saw a good-sized river a couple of miles farther on, flowing northeast. We stopped just over the crest of the hills and sat down under a stand of great beeches to share our food, while Brownie had a bait of oats from a nose bag. Melle called our companion Cowboy-dí, which made him grin; he called her Sonny. She sat beside me, but talked to him. They talked at great length about horses and cattle. I noticed that she kept asking him questions, as children will do, out of real curiosity no doubt, but also it meant she didn't have to answer any questions about herself or me. She was canny.

We could see a boat or barge now and then on the river, and our companion said, "There you are. Go on along to town and get yourselves onto a boat and that'll take you far as you want, eh?"

"Where's town?" Melle asked.

"On down along there," he said, waving vaguely at the river where it disappeared in a long bend among low hills. "I guess I better not go on with you. I don't think any of our cattle got any farther than this. But you go on down to town and get yourselves onto a boat and that'll take you as far as you want. Eh?"

I thought it strange that he said it again exactly the same way, as if he'd memorised it, as if he'd been taught how to lead us into a trap.

"That's a good idea," Melle said. "Isn't it, Avvi?"

"Could be," I said.

She had a quite emotional parting from the horse,

patting and petting it and embracing its long, mild head, and she and the cowboy said goodbye affectionately though without touching. She watched him ride off over the crest of the hills, and sighed as we started down. "They were beautiful," she said.

I felt ashamed of myself, but still couldn't relax from my wariness.

"Will we find the town and get on a boat?"

"I don't think so."

"Why not?"

I found I couldn't express my reasons. We must go on, we must escape the man who was following us, but no way of travel seemed safe to me.

"Or we could get horses, like he said. Only, are horses very expensive?"

"I think they are. And you have to know how to ride them."

"I do now. Sort of."

"I don't," I said shortly.

We walked on; it was easy going, downhill, and Melle flitted right along. At the bottom of the hill a dim footpath led off towards the river, and we followed that.

"So it would be better to get on a boat," Melle said. "Wouldn't it?"

I felt my sense of responsibility for her like a stone on my back, weighing me down. If it was just myself I'd run, I'd hide, I'd be gone, long gone....I was angry with her for holding me back, slowing my steps, arguing with me about how to go. "I don't know," I said.

We went on, I always aware of shortening my pace to hers. We were now on a cart track, coming nearer the river, and saw the roofs of a small town ahead to the right, and soon the wharves, and boats tied up.

I'd asked the Lord Luck to give this child the blessing he'd given me. Was I to distrust him, too? Only a fool acts as if he knows better than Luck. I'd always been a fool, but not that kind.

"We'll see when we get there," I said, after a half mile of silence.

"We can pay for it. Can't we?"

I nodded.

So when we came through apple orchards into town we went straight down to the riverfront and looked about. No boats were tied up and nobody was on the dock. There was a small inn just up the street, its door standing open, and I looked in. A dwarf, a man no taller than Melle, with a big head and a handsome, scowling face, looked round the bar. "What'll you have, Marshy?" he said.

I all but turned and ran.

"What's that with you? A pup? No, by Sampa, a kid. Both of you kids. What d'you want then, milk?"

"Yes," I said, and Melle said, "Yes, please."

He fetched two cups of milk and we sat at a small table to drink it. He stood by the bar and looked us over. His gaze made me very uneasy, but Melle didn't seem to mind it, and gazed right back at him without her usual shyness.

"Is there a black cat?" she asked.

"Why would there be?"

"It said on the sign over the door. The picture."

"Ah. No. That's the house. Sign of the Black Cat. Blessing of Ennu, it is. Where are you bound, then? On your own, are you?"

"Downriver," I said.

"You're off a boat, then." He looked out the open door to see if any boat had docked.

"No. Walking. Thought we might go by water if there's a boat would take us."

"Nothing in now. Pedri's barge will be in tomorrow."

"Going downstream?"

"Clear to the Sally," the man said; so it seemed they called the Sensaly in this country.

He refilled Melle's cup, then stumped to the bar and

came back with two full mugs of cider. He set one down in front of me and raised the other in salute.

I drank with him. Melle raised her cup of milk too.

"Stay tonight if you like," he said. Melle looked at me bright-eyed. It was coming on to evening. I did my best to forget my fears and take what Luck gave us. I nodded.

"Anything to pay with?" he asked.

I took a couple of bronzes from my pocket.

"Because if you hadn't, I'd eat the kid, see," the dwarf said in a matter-of-fact tone, and lunged with a hideous, gaping, threatening face at Melle. She shrank back against me with a great gasp, but then she laughed— sooner than I could smile at his joke. He drew back, grinning. "I was scared," she said to him. He looked pleased. I could feel her heart beating, shaking her small body.

"Put it away," he said to me. "We'll settle up when you go."

He sent us upstairs to a little room at the front of the house; it looked out through low windows over the river and was clean enough, though full of beds, five of them crammed in it side by side. He cooked us a good supper, which we ate along with a couple of longshoremen who ate there every night. They didn't talk, and the host said little. Melle and I walked along the wharves for a while after supper to see the evening light on the water, and then went up to bed. At first I couldn't get to sleep, my mind racing and racing among fruitless thoughts and fears. At last I dropped into sleep, but never very deeply—and then I sat up, blindly reaching for my knife, which I'd set on the floor beside my cot. Steps on the staircase, stopping and starting. The door creaked.

A man came into the room. I could just make out his bulk in the faint starlight from the windows. I sat still, holding my breath and my knife.

The big dark shape blundered past my bed, felt its way over to the end bed, and sat down. I heard shoes thump on the floor. The man lay down, thrashed about a bit, muttered a curse, and lay still. Pretty soon he began to snore. I thought it was a ruse. He wanted us to think he was asleep. But he kept it up, deep and long, till daybreak.

When Melle woke and found a strange man in the room she was very frightened. She could not wait to get out.

Our host gave her warm milk for breakfast, and me warm cider, along with good bread and fresh peaches. I was too restless and uneasy to want to wait for the barge. I told him we'd be going on foot. He said, "If you want to walk, walk, but if you want to float, she'll be along in an hour or two." And Melle nodded; so I obeyed.

The barge came into the wharf in the middle of the morning, a long, heavy craft with a kind of house amidships that made me think of Ammeda's boat in the Marshes; the decks were piled with crates, hay bales, several cages of chickens, all kinds of goods and parcels. While unloading and loading went on I asked the master if we could take passage, and we settled soon enough on a silver piece for fare all the way to the Sensaly, sleeping on deck. I went back to the Black Cat to settle our bill there. "A bronze," the dwarf said.

"Two beds, food and drink," I protested, putting down four bronzes.

He pushed two back to me. "I don't often get a guest my own size," he said, unsmiling.

So we left that town, went aboard Pedri's barge, and set off down the river Ambare at about noon. The sun was bright, the bustle of the docks cheerful, and Melle was excited to be onboard a ship, though she kept at a distance from the master and his assistant, and always very close to me. I felt relieved to be on the water. I said in my mind the prayer to the Lord of the Springs and Rivers I'd learned from my uncle in Ferusi. I stood with Melle watching the longshoreman free the rope and the master haul it in while the gap of roiling water slowly widened between the boat and the dock. Just as the barge began to turn to take the current, a man came down the street and out onto the docks. It was Hoby.

We were in plain sight standing against the wall of the boathouse. I dropped down to sit on the deck, hiding my face in my arms. "What's wrong?" Melle asked, squatting down beside me.

I dared a glance over my forearm. Hoby stood on the dock looking after the barge. I could not tell if he had seen me.

"Beaky, what's wrong?" the child whispered.

I finally answered, "Bad luck."

· 15 ·

The town passed out of view behind us around the bend of the river. We drifted easily downstream in the hot sunlight. As we stood at the rail of the barge I told Melle that I'd seen a man I knew, who might know me.

"From Barna's house?" she asked, still whispering.

I shook my head. "From longer ago. When I was a slave in the city."

"Is he bad?" she asked, and I said, "Yes."

I didn't think he'd seen me, but that was small reassurance; he had only to ask people on the dock, or the host of the Black Cat, if they'd seen a young man, dark skin, big nose, looks like a Marshman.

"Don't worry about it," I said. "We're on the boat, he's on foot."

But that wasn't very reassuring, either. The barge went at the pace of the river, steered with a long sweep and rudder at the stern. It put into every town and village on the riverbank, taking on and putting off cargo and passengers. On its upriver journey it would be pulled by horses on the towpath by the river and would go even slower, the master told me. That was hard to believe. The Ambare, taking its course through great level plains, didn't exactly run; it wandered and meandered, it moseyed along, in places it oozed. Drovers used the towpath to move their cattle; sometimes we'd slowly come up to a herd of brown and brindle cows clopping along at a cow's pace, headed downstream like us, and it would take us a long, long time to draw ahead of them.

The days on the water were sweet and dull and calm, but every time we drew into the wharf of a village my fear rose up again and I scanned every face on shore. Over and over I debated with myself whether it would be wiser to debark at some town on the eastern bank and make our way afoot to the Sensaly, avoiding all towns and villages. But though Melle was by now in much better shape than she'd been when I found her, she still couldn't walk far or fast. It seemed best to float, at least until we were within a day's journey of the Sensaly. The end of the barge journey, at the rivermeet, was a town called Bemette, and that town I resolved at all costs to avoid. There was a ferry across the Sensaly there, the barge master told me. A ferry was what we needed, but that's where Hoby would be waiting for us. I only hoped he would not be waiting for us sooner than that. On horseback or by wagon or even walking hard, he could certainly outpace the barge and arrive before we did at any of the villages on the western bank.

Pedri the barge master paid us little heed and didn't want his assistant to waste time talking to us. We were cargo, along with the boxes and bales and chickens and also, between village and village, the goats and grandmothers, and once a young colt who tried, the whole time he was on the barge, to commit suicide by drowning. Pedri and his assistant slept in the houseboat, taking watch and watch while the barge was afloat. We made our own meals, buying food at villages where we stopped. Melle made friends with the chickens, who were being sent all the way to Bemette; they were some kind of prize breeding stock with fancy tails and feathered legs, all hens. They were perfectly tame, and I bought Melle a bag of birdseed to entertain them with. She named them all, and would sit with them for hours.

Sitting with her, I found their mild, continual conversation soothing. Only when a hawk circled up in the sky over the river, all the busy little cluckings and talkings stopped, and they huddled under their perches, hiding in their ruffled feathers, silent. "Don't worry, Reddy," Melle would soothe them. "It's all right, Little Pet. Don't worry, Snappy. It can't get you. I won't let it."

Don't worry, Beaky.

I read in my book. I said old poems to Melle, and she learned to recite *The Bridge on the Nisas*. We went on with the *Chamhan*.

"I wish I was really your brother, Gav," she murmured to me one night on the dark river under the stars. I murmured back, "You really are my sister."

We put ashore at a wharf on the eastern bank. Pedri and his hand were busy at once unloading hay bales. There was no town as such, but a kind of warehouse-barn and a couple of old cowboys guarding it. "How far is it to Bemette from here?" I asked one of them, and he said, "Two, three hours on a good horse."

I went back aboard and told Melle to gather up her things. My pack was always ready, filled with all the food I could carry. I'd paid the fare before we started. We slipped ashore, and as I passed Pedri I said, "We'll walk from here, our farm's just back that way," pointing southeast. He grunted and went on shifting bales. We walked away from the Ambare the way I'd pointed till we were out of sight, then turned left to bear northeast, towards the Sensaly. The country was very flat, mostly tall grass, with a few groves of trees. Melle walked along beside me stoutly. As she walked she muttered a soft litany, "Goodbye Snappy, goodbye Rosy, goodbye Gold-eye, goodbye Little Pet..."

We walked on no path. The country did not change and there were no landmarks, except, very far off north-ward, a blue line that might be clouds or might be hills across the river. I had nothing but the sun to tell me the direction to go. It came on to evening. We stopped at a grove of trees to eat supper, then rolled up in our blan-kets and slept there. We had seen no sign of anyone fol-lowing us, but I was certain that Hoby was on our track, that he might even be waiting for us. The dread of see-ing him never left me, and filled my restless sleep. I was awake long before dawn. We set off in the twilight of morning, still heading, as well as I could steer us, north-east. The sun came up red and huge over the plains.

The ground began to get boggy, and there were low places of marsh and reed. About midday we saw the Sensaly.

It was wide—a big river. Not deep, I thought, for there were shoals and gravel bars out in midstream, and more than one channel; but from the shore you can't tell where the current quickens and has dug deep places in such a stream.

"We'll go east along the river," I said to Melle and to myself. "We'll come to a ford. Or a ferry. Mesun is still a long way upriver from here, so we're going the right direction for sure, and when we can get across, we will."

"All right," Melle said. "What's the river's name?"

"Sensaly."

"I'm glad rivers have names. Like people." She made a song of the name and I heard the thin little chant as we walked, *Sen-sally, sen-sallee...* Going was hard in the willow thickets above the shore, and so we soon went down to walk on the river beach, wide floodplains of mud, gravel, and sand.

We could be seen more easily there; but if he was on our track there was no way to hide. This was an open, desolate country. There were no signs of humankind. We saw only deer and a few wild cattle.

When we stopped for Melle to rest I tried fishing, but had little luck, a few small perch. The river was very clear, and as far as I waded out in it, the current was not strong. I saw a couple of places I thought might be fordable, but there were tricky-looking bits on the far side; we went on.

We walked so for three days. We had food for about two more and after that must live by fishing. It was evening, and Melle was tired. I was too. The sense of being pursued wore me down, and I had little sleep, waking again and again all night. I left her sitting on a sandy bit under a willow and went up the rise of the bank, scouting as always for a ford. I saw faint tracks coming down across the beach, ahead of us; indeed there looked to be a ford there in the wide, shoal-broken river.

I looked back, and saw a single horseman coming along beside the water.

I ran down to Melle and said, "Come," picking up my pack. She was frightened and bewildered, but took up her little blanket pack at once. I caught her hand and brought her along as fast as she could go to the track I had seen. Horses and wagons had crossed the river here. I led Melle into the water, saying to her, "When it gets deep I'll carry you."

The way to go was plain at first, the clear water showing me the shallows between shoals. Out in the middle of the water I looked back once. The horseman had seen us. He was just riding into the river, the water splashing up about his horse's legs. It was Hoby. I saw his face, round, hard, and heavy, Torm's face, the Father's, the face of the slave owner and the slave. He was scowling, urging on his horse, shouting at me, words I could not hear.

I saw all that in a glance and waded on, crosscurrent, pulling the child with me as best I could. When I saw she was getting out of her depth I said, "Climb up on my shoulders, Melle. Don't hold me by the throat, but hold tight." She obeyed.

I knew where I was then. I had been in this river with this burden on my shoulders. I did not look around because I do not look around, I go forward, almost out of my depth, but still touching bottom, and there is the place that looks like the right way to go, straight up to the shore, but I don't go that way, the sand gives way beneath my foot. I must go to the right, and farther still to the right. Then the current seizes me with sudden terrific power and I'm off my feet, trying to swim, and sinking, floundering, sinking—but I have foothold again, the child clinging to me hard, I can climb against that terrible current, fight my way up into the shallows, scramble gasping up among the willows whose roots are in the river, and from there, only from there, I can look back.

The horse was struggling out in the deep current, riderless.

I could see how all the force of the river gathered in that channel, just downstream from where we had found our way.

Melle slipped down from my back and pressed up tight against me, shuddering. I held her close, but I could not move. I crouched staring at the river, at the horse being carried far down the river, swimming desperately. Now it began to find footing. I watched it make its way, plunging and slipping, back to the other shore. I scanned the water, the islets, the gravel bars, upriver and down, again and again. Sand, gravel, shining water.

"Gav, Gav, Beaky," the child was sobbing, "come on. Come on. We have to go on. We have to get away." She tugged at my legs.

"I think maybe we have," I tried to say, but I had no voice. I staggered after Melle for a few steps up into the willow grove, out of the water, onto dry land. There my legs gave way and I pitched down. I tried to tell Melle that I was all right, that it was all right, but I couldn't speak. I couldn't get air enough. I was in the water again, under the water. The water was clear and bright all round me, then clear and dark.

◆　◆　◆

WHEN I CAME to myself it was night, mild and overcast. The river ran black among its pale shoals and bars. The little damp hot bundle pressed against my side was Melle. I roused her, and we groped and crawled up through the thickets to a kind of hollow that seemed to offer shelter. I was too clumsy to make a fire. Everything in our packs was damp, but we took off our wet clothes, rubbed ourselves hard, and rolled up in our damp blankets. We huddled together again and fell asleep at once.

My fear was gone. I had crossed the second river. I slept long and deep.

We woke to sunlight. We spread out all our damp things to dry and ate damp stale bread there in the hollow among the willow thickets. Melle seemed to have taken no harm, but was silent and watchful. She said at last, "Don't we have to run away any more?"

"I don't think so," I said. Before we ate, I had gone down to the shore and, concealed in the thickets, scanned the river and the shores for a long time. Reason told me I should fear, reason said that Hoby might well have swum across and be hiding near; but all the time unreason told me, You're safe; he's gone; the link is broken.

Melle was watching me, with a child's trust.

"We're in Urdile now," I said, "where there are no

slaves. And no slave takers. And…" But I didn't know whether she'd even seen Hoby behind us in the river, and didn't know how to speak of him. "And I think we're free," I said.

She pondered this for a while.

"Can I call you Gav again?"

"My whole name is Gavir Aytana Sidoy," I said. "But I like Beaky."

"Beaky and Squeaky," Melle murmured, looking down, with her small, half-circle smile. "Can I go on being Miv?"

"It might be a good idea. If you want to."

"Now are we going to see the great man in the city?"

"Yes," I said. And so when our things had dried out we set off.

Our journey to Mesun was easy enough, as indeed all our journey had been, but wonderfully freed from the dread that had dogged and darkened my way between the rivers. I had no idea what I was going to do when I got to Mesun, how we were to live; but to ask too many questions seemed ungrateful to Lord Luck and Lady Ennu. They'd been with us so far, they wouldn't leave us now. I sang Caspro's hymn to them under my breath as we walked.

"You don't sing quite as well as some people," my companion remarked, with some diplomacy.

"I know I don't. You sing, then."

She lifted up a sweet, unsteady little voice in a love song she'd heard in Barna's house. I thought of her beautiful sister, and wondered if Melle too would be beautiful. I found myself thinking, "Let her be spared that!" But surely that was a slave's thought. I must learn to think with a free mind.

Urdile was a pleasant country of apple orchards and poplar-bordered roads, rising up slowly from the river to the blue hills I'd seen from far away. We walked, and sometimes got a lift on a cart, and bought food at village markets, or were offered milk by a farm woman who saw us pass and pitied the dusty child. I got scolded for dragging my little brother out to tramp the roads, but when my little brother clung to me and glared loyal defiance, the scolder would melt and offer us food or a hayloft to sleep in. So after five days, returning towards the river, which had curved away from our road, we came to the city of Mesun.

Built on steep hills right above the river, with roofs of slate and red tile, and towers, and several ornate bridges, Mesun was a city of stone, but it was not walled.

That seemed strange to me. There were no gates, no guard towers, no guards. I saw no soldiers anywhere. We walked into a great city as into a village.

The houses towered up three and four stories over streets full of people, carts, wagons, horses. The din and commotion and crowding seemed tremendous to us. Melle was holding my hand tightly, and I was glad of it. We passed a marketplace near the river that made Etra's market seem a very small affair. I thought the best thing to do was find some modest inn where we could put down our packs and clean ourselves up a bit, for we were a frowzy, filthy pair by now. As we went on past the market, looking for inn signs, I saw two young men come swinging down a steep street, wearing long, light, grey-brown cloaks and velvet caps that squashed out over the ears. They were exactly like a picture in a book in Everra's library: *Two Scholars of the University of Mesun*. They saw me staring at them, and one of them gave me a slight wink. I stepped forward and said, "Excuse me, would you tell us how to get to the University?"

"Right up the hill, friend," the one who'd winked said. He looked at us curiously. I didn't know what to ask him. I finally said, "Are there lodging houses up there?" and he nodded: "The Quail's the cheapest." His friend said, "No, the Barking Dog," and the first one said, "All depends on your taste in insects: fleas at the Quail, bugs at the Dog." And they went on down the street laughing.

We climbed up the way they had come down. Before long the cobblestone way became steps. I saw that we were climbing around a great wall of stones. Mesun had been a fortified city, long ago, and this was the wall of the citadel. Over the wall loomed palaces of silver-grey stone with steep-pitched roofs and tall windows. The steps brought us up at last onto a little curving street lined with smaller houses, and Melle whispered, "There they are." They stood side by side, two inns, with their signs of the quail and the savagely barking dog. "Fleas or bedbugs?" I asked Melle, and she said, "Fleas." So we took lodgings at the Quail.

We had a most welcome bath and gave what spare clothing we had to the sour-faced landlady to be cleaned. We were on the watch for fleas, but there seemed to be less than in most haylofts. After a scanty and not very good dinner, Melle was ready to go to bed. She had borne the journey well, but every day of it had taken her to about the limit of her small strength. The last couple of days she had had spells of tears and snappishness, like any tired child. I was pretty stretched myself, but I felt a nervous energy in me, here in the city, that would not let me rest. I asked Melle if she'd be worried if I went out for a while. She was lying holding her Ennu figure against her chest, her beloved poncho pulled up over the bedcover. "No," she said, "I won't worry, Beaky." But she looked a little sad and tremulous.

I said, "Oh, maybe I won't go."

"Go *on*," she said crossly. "Go *away*! I am just going to sleep!" And she shut her eyes, frowning, her mouth pulled tight.

"All right. I'll be back before dark."

She ignored me, squeezing her eyes shut. I went out.

As I came out into the street the same two young men were coming by, a bit out of breath from the climb up, and the one who'd winked saw me. "Chose the fleas, eh?" he said. He had a pleasant smile and was openly curious about me. I took this second meeting as an omen or sign which I should follow. I said, "You're students of the University?"

He stopped and nodded; his companion stopped less willingly.

"I'd like to know how to become a student."

"I thought that might be the case."

"Can you tell me—at all—how I should— Whom I should ask—"

"Nobody sent you here? A teacher, a scholar you worked with?"

My heart sank. "No," I said.

He cocked his head with its ridiculous but dashing velvet cap. "Come on to the Gross Tun and have a drink with us," he said. "I'm Sampater Yille, this is Gola Mederra. He's law, I'm letters."

I said my name, and, "I was a slave in Etra."

I had to say that before anything else, before they were shamed by finding they had offered their friendship to a slave.

"In Etra? Were you there in the siege?" said Sampater, and Gola said, "Come on, I'm thirsty!"

We drank beer at the Gross Tun, a crowded beer hall noisy with students, most of them about my age or a little older. Sampater and Gola were principally interested in putting away as much beer as possible as fast as possible and in talking to everybody else at the beer hall, but they introduced me to everyone, and everyone gave me advice about where to go and whom to see about taking classes in letters at the University. When it turned out I knew not one of the famous teachers they mentioned, Sampater asked, "There was nobody you came here wanting to study with, then, a name you knew?"

"Orrec Caspro."

"Ha!" He stared at me, laughed, and raised his mug. "You're a poet, then!"

"No, no. I only—" I didn't know what I was. I didn't know enough to know what I was, or wanted to do or be. I'd never felt so ignorant.

Sampater drained his mug and cried, "One more round, on me, and I'll take you to his house."

"No, I can't—"

"Why not? He's not a professor, you know, he keeps no state. You don't have to approach him on your knees. We'll go right there, it's no distance."

I managed to get out of it by insisting that I must be going back to my little brother. I paid for our beer, which endeared me to them both, and Sampater told me how to get to Caspro's house, just up another street or two and around the corner. "Go see him, go see him tomorrow," he said. "Or, listen, I'll come by for you." I assured him I'd go, and would use his name as a pass-word, and so I got away from the Gross Tun and back to the Quail, with my head spinning.

Waking early, lying thinking as the daylight grew in the low room, I made up my mind. My vague plans of becoming a student at the University had dissolved. I didn't have enough money, I didn't have enough training, and I didn't think I could become one of those lighthearted fellows at the Gross Tun. They were my age, but we'd reached our age by different roads.

What I wanted was work, to support myself and Melle. In a city this size, without slaves, there must be work to do. I knew the name of only one person in Mesun: so, to him I would go. If he couldn't give me work, I'd find it elsewhere.

When Melle woke I told her we were going to buy some fine new city clothes. She liked that idea. The sour landlady told us how to get to the cloth market at the foot of the hill of the citadel, and there we found booths and booths of used clothing, where we could get decked out decently or even somewhat grandly.

I saw Melle looking with a kind of wistful awe at a robe of worn but beautiful patterned ivory silk. I said, "Squeaky, you don't have to keep being Miv, you know."

She hunched up with shyness. "It's too big," she murmured. In fact it was a robe for a grown woman. When we had admired it and left it behind she said to me, "It looked like Diero." She was right.

We both ended up with the trousers, linen shirt, and dark vest or tunic that men and boys in Mesun wore. For Melle I found an elegant small velvet vest with buttons made of copper pennies. She kept looking down at her buttons as we climbed back up to the citadel. "Now I will never not have some money," she said.

We ate bread with oil and olives at a street vendor's stall, and then I said, "Now we'll go and see the great man." Melle was delighted. She flitted up the steep stone street ahead of me. As for me, I walked in a kind of dogged, blind, frightened resolution. I had stopped back by the inn for the small packet wrapped in reed-cloth which I now carried.

Sampater's directions had been good; we found what had to be the house, a tall, narrow one set right against the rock of the hill, the last house on the street. I knocked.

A young woman opened the door. Her skin was so pale her face seemed luminous. Melle and I both stared at her hair—I had never seen such hair in my life. It was like the finest gold wire, it was like a sheep's fleece combed out, a glory of light about her head. "Oh!" Melle said, and I almost did too.

The young woman smiled a little. I imagine that we were rather funny, big boy and little boy, very clean, very stiff, standing staring round-eyed on the threshold. Her smile was kind, and it heartened me.

"I came to Mesun to see Orrec Caspro, if—if that is possible," I said.

"I think it's possible," she said. "May I tell him who…"

"My name is Gavir Aytana Sidoy. This is my—brother—Miv—"

"I'm Melle," Melle said. "I'm a girl." She hunched up her shoulders and looked down, frowning fiercely, like a small falcon.

"Please come in," the young woman said. "I'm Memer Galva. I'll go ask if Orrec is free—" And she was off, quick and light, carrying her marvelous hair like a candle flame, a halo of sunlight.

We stood in a narrow entrance hall. There were several doorways to rooms on either side.

Melle put her hand in mine. "Is it all right if I'm not Miv?" she whispered.

"Of course. I'm glad you're not Miv."

She nodded. Then she said again, louder, "Oh!"

I looked where she was looking, a little farther down the hall. A lion was crossing the hall.

It paid no attention to us at all, but stood in a doorway lashing its tail and looked back impatiently over its shoulder. It was not a black marsh lion; it was the color of sand, and not very large. I said with no voice, "Ennu!"

"I'm coming," a woman said, and she appeared, crossing the hallway, following the lion.

She saw us and stopped. "Oh dear," she said. "Please don't be afraid. She's quite tame. I didn't know anybody was here. Won't you come on in to the hearth room?"

The lion turned around and sat down, still looking impatient. The woman put her hand on its head and said something to it, and it said, "Aoww," in a complaining way.

I looked at Melle. She stood rigid, staring at the lion, whether with terror or fascination I couldn't tell. The woman spoke to Melle: "Her name is Shetar, and she's been with us ever since she was a kitten. Would you like to pet her? She likes being petted." The woman's voice was extraordinarily pleasant, low-pitched, almost hoarse, but with a lulling in it. And she spoke with the Uplands accent, like Chamry Bern.

Melle clutched my hand more strongly and nodded.

I came forward with her, tentatively. The woman smiled at us and said, "I'm Gry."

"This is Melle. I'm Gavir."

"Melle! That is a lovely name. Shetar, please greet Melle properly."

The lion got up quite promptly, and facing us, made a deep bow—that is, she stretched out her forelegs the way cats do, with her chin on her paws. Then she stood

up and looked meaningfully at Gry, who took something out of her pocket and popped it in the lion's
mouth. "Good lion," she said.

Very soon Melle was petting the lion's broad head
and neck. Gry talked with her in an easy, reassuring
way, answering her questions about Shetar. A halflion,
she said it was. Half was quite enough, I thought.

Looking up at me, Gry asked, "Did you come to see
Orrec?"

"Yes. The—the lady said to wait."

And just then Memer Galva came back into the
hall. "He says to come up to his study," she said. "I'll
show you up if you like."

Gry said, "Maybe Melle would like to stay with
Shetar and us for a while."

"Oh yes please," Melle said, and looked at me to see
if it was all right.

"Yes please," I echoed. My heart was beating so hard
I couldn't think. I followed the pale flame of Memer's
hair up a narrow staircase and into a hall.

As she opened the door I knew where I was. I
know it, I remember it. I have been here many times,
the dark room, the book-littered table under a tall window, the lamp. I know the face that turns to me, alert,

sorrowful, unguarded, I know his voice as he speaks my name—

I could not say anything. I stood like a block of stone. He gazed at me intently. "What is it?" he asked, low-voiced.

I managed to say I was sorry, and he got me to sit down, and clearing some books off another chair, sat down facing me. "So?"

I was clutching the packet. I unwrapped it, fumbling at the tightly sealed reedcloth, and held his book out to him. "When I was a slave I was forbidden to read your work. But I was given this book by a fellow slave. When I lost everything, I lost it, but again it was given me. It came with me across the river of death and the river of life. It was the sign to me of where my treasure is. It was my guide. So I— So I followed it to its maker. And seeing you, I knew I have seen you all my life—that I was to come here."

He took the little book and looked at its battered, water-swollen binding, turning it in his hands. He opened it gently. From the page it opened to, he read, "'Three things that, seeking increase, strengthen soul: love, learning, liberty.'" He gave a sigh. "I wasn't much older than you when I wrote that," he said, a little wryly. He looked up at me. He gave me back the book, saying, "You honor me, Gavir Aytana. You give me the gift only the reader can give the writer. Is there anything I can give you?"

He too spoke like Chamry Bern.

I sat dumb. My burst of eloquence was over, my tongue was tied.

"Well, we can talk about that presently," he said. He was concerned and gentle. "Tell me something about yourself. Where were you in slavery? Not in my part of the world, I know. Slaves in the Uplands have no more book learning than their masters do."

"In the House of Arca, in the city of Etra," I said. Tears sprang into my eyes as I said it.

"But your people came from the Marshes, I think?"

"My sister and I were taken by slavers..." And so he drew my story from me, a brief telling of it, but he kept me at it, asking questions and not letting me rush ahead. I said little about how Sallo died, for I could not burden a stranger with my heart's grief. When I got to my return to the forest, and how Melle and I met there, his eyes flashed. "Melle was my mother's name," he said. "And my daughter's." His voice dropped, saying that. He looked away. "And you have this child with you— so Memer said?"

"I couldn't leave her there," I said, feeling that her presence required apology.

"Some could."

"She's very gifted—I never had so quick a pupil. I hope that here…" But I stopped. What did I hope, for Melle or myself?

"Here certainly she can be given what she needs," Orrec Caspro said promptly and firmly. "How did you travel with a young child all the way from the Daneran Forest to Mesun? That can't have been easy."

"It was easy enough till I learned my…my enemies in Arcamand were still hunting for me, on my track." But I had not named Torm and Hoby till then. I had to go back and say who they were, and to tell that my sister's death had been at their hands.

When I told him of how Hoby had hunted me and followed us, and of crossing the Sensaly, he listened the way the fellows in Brigin's camp listened to *The Siege and Fall of Sentas*, holding his breath.

"You saw him drown?" he asked.

I shook my head. "I saw the horse with no rider. Nothing else. The river's wide, and I couldn't see along the near shore. He may have drowned. He may not. But I think…" I didn't know how to say it. "It's as if a chain has broken."

Caspro sat brooding over my story a while. "I want Memer and Gry to hear this. I want to hear more about what you call the remembering—your visions— Seeing me!" He looked up and laughed, gazing at me with amused and wondering sympathy. "And I want to meet your companion. Shall we go down?"

There was a garden beside the house, a narrow one, wedged between house walls and the cliff that towered up behind. It was bright with late morning sun and late summer flowers. For an instant I remembered the flowers. There was a very small fountain, which dribbled rather than ran. On the flagstones and marble benches around it the two women, the girl, and the lion sat talking—that is, the lion had gone to sleep, while Melle stroked her dreamily, and the women were talking.

"You met my wife, Gry Barre," Caspro said to me as we came into the garden. "She and I are Uplanders. Memer Galva came with us from her home, the city of Ansul; she's our guest this year. I teach her the modern poets, and she teaches me Aritan, the ancient tongue of our people. Now introduce me to your companion, if you will."

But as we approached, Melle scrambled up and hid her face against me, clinging to me. It was unlike her, and I didn't know what to do. "Melle," I said, "this is our host—the great man we came to see."

She clung to my legs and would not look.

"Never mind," Caspro said. His face was grim for a moment. Then, not looking at Melle or coming close to her, he said pleasantly, "Gry, Memer, we must keep our guests a while so you can hear their story."

"Melle told us about the chickens on the boat," Memer said. The sunlight on her hair was marvelous, radiant. I couldn't look at her and couldn't look away from her. Caspro sat down on the bench beside Memer, so I sat down on another bench and got Melle to stand beside my legs, in the circle of my arms, thus defending both her and myself.

"I think it's time for a bite to eat," Gry said. "Melle, come with me and give me a hand, will you? We'll be back in a moment." Melle let herself be led away, still turning her face away from Caspro as she went.

I apologised for her behavior. Caspro said simply, "How could she do otherwise?" And as I thought back on our journey I realised that the only men Melle had spoken to or even looked at were the dwarf innkeeper, whom she may have thought a strange kind of child, and the cowboy, who had slowly earned her trust. She had kept clear away, always, from the bargemen, and any other men. I had not seen it. It wrung my heart.

"You're from the Marshlands?" Memer asked me.

All these people had beautiful voices; hers was like running water.

"I was born there," was all I could get out in reply.

"And stolen by slavers, when he was a baby, with his sister," Caspro said, "and taken to Etra. And they brought you up there to be an educated man, did they? Who was your teacher?"

"A slave. Everra was his name."

"What did you have by way of books? I don't think of the City States as homes of learning—although in Pagadi there are certainly some fine scholars, and fine poets too. But one thinks of soldiers more than scholars there."

"All the books Everra had were old," I said. "He wouldn't let us read the moderns—what he called the moderns—"

"Like me," Caspro said with his brief, broad smile. "I know, I know. Nema, and the Epics, and Trudec's *Moralities*...That's what they started me on in Derris Water! So, you were educated so that you could teach the children of the household. Well, that much is good. Though to keep a teacher as a slave..."

"It wasn't an evil slavery," I said. "Until—" I stopped.

Memer said, "Can slavery not be evil?"

"If your masters aren't cruel people—and if you don't know there's anything else," I said. "If everybody believes it's the way things are and must be, then you can not know that…that it's wrong."

"Can you not know?" she said, not accusing or arguing, simply asking, and thinking as she asked. She looked at me directly and said, "I was a slave in Ansul. All my people were. But by recent conquest, not by caste. We didn't have to believe we were slaves by the order of nature. That must be very different."

I wanted to talk to her but I couldn't. "It was a slave," I said to Caspro, "who taught me your hymn to Liberty."

Memer's smile brightened her grave, quiet face for a moment. Though her complexion was so light, she had dark eyes that flashed like the fire in opal. "We sang that song in Ansul when we drove the Alds out," she said.

"It's the tune," Caspro said. "Good tune. Catchy." He stretched, enjoying the warmth of the sun, and said, "I want to hear more about Barna and his city. It sounds as if there was a bitter tragedy there. Whatever you can tell me. But you said you became his bard, as it were, his reciter. So then, you have a good memory?"

"Very good," I said. "That's my power."

"Ah!" I had spoken with confidence, and he responded to it. "You memorise without difficulty?"

"Without trying," I said. "It's part of the reason I came here. What's the good of having a head full of everything you ever read? People liked hearing the stories, there in the forest. But what could I do with them in the Marshes? Or anywhere else? I thought maybe at the University..."

"Yes, yes, absolutely," Caspro said. "Or perhaps... Well, we'll see. Here come *mederende fereho en refema*— is that right, Memer?— In Aritan it means 'beautiful women bringing food.' You'll want to learn Aritan, Gavir. Think of it, another language—a language different from ours!—not entirely of course, it's the ancestor of ours, but quite different—and a whole new poetry!" As he spoke, with the unguarded passion that I already saw characterised him, he was careful not to look at Melle, only at his wife, and not to come near Melle as he helped set out the food on an unoccupied bench. They had brought bread and cheese, olives, fruit, and a thin, light cider to drink.

"Where are you staying?" Gry asked, and when I said, "The Quail," she said, "How are the fleas?"

"Not too bad. Are they, Melle?"

She had come to stand close to me again. She shook her head, and scratched her shoulder.

"Shetar has her own private fleas," Gry told her.

"Lion fleas. She won't share them with us. And the Quail fleas won't bite her." Shetar had opened an eye, found the food uninteresting, and gone back to sleep.

Having eaten a little, Melle sat down on the paving stones in front of me but close to the lion, within petting distance. She and Gry kept up a murmured conversation, while Caspro talked with me and Memer put in a word now and then. What he was doing, in a mild and roundabout fashion, was finding out how much of a scholar I was, what I knew and didn't know. From the little Memer said, I thought she must know everything there was to know in the way of poetry and tales. But when we came to history she declared ignorance, saying she knew only that of Ansul, and not much of that, because all the books in Ansul had been destroyed by the conquerors of the city. I wanted to hear that hideous story, but Caspro, mildly perseverant, kept on the course of his questions until he'd learned what he wanted to know, and even won from me a confession of my old, foolish ambition to write a history of the City States. "I don't think I'll ever do that," I said, trying to make light of it, "since it would involve going back there."

"Why not?" said Caspro, frowning.

"I'm a runaway slave."

"A citizen of Urdile is free," he said, still frowning. "No one can declare him a slave, no matter where he goes."

"But I'm not a citizen of Urdile."

"If you'll go to the Commons House with me to vouch for you, you can become one tomorrow. There are plenty of ex-slaves here, who freely come and go to Asion and the City States as citizens of Urdile. But as for history, you might find better documents in the library of the University here than in the City States."

"They don't know what to do with them," I said sadly, thinking of the wonderful records and annals I had handled at the Shrine of the Forefathers.

"Perhaps you can show them what to do with them—given time," Caspro said. "The first thing for you to do is become a citizen. Next, enroll in the University."

"Caspro-dí, I haven't much money. I think the first thing for me to do is find work."

"Well, I have an idea about that, if Gry agrees. You write good copy-hand, I expect?"

"Oh yes," I said, remembering Everra's relentless lessons.

"I need a copyist. And a man with a really good memory would be of great use to me too, since I've been having some trouble with my eyes." He said it easily, and his dark eyes seemed clear enough, but there was a wincing in his face as he spoke, and I saw Gry's quick glance at him. "For instance, now...if I was needing a reference from Denios for a lecture, and couldn't remember what comes after *Let the swan fly to the northlands*—?"

I took up the lines—

Let grey gander fly beside grey goose,
North in the springtime: it is south I go.

"Ah!" Memer said, all alight. "I love that poem!"

"Of course you do," Caspro said. "But it's not a well-known one, except to a few homesick southerners." I thought of the homesick northerner, Tadder, who lent me the volume of Denios where I'd read the poem. Caspro went on, "I was thinking that having a kind of live anthology about the house could be very useful to me. If such work seemed at all attractive to you, Gavir. Anything you didn't have by heart you could help me look up, of course. I have a good many books. And you could be getting on with your work at the University. What do you think, Gry?"

His wife was sitting down on the pavement with Melle. She reached up and took his hand, and for a moment they gazed at each other with a calm intensity of love. Melle looked from her to him. She looked hard at him, frowning, studying him.

"It seems an excellent idea," Gry said.

"You see, we have a couple of spare rooms here," he said to me. "One of them is Memer's, as long as she'll let us keep her—through next winter at the very least. There are a couple of rooms up in the attic, where we had two young women from Bendraman living until just lately, students. But they went back to Derris Water to astonish the good priests with their learning, so the rooms are vacant. Waiting for you and Melle."

"Orrec," said his wife, "you should give Gavir time to think."

"Dangerous thing, often, time to think," he said. He looked at me with a smile that was both apologetic and challenging.

"I would— It would— We would—" I couldn't get a finished sentence out.

"To me it would be a great pleasure to have a child in the house," Gry said. "This child. If it pleased Melle."

Melle looked at her, then at me. I said, "Melle, our hosts are inviting us to stay with them."

"With Shetar?"

"Yes."

"And Gry? And Memer?"

"Yes."

She said nothing, but nodded and went back to stroking the lion's thick fur. The lion was faintly but perceptibly snoring.

"Very well, that's settled," said Caspro in particularly broad Uplands dialect. "Go get your things out of the Quail and move in."

I was hesitant, incredulous.

"Did you not see me, half your life ago, in your visions, and I spoke your name? Were you not coming here to me?" he said, quietly but fiercely. "If we're guided, are we to argue with the guide?"

Gry watched me with a sympathetic eye.

Memer looked at Caspro, smiling, and said to me, "It's very hard to argue with him."

"I—I don't want to argue," I stammered. "It's only—" And I stopped again.

Melle got up and sat down by me on the bench, pressing close against me. "Beaky," she whispered. "Don't cry. It's all right."

"I know," I said, putting my arm around her. "I know it is."